The Gift of Us

A SMALL TOWN CHRISTMAS ROMANCE, STEAMY EDITION

LULA WHITE

First Edition 2025

www.lulawhitebooks.com

ISBN: 978-1-959784-13-5

A Great Historical Christmas Book *Amazon Reviewer*

This book had me in all my feelings. I had to put it down a couple of times because I didn't want to know what happened. I fell in love with Seven. Also love the history lesson about the town of Elaine. I always know that I will get a history lesson from the author, lost history. definitely a must read.

Lula Strikes Again With Another Christmas Love Story *Amazon Reviewer*

This whirlwind affair hits Elaine, AR, with flair, chile. There is lotto, mud wrestling, and frogs. Yes, frogs. Baby, the build up to the action scenes are everything.

Awesome Read *Amazon Reviewer*

Love all of Lula White books. She puts her heart and soul into connecting to her readers. The content is amazing and worth every minute of your time.

I Never Skip A Lula White Novel! *Amazon Reviewer*

Man, this was good. I was stressed. OUT but also delighted and entertained. The writing was beautiful, the plot was messy like I like it, the steam was......STEAMING. Well done!

Dear Elaine

To the superheroes and sheroes of Elaine, Arkansas,

Your bottomless hearts, your kindness, your sheer force of will, your businesses, stories, love, inspiration, and your strength...

...are too electric and immense and Earth-shattering for this world to hold.

Thank you.

Thank you.

Warriors of the Arkansas Delta, you are the gift. You deserve your breakout movie where your truth will inform and enlighten the world of your value to this nation. You deserve justice on every level—from reparations to site markers where the atrocities actually occurred, formal apologies, a memorial funded by the State of Arkansas, the town of Helena, as well as the United States Army, and the United States.

Your redemption and recognition are coming, whether or not we see it in our lifetime. I will support you and fight for you in any way I can.

Readers who care, please support this town and its people who are descendants of this atrocity, even if it's just by spending ten minutes researching and sharing a post to pass on the knowledge. More information about how to support them and connect with them is in the "People & Resources" Section.

An especially heartfelt hug to the following people for encouraging me to push forward when I doubted if I should do this, or for making time to answer my questions, or for taking me out to the land and sacred sites where these beautiful souls paid the ultimate price.

Thank you for allowing me into the heart of Elaine.

Mayor Lisa Hicks-Gilbert

Professor Brian K. Mitchell

Kevin Dedner

James White

Nancy Hall Neal

Harvey Williams

Lenora Marshall

Contents

Playlist

I really wanted to honor the Delta as the birthplace of the blues genre. Playing a notable role in the background of this story are Arkansas musicians who had a hand in shaping blues, country, gospel, and rock n' roll. Sister Rosetta Tharpe serves folksy fire on her guitar, and I was in awe to learn she was ostracized in some gospel circles because of her electric bluesy gospel style. Plus, it was frowned upon then for a woman to play a guitar. I can't imagine the treatment she must've received. This type of bravery has always inspired me from anybody willing to carry their big dreams past small minds. And the fact that she was born in Cotton Plant, Arkansas... says it all.

Geeshie Wiley's *Last Kind Words Blues* might be my favorite piece on here. This song plays in my head when Sunday and her family walk up the steps of the Phillips County Courthouse for the hearing on the ticket. Her vocals over the guitar are solemn and final, as if everything we know about the South comes to bear on this moment.

There's so much strength in these vocals, and lightning in

their instruments. That era was a gut-wrenching time to be Black, and their voices surely won't let you forget it.

Cedell Davis's *She's Got the Devil In Her* was my little jokey joke to keep things light after Sunday's and Seven's mud fight. He was born in Helena.

Also born in Helena is Roberta Martin, whose *Ride on King Jesus* and *God Specializes* take me back to my grandma's church. In her kitchen, my grandmother played the gospel on her radio on Sunday mornings while getting ready for church. I've listened to Ms. Martin a few times and will keep listening as I get older because it's the kind of medicine you won't find in a pharmacy.

Not everybody on here is from Arkansas, and it's not all Christmas or blues sounds. So you've got a good bag of holiday vibes, mixed with Southern musical gumbo, and flavors of more modern R & B and country.

Even if you're reading this outside Christmas season, you can dig into these roots and make yourself at home. Stay blessed and thanks for stopping through.

The list is on the next page, and here's the link on Spotify. If you've got this in print, you can look up Author Lula White on Spotify and scroll through my playlists. There's one for just about every book.

Playlist

Merry Christmas Baby by Robert Nighthawk

Arkansas by Chris Stapleton

Fattening Frogs for Snakes by Sonny Boy Williamson II

She's Got the Devil In Her by CeDell Davis & Ayron Jones

Christmas Morning Blues by Sonny Boy Williamson II

'Tis the Season by Rare of Breed

My Lord Do Just What He Say by Jessie Mae Hemphill

A Rocking Good Way by Odessa Harris

We Bring You Joy by Luke & H-Town

Silent Night by Sister Rosetta Tharpe

Jingle Bellz by Starr & Juelz Santana

Snowed In by Chance the Rapper & Jeremih

Player's Ball - Christmas Radio Mix by Outkast

Cider & Hennessy by Jordin Sparks & Kenneth Paige

My Favorite Things by Mary J. Blige

I Want to Come Home for Christmas by Marvin Gaye

Rudolph the Red Nosed Reindeer by DMX

I Want to Come Home for Christmas by Ne-Yo

8 Days of Christmas by Destiny's Child

Sleigh Ride by TLC

Carol of the Bells a.k.a. Opera of the Bells by Destiny's Child

Over to My House by Elvie Thomas & Geeshie Wiley

Your Funeral and My Trial by Sonny Boy Williamson II

Blues for Christmas by John Lee Hooker

Christmas on Death Row by Death Row All Stars, Tha Dogg Pound, & Jane Handcock

A Merry Black Christmas by Leon Bridges

Selling My Porkchops by Memphis Minnie

Married Man Blues by Jessie Mae Hemphill

Trapmas Medley by Jordin Sparks

Merry Christmas Baby by B.B. King

Tallahatchie River Blues by Mattie Delaney

Ride on King Jesus by Roberta Martin

God Specializes by The Roberta Martin Singers

Santa Claus by Sonny Boy Williamson II

Loving In the Moonlight by Jessie Mae Hemphill

Cross Road Blues by Robert Johnson

Lockwood's Boogie by Robert Lockwood, Jr.

Last Kind Words Blues by Geeshie Wiley & Elvie Thomas

Walkin' Blues by Robert Lockwood, Jr.

Have Yourself A Merry Little Christmas by Luther Vandross

White Christmas by Sister Rosetta Tharpe

Up Above My Head by Sister Rosetta Tharpe

One

LIKE I DONE TOLD Y'ALL

Sunday

"Yesssss, Merry Christmas, pretty babaaaaay…" Sunday cranked up Robert Nighthawk on her mama's old kitchen radio. None of her sleepy heads were up yet, despite her turning on their lights minutes ago. "Get them pretty behinds on out them beds!" Flinging open door number one, she flipped the light switch on and off several irritating times.

"Sun, stop!" her sixteen-year-old brother tossed off his covers and stumbled from the mattress. "I got nine more minutes," Narado mumbled, flipping the light switch. On his way back to the bed in the dark, his long feet tripped over his sheets, and he landed in a thud on their hardwood floor.

Staying on beat, right along with Nighthawk, Sunday kept singing. "Oh, yeahhhh, pretty babaaay, that's what you get when that butt's up all night on the phone with them girrrrrlssss!" She raised her voice extra loud and off key. "That booty better be on that school bus, boyyyyyy, 'cause ain' nobody drivin' if you miss ittttt, and Peady ain't neithaaaaah."

She threw open door number two. "Yessssss, Merry Christmas, get that butt right on uppppp!"

"MeMawww!" Sunday's seven-year-old niece, Tori, whined for her grandmother.

Sunday scooted back to the kitchen in her slippers and snatched up the farm's financial statements before the kids came in and saw. She shoved them in her tired leather briefcase that was older than she was. Next up were the bowls, oatmeal, and dry cereal she set on the table in their family's cramped dining room.

The angel on the wall supervised Sunday's morning routine. A wide, Christmas-sized laugh opening his face, his one good eye twinkling and up to no good, he was probably in Heaven pouring hot toddies and wiping out everybody at pitty pat.

"Good mornin', Daddy," his third-oldest murmured while counting out lunch money for her three littles. "Your tadpole needs you today." Unfurling cash from her purse, her heart almost came to a standstill. She prayed the bills didn't run out before she counted enough. "Bring Geemaw, Pop Pop, and Aunt Bird, too. And Nessa. I'm gonna need backup."

He'd smiled at her. The bills stretched into money to cover their school meals. For today.

"We puttin' up the Christmas tree tonight finally?" Tori ran in and tossed her backpack on the floor. "You promised."

The kid was so excited about the Christmas tree she banged their unsteady table and knocked her bowl and spoon on the floor.

"Pick that up and wash it out." A distracted Sunday was still ensuring her statements were in the right order.

Tori remained undeterred on her way to the sink. "So we're putting up the tree?"

"You can't wait a few more days?" That Christmas tree

stood on its last legs, and Sunday's pocketbook sat on empty for the money to buy a new one.

"But Auntie, it's Christmas time now. I waited all year already. Three hundred and forty-five days. We supposed to have it! And presents! Ugh!" Tori jumped back from the sink like the water had attacked her. "Ughhhh!"

"What?"

"It's nasty!"

"Nasty where?" Sunday rushed over. Brown liquid sputtered out of the faucet. "Oh!" Immediately, she grabbed the handles to turn them off.

"What's wrong?" Her mother came in and went for the coffee pot to fill it with water.

"Don't bother." Sunday tried running more water in hopes it would clear. "We got a busted pipe somewhere."

"Again?" Mama set the pot back down.

Sunday twisted the knobs, only for the water to spurt out muddier. "Again. Tori, no cereal if you can't wash your bowl. It'll be hot pockets this mornin', baby."

"Argh!" Narado yelled from the bathroom. "Mama, this water is nasty!"

"Shut it off, Nook! Boil some water and do a bird bath for this mornin'!" their mother called to him.

Sunday searched the drawers for a flashlight to check the pipes. This was the last thing she needed. "It's always somethin'."

Her mother snatched the flashlight and waved her off. "You don't have time for all that. Ain' nothin' you can do right now. Go get yaself ready for ya meetin'."

Nerves already as jumbled as cheap Christmas tinsel, Sunday took off for her bedroom in the garage to get ready. She only needed to stay calm. Their spring planting depended on it. She cranked up Destiny's Child's "Days of Christmas." "Merry merry merry merry Christmas..."

There was nothing merry about the dresses she'd inherited from her sister. Long grown out of her own dresses from her twenties, now Sunday could hardly fit into Vanessa's. Four dresses later, she shoved her stockinged feet into some flat ankle boots for her meeting at Friends of the Delta Savings and Loan.

"Stop tuggin' on it." Her mama turned Sunday around, straightened the knitted fabric bunched around her waist, and fixed the tied belt. "And quit that worryin'. Minnie's gon' get you another good deal."

"If she don't pop first." Sunday referenced her old high school classmate who was close to her due date on baby number five. Sunday prayed, for everybody's sakes, the little girl stayed in there just seventy-two more hours so her mama could push the Conklins' refinancing paperwork through with no hassles.

"Reggie! Nookie!" Sunday clapped and called for her nephew and younger brother. "Every minute you're late is one less present you open."

Instantly, doors flew open, and bare feet hopped down the hall faster than jackrabbits on the run. Narado, nicknamed Nookie, was still shoving on a sweatshirt.

"Mama, tell Sunday she play too much!"

Their mother turned on the television just in time to see the mayor of Elaine issuing a statement about the water. "Well, here we go right here. It'll be another water boil. Right before Christmas."

Sunday wrestled with her kinks to tuck them back into her flat braids. "We've got too many shipments to send out. We need that water to be clean."

"Auntie, did you see my Christmas list I left on your dresser?" Tori asked between bites.

Having looked it over and cringed at how pricey it was,

Sunday brushed off the question with one of her own. "Did you get mine?"

"Auntieeee." Tori's grin was so sweet and pure, Sunday would've done anything to keep it there. "Well? Did you?"

On quite a few weekends, Sunday *had* done anything necessary for these three.

"Yes, ma'am, I did. Let's see how Santa feels when I tell him you messed up your brand new choir robe playing outside in the ditch."

Tori's jaw dropped over her hot pocket. That goofy, animated grin she shared with her father reminded Sunday of her older brother. "Auntie, you don't have to tell Santa Claus all that."

"Should've thought about that when I asked you to take it off before you played with Celia. Finish your food so you can be ready for the bus."

"Sun, did you say you're going to Helena today?" Nookie grabbed a hot pocket and slammed the microwave door.

"Yes. And no, you're not gettin' the new Grand Theft Auto. It's too violent."

"You still wrong for that, but it's not why I asked." He surprised her. In his hand was six dollars. "On your way back, can you pick up three lottery tickets from Kwik Stop?"

Sunday and her mother swapped concern.

"Where you get some money from?" Their mother rolled her neck.

"And you are not old enough to gamble," Sunday added.

"He don't spend his lunch money on lunch." A fat, greasy grin spread over Reggie's mouth.

Sunday eyed her little brother. "Then, how have you been eatin'?"

With Reggie's jaws chomping full of food, he kept talking. "Essence and Katanya cook for him. They bring his food to school. So he can use his lunch money for other stuff."

Irritated, Nookie threatened him with a juice carton. "Watch yaself, boy. Wait until I get my lick back."

Sunday snatched the carton, not caring about his upset. "You spend your lunch money on stuff like what? Boy, I'm around here scrapin' for you to eat and you're not usin' it?" The audacity of this kid to take her efforts for granted. "And if Essence and Katanya are cookin' for you, what are *you* doin' for *them*?"

Everybody stared down the table at a stricken Nookie, his shoulders hunched all the way up to his ears.

"We just be talkin'. I help 'em with their homework."

His scratchy voice rose high enough for Sunday to want to pop his bubble.

"*What* homework? We can hardly get you to do yours."

Nookie checked his watch and shot up from the table. "Oh, will ya look at that?" He cast his oldest sister a stank eye. "Somebody said if I miss the bus they're not drivin' me, so gotta bounce."

The others followed suit.

"We'll talk about this later. On your life, I promise you that." Sunday wondered how he'd grown up so fast. It seemed only yesterday she and her sisters were changing his diaper. "You *are* goin' to college. Won't be no babies."

"You gettin' the lottery tickets or not?" Nookie threw the dollars on the table like he had more where those came from. "The drawin' is tonight, and the Mega Millions is one hundred and ninety-six million. If I win, I can have as many babies as I wanna."

Sunday jumped after him, and Nookie ran. Her little brother cranked the Christmas music back up, and mocked her from the opposite side of the table while he slid on his jacket. He was long past the age where she could still catch him. Now he sang just as loud and off key as Sunday had earlier. "Firesiiiiiide blazing briiiiiiight...we're carolinggg... through the niii-hhiii-hiiiight!"

"Go get on that bus before I sterilize you." Sunday readied herself to leave. "You'll never walk again. Never mind havin' kids!"

"What does sterilize mean?" Tori asked, putting on her backpack.

Reggie opened the door and walked onto the porch. "Oh, that's a sweet drone."

Nookie followed him out. "What drone?"

Sunday watched them fall silent, like they'd entered some trance.

"What's out there?" Mama cleared the table.

Dipping low and then buzzing high, it cavorted across their rows of empty fields, soybeans stalks, and on toward their wooden guest cabins, aiming straight for the Old Towne Lake. It disappeared among the endless forest of cottonwood and hickory trees lining the outer perimeter of their land. But it was wintertime. Most of the leaves had disappeared, so they could still see the drone zipping through naked tree branches.

"I want me one." Reggie watched jealously. "I wonder what kind it is. That looks so dope."

But Sunday's veins were heating up. The uninvited object was an invasion.

"Who's controllin' it? What's it filmin'?" Nookie grabbed the binoculars they used for catching possums and skunks. "Somebody's sittin' in our field!"

"What? On our property?" Mama pushed onto the porch. "Reggie, you left the front gate open last night?"

Eleven-year-old Reggie's face dropped. "My bad, MeMaw, I probly did."

Sunday took the trespass personally. They could only have come from one family. "Who the hell are they to come on our land?" That murky water could have been pooling up in Sunday's chest.

Nookie kept reporting. "He's in a truck, Sun. Gimme Earl."

They all watched the tiny aircraft zip out of the woods and dally over their soybean and corn fields.

The oldest Conklin child was about to bust. "I'll do it. Fool's got a lotta nerve."

"Nah." Nookie turned to go back in the house. "I can do it."

"Nook, I said, 'no.' You just keep watchin' it. Them Adlers think they can do whatever they please." Sunday jerked open their tiny hallway closet with a vengeance.

B.B. King blared into their yard when Sunday pushed back out of the screen door.

"Merry merry merry, Christmas, baby!" B.B.'s soul exploded, and out came a soundtrack for Sunday to aim to.

"Girl, what kinda crazy is you!" Mama hollered.

B.B. King blew from his windpipes and strummed his electric guitar.

Sunday hoisted up Earl, the hundred-and-nine-year-old rifle that had made Earl Conklin a household name. She aimed. "Cover your ears."

"Hell nah," Narado said. "Take it down."

"Watch ya mouth." Sunday pulled the trigger. *Boom!* The first shot ripped across the quiet, gray morning and sent starlings fleeing from the trees.

The little drone escaped and began racing off their property, toward the highway. Sunday marched into the yard and hoisted the old relic again. "Oh, the hell you will."

"Shoot it, Auntie!" Tori jumped up and down.

Boom! That shot grazed it but the device swirled around and resumed its flight path.

Frantic, the guy parked on Sunday's dirt road jumped

from the back of his truck. He held up his arms to try and catch his aircraft. As far apart as they stood from one another, Sunday saw him stretch high in desperation. The drone lowered.

Staring down the barrel, Sunday held her arms steady and even, shoulder level, fingers and palms as limber as lion claws.

Boom!

The drone fell into the bewildered kid's arms, in tatters.

"Like I done told y'all...we ain't sellin'!" She picked up Nookie's backpack and handed it to him. "Have a good day at school, and behave like you've got sense."

ONE SMALL PROBLEM

"That sounds perfect." Seven kept his voice low, so no one in his house overheard him. "The girls will go nuts."

"Ten days? You're going all the way to France. Why don't you throw in a full two weeks, my guy?" Seven's travel agent, Macio, typed on the other end of the line.

Seven thumbed his wedding ring that had been on his finger so long it couldn't come off. Maybe he should have taken the full two weeks. He and Arista needed it.

"Nah. Arista will want to stop through Houston and see her folks before we come back. Since she won't be with them for Christmas or New Year's." At the sound of feet pounding down his stairs, Seven rolled his eyes and called to his nine-year-old son, "Dillon, how many times do I have to tell you? No shoes in the house, man."

"Bran's almost here. I don't have time to stop at the door." Dillon rushed to the kitchen to heat up a breakfast burrito for the road.

"If you wake up on time, you'll have more of it."

"Did you write the check for the field trip?" his son asked from the other side of the house.

"On the mantle."

Seven's cell phone buzzed.

NICKY

You got your ticket?

Seven ignored it and returned to Macio. "And can I get one of those personal shoppers to surprise Arista and the girls with some stuff?" He peeked around the corner to ensure he was still clear. "Somebody who knows about...you know... bedroom threads. Lace." It was Seven's favorite fabric, but after Arista had that last baby, she'd stopped wearing lingerie, despite him gifting her several sets *and* matching heels. They'd been limited edition from London. "And for our boat ride dinner, you sure it'll have a cover for us to be... private? Don't forget the activities for the kids to get into on their own. Chaperoned of course."

"Say less. I got you, bruh." Macio's keys kept tapping on the other end. "Your family's gonna love this."

A foreign excursion had to work. Seven's therapist had suggested getting them all out of Dallas, away from friends, family, and distractions. And getting Arista away from her sister and the television station. "Oh, and the art supplies! Easel? Chalk? Charcoal? Paper?"

"Done. It'll all be ready for ya. You're gonna draw Arista or something?" Macio asked. "Now, that's hot!"

Seven didn't confirm or deny. He could only chuckle. Hopefully, his wife would think so.

His middle child, Raegan, entered his office, planted a kiss on his cheek, and stuck her hand out.

"I need to run, man. My parole agents are looking for me."

"You'll have a final itinerary by tomorrow. Arista is gonna

lose it on this one, bruh. And y'all haven't been on vacay in a minute. Whooo…"

"Excellent. That's the plan anyway." Seven stood up and fished out Raegan's basketball game money. "Thanks for everything, dude." Later today, he'd stop by Arista's office and surprise her with the Christmas trip, so she could start getting herself and the kids ready. For now, Seven stared at his fourteen-year-old. "What am I getting for this twenty dollars?"

Cheesing extra hard through her braces, she exchanged the bill for a piece of paper she set in his hand. "All my love and affection."

Seven held up her Christmas wish list. "You mean I get to spend some more money."

How could she serve him sweetness *and* attitude at the same time? "Daddy, who else am I gonna ask?"

"You don't have to ask anybody. You could just go get a job. How about tryin' that out?"

She smacked her glossed lips. "I'm only fourteen."

"In a lot of countries, kids your age have been working so long they're already retired. Home by nine, Sun Ray, or you're gettin' embarrassed." Seven called her by his nickname for her.

She threw him two thumbs up. "If you embarrass me, you're embarrassin' yourself, Daddy."

"Oh ho hoo, it's like that?" He rocked on his heels, faking shock at his child who was the most like him.

"Ash, take it off. I'm not playin' with you!" Arista fussed at their sixteen-year-old on their way down the stairs. "You're not leaving this house in that."

"It's as long as my cheer skirt." Ash swung her twenty-four-inch sew-in and her nine-inch nails over the banister. "Daddy, will you tell her this skirt isn't that short?"

He eyed his oldest, whose diaper it seemed he was changing mere moments ago. She was now an object for men to lust over. And Dad knew the score. Even if she took it off, she might go to school and sneak on another.

"Why don't you put some shorts on under it?" he suggested. At least this way, he could negotiate and let her feel she'd had a choice.

Ash's big huff was his reply.

"You wanna wear the skirt or not?" Seven reiterated.

She marched back to her room. While she did that, he and Raegan stifled their silent comedy jam about Ash's excessive makeup outperforming the makeup on drag queens.

"I'm not the one you need to worry about," Ray whispered on her way out. Chill, smart, and whip-fast with the comebacks, Raegan was his favorite, but he could never say that out loud.

Once the parade of younguns had filtered out, he headed to the kitchen where Arista was blending a smoothie. He wondered if he should surprise her with the trip now, or later by candlelight.

He sidled up behind her. "You wanna see what that Stillwell's do tonight? Before we come home. We can do a li'l somethin' after the kids go to bed?"

She peered up from her phone and her thick, glossy lips spread into the same grin he'd been seeing for seventeen years. "Oh, you got your Cialis refilled?"

And I see you're still rocking your perimenopause beard. He bit his tongue. "You want me to hand you a wire plier so you can just crack my nuts, or should I put 'em on a platter first?"

To swallow his irritation and not retaliate with a wisecrack of his own, he went for his coffee.

"Sev, I'm kidding!" She grabbed his arm and tugged him back. "I'm just playin'."

"But you're not funny, Ri." Bedroom action these days was more grueling than a second or third job, and here he was still trying to put in work. Only so Ri could go for his jugular.

"It is a li'l funny, though." She snickered a final time and tasted her smoothie, not bothering to come over and soothe him physically. "On the real, though, Sev, it would have been nice if you had backed me up a few minutes ago."

"I did back you up!"

"No, you didn't. You took Ash's side by letting her keep the skirt on."

"I found middle ground where she could have what she wanted and we could remind her of her presentation."

"She is not grown. We're the adults. You're always negotiating, so when I put my foot down—no negotiation—I'm the bad guy."

"Then, maybe don't put your foot down so much. She's sixteen and needs to gain confidence to make these decisions for herself. Our role isn't to *give* her her identity, but to create space and parameters for her to safely craft her own."

Arista coyly slid her hair behind her ear. "I'd rather just give it to her. She'll thank me when she's got her own kids."

"Woman, cut." He sipped his coffee. "You down for dinner with me and Cialis or not?" But he hadn't gotten his prescription. He'd never put in the order for another round. He hated the searing headache, his muscles so tight and creaky that he could hardly move, and feeling like his heart would burst. Tonight, he wanted to try performing on his own, but he wouldn't tell her that.

She hesitated. "Don't you think we should start on Christmas decorations?"

"Tonight is Friday. We can decorate tomorrow."

Ri grabbed her gym bag and threw it over her shoulder. "Okay, yeah. Let's do it."

Okay, yeah?

"You want to meet here at the house or at the restaurant?" He sipped his coffee and drank in her reaction.

"Huh?" She stopped at the door.

"Stillwell's tonight."

"Sorry, babe, my mind is somewhere else. I need to get to the station."

They went in for their standard kiss. Sucking on her lips, he closed his eyes, cleared his head of all the boring, routine stuff she'd said, and tried to relax. This was his wife, the mother of his children.

"I've got a little somethin' for you and the kids."

She had already whipped her bob away.

"Yeah, babe, you have a good day, too."

France would help. For sure.

Somewhere, his phone was vibrating.

NICKY

Lottery ticket, dude. Don't forget. Ur playin Lewis's bday.

ME

Bet.

NICKY

Wanna ride to Shreveport?

Seven rolled his eyes.

ME

Hell nah. One of us is raising our kids.

NICKY

My check is raising mine.

His phone vibrated again. It was his sister.

CHARIAN

U got ur tix?

SEVEN

I'm gettin it.

Alone now in their "dream house," Seven climbed into the attic and dragged out the Christmas decorations before his shower. He couldn't let these walls close in on him. Their marriage had become too routine—birthday parties, holiday gatherings, and head-splitting baby gender reveals. What was even the point of that?

With the kids being older now, he and Arista could pick up some side projects—buying some land for a golf resort, starting a Black-owned solar power company, or investing in an urban farm and sustainable living. In short, he was bored. Once they ditched this daily grind, they could talk possibilities.

He wouldn't surprise Ri with the flight itinerary at dinner. He decided to have it waiting for her on the bed when she came home. He searched for her personal travel bag in her closet. It wasn't there. No biggie. Sometimes she stayed at her sister's, especially when she traveled to other towns for a news story. It was likely still in her car trunk. He used another bag instead, and propped it up to be the first thing she saw when she entered the door. Next, he hunted for her crystal Christian Louboutin Kate Max Strass heels he'd bought her two years ago. She could put them on for him once she found the France tickets.

Hm, he thought. The neat freak must have moved her shoes while reorganizing last month. He grinned. Or, his wife had already planned a surprise of her own.

Headed to his office at the mortgage lender, he had more pep in his step. In three short weeks, they'd be in Saint Tropez.

"Sev, my man! I'm glad to see you!" His immediate boss

and longtime buddy, Ian, entered Seven's office before Seven set down his things.

"What's going on, my guy? You're a little jumpy over there. You good?"

Ian couldn't stand still, pacing and cresting his fingers. "Actually, we have a fire that needs to be put out with one of our, uh, top clients."

"Oh, yeah, which one?" Only halfway listening, Seven turned on his computer to make the reservation for Stillwell's tonight. Maybe he should have gotten that Cialis prescription after all. What if he couldn't get into it? Then he'd have to see Arista's disappointment again. *Don't think like that. Relax.*

"Seven, man, did you hear me?" Ian interrupted. "I said it was the Adler family over in Eastern Arkansas."

"Ya don't say." Seven still needed to submit a leave request for his time out of the country. "Isn't the Adler account your baby? The one you don't let anybody else touch?"

Ian scratched his chin. "Yeah, but right now, they need special handling. It's near a place called Elaine. I think you'd be perfect to help us push this project through. We could really use you on this one."

"Oh, yeah, man. Sure." The Stillwell's reservation wasn't going through, so Seven picked up the phone to call the restaurant directly. He really needed for Ian to bounce so he could handle his business. "Have Marsha pull the numbers and set up the call, and I'll do the rest." He started dialing the restaurant.

"Actually, Seven, I told our Helena office you'd be there this afternoon."

Seven fell back in his seat.

"Hello?" A Stillwell's hostess had answered on the other end of the line. "Hello?"

"You should have talked to me before you did that, man," Seven chastised his boss. "Why can't you do it?"

"Like I said, this needs special handling." Ian swallowed and his face turned weirder. "By somebody Black."

Seven saw red. "I don't know anybody there." But of course, Ian would think everybody that's Black knew each other. "How do we help the client by sending a stranger there who's ignorant about the project, the land value, the community? Man, that doesn't make any sense. Send Josh to do it."

Seven needed to be home with his wife and kids. He picked up the phone to buzz in an underling. Ian took a risk and stepped forward.

"Now, listen, Seven. I know this is inconvenient. But Elaine has a particular history and there's still a lot of raw feelins down there. It *must* be somebody Black." Ian explained with his hands, swirling them around one another. "Get 'em to let down their guard. Let 'em know we're on their side. We're the good guys who wanna help. Say whatever you wanna say to loosen 'em up."

Seven's realization hardened into a lump of coal in his chest. "Oh, so you don't want me to work directly with Strom Adler. You want me to glad-hand some Black people who are giving the Adlers a problem? You need an errand boy."

"More like a...a mediator. It's in their best interest. It would bring jobs, new investors, fresh money to a community that desperately needs it."

As if on cue, Marsha the secretary entered the office with a file and the client's thumb drive, setting it on Seven's desk. With her back to Ian, she offered Seven a tacit apology with her eyes.

Ian continued, "This family is thousands of dollars in debt. Barely keeping their heads above water. They've been a thorn in our side for decades. If we could close on this property for the Adlers, you and me both would come up very nicely."

Seven picked up the file and looked inside. "Conklin

Family Fields." He ran down the list of what they were farming and was instantly startled. "Frogs?"

Ian chuckled. "Yeah. Frogs. This family's been in over their heads for a long time. They're all that's sittin' between us and a nice payday. With that smooth tongue of yours, you'll probably be back home by tonight." Ian pinched air with his index finger and thumb. "We just need to knock out this one small problem."

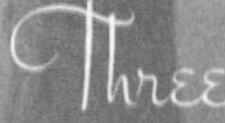

Three

PHILLIPS COUNTY

SEVEN

"Frogs?" Arista tucked her laughs behind her hand in the FaceTime. "That's a thing?"

"Apparently so." Seven tossed a couple nights' worth of slacks and Friends of the Delta golf shirts in his own travel bag now. "You wanna come with me?"

"Elaine, Arkansas? What's there? Do they have an outlet mall, an amusement park, or a spa or something?"

"No, but they will have your husband." He clawed out the map Marsha had given him. Moving his finger along the map, he found Elaine hovering near the banks of the Mississippi River. "Some place called Phillips County, an hour and a half from Memphis." Turning off the house lights and setting the alarm, he headed out to the company car waiting to take him to the airport.

"Send me pics of you and the frogs. The kids and I will have the Christmas decorations up when you get back. I'll leave Santa and the reindeer for you."

Within arm's reach of him was their holiday escape to

France. She'd find it tonight when she came home. They could start on the details—of the trip and reviving their love life—when he got back.

He couldn't blame her for not wanting to go. Who in their right mind would willingly visit the backwater of the South?

Neither the town of Elaine nor the bank's satellite office in Helena had an airport, so two hours later, he touched down in Memphis. After driving *another* hour and a half, the son of Chicago approached an incredibly long gateway that seemed to never end. From Tunica, he crossed the Helena bridge over the mighty Mississippi River. Seven didn't believe he had ever seen it before.

He wished he'd brought his Nikon camera. The glittering water stretched wider than the heights of most buildings he'd seen, far more massive than he'd imagined in middle school reading Huckleberry Finn. It sparkled between vast carpets of trees still serving autumn cinnamon and nutmeg on either side of its banks. This place felt like it was cut off from the rest of the world. Seven had needed to drive from Tennessee to Mississippi and *then* over into Eastern Arkansas.

Finally, he passed a highway marker, nearly swallowed up in tall weeds, that told him he'd entered Helena-West Helena. A folksy "Welcome to Helena" sign sat in front of the Welcome Center that was more of a picnic pavilion. A block up the road was "Freedom Park." Hardly the size of his yard, it was mostly bare, save for a few benches, an old Civil War cannonball, and rusting iron cutouts of soldiers. Seven wondered if Helena ran out of money before they could buy the merry-go-round, slide, or jungle bars for "the park."

"Elaine, Arkansas?" Seven's mother shrieked over the phone while he drove to Friends's satellite office. "What on Earth did you agree to go there for?"

"I wasn't asked, Ma. I was volun-told."

"Black people still live in Arkansas?" Pop said on the other phone back at their house in Chicago. "I thought most of 'em had left. Or...you know..."

"No, I don't." Seven steered into what seemed to be a ghost town. "What?"

Pop hedged. "Nobody else knows what happened to some of 'em, either."

"Just be careful down there, son," his mother warned. "Don't stay any longer than you have to."

"You don't have to tell me twice." Driving toward the town's main artery, Cherry Street, his mouth fell. With their darkened, blown-out windows, collapsed rooftops, and overgrown weeds, the Colonial Revival, match-box buildings were shadows of a time long passed. Where was everybody? "By the way, Ma, in case somebody asks, do we know anybody around here?"

Her heavy sigh was an answer he hadn't expected. He waited.

"No. Call me when you leave and let me know you got out of there safely."

The two-hundred-year-old antique town of Helena was only bigger than the other rural dots along US 61 by just two or three more buildings. He rolled up to the town center that didn't contain enough people to fit in a Hallmark movie.

From one side of the street to the other, simple strings of red tinsel hung over Seven's head, and looped around every vintage light pole, topped with green tinsel Christmas trees. It was a humble attempt to dress up a skeleton for the holidays. One boot at a time, he stepped into a Norman Rockwell painting of a community that hadn't been touched since 1940.

"It's all good. I'll just convince these people to use their common sense, and after we close this deal, I'll be right back on the airpl—"

The door to the bank's storefront office swung open so fast Seven didn't have time to jump back, and it banged into him. Out barreled a stout woman whose smooth face of hessonite garnet caught him off guard while her body nearly stomped over him.

"Excuse me," Seven said to her behind.

In a dress and wool coat that wanted to be on somebody else, they hiked up in the back, swishing from one side to the other, while she and her can of whoop-ass marched to an abused, muddy F-150.

"Yes, you're excused," Seven said louder and waited for her manners.

She threw her purse and herself inside and slammed the door.

Seven turned to walk in the office. Outside, tires backed out and burned rubber all the way down the street. Once he had received printouts for the property, his hotel reservation and maps, he filled his belly with barbecue from Downtown Bar. Though he was tired from all the traveling just to get here, he refused to wait until the next day to see this place. He would head out to the Conklin Fields this evening, and he wouldn't tip them off with a phone call.

An hour later, the sun had vanished. Lost on the dark Highway 44, he still wandered up and down the woods on a two-lane. The reception on his phone was going in and out. Streetlights on the main highway didn't display all the tiny dirt turnoffs hidden among the cornfields and soybean crops.

"Ancestors, how did you ever do this?"

Hugging his steering wheel, squinting to see sharp curves and animals in the middle of the street with his high beams, Seven scanned left and right for the Headless Horseman to jump out and knock his head off.

Up ahead was a sight for his tired eyes. Lights! He gratefully exhaled the breath he'd been holding, never happier in his life to see a gas station.

At six-fifteen in the evening, Arista should have made it

home and found her Christmas gift. What if she'd tried to call and couldn't reach him? He had one bar for reception, and used it to dial her. His phone dialed, but there was no answer. Yet, the missed text messages quickly rolled through.

NICKY

We bout to git this money. If I win & u ain buy a tix, don't ask me for nan.

CHARIAN

U really on a plantation? Bring back frog legs.

RAEGAN

Dad, where u at? Dnt wnt 2 stay at Aunt Fran house. It's only one tv, so we hv to watch Jeopardy n she farts in her sleep.

Fran's house? Arista's aunt?

ME

Y r u over there? Where's ur mama?

ME

Where ur bro n sis?

He waited for his Sun Ray to respond, but his messages came back as undeliverable. He grabbed a handful of Christmas peppermint Hershey kisses, some pork rinds, and two gas station hot dogs for a late dinner. There was no way he'd locate a barbecue joint in this darkness.

The kink in his neck was tightening.

"I'd also like a Powerball ticket with the numbers…" Seven thought a moment, and blurted out a date he'd heard often. "071899." The date was associated with his great-great-grand-father, Lewis Sheridan.

On his way out, he tried Arista again to see if she'd gotten home. No answer, so he dialed Raegan and Ash.

"Hello? Daddy?" his Sun Ray answered.

"Ray?"

"Daddy, you on the way? You comin' to get me?" Her eagerness danced through the phone and straight into Seven's heart.

Somewhere outside, an annoying truck revved into the carport, and he strained to hear his girl over the scream of bad brakes.

"No, baby girl, I'll get back there tomorrow. No later than Sunday. Where'd your mama say she was going?" He waited for an answer. "Ray?"

"Da..."

A storm jogged by him and bumped him on its way to the counter. More concerned with his daughter, he ignored it.

"Can you hear me?" He moved near the doorway of the gas station, stepping inside and then outside, to catch a signal. "Can you hear me now? Ray? Raeg—"

The storm blew by him again, almost knocking Seven on his behind. He faced the woman from this afternoon. In a pair of waterproof rubber boots, this time, she wasn't wearing a dress that struggled to keep up with her. In her arms, she carried every type of junk food that guaranteed diabetes.

His lottery ticket lay on the floor with another ticket. Irritated, tired, and bordering on getting in that rental car and driving back to Dallas, Seven refused to let this woman keep disrespecting him.

"I don't know if y—"

"I am so sorry. My bad. I wasn't payin' attention." Her voice did not match her march. She dropped to the floor and picked up both of their lottery tickets, shoving Seven's back in his hand and hers over her sweater, into her bra.

Glistening, she smelled like her skin was leaking moonshine. Before the distraught woman of barely thirty could avert her eyes, Seven noticed they were glassy and filled with emotion, maybe hurt or worry, or both. Tracks of tears wet her cheeks.

Hell, how could he fuss now? "It's all right. By chance, can you tell me which way is Conklin Fields?"

Now, she inched back, staring at him like he'd cursed her. Just as she opened her mouth to answer, her gaze fell to his polo shirt, just inside his coat. He watched her scan his "Friends of the Delta Savings and Loan" logo, and she snapped her mouth shut. The woman jerked away from him faster than if Seven had rabies.

"Ain' no Conklin Fields around here." Hell on wheels, she was off again.

Seven reeled at her answer. The Elaine town sign had said the population was only six-hundred and thirty-six. In a town so small, how did she *not* know the location of all that property? Maybe she wasn't from here and was simply passing through, just as he was.

"Thanks anyway. I hope you feel better," Seven called after her. He shoved his ticket in his coat pocket on the way to the clerk's counter. "You know where I might find a Sunday Conklin?"

The clerk deadpanned, as if Seven had two heads. "That *was* Sunday Conklin."

Damn. Now it made sense why this chick ran him down at the bank earlier. He rushed out the door. "Ms. Conklin! Can I talk to you for a…"

Even her F-150 was mad, revving up and burning rubber with something to prove.

Seven didn't come all this way for nothing. He threw a twenty on the counter, grabbed a Razorback t-shirt and started after her tail lights up ahead, now red specks in the dark.

He turned his headlights off and pursued until she turned

onto one of those narrow, lightless roads that disappeared in a field of darkness.

Parked along Highway 44 were several pickup trucks and a few buses, including school buses and church buses. Up ahead, she paused and then drove onto the property, her headlights illuminating long rows of greens. What was this? Some kind of party?

A mechanical gate guarded the entrance, protected by a giant, iron frog wearing a goofy smile and a sign, *The Frogs Come Out At Night.* Around it was a Christmas wreath of blinking, red lights.

Seven thought of pressing the intercom, but it would be futile. She'd already seen him wearing the Friends bank logo. He needed another way in.

Santa really must've been sitting nearby. Right then, bright lights emerged from the dark. An old school bus joined the parade of others, and off puttered elderly people. Their heads bopped to a high-energy harmonica that backed up an old man singing about frogs and snakes. The tune must have dated back to the 1940s or 1950s. It was seven o'clock on a winter night, albeit not that cold. What were they doing out here? Some of them carried long, sharp sticks. And their driver unloaded backpacks and small luggage. They must have been important because the gate to the Conklin Fields was opening again.

Someone drove out from the property and threw open her arms. She definitely wasn't the wrecking ball Seven had seen at the gas station.

"Good evenin', froggers! Y'all ready to catch some Christmas frog legs?" This younger, friendlier version of Sunday had a bit more decorum.

"Yehhhhh!" Cheers sailed into the night sky.

Moving fast, Seven rushed into the Arkansas Razorbacks sweatshirt he'd just bought. The moment he threw open his car door to exit, one of the older women stumbled in the back of the group. She limped a bit, seeming to be in hip pain that she hid from the others, unaware that Seven had seen her from several cars away. Others in her group yapped on, not noticing how she lagged behind.

Seven tossed his backpack of soil-analyzing equipment over his shoulder and snuck toward the grandmotherly lady. "Ma'am, do you need some help?"

Startled, the woman glared at a man who appeared out of nowhere. "No, I do not. Whah you come from? You new?"

Seven would have to start believing in Santa again after these breaks he was scoring.

"Yes, ma'am, I'm a new, uh..." What had the girl called them? "Frogger. I'm a new frogger, and I heard about this place. Thought I'd come check it out." He had no idea what a "frogger" was, but if it got him inside, he'd go with it. "I noticed you're having some trouble. I'd be worried if my mother was out here so late in these dark woods. How about a helping hand?" He offered her his arm.

The old woman straightened her aging back, though she still leaned on her stick. "Don't you worry 'bout me. I been doin' this since long 'fo you was born. I'm right where I'm s'pose to be."

"You mind if I join ya then? And you can teach me how to find some good, fat ones."

"Turns out tonight's your lucky night. It's nice and cool. They about to come up outta that mud and start singin'. Ya found the right instructa. You from 'round here? Feel like I know you."

"N-no, ma'am, I'm from Chicago. Always heard about this place, though." He ignored the guilty pangs of deceiving a sweet little old lady.

"Where's ya giggin' stick?" She checked around Seven's body.

Gigging stick? He was about to be exposed. Should he just tell the truth? No. He needed to enter this property, scope it out, and assess it for an offer that no family would turn down. Then he could go home. And off to St. Tropez.

"After work, on the fly, I decided to—"

Even in the dark, the old woman's eyes cut through him and planted him where he stood. "It's alright, young man, ya don't have to lie." She gripped his arm and planted him where he stood. "You can borrow a stick when we get to the lodge. If this land was callin' to ya, it's a reason ya here."

Seven swore nothing was calling to him just now. This was dirt, plain and simple, another sale he needed to close. He couldn't see it in the dark, but it felt vast, endless, and lush with money to be made off its fertility and uses. The trees alone, for lumber and construction, would attract a pretty penny. The sale of this place would be the icing on his France trip with Arista and the kids. So, he'd play along. All he had to do was stay out of Sunday Conklin's sight.

"You know, I did feel really peaceful when I walked up here."

"Mmhm." The elder's forehead lifted. "This land'll sho nuff do it to ya."

Arm in arm with her, he joined the group, walking right through the gates that closed him inside the Conklin Fields.

* * *

Sunday

"Stab him. Gon 'head! Don't let him run!" Sunday almost snatched the gigging stick from the teenager. It seemed today would never end. After her disastrous bank meeting this morning, she longed to sob under the bed covers. Instead, she had to deal with other folks' kids. She should have just impaled the doggone thing herself. "Stab him!"

The eighth-grader poked at the weeds softly, like she was roasting s'mores.

"Chile, what is you doin'?" Mama Piggee asked. "Impalin' it or ticklin' it? We can't let these boys win this thang! When I was your age, I could do this with my eyes closed!"

Other students fell against trees, not bothering to hold in their laughter.

Sunday's younger sister, Paris, dropped her head and leaned on her gigging stick. "We're gonna be out here all night."

"Get outta the way. Gimme that stick and I'll show you young gals how to do it!" Mama Piggee pumped her fists. To demonstrate for the group that she still "had it," the retired school cafeteria lady moved in. But the cold mud wouldn't let her be great. Unable to maneuver the stick as easily as she thought, she tripped and threw herself forward, face first.

"Ooh!" some of the group crowed. Somebody gripped her by the hood of her jacket and caught her from diving all the way into the mud.

"Careful there, Ms. Marleen," Sunday cautioned, calling their family friend by her first name, "looks like you need a little warmin' up yaself."

"She needs more than that," Paris murmured.

Sunday rarely led tours anymore. Since her workers who led night tours needed holiday time for shopping and their children's school events, Sunday and Paris had to cover tonight.

She should have been at the house, calling up every group on her contacts list to come and poke some frogs. They needed to muster up money to plant the cover crops they'd test out this spring for the first time. If they didn't get it right, she'd keep losing her good soil to floods.

"Miss Sunday?" One of the youth broke into her thoughts. "Will you show us how you stab the frogs?"

"I'm sorry, y'all. It's been a long day. I'm strugglin' tonight." Sunday turned to Reggie. "Reg, show 'em how we do it."

"Oh, girl, you stop it and get on out there," Mother Fordham fussed. "There's a nice young fella here with me tonight. He's new to this froggin' thang. It's his first time in Elaine. *You* show him how it's done? Young man?" The town's second-oldest resident spun around. But no one was there. "Young man? Now, he was just here talking with me."

Paris rolled her eyes. "She's always been loose a couple screws."

"Shhh." Sunday surveyed the area.

Avonia Fordham was a distant cousin of their father's, and not many of the older generations were left. However "loose" the woman's mind, Sunday was grateful for a holdover from a different time.

Reggie started scouring the mud along the shoreline of Old Town Lake. Instinctively, Sunday pointed to an area she was certain the frogs were hiding.

"No helping him, Miss Sunday, unless you're gonna do it yourself." One businessman laughed.

"What're you scared of, Sun?" a teacher teased.

Mama Piggee motioned the way older people tended to. "Sunday, help these young ladies push their count up. Give these here gals some direction and show 'em what your grannies showed *you*."

Deep down the chimney of Sunday's soul, that callout burned. She wasn't any of her grannies. Not even close. If she had half their wits, she wouldn't be in this situation.

For these tour groups to keep booking, she'd have to give them a show. Sunday rolled up her sweater sleeves and started off with her nephew.

Reggie grinned. "Auntie, let's bet on who'll catch the biggest one in five minutes. If I win, I want the new Playstation Five for Christmas."

"And what do I win if I catch the biggest?" Anticipating his answer, she smacked her lips playfully. This was the fun side of being in business with her family.

"A whole lot more love from me." Reg served his trademark goofiness.

Laughs broke the forest quiet.

"Nice try." She thought of a task he hated doing. Something juicy. "If I catch the biggest, you're cleaning the frog tents."

"*What?*" Disgusted, Reggie stared at her. "That's a whole lot of work for one little catch, auntie!"

"But you want me to bet a six-hundred-dollar game for that same little catch. Fair is fair, homie."

Sunday scanned frogs of all kinds and sizes, but she knew where the big, lazy ones liked to hunker down. Granny Ruth had taught her the sounds, and right then, she listened. Every frog in the Delta sang a different song, even if some of it amounted to ugly croaking, mooing and barking. Over the dead grass, floating moss, and into the low-hanging branches, she crept to where frogs loved to burrow in the cooler months. Since the weather wasn't freezing, quite a few of them still hovered just beneath the surface, between the water line and the mud line.

Spectators tailed her, their cell phones recording.

Where were her big boys? Several sets of bubble eyes peeped at her from beneath the mud, but she searched for a wider head. A few yards away, Reggie scouted for his own. She wasn't after a Spadefoot or a Cajun. Skipping the good ones was hard, but in her heavy duty, rubber coveralls, she waded from the mud into the shallow water, toward clusters of bushes.

Her flashlight caught a pair of eyes staring back at her, lounging in the cool space under a bush, along a tupelo. He froze in the light and didn't hop off.

"Sun. Sun," one of the tourists whispered. "Here." Somebody offered her a gigging stick.

Ignoring them, she lowered herself until he was within arm's reach. She snapped out her arm and clutched him so he couldn't squirm, snatching him from under the bushes.

"Ew!" One girl covered half her face. "She did it with her hand."

"Now that's the kinda woman I like, somebody who ain't scared to grab big, slimy stuff," one of the boys cracked.

"Watch your mouth there, young man," Principal Overton warned. "You're not slick."

Sunday and Reggie waded back to the meeting spot.

"Hold em up!" Principal Overton was comparing them.

"Ready to clean them tents?" Sunday teased. "You do all right, nephew, but you've got a lot more learnin' in front of ya."

Miss Piggee brought a measuring tape and started with Sunday's. "Six inches long, four inches across." Next, she moved to Reggie's frog. Her jaw fell slack and she squinted. "Well, I'll be doggone. Six inches long, *five* inches across!"

Reggie shot out of the mud as fast as one of his bottle rockets on Fourth of July. "Yes!" In his scratchy, 'tween voice, he was too old now to scream. "I won! I'm better at giggin' than you now, auntie! I'm gettin' a Playstation! You don't even have to put it under the tree for me, auntie! I'll take mine now!"

The tourists clapped at his excitement.

"Careful now. That just means you got yaself a good teacher here." Principal Overton sounded like he was back in the hallways of Elaine High School again. "Both of y'all caught some mighty big ones."

"That's gon' be some good eatin', too." Mama Piggee held open the ice chest. "These swamps run in that Conklin-Straughter blood."

Sunday eyeballed Reggie. "Where did you find that frog?"

"That's for me only to know, auntie." Still celebrating, Reg did one of his social media dances in the mud. "You gonna have my game system waitin' on me tomorrow after school?"

Now, Sun swapped a nervous glance with Paris, whom they'd nicknamed Peady. Finding the funds to pay for a Playstation would add one more crook to Sunday's neck. The thirteen-year-old would be fortunate if he received the game before he turned eighteen.

Miss Fordham asked, "Sun, how you let this bighead boy out-hustle you?" She turned aside. "You see that there, young man? If that boy can catch a good one, you can—" Yet again, the woman looked and found no one beside her. "Whah'd ya go?"

Sunday wondered what was happening with Miss Fordham. "Miss Fordham, who're you over there talkin' to?"

"What in the world?" Ms. Piggee peered at Ms. Fordham. "Where did that gentleman go? He was just right there. I saw him, too!"

Next to Miss Fordham, Sunday shined her flashlight at an extra set of foot prints in the mud. They trailed away from the swamp and in the direction of her fields.

Ordinarily, she wouldn't have paid it any mind. Plenty of experienced giggers booked weekends to venture out on their own. But who would stand there with Ms. Fordham and disappear without a word? Going toward Sunday's crops. Someone who had not booked their trip and snuck in with a tour group?

After what happened this morning with a trespasser

parking on her land, flying a drone over it, and then the awful bank meeting, Sunday's internal radar fired off.

"Sun, I'm exhausted. I'm about to hit this ground. Let's head to the house." Peady rubbed her eyes.

"Bring me Earl."

"What?" That snapped Peady's eyes wide open. "What'd you see? A bear? Wolf? Coyote? *What*, Sun?"

Sunday kept quiet, keeping her suspicions to herself. Peady would try and talk her down, and Sunday had no more patience for talking. "Just bring him to me."

Four

BANK MAN MEETS EARL

SEVEN

Seven heaved his water-soaked boots further down the perimeter between the woodlands and the field. He had ventured pretty far away from the group, and his elderly companion, but since they were at least seventy-five heads strong, nobody had noticed him slip off.

His expensive Lucchese cowboy boots he'd worn to the desert in Nevada, ranches in Texas, and the wine valleys of California, were no match for this Delta clay soil. The upside was he'd gotten what he'd come for. The clay soil quality of this place was as lush as Ian had said. Situated near the Mississippi River *and* this Old Town Lake, the grass around here must have turned so emerald in the summertime, a man could see it glow all the way from Mars. Seven envisioned waterskiing, boating, fishing, hunting, walking and biking paths, too.

Who in their right mind would use such a nice piece of real estate for frogs? No wonder it was failing. She owed well over three hundred thousand dollars on it, and her payments had fallen behind. The way Seven saw it, this chick should count her lucky stars the bank was offering her a way out.

He dug his hands in the cool top soil and let it fall through his fingers. The energy inside him reacted. Out here in the dead of night, he was hit with memories of fizzy, orange soda pop on his tongue, sugary popsicles turning his fingers blue, and lightning bugs flitting around him. In a most visceral flashback, he felt a surge of terror at a large, black wasp chasing him, while he ran away with sticky, smoked barbecue brisket he'd rubbed on his t-shirt. Where'd that visual come from? How old had he been?

The Conklins' frogs were singing to Seven from the lake. Though he didn't quite understand the frogs, Seven could see how somebody would hesitate to give up this peacefulness. He'd read the family's file on the plane ride—a father who'd been dead sixteen years, a disabled mother, an older brother in prison, and only two years ago, her older sister killed. Sunday must've had the whole world on her shoulders. In the buyout negotiations with the bank and the Adlers, Seven would ensure she was handled delicately. After all they'd been through, these folks deserved sympathy, especially at Christmas. They were helpless. He shoved his soil analyzer device back in his knapsack to return to the group before they realized he was gone.

A single click echoed through the night. Hard steel pushed against his skull.

"Drop that thang right where it's at and put yo' hands up where I can see 'em."

That guttural voice, so apologetic back at the gas station, now leaked gun powder. She couldn't have been holding what she pretended to be.

Seven laughed with relief. "For a moment, I thought you were serious. This here is a dope place you have."

A single shot blasted into the same starry sky he'd just

gazed at. His heart out-flapped the birds' wings flying from the trees.

"Who ain't serious?"

"Sunday!" somebody else hissed a few steps away.

"I said drop it and put your hands up."

How had she crept up on him in that thick, rubber getup she was wearing?

Seven felt like an idiot dropping his device on the ground and lifting his hands as if he were some criminal. "Ms. Conklin, I was just admiring your spread."

"Raise up slow."

Was this for real? "Sunday...Ms. Conk...Sunday, you've probably got a lot on your mind. I understand. You need some help with all this trouble you're in."

"I won't tell ya again. The next one will be in your behind. You are a trespasser, sir. You've snuck onto my property. Now you're makin' yaself at home. What you want next? A cold brew and a plate?"

"Actually, I am hungry. I've been traveling all day, and the cellular reception around here is bad so I'd like to use your phone to call my kids and wi—"

The gun blasted again, and his backpack holding his device exploded.

"Damn, woman, that wasn't yours to shoot!" Seven snapped.

"And my property ain' Strom Adler's to invade! You lucky I don't exercise my right to shoot you."

He eased up from where he kneeled in the dirt. "Your lawyer must be as smart as your farming. You don't have a right to shoot me. You can't use deadly force for a mere trespass."

"It'll be your word against mine."

"How much is your word worth around here?"

"Start marchin'."

Still seething at how she'd destroyed his analyzer, Seven resentfully obeyed, collecting his shattered device and bag with a giant hole through it.

"Is this how you act with all the guests to your home?"

"Who invited you?"

He walked in his fancy cowboy boots filled with mud and water. "Look, Sunday, I could help you ease everything on your mind."

"Says every man who can't be found nine months later."

She had some humor about her.

"I'm not talking about that. I'm with Friends of the Delta Savings and Loan. One of the lead finance guys in the company. I specialize in smoothing out the money part."

"So the bank did send somebody onto my property? You must want this bullet real bad."

Walking in thick mud with a gun to his head, Seven stumbled, falling almost to the ground. Miss Sunday nudged the barrel into his back and urged him back on his feet.

"The bank sent me to see how we can help you. Sneaking in here was my idea. I saw a bunch of happy folks and I invited myself to a good time. I apologize."

"If I ever catch you here again, I'll invite myself to do some thangs also. Besides, the bank ain't interested in helpin' me or they would have done it already."

"They're trying to. You've got a respectable piece of land here, Ms. Conklin. You don't have to be in debt and struggling. Let's work something out. Even if you manage to afford your spring planting, how will you get it out of the ground and to market come October? The floods get worse every year, and your old equipment is no match. You don't have updated sprays to keep up with new diseases and more resistant bugs. Prices are steadily outrunning income. You've held this place up a mighty long time and that is to be commended. I give you two more years to keep limping along. And that's generous.

Three if you hit paydirt next year with a big buyer, the way you sometimes tend to. But why keep pressing your luck?"

Like she was emphasizing who was in charge, she shoved the barrel against his spine. "I suppose for the same reason you keep pressing yours. I'm not a quitter."

"You won't be. If we buy you out, you'd have an entire world of possibilities ahead of you. And no failing farm strapped to your back."

"You mean the Adlers. If the *Adlers* buy me out."

The two marched through the empty dirt field, with nothing more lighting the way than a wintry crescent moon. "No, I said the bank."

"The banks around here do whatever the Adlers tell 'em to. All of ya are in bed with them. Hell, the Adlers may as well be the bank. I bet you're the only Black boy that works there, huh? I ain' nevah seen no othah. So you're the token, a DEI hire."

"Black *man*, ma'am. You mean Black man."

"Tell the bank that." The woman behind him huffed. "Next time they call you to tote their water, you should let 'em know real *Black men* don't do that."

Seven's feet hurt, his cowboy boots now lead cinderblocks. Fifty-five degree air bit his skin and his arms struggled over his head. He still dragged himself through the middle of a dark field that seemed endless.

"I don't tote anything for anybody, Ms. Sunday. I do my job. You should be grateful for token DEI hires. We're the ones who speak up for stubborn nepo babies who don't know when it's time to move on."

Fed up and exhausted, he swayed and dropped to a knee.

Unswayed, Sunday stood over him with her gun. "They use your Black skin for convincing Black folks to give up our land!"

This time, when she nudged Seven with the barrel, he

caught her off guard, twisting suddenly to grab the shaft. He aimed it up at the sky in case it fired. The woman was tough. Her fingers hadn't let go. With them both holding on, he snatched her forward and threw her into the dirt next to him. She must have been made of Teflon, her fingers welded to that rifle. It fired and blew out Seven's eardrums.

He had a feeling she was one of those who *liked* to fight. Sunday snapped onto her side and started punching with one hand, while still clutching the gun with the other.

"Get off my land, and take your ugly DEI cowgirl boots with you!" She managed to steal on him with two solid licks to his chest and shoulder.

Seven threw his six feet and three inches onto her and applied everything he had to overpower her.

"I get it, all right? Drop this damn thing!"

The struggle reminded him that he hadn't been to the gym in a while. Wrestling Sunday made plainly clear how much muscle mass he'd lost while he'd been raising his kids. Pinning her down tonight would have been easier ten years ago. She clearly spent her days lugging large bags and tools, operating giant machinery that weighed tons, and repeating high-energy motions. Her heavy, rubber overalls didn't hide the firm muscles underneath that told him she could do this all day and not get tired. He definitely would not have snatched her to the ground without surprising her. Straining every vein in his neck for what felt like an eternity, he finally shoved her wrists into the dirt.

A shocked Sunday Conklin glared like she couldn't believe somebody had the audacity to fight her back. "Get offa me!"

"I know you don't want me here, and you don't want the bank sending anybody else. So deal with me now! I'm unarmed, so if you shoot me, Arkansas will bury you *under* the prison. Then, what about your aging mother, niece, nephew, younger brother, and your sister still in college? You really gonna leave all that weight for your next sister, Paris, to handle by herself? Huh?" He struggled to hold her down. "When your daddy fell off that tractor, it snuffed out your future. If you go completely broke, will London have to give up hers, too?"

The lights in her eyes seemed to turn on. His words may have been flipping her internal switches. Her body mellowed under him. Sunday was seeing the light.

"Yeah," Seven added. "That's what DEI hires do. Now, can we go somewhere and talk like adults?"

Out of nowhere, a large wad of spit hit his eye. She'd hurled too fast for him to dodge, like she'd done it so many times she didn't even have to stop and aim first. Did Seven let go of one wrist to wipe it off? No. With one wrist free, she'd do worse.

"Ignant fool! I said, get *off* me!" she screamed. "Friends Bank ruined everything! And you're a fool for lettin' them use you to take down anotha Black person! That damn bank has *destroyed* Elaine! Ain nothin' in this world worth me givin' up this land. You'll need a missile to take me out. Go back and tell 'em I said it." Chest heaving, lips and fists curled, she hollered that with her full chest.

Wheezing, out of shape, Seven's lungs hurt from sucking in too much cold night air while tussling. Then, he realized he was still on top of her.

While she was distracted with her feelings, he grabbed her gun and flung it out of her reach. Then, he rolled off her. He didn't dare sit or rest, and watched for her next move. Sunday lugged herself back onto her feet, her back to him as if somebody had instructed her to "never let 'em see you cry."

In the distance, headlights approached, riding down one of those narrow dirt roads from the other side of the field. The coming cloud of dust silhouetted Sunday's well-nourished hips that swung in the light. The dirt thrown up from the ground formed a luminous halo around her, so she appeared to float over the land of her ancestors.

Seven averted his eyes. He was focusing too hard.

The pickup truck from earlier reappeared and another pair of shoes jumped out.

"Girl, get in the truck and cut out this foolishness." An older woman jerked a finger toward the vehicle. She shielded her eyes from the headlights to study Seven. "Young man, you all right?"

Seven squinted to make her out in the dark. From her slight limp, Seven calculated she must have been Vertreese, the family matriarch now.

"Yes, ma'am," he answered.

"Come, get on. We'll take ya back to your car."

Sunday met him in the back of the pickup truck. The older woman, similar enough in stature and demeanor to be her mother, heaved herself into the passenger side. In the driver's seat sat the kid from earlier, Sunday's nephew. If Seven's memory served him correctly from reviewing the file, that would be Reggie. He couldn't have been more than thirteen. Yet, here he was driving his grandmother and auntie around in the fields.

Caked in mud from head to toe, Sunday and Seven stared each other down on the bumpy ride back to Highway 44, in case one tried to pull something on the other. A few kinks of her angry hair had escaped one of her dirty French braids and blew around in the wind.

"All of you could have a real nice Christmas that your family deserves," Seven reiterated on their ride back to the main road.

"We're gonna have a nice Christmas anyway because we have each other." The truck came to a stop. "Don't come back. This is your only warnin'."

"Just in case you wanna think about it, I'll leave the papers here." He salvaged what hadn't exploded in his shot-up bag, and spoke loud enough that her mother could hear him from the front seat. "Six million dollars is a lot of money. That's a lot of college educations. All your debt. You could leave Elaine and move to Little Rock. Buy yourself a nice, new house on Chenal Parkway. Finish that engineering degree you never got from Clark Atlanta."

At that, Sunday flinched and motioned with her gun for him to hightail it out of her truck.

Seven continued, "Here's my card." He wedged the documents underneath heavy rope and eased himself over the tailgate. "Once you calm down, we can have a talk."

He went for what was left of his soil analyzer bag. Maybe with help from a tech guy, they could salvage the readings on the SD card.

"Leave that here. I didn't give you permission to stick nothin' in my dirt."

Seven stared at the bag with the bullet hole right through it. "I need that soil grade proof to convince them to give you as high an offer as possible."

"You need it so you can tell the Adlers my dirt's good enough for all the ways they wanna use it once they've got it." The night frost had nothing on her.

With her jaw set like that, he didn't stand a chance.

"You all, have a good n—"

Thirteen-year-old Reggie had obviously been taking lessons from his aunt on how to drive like a bat out of hell. Seven's papers flew out of the trailer and drifted to the ground. He was too exhausted and stiff to bother picking them up. Instead, he removed one ruined boot at a time and tossed them in the large trashcan outside the gate. The hard ground was sharp and pebbly on his feet, but that was still better than lugging heavy wet boots on the short trek down the highway to his rental.

Once his feet warmed, he could have fallen asleep right there in the driver's seat, but he needed to call his family, and let his wife know he was okay. She'd probably found the plane tickets and had been trying to reach him. Aside from that, he was sitting on a lonely road in the South.

Despite that ridiculous exchange just now, Seven's insides hummed. That rumble in the dirt had charged him up. Out on the land, frogs and owls serenading him, the forest engulfing him, every star in the sky visible, Sunday's feisty outrage...her hips...

...no.

He shook that thought from his mind. His fascination, one he couldn't yet put his finger on, must have been connected to the ground beneath him. Even in the car, it felt like the land was playing sheet music his blood was dancing to. What was this town of Elaine he'd never heard of?

To stay awake, he turned on the stereo, and an electric guitar screamed at him. A raw blues man moaned with no fanfare, *She's Got the Devil In Her*. After all he'd just been through, Seven might not have agreed with a song so much in his life.

But certain parts of him were waking up. He peered down at the crotch of his jeans. Hot damn.

He hadn't seen that in some time. Seven needed to go call Arista.

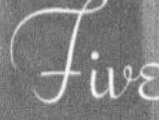

Five

SHUT YO MOUTH!

SUNDAY

Sunday brewed her coffee before dawn was anywhere close to breaking the horizon.

I give you two more years to keep limping along. And that's generous... why keep pressing your luck?

She massaged her neck. Squabbing at thirty-six hit different than squabbing at sixteen. Her sore hips reminded her when she stooped to pick up the kids' mess from decorating the old Christmas tree last night.

That bank man had irritated her something awful, but now she snickered. He had real nerve. He couldn't have been more than forty. Clean-shaven, long, a wiry frame underneath the middle-age weight he'd likely gained from sitting on his behind in some office, he'd shocked her with his audacity to grab her gun. Everybody around here knew better. But that man wasn't from around here.

If we buy you out, you'd have an entire world of possibilities ahead of you. And no failing farm strapped to your back.

At the kitchen table, in front of her pile of unpaid bills, for a few precious moments, Sunday allowed her mind to wonder.

Six million dollars is a lot of money. That's a lot of college educations. All your debt. You could leave Elaine and move to Little Rock. Buy yourself a nice, new house on Chenal Parkway.

If Daddy hadn't died and she'd remained in Atlanta with her engineering degree.... She'd have two or three homes by now. Several vacations a year wouldn't be a problem. For her *and* her siblings.

Sunday also would have found *her* distinguished husband —educated, financially stable, respected, and heavy on the love.

Last night, she couldn't help a glance at his ring finger while his hands were up. It wore a ring.

Not that she was interested. She saw plenty of action from her standby-links she kept around the Delta. Men who got the job done and kept her topped off. But a tiny sliver of her imagined what it would be like to actually talk when it was over.

Now, she reached for the bills. The same way Daddy once did. Quite a few utilities and accounts still had his name on them.

"Daddy, Nessie, where are ya? I need you. *We* need you." Before the flood could start up good, she squeezed the tears from her eyes. "Elaine needs ya. Real bad." The knot in her throat was unraveling and she shuddered to even think the rest. "Or they're gonna finally finish the job."

She stole the next three minutes of morning quiet to dry-heave from her soul. Since the boys were piled up in the living room, she stifled the sobs so only God and her ancestors would know. Hearing the first creaks somewhere in the house, she soaked up the tears with her sweater sleeve.

Deciding what she could pay now, and what would be shut off, she stared down the hallway to the final bedroom at the end.

As a child she could never go inside, and only rarely did she do so now. Inhaling a nervous breath almost too big for her lungs to hold, Sunday ventured down the hallway until she stood at the door. There *had to be* a reason for this. Hand raised, she started to knock.

Another bedroom door opened across the hall.

"Auntie." Tori padded over to Sunday's arms. "Can we go to Walmart today, and look for my Barbie truck for Christmas?"

Sunday wondered if she should knock anyway. With lead feet, she headed back to the kitchen. "You have responsibilities today. Remember? We still have guests staying at the cabins."

Her niece's face fell upon the reminder of her "responsibilities." She caught a look at the piles of bills and "Past Due" statements on the table. "What's all that?"

Sunday turned over some of the envelopes, determined to shield the younger children as much as possible from her problems. "Important papers I have to see about. That's all."

As if Tori didn't believe her, she asked, "Am I really going to get my Barbie truck? I made straight A's and had good behavior, just like you told me." She lowered her voice. "Do you have enough money to buy the Barbie truck?"

That needle didn't feel good. "Don't you worry about that. Leave that to me. Do you mind helpin' out and goin' to greet our visitors in the cabins when they pick up their breakfast? Hand them clean gig sticks and food to feed the ducks and swans?" Distraction was the only currency Sunday had right now. "And since we're still on a water boil, make sure they've got at least three jugs of spring water in each cabin. And their intercom works to buzz us for more."

Tori nodded. "Are they gonna gimme some money like they do in summer?"

"If you brush your teeth and your breath don't smell like you were just chewing your mattress, maybe." Sunday laughed. "Hurry up and go get dressed, so you can start pulling it all together."

Sunday quickly scribbled out a couple of checks. She and Peady could discuss a small loan from Peady's fiancee who had a good job at the post office.

"Mornin'." Mama scooted in for coffee. "Who was that man you were out there actin' up with? He looked familiar."

"Some bank lackey the Adlers sent to poke around in our business."

"Anybody we know?" She stirred sugar into her cup. "He don't come off like a stranger. Looks familiar. You get his name?"

"No."

Mama stared at Sunday over her mug. "Didn't he give you some papers?"

Since Peady had spent the night to help with work, she came in next. "What did he say? And mornin'."

Sunday sipped her coffee that had turned cold. "The Adlers want to buy our land and the bank wants to arrange it."

"That's good, ain't it? Just yesterday, you were mad the bank wouldn't redo your loan." Sunday's younger sister leaned back against the sink, her hands on her hips. "What did you tell him?"

Her back to Peady and her mama, Sunday started tugging on her own boots and jacket. "Not a snowball's chance in hell."

"What did he offer?"

Of all the mornings for Peady to start caring... "Does it matter?"

"Maybe."

Nookie paused from going to put on his clothes. Tori returned from putting on hers.

Sunday stared at them all staring at her. "Six million."

Peady shifted where she stood. "When were you gon talk' to us about that?"

The sudden sharpness in Peady's tone caught Sunday off guard.

"What's to talk about? They've wanted our land for years and our answer's always been the same."

"That was back when the economy was better and these tariffs weren't bitin' us." Peady snatched on her own coat with a vengeance. "I'm not tryin' to be mean, Sun, but we also had Vanessa. She spent more time with Daddy, learnin' things, and was better at business and the public part of it than you."

Sunday couldn't pretend that didn't sting. She'd known Peady was somewhat bothered about having to come over and help. As the third daughter, she'd grown up accustomed to the older kids doing the heavy lifting with her only pitching in as needed. So her pent-up resentment at having to contribute more didn't surprise Sun. However, that open wound now had salt on it.

"You're not the only one with rights to this land, and the rest of us don't feel the same as you do about workin' it, Sun." Peady cast a glance over at Nookie. The two of them had apparently been commiserating.

Caught on the back foot, Sunday was flabbergasted. "What's that supposed to mean?"

"The next time somebody comes around here offerin' us millions of dollars, he should be talkin' to all of us. Not just you." Gloves and a hot pocket in hand, Peady headed for the back door.

"What is wrong with you?" *Not now.* All they needed was for a fight to break out right before Christmas. And when Sunday might have to ask for money.

"I got a kid, Sun. And a husband at home. You never had kids, so you've got plenty time to waste out in them fields. But I'm pregnant again."

There it was.

Peady's leg shook her whole body like it was winding her up. "You're so busy worryin' about work and money you didn't even notice. But Vanessa would have. Much as I respect family legacy and all that, them people been dead and gone. I wanna be with *my* family at night. Not out in the swamp. The next time that bank man comes here, I wanna talk to him. So don't you run him off. I wanna sell my part of the land. Whatever part of it is mine."

"Did you really need to come for my womb, though?" TKO'd by shock, Sunday didn't have any other comeback.

"The two of y'all, stop it." Mama's smile was proud. "I'm havin' me another grand baby. How far along?"

"Four months. It's a boy, and I want my kids to have somethin'."

The world was spinning hard for it to barely be sunrise.

"They *do* have somethin'." Sunday stood from tugging on her boots.

"This farm don't give out what you put in, Sun." Peady hung her head and swung it in disagreement. "I'm sorry. Please, don't be mad at me. But somebody gotta say it. You out there killin' yaself for somethin' that don't wanna live. Maybe it's time for them dead folks to rest and for you to let the Adlers have it."

Paris may as well have smacked Sunday with that wrought-iron skillet.

"You's a fool for lettin' it even come out your mouth. Take it back!"

"No." Peady's stank-eye was really a stench. "You can't even bring yourself to say 'congratulations'. You're sittin' there worryin' about who's gonna do my work. What will you do? Make London quit school like you did?"

"Y'all, that's enough!" Their mother went to her daughter

for a hug that might turn down the temperature in the kitchen.

When Peady flung the door open, they were all jarred. What sounded like shouting echoed across their fields. The visitors in the cabins were calling out to each other.

Mama peered outside. "What on God's green earth is goin' on out there?"

Somebody had been hurt? Sunday jumped after the First Aid kit. "Lord, somebody's done something stupid."

Nookie craned his neck to see. "They're dancin'."

"They're what?" With the binoculars, Sunday took a closer look. The guests walked together and laughed, like they were excited. A few of them scurried between cabins, each one of them holding something. Was it paper? "What's in their hands? Why are they so happy?"

"Sun, go see what's goin' on out there." Mama turned to her younger daughter. "Peady, if you too tired or you're not feelin' good, stay here and rest."

Principal Overton ran toward the house, out of breath when he arrived.

"Everything all right out there, Mr. Overton?" Sunday asked her former high school principal.

"Somebody in Arkansas won the..." He huffed a few times. "Powerball! They might be right here in the Delta!"

"Quit playin'!" Nookie nearly left his skin to run for the television.

"Shut yo' mouth!" Mama slapped the former principal's arm.

"We didn't hear all the numbers on the radio and the cell phone reception isn't good in those fields." The grin on his face was a wreath while he held up his ticket. "I wanted to check my numbers here."

Sunday sucked her teeth. Even if something so ridiculous was true—nobody in Arkansas ever won anything—those folks had rigged it to make sure the winning ticket was sold in some white area of the Delta. That's how everything in Arkansas was done. It was so ingrained in every aspect of their lives that a "whites only" sign was no longer needed.

In the living room, the newscaster, Les Warner's, voice was too upbeat for this side of early. "The winning numbers were sold last night at a Kwik Stop in a town called Elaine, Arkansas. I've never even heard of Elaine, Arkansas. Have you, Monica? What part of the state is that?"

Sunday nearly dropped her coffee mug.

"Sweet Jesus! You hear that?" Mama slapped her hands together, the sound ringing through the house. Celebration rang out all around her.

On television, Les interviewed the store clerk. "Sir, has anyone brought in the ticket to claim the money yet?"

"No, sir." That was the clerk at Kwik Stop!

Les continued, "This one-hundred-and-ninety-six million dollars is the *largest* jackpot in Arkansas history. Now, the entire state is waiting with bated breath for what happens next on this most epic Christmas."

Nookie backed up and eyed Sunday. "Sun, you buy that lottery ticket yesterday?"

Tori's jaw dropped, eyes large as Christmas ornaments, and she jumped up and down. "You bought a ticket, Auntie?"

Principal Overton pointed at the TV. "At *that* gas station that was just on the news?"

Her sixteen-year-old brother circled his index finger in the air impatiently for her to hurry up and remember.

She'd drank before the tour last night. Then she caught one of those bank guys sneaking out in her field. What happened between drinking and fighting?

Racking her brain, Sunday nodded. She was sure of it. There was no mistaking those ridiculous cowboy boots Bank

Man was wearing when they bumped into each other and dropped their tickets in the doorway.

"Yeah, I did."

Whooping and cheering could have deafened her.

His teeth gleaming from ear to ear, Nookie rubbed his hands together. "That's what I'm talkin' 'bout, sis."

Automatically, Sunday shoved a hand in her bra, where she temporarily stored everything of value. From one side to the other, she dug around. It wasn't there.

She'd changed clothes twice last night— when she put on her overalls, and after she got back from the tour. She didn't recall putting the ticket away either time.

Peady snickered. "You oughta know about drinkin' when you're mad."

"Well?" Mama insisted. "Where's his ticket at?"

"*His* ticket?" Sunday snapped. "He used *my* money *I* give him for lunch. Besides, he's not old enough to play the lottery anyway."

"Aside from that, where is it, Sun?" Peady insisted.

"I just have to look real quick."

"You mean you don't know where you put it." Peady's thumb steadily strummed her fingers.

"I know where," Sunday lied. "I just have to check."

Her family didn't buy it.

Neither did Principal Overton, whose eyes glowed when he pointed out the door. "So...it could be somewhere out *there?* Where we were last night? I'll help you look."

"No!" Realizing what was happening, Mama threw up her hands. "It's all right, Tommy, we got it!"

Faster than water on hot grease, he was out of the skillet, nearly falling off the porch in his scramble to tell the others.

"Aw, Sunday." Mama wrung her hands, something she hadn't done since Daddy had died and she learned how much debt he had. "Wake Reggie up so he can get out there and keep an eye on 'em. We're gonna need everybody. Sunday and Nookie, y'all take the yard and everywhere Sunday went yesterday. Me, Peady, and Tori will search the house."

Principal Overton reached the others and his lips were looser than the wooden floorboards. In the same fields where their ancestors had toiled, the neighbors' bones started snapping to life like the Rapture had come.

A heavy crease stretched over Mama's eye. "We've gotta find it before one of them do."

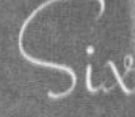

Six

MY LAWD

SEVEN

"Raegan!" Before he'd fully shaken off sleep, Seven grabbed at his phone.

When he'd finally made it to The Edwardian in Helena, at nearly one in the morning, the only person in his family he could reach was Raegan.

Several hours later, Seven awakened to what must've been a million text messages, mostly from his sister, Charian, and his Uncle Nicky. He skimmed without opening.

NICKY
Bruh, u get the tick...

CHARIAN
7-Up, yo time up if u didn't...

DAD
Son, where'd u buy ur...

Seven could care less about the stupid lottery. He was checking for one group of people. And one person.

Scrolling and scrolling, he finally saw one.

RAEGAN

im koo. Auntie farts. When u cmn hm?

ASH

At Miranda's. Cn i stay da wknd?

Of course, she is. They'll go to the arcade, the pizza parlor, and land at somebody's house doing each other's hair. Miss Popularity was good as long as she was with her friends.

ME

Fin hmwk b4 bedtime tmrw.

DILLON

At Chris house

His children were safe. Dillon and Ash were good with not being at the house. The only one who had a problem was Raegan, since she hadn't landed some place she liked. Apparently, Arista had made arrangements for all of them.

Why weren't they at the house? Seven slid his finger up and down for a message from her, especially the one where she was giddy about finding the flights to St. Tropez, or the one where she was worried about him on those dark, country roads. There it was.

WIFEY

Hey, babe, u gd? Call and lmk how frogs went.

Excited, he was ready to be worshipped appropriately, reading further up the thread for the rest, particularly the one where she was going nuts over the surprise flights she'd found by now.

Seven scrolled.

That was it?

Nestling in the sheets, he lifted them and peeked. Stiff as a brick, his manhood was ready for action. These days, it didn't stand up like that without medication first, and Seven hadn't taken any in a few days. That was all-natural right there.

He took a pic and sent it to his wife.

ME

No Cialis.

We back.

With the kids elsewhere, maybe they could do a video call. It had been a good minute since they'd done that. Years, actually. Arista was an early riser, so she'd be up by now, either on her spin machine or her treadmill.

A few minutes later, Seven still waited for her to call him squealing over his pic. They were running out of time. He had to check in with the Helena office and report his data from last night.

He positioned his thumb over her picture to call her. Instead, his Uncle Nicky's trifling image popped up, holding a stripper on each leg. If Seven didn't answer it, his uncle would never shut up.

"Dude, I bought the ticket all right? I'm not even gonna be here for Christmas, and just so you'll be quiet, I still bought it anyway," Seven said before Nick could blow off steam.

Their family played betting games at Christmas with old lotto tickets. The more tickets a person had, the more entries they got and the higher their chances of winning Christmas money.

"Negro, what you mean 'you won't be here'?" Nicky was holed up in his office. That squeaky, old leather chair would never let Nicky do anything on the low.

"I'm taking Arista and the kids to France for Christmas.

Like I said, we won't be here." Now that Arista had the tick-ets, he could go ahead and let the cat out of the bag.

"The hell that's got to do with me?"

Seven couldn't lollygag any longer. His sexual rebirth would have to wait. Hopefully, not for long. He might not convince this Sunday chick to sell willingly, but if the bank planned on foreclosing, Seven would help her out. It was the least he could do.

"You're right, Unc, it's got nothing to do with you." Seven rose from a stiff, hundred-year-old bed that Robert E. Lee must've slept in. He cracked the black-out curtains. The tiny town of Helena was filled with the ghosts of buildings, a Confederate Cemetery, and an old Civil War fortress called Fort Curtis. Along with the occasional Christmas ribbon, wreath or tinsel. Like they'd tried to decorate a haunted town. "What's popping? Didn't you know I'm out of town?"

His mother's younger brother loved playing the lottery, hoping one day he'd win and retire from his job as store manager at Savings Pro grocery. "Yes, Negro. That's why I'm callin'! Get out that bed and go check yo ticket, mane!"

"Why?" Still sleepy, Seven rummaged through his slacks for the ticket. What had he done with it? "Somebody won?"

"Is fat meat greasy? Somebody didn't just win. They won right there where you're at!"

"Really." Preoccupied, Seven still anticipated his wife call-ing. He checked himself again. Yep, his dick was still reporting for duty.

"*Really.*" His uncle mocked him. "Dude, where'd you say you was at again? Tunica or somethin' like that?"

"Helena."

"Where's that? That near Elaine? *Please*, tell me you at least drove through Elaine, or took a piss in Elaine, or got some cat in Elaine or sump'm. If you bought a ticket in Elaine,

I swear I will never talk noise to you again, and I will personally put gas in your car for the rest of my life."

This dude was a trip. Nicky had been promising that since Seven was a teenager, and he had never ponied up. "Bruh, chill. I was just in Elaine last night. Why?"

"Stop playin' wit me!" Nicky's rickety back-office chair hit the cheap linoleum floor. "You lyin'!"

"I'm not. I was there."

"Check it out. Did you use Lewis Sheridan's birthday? Because the winning numbers are—"

The phone beeped. Arista!

"Nicky, I gotta call you back. Ri's calling." If they hurried, he and Arista could get it done in three minutes.

"She can wait. You got the numbers or not, mane?" Nicky complained.

Seven's first nut with no meds was more important. This was a life-altering event. He kept that part to himself. Click.

"Baby, you won't believe how hard I am right now. I ain' even take anything. It's crazy. I got in the car last night after the site visit and my dick was 'bout to blow." Proudly, he stroked himself. "We ready fo' you, bae. You check the bed and find your Christmas gift, yet?"

"Um, come again?" a strange young woman's voice spoke through the other end.

Seven now checked the phone screen. He'd assumed it was Ri and hadn't looked before he clicked over.

On the caller ID: Paris Conklin.

"Oh!" Snap! *The hell?* "My bad, Ms. Conklin. I was, um..." He hopped into some sweatpants as if she could see him bricking in his underwear. "I thought I was speaking to my wife. You are..." Which number was she in the sisters again? He racked his brain for all the info he'd memorized on the plane yesterday.

"I'm Paris, the third sister. Right after Sunday. Is this the man who she chased off our property? The one from the bank?"

"Sunday didn't chase me. All right? I walked slowly. She was not all that welcoming, though."

His line beeped, and this time Seven checked. At this point, he needed Arista to call. And not necessarily because he was worried for her safety. She had plenty of friends and family around the DFW who could reach her faster if she was in trouble. Her safety was a given.

He checked the screen for the mother of his children. Nicky's face awaited. Annoyed, Seven hit 'Send to voicemail.'

"That ain't the way I heard it," Paris said. "But anyway, somebody brought me your papers from outside our gate. I know how my sister can be. I wanna know what the offer was."

Say what? Caught off guard, Seven put his head back in the game, so he could be sure he was hearing what he thought he was hearing.

"I can't guarantee a firm number since I only analyzed a little soil. But just from eyeballing it, and from what I saw on my analyzer before your sister destroyed it, I feel comfortable floating six million. If the crop yields, structures, water, and such are good, you could get more."

"Tell him we'll take it," some guy said in the background.

"Shhh." Ms. Conklin shushed somebody. She was in a room with other people listening in. That guy was likely Narado, the youngest. It couldn't have been their older brother, Will, since he was still in prison.

"I can't speak for my sister," Ms. Conklin continued, "but I'm tryin' ta hear my share if I sell my part."

"Yeh, me too," the young guy with her said.

"Shhh. And I wanna do it quick." Paris's words sped up, and her voice tightened, as if she feared someone catching her. "Before she can hire a lawyer and stop me."

Whoa, Nelly. So, there was division among the Conklin siblings.

Seven's phone started beeping again. This time, he just let the call go. He didn't dare miss this small window of opportunity. If he pushed this deal through, he and Ri would be traveling to a lot more places than France.

"All right then, Ms. Conklin. For me to get a reliable estimate of the property, I'd need to analyze your land with my machine. Your sister shot up mine. And even then, that's only an initial estimate to start the conversation. Your land has a couple of mortgages on it. And about three liens I'm aware of. We'd need a full appraisal and audit of the farm, so the bank can see what you're working with. I'd have to bring in my guys before we could give you a formal offer in writing."

"Bet. Let's start with your machine then. We'll go out there with you and make sure she don't shoot it up again."

A partial deal wasn't ideal, but this was more progress than the bank had made with this bunch in a generation. Maybe this piecemeal approach would be best. If Sunday's siblings sold and walked away, she'd be alone carrying the financial and work obligations, which added pressure. The cash would be harder to turn down once Sunday saw her siblings spending it.

"I'll be there in an hour."

When he clicked off, he had another missed call from Nicky. One from his sister, Charian.

And one from Arista. She'd called. His stomach untwisted.

WIFEY

Stayed @ Erin's. Xmas shopped 4 u & kids. Frogs ok?

Of course, she took the night to Christmas shop with her sister. He should've known.

ME

My frog REAL ok. 😈

He waited. No response.

And now, no time.

The Conklin siblings were waiting, and he needed to phone the Helena office for another machine, and a couple of guys to meet him in Elaine *now*.

If Seven played his cards right, and snagged even a fraction of this property for the bank's biggest client, he could turn his marriage around and give his children the best Christmas they'd ever had.

* * *

SUNDAY

"Folks, get out of our trash, or Imma call the sheriff! I swear it. That's enough!" The Kwik Stop manager plugged his hands on his hips.

"Y'all ain't announced a winner, so the ticket is still around here somewhere!" One of the diggers held onto a trash can lid.

The Kwik Stop carport overflowed with pickup trucks, some spilling onto 44, so people could hunt for the ticket.

"Imma keep on huntin' and the sheriffs can arrest me," one of the diggers replied. "My wife can bail me out with our hundred and ninety-six million dollars."

Sunday and her mama rolled their eyes. They had already torn up the house and retraced Sunday's every step from last night, including coming to the Kwik Stop to search. But with all these people here doing the same, it was impossible.

"Mr. Tracy," Mama pled with the manager, "you sho' you

can't just look at your video camera and see who bought the ticket? That'll take care of all this."

"Ms. Conklin, I done told ya already that's a violation of the winner's privacy. You either gotta show me a court order or the winnin' ticket, and then, I will be happy to oblige ya nah."

On the ride back to the house, Mama kept her lips tight. But her silence chastised Sunday loudly.

"When the rest of 'em ask where's it at, tell 'em you ain' win," Mama instructed before Sunday left for the fields to take over the gigging tour.

Sweating in this cool weather, Sunday turned up her flask. She'd already guzzled it. They'd been so busy searching, she'd forgotten to fill it up.

Her mother snatched it. "Gimme this durn thang. Don't need it no way at no 'leven in the mornin'. Worse than ya daddy. Get your head togetha so you can remember where that ticket went."

"Auntie."

Before Sunday headed out, a whisper stopped her in her tracks. At her hip, Victoria had slipped her skinny arms around Sunday's waist.

"Ma'am, I thought you were helpin' the guests."

"I forgot to ask you or Auntie Peady to do my hair."

Another task was the last thing Sunday needed right now. "Let's wait until tomorrow night before you go back to school. If I do it today, and you spend the whole weekend playin', it'll be messy come Monday mornin'."

Tori shook her head and gripped Sunday in the gut with her kitten eyes. "I want it to look pretty today."

What was going on? "Where's this comin' from? Your hair is fine, first of all."

"No, it's not. Damon said my plaits look like turds." She hung her head, and didn't bring it up again, nearly compelling

Sunday to start marching through the fields like Miss Sofia in *The Color Purple*, until she reached that boy's house in the residential side of town.

"Look at me."

Tori's head rose with the lightness of a bowling ball.

"Your hair is gorgeous, and don't let nobody tell you different."

"It's nappy and ugly. I want a perm." She toyed with Sunday's belt loop.

Appalled, Sunday snatched Victoria's chin up again. "No, ma'am, we don't do that. We don't change ourselves for other people's dumb opinions."

"You do it." The seven-year-old's pupils were too searching and innocent for that to be offensive. "You change how you act for people all the time when you think you gonna get some money. I want a perm so Damon don't laugh at me no more."

"*Any*more. Don't laugh at you anymore." Sunday would have a firm talk with his older brother. If she didn't snatch him on sight. "They shouldn't have been laughin' in the first place. I'll fix your hair later when I get back, and we'll put some curls in it."

Her niece's eyes found light. "Okay."

Sunday ignored the pangs of guilt that she had so little time. Or money for them to have it professionally styled more often.

With nothing to numb her, Sunday got in the truck to go find the group. Mild for a December, the crisp morning felt more like early fall than the top of winter. But Sunday wasn't complaining. Warmer weather meant the frogs hadn't burrowed too deep into the mud, and she could keep booking tours until frogging season ended on December thirty-first.

Reggie jumped in the back of the trailer and shoved his head through the window. "Don't worry, Auntie Sun, if you lost Nookie's ticket, we can just sell, like Peady said, and we'll be real rich. She's gon' talk to that man while you're on the tour, and find out how much he'll pay."

All that stopped Sunday from smashing the brakes was her brother's son hanging in the window. "What'd you just say?"

The kid's face shook once he realized he'd talked too much. "Nothin'."

Come to think of it, how had Peady even known who that man was from last night? She was nowhere around when he'd mentioned a dollar amount. Sunday glared at Reggie, who'd been driving Daddy's truck to pick her up last night. He'd heard the entire exchange.

"Boy, you tell me right nah what they been at that house doin'."

While she and Mama had been hunting everywhere for the ticket, what were Peady and Nookie up to?

The boy swallowed for his life. "Peady called that man and told him to come back. She's gon' let him walk around and tell her how much she'll get for her part of the farm."

That was a gigging stick right through Sunday. For a quick fix, she reached inside her boot. Dammit!

"Geemaw took your flask. Remember?"

Sunday had no choice but to remember. Every cell in her body wore the imprint of every mistake she'd ever made. And she had nothing to numb them.

She shifted the truck into reverse. That man would be walking around in her family's sacred fields they'd protected for a century. With access to one of America's biggest secrets.

That's all the Adlers really wanted for Christmas. To make sure that secret never saw the light of day.

Before she charged out to the fields, something told Sunday to hold still. *Aunt Bird, Daddy, what do I do?*

The Conklins couldn't fall apart for Christmas. Not after

all they'd been through, and not when they were so close to finally turning this land profitable again.

Sunday shifted the truck back into "drive" and rode to the tour group at the edge of Old Town Lake.

"Mornin' everybody."

"You's runnin' late. That ain' like you. You all right, baby?" Mama Piggee asked.

"A li'l tired. We had some excitement these last few hours."

"So I heard!" Ms. Tabitha's eyes almost left their sockets. "Brother Overton mentioned you had a lottery ticket. How it work for ya?"

"I ain't win nothin'." Not that good of an actress, Sunday lugged her whole heart past them. "Maybe one day."

"Welp, somebody won sump'm. If it wasn't none o' us, then who was it?" Mama Piggee shifted from one hip to the other.

Principal Overton, who'd taught Sunday her math, urged her onward. "I suppose we'll find out soon enough. Let's get out there. Angela wants these fresh frog legs tonight."

They started into the weeds in their high rubber boots, gigging sticks, and rain jackets.

Sunday bent over to pry apart some bushes and poked for any hidden critters underneath.

"Say, Sunday?" one of the girls called to her.

She led them through bushes. "Yeah?'

"You got a receipt about to fall out of your back pocket."

"Oh, thank y—" Sunday stopped. Her entire body remembered.

Last night, she'd had the ticket in her bra, and while changing for the tour, moved it to these overalls. She changed her mind and wore a different pair of overalls to save these for today, but left the ticket in these.

"Aunt Sunday, you see somethin'?" Reggie called from the back of the group.

Almost too scared to look, she took the paper out. It was the ticket!

Her eyes scanned.

"Sump'm wrong, chile?" Mama Piggee peered over her shoulder. "Whatcha got there?"

What were the winning numbers? "Nothin'."

"I think she found her ticket," one of the girls replied.

"I thought you said you didn't win nothin'," Principal Overton said.

"I didn't."

One of the others studied her harder. "Then, why ya got it out here lookin' at it? You sho?"

"I'm sure."

Sunday tried to put it back in her pocket, but Mama Piggee held out her hand.

"You don't look sho. Give it here. Lemme see," she said. "I put the winnin' numbers in my phone, in case somebody out here found it and we didn't have good reception."

"That's all right." Sunday tried to shove it in her back pocket and missed. It slipped to the weeds.

Somebody else picked it up.

"Give that to me!" Sunday jerked for it.

"Aw, chile, hush. We can tell ya ain' even know ya had it." Mother Fordham held it up.

Mama Piggee pulled up her phone and called out the numbers. "Zero, seven, one, eight, nine, nine."

The wind had stopped whistling. Crickets halted their chirp. No "hoo-oo" floated from nary an owl. Even the frogs had shut down their croaking.

While they checked, Sunday had stared into the distance, trying not to care. Not wanting to be fool enough to believe the impossible. She was tired of her hope reaching higher than reality.

Miss Fordham stumbled. "I'll be. The numbers match." Avonia Fordham faced Sunday. "My Lawd."

Uncertainty and shock danced among their eyes. Then they transformed the air with the first breaks of hollering.

Daddy...Geemaw...Grandpa Earl...

All those years of barely getting by, being laughed out of town meetings, of lawsuits kicked out of court, their plans snuffed out at every turn, the humiliation of having to smile when not a damn thing was funny, of keeping quiet so the loss wasn't deeper or the load on their backs heavier, when the Adlers always won.

"Ira Conklin shoulda been heah to see th..." An emotional Mother Fordham struggled. "God done did it."

Over the water where the bodies still lay, in a baptism they thought they would never see, Mother Fordham passed back to Sunday the ticket of the biggest lottery in Arkansas history.

ONE LIT CHRISTMAS

SUNDAY

Dirt danced around them while Reggie drove Sunday to the small group of people on the other side of their land. On their way down the fields, the unplanted rows didn't feel like work today. They felt like potential.

Reggie stopped the truck in front of the meeting Paris was leading, where the bank man bent over a different machine today.

Paris, her husband, Kevin, and Nookie all approached Sunday as if *she* were the interloper.

Behind them, the bank man stood up, on edge, his jaw clenched as if he expected her to charge at him. The slight gleam in his eyes signaled he may have wanted her to. He couldn't have been shorter than six foot two, maybe three. Sunday's gaze dropped to see if he was back in those Sheriff Woody cowboy boots. Somebody must have loaned him proper attire. A pair of rustlers on him, a long sleeve Henley that was a smidge too tight displayed what was going on underneath. He apparently lived good, with workout equipment *and* a full fridge of whatever he wanted. Sunday was truly in a good mood, because his attitude while he stood on *her* property doing the Adlers' bidding, was having an effect other than pissing her off. Salt and pepper in his goatee and a full head of hair, his eyes telling her he didn't serve 'boy' energy, Bank Man didn't clean up too bad. Were his eyes traveling?

It didn't matter. Sunday hadn't come for him. *And* he worked for the Adlers.

"Now, why are you out here, Sun?" Paris squared her shoulders, like when they were kids. "He's not doin' nothin'. Just checkin' the quality of what we got."

Kevin moved to stand between Sunday and his wife. "Come on, Sun, let the man do his job. He's not hurtin' anything. P got just as much right to this here as you do."

Nookie was still stewing. "Sun, don't come out here loud-talkin' like you ain' just lose a whole two hundred-million-dollar ticket today."

Sunday checked for whether the bank men caught that, and thankfully, they were so engaged in conversation, they hadn't paid attention.

"Auntie, tell 'em!" Reggie said that with his entire body.

The others waited for what was up.

"Unless you got my ticket, I don't need to know." Nookie rolled his eyes.

Right before she showed them, she noticed Bank Man and his crew had now paused from working to ear hustle.

"Let's move on, by ourselves," she cautioned.

The last thing they needed was for the Adlers to find out and make phone calls to shut them down, the way they always did.

"For what, Sunday?" Exasperated, Nookie didn't want to play.

The Conklins walked forward, placing distance between themselves and the bank workers.

In a circle of her family, her back to the bank people, Sunday pulled out the ticket. "We won."

Her siblings checked Sunday's face.

Squeezing his head, bending over, shooting back up again, he spun around and Sunday thought he would rocket into the sky. "Whoooooo!" he screamed, and leaped so high he almost did fly. "This 'bout to be one lit Christmas!"

"You lyin'," Peady whispered.

"Let me see it." Nookie took the ticket and pulled out his phone to check the numbers.

"You don't have to sell your share now, Peady." Sunday's eyes welled up as sixteen years of heartache came spilling out. "You can keep this and put a house on it, two or three now if ya wanna, and rent 'em out. Or that beauty spa you always talk about. But if you really don't want to deal with any of this anymore, or even stay here in Elaine, Peady, sell it to me."

Nookie walked around, hunting for a stronger reception to pull up the winning numbers and see for himself. "Let's go to the house and use the internet."

Sunday took the ticket back from Nookie. "Let's do it."

"Wait a minute. Hold up." The air changed. "What you doin'? It's mine, Sun. You already lost it once. You know you don't play no lottery."

"Nook, how you gon' cash it? You're sixteen, a minor. Not allowed to gamble." Sunday gave him a minute to see reason before he could start smelling his piss. "Number two, whose money did you use to buy this? So is it really yorn? And three, who's been breakin' their neck to make sure you eat for the sixteen years you been here?"

Throwing his hat on the ground, he punched air. "Urghh!"

"Sunday's right." Peady nodded. "It should be all of ours. Not just any one of us. You might have bought the ticket, Sun, but you ain' been doin' all this by yaself. How much is it again?"

Her husband held up his phone. "I got a signal. It's one hundred and ninety-six million, four hundred and fifty-four thousand, two hundred and seventy-one dollars and thirty-eight cents. Before taxes and all that. The winning numbers are 071899. You got that?"

Nookie, Peady, Sunday, and Reggie all stared at the ticket as he read them off.

Complete quiet surrounded them. They all realized it at the same time: Christmas would be a whole lot different this year.

"Aaaghhh!" The four woke up the ancestors, jumping around in a circle, screaming at the top of their lungs, hugging, grabbing each other, dancing, whipping the air, two-stepping and shimmying on the same land where their forebears had picked cotton.

The elders left the frog gigging and rode over in their trucks. Sitting atop the edge of the trailer, Mama Piggee slapped her hands together.

"This day been a long time comin'! When the party gettin' started? The whole wide world is gon' hear from Elaine tonight!"

Principal Overton was behind the wheel of another truck. "What y'all out here plannin'? What we doin' first? Where we goin?"

"When y'all takin' the ticket up to Li'l Rock and cashin' it in?" Mother Fordham asked.

Sunday's chest hurt from all the dancing. "Let's ride to the house and tell Mama first. Then, we should hire us a lawyer, and an accountant, and make sure we're doin' this the right way."

Principal Overton cried and did the church clap. "That's what I'm talkin' 'bout."

"Sho is a fine time fo' my Odessa!" Mother Fordham reached for the stereo and churned up Odessa Harris, a country blues legend from Helena, and *A Rockin' Good Way* kicked off the festivities. "Let's get on to the house, fry up some frog legs, catfish, okra, cook up some gumbo, and throw us togetha a big ole cookout! Issa bout ta be crackin' up in heah tonight!"

"What you mean, 'frog legs'?" Nookie asked. "We rich now. I'm orderin' me some caviar!"

"Boy, that stuff is nasty. I won't give you one minute before it comes back up again," Principal Overton laughed.

This party was more than a century overdue. Sunday looked up at the sky in hopes all the passed-away souls were up there tearing the roof down. Long-awaited justice was finally coming to Elaine. Then another thought struck.

"Hold it! Wait! We can't let on what's happenin'."

"Why not?" Nookie insisted on knowing. "As long as them Adlers been throwin' their money in our faces, Downtown Helena should be our first stop."

Sunday shot out a finger. "No! Not until that money is sittin' in the bank. We shouldn't be makin' a bunch o' racket until it's transferred to *us*. And we've got it in our control."

Principal Overton agreed. "That's a good point. Them Adlers know everybody with power in this state. If they find out y'all have the winnin' ticket, all it takes is a phone call, and them numbers will magically change. 'Oh, we're sorry. There's been some mistake.'" He wagged his head mockingly.

Peady's leg kept pumping her thoughts. "We should find a bank that's not based in Arkansas."

"And lawyers representin' y'all who ain' from 'round here," her husband added.

Everyone nodded in silence.

Sunday met every eye in the circle. "So it's understood then. We keep our heads down until we've got the money. No partyin', no socials." She stared at Nookie. "No girls."

He bobbed his head up and down.

"Y'all still got tours goin' and groups out giggin' on the land," Kevin said. "I'll go keep watch."

Arms tight around each other, the group had never hugged so hard, nor so happily.

A few yards away, Bank Man stood confused where they'd left him. With new energy in her step, Sunday strutted toward him. Her forehead stopped in front of his throat, close enough to grab it and choke him. But from prison, she wouldn't be free to cash in her ticket come Monday.

"Miss Sunday, whatever is going on, you sure do seem a lot better now than you were last night."

"We're not sellin' to you. You came all this way for nothin', and you can go tell Strom Adler I said it."

"I haven't ever met Strom Adler. I work for Friends of the Delta Savings and Loan."

No longer irritated at her core, Sunday could listen to him now. And hear. Today, she heard a different voice. Smooth, older, self-assured, it was nevertheless...frustrated. Tense. Tired. Like he had some pent-up angst in those vocal cords. Sunday had been with enough men on enough drunken nights to know.

His lips were dry from winter ashing them up. Other than that, they were pretty. "So do you mind me asking how you'll pay all that debt, and what's changed in the last thirty minutes to put you on cloud nine?"

"Our ancestors are finally getting what they're owed." She stared him up and down. "Now, do you mind if I ask *you* somethin'?"

Apparently not expecting that, Bank Man served an amused half-grin. "I'll probably regret this but go on."

Sunday leaned in and sniffed, screwing with his head. "How long has it been? A month? Two months?"

Confused, he stared at her, obviously not having a clue what she meant.

"How do you take care of yaself all them nights yo' wife don't give you none?" As far as Sunday could tell, he was practically wearing his testosterone build-up.

Bank Man's body was objecting before he could think of a comeback. "My marriage is none of your damn—"

Sunday's boots had already started walking. One of the others offered their hand to help her onto a truck, but she didn't need it. Sunday Conklin gripped the rail, same as when she was a girl, stepped onto the tire, and flung her elation in the air, throwing herself onto the trailer bed. On their way off, the trucks kicked out dirt.

She was rich. Not just a little bit, but a lot. The ancestors had won. Christmas was here, and it would be the biggest celebration the Delta had ever seen. As Reggie drove off, Sunday saluted Bank Man, leaving him in the dust.

THIS LAND CONCEIVED HER

SEVEN

How was it that, out of nowhere, a person so miserable just yesterday suddenly was in charge of the elf choir today?

Sunday Conklin looked, talked, and walked like this land conceived her in its buck shot clay, from the russet pigment in her skin, hickory in her eyes, almond shade of her heavy lips, umber kinked hair on her head, sprinkled with strands as gray as burnt incense ash, down to the row crops she was growing on her backside.

"I wonder what's going on with them," Seven muttered to the soil techs he'd brought with him.

"I wonder how them frog legs taste." The soil tech had already thrown his backpack over his shoulder.

"I bet they're hittin', too." The second tech packed up.

Seven stared at them both. "Where are you two going? We've got to head back to the office and file reports."

One of the techs pointed toward the house. "That old lady, Ms. Fordham, invited us for something to eat."

It was now one in the afternoon. Since he had awakened

that morning and started work with no breakfast, Seven was hungry himself. A good restaurant was hard to come by around here for miles. So was a decent cell phone signal to check in with Arista and the kids. The drive back to Helena was twenty-five minutes. He didn't see the harm in joining the guys for a break.

Seven stepped into the Conklin's yard in disbelief. Was that an actual wire clothing line? Out of nowhere, fresh bleach and detergent entered his nostrils and took him back to childhood. He'd grown up in Chicago's Albany Park with *two* washers and dryers in their home for his mother's parties and social gatherings, but still, he'd smelled this outdoor-dried-clothes scent before.

The Conklins' humble house appeared to be held up by clothes pins and hogties. He'd known they were drowning in financial obligations, but it seemed this family had never even poked their heads above the water to breathe oxygen or see the sun.

While time froze, Seven entered another dimension. Outside the little house that was certainly on the prairie, a large propane tank heated their home. That was standard for a lot of rural areas due to not having a natural gas line. But the paint chipping and fading along the walls had to be a health hazard. And the Christmas tree...

Seven averted his eyes. How were people in America still living this way? This extent of despair wasn't just poverty. This was insidious.

"What's takin' you so long? How 'bout you pass them plates down, bruh?" Narado asked him. If Seven's memory served him right, Narado hadn't been born when his father was killed under a tractor.

"My bad, man." Seven set aside his new analyzer sack and grabbed paper plates. He passed them down the line of people who seemed to be intimate friends of the Conklins.

A little girl held her plate up for Sunday to drop frog legs on it. "Gimme another one, auntie."

Seven wondered which of the Conklin grandchildren was she—Vanessa's daughter, Paris's daughter, or William's. On his plane ride, he hadn't had enough time to memorize the younger children.

"Baby, eat what's on there first." The soft, cajoling tone seemed to come from an alien, somebody caring, a nurturer. It didn't belong to the woman who'd held Seven at gunpoint and wrestled him last night. "And then come back if you want more." Sunday stopped herself and thought a moment. She changed her mind and dropped another set of frog legs on the girl's plate, like she'd had another conversation with herself.

"Whah dem bones at?" another man asked, and pulled out a small folding table. "Who want some?"

The dominoes, dice and playing cards were brought out. Was this turning into an impromptu get-together?

Before he held out his plate, Seven scanned for any pets, and how the utensils were being handled.

"Bank Man, what are you doin' here in my house? I thought I asked you to leave." Sunday stood on the other side of the buffet table ladling food.

What *was* he doing here?

"I, um, my guys—"

"I invited 'em." Mother Fordham, aged and infirm as she was, somehow appeared right at Seven's side from nowhere. "The men looked hungry and it's a ways back to Helena. We was all comin' ta eat. Didn't make sense leavin' 'em out thah."

"Motha, with all respect. They shouldn't even be here. He can't eat the same food he's workin' to take."

Seven didn't move an inch. "Offering you millions of dollars is not taking anything. The bank is *giving* you a chance at a much better life than this."

Mother Fordham grabbed her wrist before Sunday could get the next word.

"He's my guest. Treat him the way yo' grandmotha would have. No matter who walked thru that door, they got sump'm ta eat."

Paris came over then. "He's my guest, too, Sunday. I invited Mr. Hardcastle here so we could *all* talk to him." Her eyebrows rose, seeming to signal more that she wasn't saying aloud. "Regardless of what's goin' on now, we've got business to settle with Friends, so don't it make sense to treat 'em a li'l betta?"

Judging by how Sunday ground her disdain back and forth between her jaws, Seven halfway expected her to switch her ladle to the other hand and break it on his head.

"I saw you lookin' around to see if we're clean. We might not offer your bougie banker restaurant accommodations, Bank Man, but we *are* sanitary." She dropped the frog legs on his paper plate, followed by a splat of macaroni and cheese.

"I didn't tell you how I like my restaurant a—"

"I don't care."

Without his permission, Seven's attention dropped to the full rack on her chest. He needed to go find his wife. He lifted his gaze again. "You and I kicked off on the wrong foot last night."

"That tends to happen when you sneak onto folks' property tryin' to steal it."

"Not steal. Buy."

"Forgive my error. I should be a lot more grateful for that *seven point five* percent thirty-year adjustable rate mortgage, *on top of* the one point four percent mortgage insurance y'all charge. Where are my manners?"

Those rates were high. He hadn't paid as much attention to the financing she'd gotten on the front end, only on her business income she was earning now. To be honest, he'd focused more on her struggles that he could use to his advantage. He hadn't looked into where Friends might have gained the upper hand over her.

"'Scuse me, Auntie." The sweetest voice melted the snow between them. Tori protruded from Sunday's side and patted her aunt's tummy. "When are you gon' do my hair? Remember you said you would press it and gimme curls."

Seven witnessed the moment every parent dreads, when they realize they either won't have time, or if they will, they'll be dog tired. That reality rained down Sunday's face.

"Baby girl, I've been workin' all day. But don't worry. Real soon, I'm takin' you to the best hairstylist you've ever had, and she's gon' make your hair so pretty you look like Doechii."

Rather than jump with excitement, the girl rolled her eyes. She'd obviously heard that one too many times. Those eyes drifted to the other side of the cookout where a group of boys laughed and horsed around. Seven didn't need any further information. As a father of two girls, he'd lived it.

"Say, mane," somebody called from the end of the makeshift buffet. "Move the line."

Seven wasn't finished talking to Sunday. "My bad."

The Four Tops blared from a relic Seven hadn't seen in a minute—a nineties boom box in the corner with a CD player on top. A fairly intimate gathering was mushrooming into a full-blown cookout, for no apparent reason, in the middle of Saturday afternoon. People kept filtering in. How was this tiny house able to hold so many people? Why were they coming? There was no cake or party favors.

Once he'd moved on with his plate, he peered back at the buffet table. Sunday's grin glittered prettier than the Old Town Lake had last night. When she was especially amused, a dimple showed up deep in her right cheek and rewarded the world. Her arms opened for the townsfolk and extended relatives who'd clearly known her *and* her people before her.

"Bruh! These frog legs go so hard." One of the soil techs dunked the legs in garlic butter dipping sauce that dripped over his lips when he shoved them in his mouth. "They're doin' somethin' extra with this sauce." Smacking and sucking his fingers, he bobbed his head and swayed to the Jackson Five. "Plus, they got a couple honeys in here I ain' never seen."

Seven peered outside the window in the backyard leading to the fields. A light rain had started to fall, and some guys had begun putting up a tent.

Damn. He'd have to drive back in the rain, which only added to the pile of things going wrong this weekend.

"Baby, how's the legs?" The comfort in Mother Fordham's voice was growing on him.

"Good. Really good," he lied since he hadn't tasted them yet. "Thank you for protecting me a few minutes ago. That Sunday is a tough nut to crack."

"She's a proud bird, she is. But this family's been through it. You just dealin' with the mother hen in her is all. Ain' nothin' she wouldn't do for none o' these folks in here. Now. I have to ask, son. You sure you ain' kin to nobody roun' here?"

"No, ma'am, I actually asked my folks just yesterday, and my mother says we're not."

Elders had a way of squinting like they could read a person down to their DNA, and that skill had not skipped Mother Fordham. "You is kin to somebody 'roun' here. I just ain' put my finga on who yet. What's yo' motha's name?"

She was a sweet old lady, and she was the reason Seven still stood here with a prayer of this deal going through, so even though she couldn't have been more wrong, he indulged her.

He shrugged. "Sheridan. My mother's maiden name is Sheridan. Dad is Hardcastle, of course. Her people came from somewhere in the South a long time ago. I think his name was Lewis Sheridan, my great-great grandfather, ma'am."

Her eyes wondered in her head, before she shook it. "Nevah heard of 'im. Nah where you say you come from?"

"Chicago, ma'am," he reminded her. "I believe he was born in 1899. Moved from the South to Chicago in 1919 for a better life. That's all I know of him."

Her jaw slackened, and her chewing slowed, like she was reading her internal tea leaves. "Mm." The sage elder studied him, and stunned him when she grabbed his arm just, as she had Sunday's. "Hm. Yo' spirit ain' no stranger. You ain' come here for no business. You came here 'cuz you got debt to pay."

"Mother Fordham, I promise you, I'm debt free. Perfect credit score. Not even a mort—"

"I ain' talkin' 'bout this world. I'm talkin' 'bout tha otha. The truth called you back here, son." Her crooked veins were wrapped around his arm, around his veins, for the blood in her veins to cross his. "You's familiar. I just ain' placed how yet."

More than her words shook Seven at whatever umbilical cord connected him to his bloodline. Was he catching the Holy Ghost right here at an impromptu kickback? What was he supposed to do with that?

Inside his rib cage, underneath his chest muscles, a tiny on-and-off switch to his existence seemed to flip off and on in agreement, his first time ever feeling that.

Thunder and lightning outside broke the spell between the two. The rain had picked up, and another shot of lightning forked across the sky. Seven realized the increasing likelihood he wasn't getting back on the road for at least a few hours until this passed.

"I knew we should have headed back to Helena."

"What are you rushin' off for, Mr. Seven?" One of his soil techs licked his lips while eye-screwing one of the girls who eye-screwed him back. "The party ain't even started."

"I've got a wife and kids back in Dallas. That's my party. I need to wrap this up." Seven checked his phone again for reception. A couple of text messages had made it through.

NICKY

CALL ASAP. IMPT!!!!!

CHARIAN

Bro, where u at?!?!!!

Seven didn't see any texts from his wife or parents, and the kids had likely landed at friends' houses where they preferred to be anyway. So Nicky and Charian were probably being dramatic. Just in case, he took out his phone and tried to call.

"Seven! Nephew, you check your—"

Nicky started, but the reception stopped him from finishing.

"Nick? Nicky?" Seven plugged his ear with an index finger, and stepped away from loud kids and louder music. "I checked what?"

The call dropped. Damn these rural areas. Seven tried dialing Charian.

Principal Overton came and stood in the doorway. "Everybody who's got arms, come on out here and help get this tent up!" He stared straight at Seven. "Young man, do a li'l work for somebody 'side them Adlers."

Another person called out, "Sunday's got a whole huntin' lodge out there. Why can't we use that?"

"No!" Sunday stared around at the growing afternoon visitors. Why did she seem so flustered? "We've still got guests out there, and they're not from Elaine. Our business stays right here."

What business? There was definitely inside information among the townsfolk that Seven wasn't privy to.

"Can I go out and check if anybody's usin' the lodge? If they're not, can we please?" Nookie asked.

Hesitant, maybe even nervous, Sunday seemed agitated at her own party. Still, she nodded. "Only once all the hunters are gone."

He could only wonder what occasion called for them partying despite the cold rain in December. Though the temperatures weren't quite freezing, they were chilly enough to stay inside. Ignoring his own questions, Seven and his soil techs joined the community of Elaine, to put up a tent for the people who couldn't fit in Sunday's house.

By the time Seven and the other men finished standing up poles and tying cords, his coat was wringing wet, clinging to his back. Not a single inch of him was dry.

He looked up just as Sunday turned around from another conversation and accidentally served him her real side. He caught the leftovers of her smile. The corners of her mouth twitched, like she knew a secret he didn't. That moment lingered longer than she might have intended.

For Seven, that one second was too long, too pregnant with curiosity, and maybe even admiration. It cracked the door between them so fast his body jumped through it before Seven's brain could pull it back. Between his thighs, his manhood started paying Sunday its respects.

Too bad their circumstances weren't different.

Nine

YOU AIN STUCK HERE

SUNDAY

Sunday couldn't have been more irritated at her siblings and their friends. They had all agreed to keep quiet.

Yet, their small house was packed from wall to wall with people planting fat kisses on Sunday's cheek, and men crawling out of the woodwork who she hadn't messed with in years. They were driving in from other towns—Stuttgart, Snow Lake, Lula, Pine Bluff, Little Rock, Memphis, and Clarksdale. Only now, she could have her pick of the lot. She didn't have to sleep with whatever was available, uncertain of when a better man would roll in.

Sunday was in too good a mood to be mad at whoever's lips were flapping. She had already begun making Christmas plans. All the people she loved surrounded her, and Elaine's long overdue day in the sun had finally arrived, right on time for the holidays, *despite* the rain. In farming, rain represented cleansing, renewal and fertility. It prevented droughts and nurtured the harvest. Elaine would get its renewal. The past horror and brutality would be washed away.

"Sundie." Mama came over with fresh towels, jeans and flannel. On top of it, she set a key to one of the cabins, the best one. "Take this out there to that man from the bank."

Sunday's joy took a detour. "Whoa," she objected at the sight of the key. "He's not stayin' here."

Her mama leaned in on her. "Where else you think he goin' in all that rain?"

"Back to wherever he came from."

Mother Fordham and Mama Piggee came over to make it a team huddle. For some odd reason, they liked this interloper —Hardcastle—or whatever was his name.

"Motha Fordham thinks he got people here," Mama explained.

Sunday objected. "Ain' no Hardcastles ever been 'roun here."

Mother Fordham's finger shot up. "Sheridan. Lewis Sheridan. Now I ain' never heard of him, but that bank man's face look familiar. And I wonder if he came from one of the folks who ran off, and he don't know it. Say he from Chicago."

Mama Piggee thought aloud. "You know, thirty years ago, it was a family came down from Chicago and they brought a body with 'em. They said he was born here and wanted to be buried here with his people."

Lights came on in Mother Fordham's eyes. "You sho' right! But that man was um..."

Internally, Sunday took a mental walk. She suffered through these conversations all the time, where they stood for an eternity, laboring to recall people dead and gone. She had things to do. Gifts to buy. Financial and legal professionals to call. Farming business consultants to hire. She was a multimillionaire now.

Architects and building contractors to hunt for, who could draw her up and build her the house of her dreams, with an infinity pool, a garden, and a two-story home with a sunroom, large dining room to fit everybody, heated bathroom floors, music coming out of the walls, clap-on-clap-off lights so she didn't have to get up, and a bidet. Whew, that especially was going to feel *so* good.

Still, she maintained her respectful tone. "Motha, you and him can't talk about it on the phone?" Even if Bank Man was a little bit fine with his bowlegged walk, his loyalty to Strom Adler took him out of the running. As far as she was concerned, it didn't matter if he came from the moon.

The Adlers would wish they'd never heard the name Conklin. Sunday also needed to pick her Monday outfit that she'd wear to Little Rock and turn in the ticket. A hairdresser was coming to the house tomorrow to do her up. She and her siblings had decided to remain anonymous, but Sunday wouldn't let the biggest moment of her life pass without her looking the part.

"Gitcha head out them clouds, gal. You ain't got the money yet." Mama Piggee's smirk was waiting for Sunday once she settled back on Earth.

Mother Fordham shook her head. "I got a feelin' 'bout this heah man. He is where he s'pose to be this weekend. Ain' 'bout no bank neitha."

Out of respect, Sunday controlled her side-eye. She had to admit Mother Fordham's "premnishuns" were never wrong. Sunday had experienced the most potent one herself. Seventeen years ago.

"Reggie!" Sunday called out so she could pass her mother's chore on to somebody younger.

"No." Her mama shoved the clothes at her. "It needs to be you. You the one who aimed a gun at him. You go over there and make it right."

"Make what right? He trespassed on our land."

Her mother cut down her second-oldest daughter's wall in

a way only mothers could. "You might have a little money now, girl, but that ain' gon' solve every thang fo' everybody else. Other folks 'roun here still gotta deal with that bank. All the Black people who *ain't* win the lottery still gotta take out loans at that bank. They gotta buy houses through that bank. You ain' got no bank for 'em yet. That bank can still mess over a lotta good people, and punish them out of spite over you. Take these dry clothes over there, and make nice with that man, so nobody else suffers just cause you ain't thinkin' straight."

Sunday took the clothes. The carport had filled up now. After scanning all the heads, she finally found him, hemmed up by one of the neighbor women wiping rain off of him. It was understandable. He was educated, had a good job, all his teeth were in his head, *and* they were straight.

She threw on a parka and moved toward him. Her eyes slipped and noticed how his drenched Henley stuck to his back, defining every extra, grabbable layer of meat over decent muscle structure. He'd used them to put up a respectable fight last night. But he clearly hadn't asked Tonya to respect his wedding ring, though, confirming Sunday's suspicions the poor man wasn't getting any.

"Tonya, my bad, girl," Sunday interrupted. "I need to take Mr. Hardcastle to a cabin. And then, he's all yours."

Awestruck, Bank Man stared at Sunday. "You're inviting me to stay and you didn't call me Bank Man."

"My mama's the one inviting you. She said I have to be nice."

Bank Man thought it was funny. "My name is Seven if you wanna call me—"

"I don't. Wanna call you anything. At all."

"How could I forget?"

"I'll make sure you can't."

However, Tonya held in her eyes all the little stars that

weren't shining tonight. "Mr. Seven, you can call *me* if you need to."

"Thank you, ma'am, I appreciate that. I'm fine. Ms. Sunday's bark is bigger than her bite. I'll manage."

Sunday handed him a parka.

"Mr. Hardcastle!" Mother Fordham wobbled over. "We need help over at the lodge. After ya check in ya cabin, come on back. We got plenty mo' fo ya to do."

Opening an umbrella, Sunday started off in the rain. "I see your soil guys found somewhere to lay their heads. *Both* sets of heads."

"When you've got eight cabins on your property in a rural town, it should be no surprise. How'd you come to have eight of these anyway?"

"My daddy had 'em built a couple of years before he was caught under a tractor." She hopped in her truck and took off before Seven closed his door. "He planned on putting nice, pretty things out here, like an arboretum where kids could learn the science of plants. And local school kids could earn college credit for studying farming and soil health." She wondered why so much information had spilled out of her from just one question.

Maybe she wanted to counter any stereotypes of country folks as being too backward to dream. That's certainly how bank people treated them. She inwardly chastised herself for caring what he thought.

"I'm sorry about your father."

"Me too."

"The bank has a lot of respect for him. Seems he was an honest man who did a lot around the Delta. Your family name goes back for generations in the records. I'm guessing that's why they give you so much leeway."

"But not enough leeway to bring down that interest rate. And we never had a choice. Friends was the only bank who would deal with us. Trust me. We tried our hardest to go somewhere else. But all you finance guys know each other."

Come next week, though, Sunday would have the kind of money no financier would ignore.

"Friends has canceled fees and penalties the times you've been late, Sunday, out of respect for all you've been through. That's why they're giving you a chance to—"

Sunday stopped the truck, and threw him forward. "Don't use the words 'respect' and Friends in the same sentence around me again. Friends has put more people out on the street, forced them out of their businesses, out of their homes and sponsored more wholesale land theft, and terrorist acts than any other bank in Arkansas. I'm not sure what you know 'bout all that, but until *you* know what *I* know, don't come here thinkin' you're about to tell me *nothin'*."

She pressed that energy on the gas pedal for their bumpy ride in the downpour.

"You're right. I don't know much of what you're talking about. I should have done a better job of finding out before I came. My office asked me to fly here and said this wouldn't be a big deal. I had the impression this transaction was almost tied up."

"You thought because we're Black in the country, we'd jump at some money, and you didn't worry 'bout the rest."

He opened his mouth and hesitated. She wondered what lie would come out in denial.

"I did. It was classist and arrogant. I apologize."

No. No, no, no. Don't sound humble.

He continued, "I've heard Delta life is rough. And a lot of terrible injustices happened in these parts I could probably never imagine. What I do know is I'm a father myself, just like your father was, Sunday. No father wants his children miserable and impoverished out of some misplaced sense of loyalty or legacy. Not any sane man anyway. It looks to me like you're unhappy every time you and I cross paths. Is that what your father would have wanted? What's the point of you doing all this and it's not bringing you joy?"

"He sure didn't want Strom Adler chasing his kids off the land he worked hard for. We're here. It's this one." A few barnyards away, she pointed to another building. "The lodge is just over there when you're ready for Motha Fordham."

Instead of going for his door handle, Seven remained.

"Land you're striving to keep up. I'm just wondering which was more important to him—this land or your joy. When was the last time you left here and went somewhere else? To the Caribbean or Hawaii? Or to a spa."

Not in sixteen years since she'd had to come home from school. She squeezed her irritation into the steering wheel, ready for him to go. "Friends fo' sho sent the right man to come sweet-talk me. Folks around here don't need a vacation. They need you to tell that bank to give us the same privileges and rates they give those white boys up the road in Helena. The same financing *you* would ask for *your* daughters to have. But I won't need Friends much longer, so I'm feelin' better already."

"You gonna be at the lodge?"

"Why?" Sunday couldn't help a glance at the knots in his jeans that had grown since he'd jumped in the truck. "You want me to shoot somethin' else of yours next time?"

He actually laughed at her threats that annoyed everybody else in her house. "That machine wasn't mine. It was Strom Adler's."

A chuckle flew out of her before she could stop it. Okay, so he had a funny or two in him.

His teeth *were* perfectly straight. And white. His low-cut salt and pepper fade carried waves from being brushed down. "Just wondering how I'll get on without your sunny personality."

"I'm sure Tonya can help you figure it out." She switched gears to signal it was time for him to get out. Before she started thinking of ways to send Friends's water carrier back to them ruined.

"Since I'm stuck here, you got any of that moonshine you had on you last night?"

Tuh. It had been that obvious?

Sunday studied him a moment. "You ain' stuck here. You just ain' tried hard enough to leave." The entire ride across the field, Sunday noticed he hadn't pulled out his phone to check for his wife.

His pearly whites faded instantly.

He was obviously conflicted about something, and his tension blasted a radio signal Sunday could have picked up from the other side of the planet. She'd tuned up the married ones, too. The ones whose marriages had *been* dead, but they cringed at divorce, so like a stalled car on the road, they pushed it aside until they figured out what to do with it.

"And what moonshine?" she asked. "What are you even talkin' 'bout?" Why would she be dumb enough to trust an Adler bot? He might write it up in his report.

Now it was his turn to stare. "You were wearing it all over you last night, but okay. May I ask what changed since last night that you don't have to worry about Friends anymore?"

Behind them, trucks pulled up in the rain, with the townsfolk of Elaine bringing their party to the lodge.

To think, town celebrations would jump in the most wonderful ways now. Sunday almost leaped out and spun around in the rain, but she restrained herself. "You'll find out soon enough."

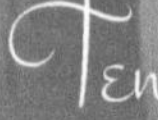

CHRISTMAS IN ELAINE

SEVEN

Seven paced around the cabin. For the last fifteen minutes, he'd doused himself with cold water from the little refrigerator, and his erection *still* hadn't gone down.

He hadn't had this problem since...he couldn't remember. Actually, this was a wonderful problem to have, if only he could get it to do this at the right time for the *right* woman.

He had never stepped out on Arista, nor she on him. But these last few years had been rough. He had friends who slipped out every so often, and friends who kept a "snack" on the side for when wifey got to tripping. Seven considered himself a man of honor. Arista married a man committed to her for a lifetime. Including and especially the nights he lied awake questioning what they were now. Despite the lack of energy in his bed, he'd stayed committed.

Yet, these last twenty-four hours, fighting for his life in the middle of a dirt field in Phillips County, Arkansas, had brought Seven back from the dead. A good tussle that forced out *every*thing he had to give—no pretentiousness, no titles or status or money, just sheer grit and force of will—had been a dopamine hit like no other. Their exchange erected a part of him he had feared was fading. He was still a man. Nothing was wrong with him. The proof bobbed up and down, staring right back at him and ready for action.

"Come on, man, turn down. You're not getting wet for at least another couple days. Chill."

A heavy knock at the door startled him.

"Mr. Hardcastle, ya forgot about us already?" Mr. Overton asked from outside.

Yanking on some jeans, Seven opened his door to find the former principal under his umbrella on the porch.

"We're waitin' for ya over at the lodge for the, uh, tall people assignments."

Did these folks ever get tired?

"I'm on my way. I'll be there shortly."

"Good to hear." Mr. Overton lowered his umbrella and brushed past Seven, entering his cabin. "I'll just wait here for ya." The man looked around. "Were you in here talkin' to somebody? I don't see ya on the phone."

"I hung it up. Battery was dying."

"Mm." The principal stood and waited, not allowing Seven to mosey over there on his own time.

Flabbergasted, Seven took the dry clothes to the bathroom to change. These cabins were quaint, homey, well-built and well-maintained. Despite the town having a water boil warning, the toilet was quick to flush, no mold or mildew, fresh bedding was topped with Christmas chocolates, a cinnamon aroma emanated from somewhere in the room, a cozy reading chair in the corner with a washable cover over it, and even deer food and bread crumbs to feed the ducks and swans on Old Towne Lake. It had even come with a note:

Welcome! We kindly ask that you please not feed the

ducks, swans or deer with human table scraps. We want them with us as long as possible. Thank you for visiting The Conklin Fields. We hope you find a quiet, hidden piece of you here in the treasure box that is Elaine.

Her sister must have written that. Or her mama. Or the sheriff. Anybody other than Sunday.

In the bathroom, Seven checked his phone for what messages had rolled through, but it had died. With all his ripping and running, he'd forgotten to charge it. Maybe somebody would have a charger at the lodge.

When they arrived, the principal threw open the door, and the noise almost blasted Seven back to Dallas. What kind of Christmas music filled these halls? Was that Snoop Dogg rapping some kind of Jingle Bells hip hop remix?

The party was growing bigger by the minute. People stood on ladders, stringing lights and tinsel across the ceiling. Seven peered up and noticed old toys hanging over his head.

He was afraid to ask, "Mr. Overton, what are those?"

"They're from long time ago."

"How did they wind up here? Whose are they? The Conklins'?"

Mr. Overton also scanned them. "They're everybody's. All the folks who died around Elaine and their family didn't come, so they left an empty house. Then, there's folks who the Klan run outta town, too scared to come back. Some were killed. Some disappeared in thin air, here one day, gone the next. Others packed up their families and took a job where there's more money, left their house the way it was. There were folks who got sick, and didn't have long so they donated it. It's a lotta stories hangin' up there. Those toys remind us of who all was here, and didn't get to see this blessed day."

"This blessed day?" Seven wondered. "If you don't mind

my asking, what day is today?" Some local holiday? Was that the reason for the party?

"Welp, we'll just call it Elaine's liberation day."

Ha. Seven hadn't heard of anything special. "Oh! You mean with the lottery? That's right! Somebody did win! You know 'em?"

Mr. Overton stiffened his lips, sealing them from spilling anything more.

"Mr. Hardcastle," a gentleman approached. "My name is Harvey with Delta Dirt Distillery. Friends of the Delta Savings and Loan services my business's loan. Pleasure to meet ya."

Finally, a friendly welcome. "Good to meet you as well. A distillery, huh? What are you distilling?"

"Whiskey and vodka. We make it from sweet potatoes off my family's farm."

"Say what now?" Intrigued, Seven couldn't help being impressed. "Sweet potatoes?"

Harvey grinned wide enough to grow vegetables on both rows of teeth. "Yes, we certainly do. We brought some with us to celebrate the special occasion. If you'd like to try it, we'll be throwing together mixed drinks—egg nog, cider, hot chocolate, hot toddy, and hot buttered rum. If you'd like to take some back to your colleagues in Dallas, we'll even gift you a complimentary bottle. But you've got to share it now. Help us spread the word about Delta Dirt. Don't keep it to yourself."

Another hand extended to Seven. "Mr. Seven, how are you? I'm Nancy Hall Neal, and I grow soybeans, corn, peas, and other vegetables on my land. I also come from a family that goes back a few decades around here. We're the Halls of Snow Lake. We're glad you're here."

Taken aback, Seven was flabbergasted. "*Glad? Really now?*"

"Of course. Why wouldn't we be?"

He stared around in search of Sunday. "Let some folks tell it, I'm Satan in the flesh."

She chuckled. "Oh, you must be talking about Sunday? Don't pay her any mind. She's like a caramel chocolate—mild on the outside, gooey once you crack her open."

Seven jerked in disagreement. "So far, she's more like a Jawbreaker. Teflon on the outside, torture on the inside."

Nancy laughed. "But you're approaching it with the right attitude. If she gives you any more problems, just give me a call. I'm over on the Knowlton Farm. It might take me a day or two to call back, and hopefully, you'll have enough limbs left to answer the phone when I do."

Seven nodded with a chuckle. "So you do know what I'm going through around here."

The lodge could have easily passed for an elementary school cafeteria. But it looked better than the pictures on the web site. The fireplace added quaintness. Wooden benches and tables were definitely for hunters. It would have been unfair to compare this place to Jackson Hole, Vale, or Lake Tahoe. For a small town in Arkansas, this lodge hit the mark. And it had potential for more. Seven could see the vision that Ira Conklin had been reaching for. How many Black communities could claim a hunting lodge? He'd visited a couple of Black-owned country clubs, resorts, golf clubs, and bed and breakfasts. But never a hunting lodge, and certainly not a frog farm.

Spiced scents of homemade eggnog, apple cider, real cocoa, cinnamon and nutmeg wafted around him.

Their voices full of pride, their chests even bigger, each farmer or worker introduced themselves like they personally attended every seed producing food in this Arkansas Delta soil. Their swagger declared that if grocery stores went away tomorrow, the South would be just fine. Each solid handshake conveyed these men and women didn't need anybody else to feed them.

Seven marveled, because if the world fell apart tomorrow, he'd be screwed.

"Mr. Hardcastle, I'm Lisa Hicks-Gilbert, the Mayor of Elaine. I heard you were here and wanted to introduce myself."

She'd caught him off guard. "Pleasure to meet you, Ms. Mayor. Now that I've met more people, I can say it's good to be here."

She held onto his hand, not aggressively, but firmly enough to emphasize she had a point worth grasping. "Yes, I heard about that. While you're here doing your work, just remember that Elaine is over sixty percent Black. We have a lot of promise in our community. All we need is the right support, sir. Maybe before you go, you can stop by my office for a coffee."

What was she implying? "Of course, Madam Mayor, but just so you know, Friends of the Delta gives your constituents a lot of loans. We make it possible for these farms around here to thrive."

"Barely." Her smile offered Southern courtesy, despite it not reaching her eyes. "I wouldn't call what our farmers go through 'thriving'."

"All right, everybody!" Paris Conklin stood atop a chair. "It's time to light the Christmas tree and put the angel on top!"

"We don't have to talk about it now," the mayor concluded. "It's the holidays and tonight is a special night. But do stop by. Will ya?"

"Yes, ma'am. I will do that." A special night?

Children jockeyed for position around the tree, and adults lifted the littles on their shoulders to see it better. Placed in a tub of water, it was a real Red Cedar, its branches still green and lush from the land, not the plastic kind he and Arista pulled out every year from the attic.

Facility lights lowered, and children's faces fell into a collective trance.

Seven remembered his kids at this age, eying a magical tree in wonderment after waiting all year. But unlike in the big city with all its lights and heights, a single twinkling tree now illuminated this entire town.

They'd hung pinecones sprinkled with glitter on the tree, along with acorns, paper cutouts of frogs, miniature trains, trucks, tractors, broomsticks, and flannel stockings. Folksy and spirited, the tree knitted together a country, color-coordinated Christmas display. Paris oversaw the festive lighting ceremony as if she was born to put on a show, obviously having arranged the children's work.

"I wanna light it!" One of the children piped up.

"I'm puttin' the angel on," another child insisted.

"You guys, share. Let somebody help you, baby," Sunday's mother suggested.

Next to her, Sunday's niece pouted. It was Tori, the one who had asked for her hair to be done. It still remained untouched. Seven scanned the room for Sunday.

Rather than lighting the tree right up, they broke into an acapella chorus of *Lift Every Voice and Sing*.

Paris kissed her toddler daughter. Paris and Sunday's mother, thumbing tears from her own cheek, hugged one of her granddaughters. She stood alongside farmers whose eyes gazed at the toys on the ceiling, the remnants of departed loved ones. Arm in arm, others swayed, teasing and giggling like tonight truly was the gift.

At the end of the song, the tree lit every face in the dark. The "angel" they placed on top was an adorned ancestor, a scarf around her head, in a white gown.

Mr. Overton waved Seven to an area of men decorating the higher areas on the walls. "Mr. Hardcastle, follow me. We need ya over here."

"Nossuh!" Mother Fordham strutted over. "I caught him first, brotha man! Go on and find one o' them students you been tryin' to save the last thirty years." She turned to Seven. "Young man, you shell purple hull peas?"

"N-no, ma'am." He'd only heard about it from his southern-born-and-bred friends in Dallas. The closest he'd ever come to unshelled peas was the produce section at the grocery store. Nobody in his blue-blooded family had been born in the South in at least four generations. In fact, a few of his family members thumbed their noses at "soul food," adamant that it was a badge of slavery and degradation they refused to adopt.

"Come on. It's simple enough. Won't hurt them city-boy fingers o' yorn too much."

She shoved her hand inside a large, brown paper bag standing as high as Seven's kneecaps, pulled out a handful of pea pods, and dumped them in a large bowl for him to shell. Every time she reached in that bag for more bunches of pea pods, Seven's stomach caved in deeper. Then she assigned him to a group of women and bored preteens who were shelling.

Within the first two pods, he learned why this chore got such a bad rep.

"You gotta split it open and slide your finger straight down the middle. It goes faster that way." The kid next to him, wearing a cast around his leg, demonstrated.

"Oh, I see. You must be a pro at this."

The kid shrugged. "Our farm is mostly peas, so, yeah."

"Mr. Hardcastle."

He looked up to find Paris Conklin with her toddler falling asleep over her shoulder.

"Ms. Conklin, hey."

"Thank you for comin' out here when I invited ya."

She stepped away from the group, so Seven rose and followed her.

"I appreciate you calling me. It can't be easy when the family doesn't all agree." He avoided mentioning Sunday specifically. "I'll be honest. I've never visited the Delta." Or Arkansas period, for that matter. Much of his business was in Texas, Louisiana, and Oklahoma, with a few accounts in the West, where there were more well-to-do Black businesses with bigger accounts. Ian was responsible for Arkansas, Mississippi, Tennessee, more of a "white man's land" for money. Seven supposed that was a big reason why he'd never been interested in coming. "I haven't known too much about this area. This has been a good time." He meant that.

Paris patted her toddler's back and lowered her voice. "I'm actually still curious about my share. What would it be? How does that work? I'm not a realtor or nothin'. We don't have to get into it tonight, but...I'm just wonderin'."

"Of course. I'd be glad to throw out some options for how you all might work out a tenancy in common and possible partition."

"Thank ya for that."

"Auntie Peady, where's Aunt Sunday?" Tori popped her head between them.

"Tori, baby, she's been busy today. Why don't you go play?"

Tori's gaze fell, and she clearly wanted something but didn't feel comfortable using her voice. Her eyes meandered between the two adults studying her, and Seven watched her courage wilt.

"You know, Ms. Paris," Seven started, "have you ever heard of the Flying Comb?"

For a moment, Paris drew a blank. "No, sir, I can't say I have."

"I have two daughters myself, and when my wife was out on assignment, Flying Comb had to sweep in and do emergency landings on some heads. That ever happen to you?"

Paris caught on. In exaggerated fashion, Paris dropped her jaw and eyed Tori. "What you say now, Mr. Hardcastle? You're a girl dad who can do hair, too? What is this Flying Comb you speakin' on?"

"Well, Ms. Conklin, I can't really explain it. Gotta take a seat and see how the plane will land. If you've got a doll somewhere who can be my flight attendant and make sure the cocoa stays hot, even better. You got some oil, gel, and hair-safe plastic bands? I'll see if I can fuel up the Flying Comb."

Her eyes grew hopeful, a smile cracking on her face, but just as fast, Tori lowered her expectations. "You're a boy. Boys don't do hair."

Paris jumped on the opportunity. "I know some boys who can do hair better than girls can, T."

"Since you don't believe me, we can stay right here with these ladies, and they'll watch the Flying Comb go to work," Seven suggested. "That way, when I'm finished, they'll back up my skills. You can't be telling stories that it didn't happen, or saying one of your aunts did it, either. It was the Flying Comb."

Tori's grin grew by the second. "You don't have a comb that flies. Combs don't fly."

"Mine does." He pointed at the women shelling peas and cackling. "That's why I'll have me some witnesses."

Paris grinned. "T, why don't you try it and see, baby girl?"

Though hesitant, she was curious and wanting her hair neater. "Okay."

Seven didn't know any of these people very well. He had been here less than two days. But when he retook his seat in the circle and whipped out his Flying Comb—not as a real estate finance manager, but a dad and a Black man—he was pleasantly surprised. Entering Elaine, he hadn't realized he'd been so tense. Yet, tonight, among strangers at a rural, folksy Christmas celebration on a Saturday night, he had mellowed out.

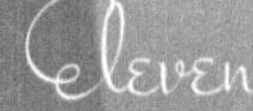

Eleven

FLYING COMB MAN

SUNDAY

"Hey, Sun, congratulations, gal. What ya doin' with yaself tonight?" A "big n' sexy" pushed his head through Sunday's window as she returned to the lodge.

The whisper campaign was spinning out of control, but fortunately so far, nobody outside Arkansas's Black network had contacted her. It was only a matter of time, though.

"Boy, what are you even talkin' about?" For now, she played dumb. She stepped out of Daddy's truck. Would she keep it? Yeah. A remnant of him, it gave her the feeling she was wearing his shoes. But from her daddy's dream, Sunday stepped into her new reality.

"Aw, so you don't know me nah, huh?" Another sneaky link called to her on the way inside. "That money done got to yo head already?"

Sunday patted the area atop her bra to ensure the ticket was still there. "Same way you don't know me when yo' baby mama come through on her way to Memphis, foo."

She had been on the phone all evening and secured two lawyers, one for herself and the other for the family business and properties--establishing the "corporate veil." She was about to do a ton of good for her town. But her friend, and now lawyer, Dorinda, in Little Rock, had made clear that now there needed to be a bright line between family business money and her own. Sunday had been pretty good with book-keeping, but this way, the family's debtors couldn't come for her new winnings to pay outstanding family debt. Dorinda had also referred Sunday to a Black accountant. They would also be connecting Sunday with a financial advisor and an asset manager. All of those were different people.

She giggled at the notion. *Giggled.* Sunday Conklin—from teeny, tiny Elaine, Arkansas, that most folks had never heard of— was rich enough now to giggle.

Sunday could now tell Strom Adler's purse-holder to get off her land. She was protected now, and her mother was wrong for keeping him here. The rain had lightened to a respectable drizzle, so Bank Man could make out just fine on the 44. He could take that abandoned orphan between his legs, and the hole in his chest, and go steal somebody else's heritage. Paris had invited him here for *one* task, and yet, he was making himself at home, getting comfortable with the elders, and was now at her lodge talking to Sunday's neighbors and collecting information on her.

Whatever this Bank Man needed for his bank promotion, or his career, he wouldn't collect it at the Conklins' expense. Mother Fordham would just have to be upset.

Sunday let herself into the backdoor while practicing her delivery. She reached under a locked counter for her secret stash of moonshine and poured some into a mason jar.

After the first intoxicating sip, she raised it for another and halted. Liquor could diminish the mature tone she wanted to present. She twisted the jar lid on and put it back.

"Congratulations, Sunday." People hugged her in the corridor on her way to the main hall.

"You deserve it, baby. Don't forget about us," a neighbor said.

"I'm not goin' anywhere." At the entrance to the hall, she scanned. Where might he be digging up trouble? She stepped into the party where people ate, bobbed their heads to Run DMC's Christmas rap song *Christmas In Hollis*, and cut up laughing over old stories.

Oh, this devil was good. Oh, this devil was good. He must have posted up somewhere inconspicuous. But if Sunday could grab frogs and hunt deer, rats were no match. She shook hands and exchanged hugs while pushing through throngs of well-wishers. A weird noise cut through the music.

"Vrrroooom, zoooommmmm...where's it landing next?"

Sunday's ears tuned out all else, so they could isolate the sputters, smacks, zooms, and lip-popping that followed, along with chuckles that were highly familiar to her.

"Is it landing on your forehead?" Was that a man? "Oop! He's coming for your neck!"

Several voices burst out laughing. Wildly.

"Get him!" Was that a child?

"Nah-nah-na-naaah-nahhh! Youuu can't catch me!" That was definitely a man, singing an oldie but goodie from childhood.

"Yes, I can!" Without a doubt, that irritatingly high-pitched squeal belonged to Victoria.

"No, you can't, 'cause I'm Cornelius the Flying Comb, the illest comb of all!"

Sunday stepped around the final group of people blocking her path.

Victoria stretched her arms over her head, laboring to defend herself, swatting at Bank Man who waved a comb over her, tapping her neck, cheeks, shoulders, and head—all safe spots. And the community mothers were right there watching.

Sunday's hand flew to her mouth.

"Yeah, I know. Right?" Peady crept up next to her. "I asked him if he could do CiCi and Livi tomorrow before he goes back to Dallas," she said in reference to her daughter, Sienna, and Vanessa's daughter, Olivia, whom she had adopted.

Tori's hair was...

The other girls were tapping their mothers and asking if they could have their heads done in that style—rows of flat twists up top, each rolled into a single line of bantu knots from ear to ear, and in the back, lots of well-moisturized, gelled and shiny twisties that swung around her head when Tori turned from one direction to another. She was eating up the attention, and the style ten-timed her confidence. He'd done it all with her natural hair that she could proudly display.

Tori glowed, snapping her head every time somebody called her name so that her twists would bounce. The moment she caught sight of her aunt Sunday, she raced over and grinned, her form of a humble brag. The six-year-old's eyes said, *Look at what he did that you should have done*, but her mouth knew better.

Sunday squeezed her cheeks. "Yeah, I guess you look all right."

"Ain' no 'guess', Auntie. I look *better* than all right."

Her aunt let her have that one. "Well, excuse me, then."

Rather than heading off to play with baby dolls and stuffed fur babies, Tori's very next stop was the group of boys now petering out with their handheld games.

"The Flying Comb got them weeds outta the back of there," the boy said.

Sunday and Peady stood on edge, ready at a moment's notice to go snatch a boy up if necessary.

Tori jerked her neck around. "Yeah, now the Flying Comb needs to shave them rocks off your pointy head."

Sunday and Peady laughed, waiting for how Tori would handle herself next. Smartly, their niece pivoted while he tried to think of a comeback.

"Good girl," Peady murmured.

Once Tori was safely out of there, Peady shifted toward her older sister.

"You don't have to like the way he came in here, Sun. But he ain' Strom Adler. I don't think he's ever even met the man. It's late and I'm headin' to the house to put these kids down. I'll get up early to come back and clean."

"Girl, you're pregnant. Don't worry about it. Sleep in."

A shocked Peady stared at Sunday, disbelief paralyzing her tongue.

Maybe Sunday had been too hard the last few years since Vanessa had died. She'd been too scared of the Adler boogeyman right over their shoulder, too worried the next wrong move would be their last.

"I got it." They had enough money to breathe now.

"I'll see you tomorrow." Peady glanced over at Bank Man. "Be nice. He could be helpful in these parts. We need more folks who teach about money and property, 'cause people 'roun here don't be knowin'." She reached for the others. "Tori! Reggie! Let's go. Nookie, if you leave here, let somebody know."

Their mother had already left, and the families, flirts, neighbors, and extended relatives were thinning out. As always, Mama Piggee, Mother Fordham, and any girls on the hunt for Narado remained for clean-up duty. Only tonight, there was a new addition.

"And when ya done with that, Mr. Hardcastle, ya can brang them pots ovuh here and wash whatever'll come off. Soak the othas. Sunday or Peady'll wash the rest tomorra."

Mother Fordham wouldn't let him out of her sight. He was definitely paying a price for using her to sneak in here.

But if Mother Fordham had decided he was "some no-good sucka," she would've turned her nose up and swatted her hand behind her already.

"Then, after ya move these benches and chairs back ovuh there, ya can stack up the decorations in that corna and sweep all this mess offa tha flo'."

Sunday made her way back into the corridor, tucked in the dark just enough to remain hidden while observing. He was tired indeed, and he should have been, creeping through their fields at night.

She supposed she couldn't kick him out now, though. The lady of the Conklin Fields went and grabbed her jar of moonshine. This was certainly the perfect weather to drink it.

Where he leaned on the broom while pushing it in the middle of the floor, she approached Bank Man from behind, and reached around, surprising him when she passed him a jar.

He nearly left his body.

"You think we worked him enough, Motha Fordham?" Sunday asked.

"What else he s'pose to be doin'? He'll rest plenty when they put him in the ground." But even as she said this, the elder was tugging on her rain coat and heading toward the door. "You young folk don't know what hard work is nowadays. My mama use ta be in the fields befo' the sun, plantin' with us on her back. I'll see y'all tomorra. We'll have them black-eyed peas, frog legs, and fried tomatoes."

"Thank ya, Motha, good evenin' to ya," Sunday called.

Eying Sunday with suspicion, Seven smelled the jar. "What are you planning on doing to me?"

Sunday picked up her own jar and headed for the porch. "Nothin' I couldn't have done already."

She propped the lodge door open and set a chair just inside. The temperature was dropping, precisely how she liked it. Frosty nights promised clarifying winter in the weeks ahead. Sitting here in the door, she'd be warm enough and could still listen to the tap-tap of rain washing out the old and bringing in new possibilities. From the death of old things in winter came the birth of new life.

* * *

SEVEN

Seven took his first sip of Sunday's moonshine and the potency kicked him in his back. Sucking his cheeks, he shook it out. "You made that, didn't you?"

"Damn straight." Proudly, Sunday took another sip.

Within the next few sips, he adjusted and it was actually pretty good. The grass seemed to welcome the rain spraying the fields. Out ahead, a winter shower cascaded into the forest and swamp, as if it were returning home. Scents of wet moss and wood saturated the air. Way out here, far from offices, deals, bosses, and obligations, not a single thought entered his mind.

He was exhausted enough to give up the ghost. All this country quietude, accompanied by rain, promised at least ten straight hours of slobbering shut-eye. But the busy dad and financier couldn't sleep on this. When would there be another time to simply sit and be?

"Why do you work for him?" Her eyes were fixed straight ahead.

Seven sat a few moments longer. "I don't work for him. I work for Friends. My boss is the primary manager of Adler's account and holdings, and he never lets the rest of us anywhere near that man. A couple days ago, he sent me here to see if I might have some luck with you. They don't want to foreclose."

"You mean they don't want it in the media. We've been here a long time."

Seven raised his glass in a salute and took a sip. "Yeah."

"So you like that job. Where you decide loans and what kind of financing people get. You must know the ways that bank operates. How unfair it is."

Seven recalled the times he'd discovered some upsetting kickbacks and privileges that were illegal. "I wish I could tell you they don't, but all banks do it. They can play in ways we can't."

"And you're happy in that world."

"I used to be." He took another swig. "I've been at Friends for most of my career. My first job was at one of the national banks. I hated it. Back then, I was just another paper-pusher. But after 2008, the regional banks started competing, hiring more Black executives once they learned how much money Black people had. It was fun and I could travel." Then, he married an ambitious news reporter who was just as hungry and driven as he was.

"Exactly how bored are you now?"

He snort-laughed and the liquor burned his nostrils. "And you're out here in the middle of nowhere riding bulls everyday, huh? That why you haven't tried to leave again? This out here is comfortable for you? Fighting. Struggle. Barely getting by."

"Don't start." Miss Sunday kicked off her boots, maneuvered out of her socks and wiggled her toes, their nail polish long faded.

"Serious question, though. Blacks all over the country think about the Delta, and most people would never even drive through here. Let alone live."

"Who's gon' live here if we leave? We can't all run somewhere else."

"You tried to, though." Moonshine and rain and countryside were an intoxicating combination. "You wanted something else besides this, Sunday. Don't act tough, like Elaine is all there ever was. What was the *other* dream that called you out of here?"

He wondered if she would open that part of her. It had to hurt—thinking she had broken free of the cocoon, only to have to return and crawl back inside.

She stared into her jar, swirling it like she was the strong liquor splashing to escape. "Industrial engineer. I was gonna work somewhere a few years, maybe at Fanjful, Offut or King, and learn the ropes. Then I would come home and use my skills to make this place a goldmine." Her vocal cords faltered the longer she talked. "So Daddy could finally compete on the same level with the other guys around here."

Seven felt the imbalance in those scales. "Where would you go if you left today?"

"Paris." No hesitation. "My mama named my younger sisters after the cities she and Daddy wanted to visit one day. I know I don't look like the Paris type. It's probably trashy and touristy but I wanna go because country tomboys like me don't go to those far off places. I'll finally take my mama so she can see it while she's still able to enjoy it."

Seven wondered what Arista did when she had discovered *her* France tickets on the bed. If she excitedly called her friends or sister and showed them off. He needed to head back to her and the kids by tomorrow night. She helped with English and history assignments, and he always took math and science duty.

"Paris has a lot of good spots worth seeing." Making love in. "You should go."

"I will." Her bare feet curled around one another, like she was already there in her head. "You been there?"

Atop the Eiffel Tower, he and Arista had planned to take the world by storm, before either one knew which way the winds were taking them. "I have."

"How do you sleep next to somebody in want the whole time? I don't understand how married folks do that." Sunday finally shifted her gaze toward him, like she needed to see him say the words to believe him.

"How do you know I still want?" Despite trying his damndest.

She settled deeper in her chair. "You ain't checked your phone. Even if you don't want her no more, you must lay there at night wantin' somethin'."

In his blood, in his head, through his heart, the liquor relaxed him, and stripped him of every pretense. Far from home, in a town he knew little about, there was no one who knew him to hear if he poke the truth. Surrounded by virtually nothing, the liquor was giving him permission to say it out loud.

But still, "I'm not interested in trauma-bonding with you, Sunday."

Or more accurately, he wouldn't allow his mind to wonder that far into fantasies he couldn't have. He might never come back. Best to not even go there. Will power was the only way his and Arista's marriage was surviving.

"You real devoted to your kids." Sunday took a swig of her own. "Respect for that."

They had mattered most. Private school, extracurricular activities, tutoring, family functions and connections, sleep-overs, parent circles, exposure to new things, their world and how they experienced it outvoted his, every step of the way.

"Thank you." He only had a couple of swallows left in his glass. As if it were a sign his opportunities were shrinking. In more ways than one. "Same way you're devoted to this land. Come hell or high water."

No love came without sacrifice.

"Elaine is more than what you hear on the news."

"I never heard Elaine on the news. Come to think of it, I never heard of Elaine at all until I got here, so no worries there."

Tipsy, she sputtered from laughing and some liquor dribbled over her lip. He reached out to wipe her like he would one of his kids but caught himself, and redirected his attention.

"You know what I mean," she slurred.

He kept his eyes focused on the rain falling way on the other side of the field, and nodded from a safe position. "I know what you mean."

As tired as Seven was, he could have slept here in this chair, listening to the rain, owls in the distance, crickets, and yard critters.

All he needed now was charcoal and paper. Rain, boots, straw hats, jackets on the rungs, field tools, and stray cedar branches for Christmas garland and...

Somebody had hung mistletoe over the door.

Sunday's gaze followed Seven's.

"Don't pay that no mind."

"I wasn't." Plenty other parts of him were paying enough mind that his head didn't need to.

He wondered how her lips felt to be that thick. He was a man. Quite naturally came the question, if her bottom lips were anywhere near as plump as her top set.

She must have read his mind. Sunday took her jar to the head and stood. Though she tugged her jeans up over her butt crack, her meat played peek-a-boo between the bottom hem of her sweater and the top rungs of her Levi's. Seven hadn't quite finished sopping it up with his eyes when hers shifted down. Her snort put him back in his married place.

"I'm tryin' ta help you out here. Do yo' part. We're giggin' tomorrow mornin', first thing. It's late. If you wanna sleep in, nobody'll much blame ya."

"It's midnight. You're getting up at six a.m.?"

"Four-thirty. Best to stick 'em in the dark, 'fo first light. We should be back here by eight." Her side-grin teased him. "In time fo' the girls to get the Flyin' Comb."

Seven thought he saw a hint of her dimple, but it was hard to tell out here in dim light. He finished his last two swallows and stood up.

"If I'm not out there, Mother Fordham will come knocking. I may as well wake up on my own accord."

"Smart man." Her laugh, so easy now, had been non-existent twenty-four hours ago.

"I'll take the chairs in."

"Thank ya."

The rain had finally stopped. Sunday locked up, and they put on their jackets. In one direction was her truck. In the other was his cabin.

* * *

SUNDAY

She practically heard his heart thumping from one side of his inner turmoil to the other.

"Good night, Mr. Bank Man."

He wasn't ready. And Sunday wouldn't be the one to trip up a man still trying for his family. He was still committed, even if it killed him. But not once had he checked his phone for messages, or tried to make a call, or even asked where the phone reception might be good.

"Good night, Ms. Conklin."

Nor did he inform her he would be shuttling on back home as soon as he woke up. Had he bought a roundtrip ticket to leave? How long had he planned on being here? Either he wanted that information on her land really badly, or… the ole Delta was putting down roots in him.

From behind her steering wheel, Sunday waited for him to reach his cabin. The headlights of her truck lit his path, so he didn't stumble into any mud puddles or run across unexpected visitors like snapping turtles or possums. His stiff gait would have had more rhythm if she'd helped him out.

The old Sunday would never have cared about a married man's situation. If he was over twenty-one and wanted it, and she did too, end of story. Jumping from Daddy's truck now, she questioned where was Old Sunday tonight. Old Sunday would have milked tonight for all it was worth, and had these fools begging for a marriage they never wanted.

But Bank Man arriving here the same night she became a millionaire had her thinking. Maybe he was a message from Daddy. Could her father have sent a messenger in the form of a devoted husband to show her it was time for her to level up her choices of men?

What I do know is I'm a father myself, just like your father was, Sunday. No father wants his children miserable and impoverished out of some misplaced sense of loyalty or legacy.

"Daddy, you ruinin' my good time," she muttered. "Stay out of it."

Their house sat dark and quiet. The boys would normally have been up watching movies or on the game, but even they had puttered out from all the festivities. She softly padded to the bathroom for night hygiene. Then, she'd head out to her "room" in the garage, already excited to satisfy herself.

"Sunday."

"Ah!" she hadn't noticed Mama in the corner next to the

paltry Christmas tree. That was another thing Sunday intended to replace immediately.

"Didn't mean to scare ya."

"What're you doin' up this late?" It was just after midnight and Sunday needed to hit the pillow. Tomorrow would be good and busy with all the plans she was lining up. As soon as that money landed in her account, she was buying the girls ponies and the boys Mustangs. And she had already reached out to McKissack and McKissack, America's oldest Black contractor from Georgia, to come and preserve their home while expanding it.

Rather than joy, Mama's face was pinched with worry. "You ain' do nothin' with that man tonight, did ya?"

"No."

"Is you lyin' ta me?"

Sunday rolled her eyes. She supposed she'd earned that over the years. "No, Mama."

"Good. I'm proud of ya for how you handled yaself today."

"What you mean?"

"With ya brotha and sista out there, makin' them feel a part. When I'm gone—"

"Mama, please don't."

With a flick of her hand, her mother cut off any counterargument. "When I am *gone*...y'all shouldn't be fightin' each other over none o' this here. That was one thing ya daddy got right, after *his* brothas and sistas fought. None o' that 'heir property' mess. So y'all could all work togetha. This was a real good start. I'm mighty proud o' ya. It's what Vanessa woulda done."

In the brief seconds after Sunday closed her eyes, before she drifted off to a land of no stress or worry, she let that acknowledgement soak in. Sunday had finally gotten it right. She had attained the same respect as her glorious sister. And not only that. Sunday could close the circle on what she and Vanessa had wanted for years—money. Not just barely surviving and robbing Peter to pay Paul, but overflow. Shaken together, pressed down, and spilling out of every cup. Elaine would see a new day.

For now, she slipped her fingers between her womanly lips and was shocked at the new fantasy popping into her head—Bank Man's mouth.

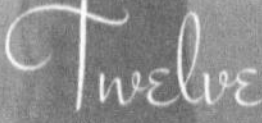

Twelve

THE REAL GIFT

SEVEN

He had changed his mind about going out frogging with the others. The bed felt too good.

Whatever this deep cedar, earthy scent was that they'd sprayed in these firm, pliable pillows, and thousand-count sheets that didn't scratch, it was doing its job. No kids were downstairs fighting over the last Pop Tart. No phone ringing with their friends calling to go stand in a long line for a new sneaker that cost five hundred dollars. No teenagers knocked on the door in realization they'd forgotten a weekend practice. No wife decided she needed to catch a "one time only" sale that required her to tear up her closet in search of the perfect warmup suit.

The dead quiet of the Delta fields blanketed Seven like he was still in his mother's womb.

Bang! Bang! Bang! Bang!

Seven's pillow was wet. He wiped drool from the corner of his mouth.

Bang! Bang!

"Mista Hardcastle! Ya still wit us?" Mother Fordham asked on the other side.

He forced his head from the pillow. "Ye..." His muscles and bones begged to go back into slumber.

Bang! Bang!

"Yes, ma'am. Five min..."

Eight minutes later, he opened his door to the elderly woman's eagle-sharp eyes waiting.

"I thought we was gon' need a bulldozer." She pushed the gigging stick at him. "The good ones already goin' down in the mud. Let's get on if we gon' catch a few decent ones." The apparent grandmother of Elaine already marched off the porch and into a waiting truck.

Driving it was Principal Overton. He reached back with a foam cup that smelled of strong coffee and zero cream. "Good mornin', young man."

"I have to tell you. I'm not feeling all that young at..." Seven lifted his wrist. Damn. He'd rushed out the door and forgotten his watch. And his phone. It was dead anyway, but he'd hoped to grab a charger off of somebody and juice up. He was confident his wife and kids were okay, but it was rare to let twenty-four hours pass without communicating. "You know what time it is?"

"Time to be thankful for another day, Mr. Hardcastle," Principal Overton eyed him in the rearview mirror. "Where ya got to go? Just the other night, you were tryin' your best to come in here. Now you tryin' to leave out?"

"Ha." Seven attempted to connect his lips to the cup while the truck bounced over the mud. "I've got a family to see after."

"Welp, you've gone this long without 'em. I don't see what another few minutes'll hurt."

Sleepy, his body lagging, Seven was irritated to be out here in the wee hours of the morning. The moment they stepped out of the truck, he was back at the perimeter of the fields. This morning's cold air bit harder than the day before, practically in the forties now, and Seven zipped his jacket.

"Looks like we picked a good weekend." Mother Fordham ignored Seven's extended hand to help her from the truck, and she eased out on her own. "Temperature is droppin' after that rain. Feel like it's gettin' cold befo' Christmas. This'll likely be our last run."

"Why your last?" Seven asked.

"Gigging season is over December thirty-first." Principal Overton slid a rifle out of the bed of the truck. "The frogs go deep in the mud to stay warm once that cold sets in, so you won't find 'em anyway. Mama is right. This'll probably be our last. Sunday will use the next two to three months after the holidays to clean the property, root out predators, choose which frogs she'll breed for sales, and set them aside to lay a nice clutch in April. Season starts all over again in June."

Not yet twilight, Seven helped carry the buckets of ice, gigging sticks, and tools such as knives and flashlights. From one pair of hands to the other, they passed the items to other froggers who were arriving.

"Mornin'." Mama Piggee slid on a pair of those ugly rubber overalls. "Weather feels like this might be the last run this year. We gon have to make it count today."

"Mornin', young tadpoles," Principal Overton said to the teenagers who appeared to sleep-walk from trucks the way Seven's children did so most mornings. "Come on over here and grab ya sticks."

"I don't want to," one of them complained. "I'd rather my grade just be a C and I can stay in the truck."

Another adult monitor straightened their back. "Problem with that is the real world don't give grades. It gives paychecks. If you go back to sleep because you don't want to, you don't get paid. Then, them bills don't get paid."

"Imma work for myself and be a rapper."

"Hits don't magically fall outta the sky, baby," Mama Piggee explained. "You'll have to get up and work, and hustle, and cry, befo' people know you're even alive. So move on out there now and start doin' things you don't want to so you can eat in the meantime. Last I heard, they ain' servin' C grades in them soup kitchens."

The adults laughed, but Miss Marleen's responsibility speech kicked Seven in his groin. What was he doing out here not calling his family? Not charging his phone. Drinking late at night with a strange woman. *And* lusting for her. Somebody who'd held him at gunpoint!

He had committed to a life with Arista, and he needed to return to it. For better or worse. That reminder sent his spirit into the mud to join the frogs. Mama Piggee had made that speech for Seven, too. Life was full of unavoidable commitments and he'd made his.

He would eke out this last activity, and make an excuse for not doing the girls' hair later this morning. He'd book a flight back to Dallas and be at the house to eat with Arista and the kids this evening, or at least to say goodnight and make sure homework was done. Seven had done his job here as best as he could. Friends now had a crack of an opening into the Conklin family through Paris, and Seven could handle the rest from Dallas over video calls.

Speaking of the Conklins, the truck that was becoming more familiar to him made its entrance, bouncing over the dirt field, splashing mud out of puddles, rumbling and revving its engine, and shining painful LED lights straight into Seven's face. Sunday's boots seemed to hit the ground with more bounce this morning, as if no amount of gravity could hold her down today.

"Mornin', everybody!" Despite the frog croaking from her throat, the weight of her life must have lifted some.

"Miss Sunday, wouldna expected you out here. Ya workers still out?"

"Yep, it's the holidays and they're with kids and family. Paris is a little under the weather. Narado went out last night. Y'all are stuck with me. I'll go easy on ya." Her cheeks on the rise, she discovered Seven. But this time, those cheeks held steady and didn't plummet. "Mr. Hardcastle. You're here."

"Barely," Principal Overton joked.

"Morning." What should he call her after they'd drank together, listened to the rain, and stared into the darkness until midnight? She was still the bank's customer, but 'Ms. Conklin' felt fake now.

"Mornin'." Was her voice lighter? She broke eye contact first, and charged toward the resentful teenagers as if they shouldn't possibly want to do anything else this early. "We ready to catch some Christmas frogs? Learn about some Delta soil? How these frogs tell us what time it is around here? They let us know what kind of growing season we've got ahead, and what the land is doin'. These frogs take care of us in a lot of ways. And they've been good eatin' in lean years."

"How frogs do all that?" A sleepy teenage student asked. "All they say is 'ribbit'."

Sleepy laughter broke the morning darkness on their way to the swamp. Flashlights searched through the trees.

Seven hung back and listened. Somewhere else on the land, other hunters had started their own independent excursions. It hadn't quite set in for him yet that people actually took time out of their lives to catch frogs.

"Of course, frogs do all that." Sunday led them deeper into the marshy high Johnson grass, now brown after autumn. "Anybody know why?"

"Their skin," one girl answered.

Sunday was surprised. "Very good. What's your name, baby?"

"Deanne."

"That's a pretty name. How did you know that?"

"I like biology. I'm gonna be a marine biologist and help preserve the planet y'all destroyin'."

Groans and grunts mixed with gentle laughter.

"We ain' destroyin' nothin', baby girl." Mama Piggee cast a side-eye at Seven. "All them big farmers, their pesticides, and factory operations are what's screwin' up the soil, banks givin' 'em more money to keep buildin' and eatin' up little folks... *that's* what'll destroy ya planet."

Seven held his peace. He wasn't new to people's anger at banks, and that he was a Black man who worked with those bigger companies. Those businesses didn't grow big by playing small. Nor did he send his kids to private school by worrying about amphibians.

"What about their skin might have helped our people survive out here? Maybe it even gave us our advantage at times?" Right at home in *her* skin, Sunday waded deeper into the chilly, muddy water rising calf-length around her rubber coveralls.

"Their skin is really sensitive and permeable," Deanne explained while taking pictures with her phone. "It absorbs anything around it, so if there's pollution or contamination in the area, a frog's skin will change, and you can tell from the color or size if the soil is bad. Black people who lived off the land might know from a frog where the good dirt would be, and where to plant. If they were on the run and gathering fruit, fish or small animals, the way frogs looked likely told them where it was healthy to eat or where not to eat."

Sunday pushed her shoulders back as if she were glad another person in the world understood the mission. "Deanne, you're gonna do amazing things, but if you ever wanna help out around here, we'd be glad to have ya."

"Thank you." Indeed, young Deanne pushed forward the

way a person did when they knew they had bigger and better plans than their current circumstances offered.

All of a sudden, Sunday aimed her flashlight straight at the mud, between high weeds. Rather than stabbing, she pointed. A young man stepped forward, looked, and without hesitation, stabbed. He stooped down, and in silence, they seemed to work in harmony. Sunday pinned the poor frog in place while the kid gained a good grip.

"Go ahead. Get ya fingers in his sides, good and deep so he won't go nowhere." Sunday coached him.

"You mean he's not dead already?" Seven asked.

"Impalin' him won't kill him. He'll jump off if you don't grab him first. Then, take out the stick."

The young man held up his catch. It was as wide and long as his hand. The elders crowed.

"Oooh! A bull frog!"

"And a nice, big, fat one, too!"

"Good job, Toby!"

Toby's grin disappeared faster than it came, almost as if he hadn't heard those accolades very often but didn't want to be the butt of jokes from his classmates, so he couldn't revel too long. After tossing his frog in the ice bucket, he avoided eye contact and moved on.

Suddenly, another student shined their flashlight into the yellowing bushes, raised her gig and sent the water spraying around her.

"Whew, chile! Now that's a woman who done already decided she ain' gettin' paid no C money!" Mama Piggee was impressed.

Sunday grew bigger with every gigging stick raised in the air and brought back down. The youth were more motivated this morning than they had been Friday night, or maybe they were ready to collect their minimum haul and get this over with. With various frogs croaking and singing, the group followed deeper into the cold swamp water.

After several minutes of "hoo-hoo's" from a local owl, a few blackbirds squawking at each other, and crickets reminding him it was still way too early, Seven heard croaking close to him. Principal Overton and the others chuckled at Seven in jest, shaking their heads.

Seven listened. Too scared to disrupt the water, he twisted in the direction of the sound. The swamp fell silent again. Damn. Maybe he shouldn't have moved.

"Pssst." Several feet away, Sunday shined her flashlight at the base of a tree along the shore, right at the water line.

Seven swallowed, wading carefully. Lifting his gig stick, he smashed it down in the water! Caught up in the excitement of his first real gig, he brought up his stick. Nothing was there. Another stick smashed the same area. The frog hopped past both of them.

"Crap!" Deanne cried next to Seven.

He was no quitter. The frog landed in another spot and hopped up again, straight onto Seven's chest, shocking him, and bounced off before Seven could make a move. Mother Fordham, Principal Overton and the others erupted with amusement.

"That frog said, 'not today you won't, joker'!" Mother Fordham howled.

Seven pursued. Faster this time, he was ready for that next landing, and Seven went for it. This time, he stabbed and left the stick inside. Dropping to his knee, reaching into the murky water, he felt around for the writhing creature and gripped it at the sides. Ensuring he had a firm grip, he lifted both the stick and the frog from the water. Deanne came over and helped wriggle out the prongs so the thing didn't slip from Seven's fingers.

"Yeh!" The others clapped.

"Ha haaa!"

Seven dropped the frog into an ice bucket, feeling like he deserved a medal. This outing in the forest, wading through swamp water, moving in darkness, nothing but Earth in his presence, brought him a sort of clarifying peace. He felt guilty for enjoying it.

"Mr. Bigshot ready to be a country man nah." One of the men teased. "How much longer you gon' be a country woman, Sundie? Time you cash in that—"

Principal Overton shook his head, as if he was silencing the man.

Any other time, Seven would have minded his own business and ignored that, out of respect. But why would somebody ask her that? Why would she be anything other than a country woman? What would she be cashing in?

Sunday turned her back and poked onward. "Let's move, family. We've only got a bit of dark left."

A sudden hush fell over the group that suddenly felt forced and awkward.

"Mr. Bank Man, you ever heard o' anybody named Sherman?" somebody asked.

Suspicious, Seven continued wading along the shore. "My name is Seven. Not Bank Man. And no, I don't know anybody with that last name."

"That sho is strange, 'cause yo face and build resemble some pictures my grandma had at her house. Of some Shermans."

Seven laughed, eying a frog that stared straight at him from among the mud and leaves. His flashlight trained on the frog, it froze, and he stabbed. "Seems everybody around here is related to somebody else. But no, I'm from Chicago."

"Shermans, ya say, Manny?" Mother Fordham ran a finger down her nose.

"Yes'm," the man replied and pushed ahead.

Her hawk eyes went to work on Seven, inspecting him for similarities to some ghost of a person who likely had no current relevance to anything. "Hmph."

As respectfully as he could, wanting to enjoy this last peace before he broke the news that he had to leave, Seven moved on.

Over their heads, an eye had opened in the purple eternity of night. Through it snuck the dawn, cascading on them in shades of lavender, orange, primrose, and apricot that cracked through the Heavens.

Sunday cocked her head back, as if basking in a sunrise that was hers alone. And indeed, morning light reflected in her chestnut irises.

"The sun's done moved since last time I's here." Mother Fordham lifted her face to the Heavens as well. "It's Christmas season."

Dawn revealed the Old Town Lake, just beyond the trees. Sky-high water tupelos ascended from the mirror that was the lake. A lone swan bathed. Fish disturbed the glassy surface.

Elaine's Black residents took in the vision.

"It sure is, Motha." Sunday grinned.

A few waded toward each other, grabbing one another's arms, briefly touching somebody's hand, or squeezing a shoulder. Calm hung over the water. The lake sat so peaceful and still, the forest and fields so tranquil, that all of Heaven and nature must have been singing a song only for these souls of Elaine to hear. Some aura or entity was very present in this swamp, and connected them all in an unspoken bond that, clearly, no one who wasn't one of them could possibly understand.

Whatever they were bonding over, or secretly celebrating, Seven sensed what he was seeing right here and now was the real gift.

Thirteen

THE SECRET SOCIETY OF SOUTHERN SOULS

SUNDAY

He had actually waded into the swamp, gigged for frogs, *chased* one of them, and grabbed them with his bare hands. A man who had a cushy bank exec job in the city, and drove home every evening to an immaculate house in one of those neighborhoods where everybody had Astroturf and backyard swimming pools, was out here picking algae off his rubber coveralls.

Tuh.

She reminded herself he was only doing his job. He was trained at pretending he cared so people would open their wallets. At that moment, mid-chuckle with Toby during some joke, he looked up. And did a double-take, apparently shocked Sunday was already staring.

"What?" he mouthed.

She shook her head. "Nothin'." Why did she mouth back?

Suspicion deepened on his face, along with a perplexed squint in his eyes. "*What?*" he insisted.

His mouth was *not* sexy. Okay, so it was. Under his

mustache. And over what was now his salt and pepper five o'clock shadow. Those perfect waves on his head were a little rougher today, closer to their natural, uncontrolled state. Sunday averted her eyes. A woman could only have so much discipline.

That morning had been such a good time she didn't want to utter these next words. "Everybody, time to wind it down and pack up." In less than twenty-four hours, she would be at the state lottery office.

Her land would look so different come next year.

"You all right, baby?" Mama Piggee asked her.

"More than all right."

"That's what I'm talkin' 'bout. What's the first thang you doin' tomorra?" The older woman lowered her voice so only Sunday heard. "After you meet with all ya new representatives ya got."

"I don't have one clue. It's so many thangs I been wantin' to do a long time. I don't know which one to do first. Book us a nice trip somewhere overseas. Or hire a contractor to build us that house Daddy always wanted and Aunt Bird woulda been proud of." Sunday took a final glance at the swamp. "Hire a private investigator, and our *own* archaeologist to finally bring up them bodies. Bury 'em right an' proper. Same way they did in New York and Tulsa. Elaine can finally see justice done."

Mama Piggee frowned. "Them folks been here a hundred years. They ain' goin' nowhere. Take yo family some place nice. Show them kids the great big world out thah. All this'll be here when you get back. Ain' everyday somebody win the lottery. Damn sho not a Black person roun these parts."

"Somebody won the lottery?"

Sunday spun in her boots to find Mr. Hardcastle had approached. Worry squeezed her chest closed.

"I wasn't trying to be nosey."

"But you were."

He was still here to do Strom Adler's bidding.

"I only heard the last part. That somebody had won. Nothing else. You know who did?"

He may not have known before, but now, Sunday watched the dots connect on his forehead.

"Wait a minute. Sunday, *you*?" A range of emotions crossed his face. "*You* won the lottery?"

No!

"Hold on." Mama Piggee stepped in front of Sunday. "You makin' a mountain outta nothin'. Ain' nobody said all that. Somebody from 'roun' here did win, but not her."

Bank Man refused to play along. "Your whole vibe changed overnight, from Friday to Saturday. The party with all your neighbors. You and your brother and sister arguing out in the field and then making some kind of agreement. All the little hints you've been dropping."

Sunday stepped to him. "I thought you said you weren't bein' nosey."

He surprised her and stepped closer, leaning over her. "I wasn't when I first came over here, but the biggest fool— which I have been— can figure all this out, Sunday. And why are you so worried what I think if you didn't win? Why didn't you just say that? If you pay off the bank, you won't have to worry about it anymore. I'm happy for you. Really, I am."

He looked like he meant that.

"I've got plans for Elaine. That's why. And I can't have these white boys trippin' us up, sendin' state inspectors, openin' audits, rewritin' the rules, like they always do whenever we finally get somethin' for us. So, I'd appreciate you not puttin' that in your report. They'll find out soon enough, I know, but let me sign the check and the money hit my bank account first, before I have to worry wit them."

All that spoke was his breathing. Pinching the bridge of

his nose, dropping his head, he was clearly conflicted about it. At least he had a conscience that didn't make the choice easy. "You want me to hide from my employer—your creditor—that you have assets now to pay your debt."

"A low-down creditor that's racist and bankrolls racists," Sunday declared. "And don't pretend you don't know. You might turn a blind eye so you don't have to see everything, but in your heart, Bank Man, you *know*!"

"C'mon, brotha man. Do us this one solid," Mama Piggee coaxed.

"Oh, I'm not Bank Man no more? I get to be a 'brotha' now." An irritated Mr. Hardcastle stared from one to the other.

Mama Piggee elbow-bumped Sunday. "Look at him talkin' 'bout some 'no more.' That ain' how they talk at the bank. You one o' us now."

Sunday faced Mr. Hardcastle. "Please." She wasn't too proud. For her family, alive *and* dead, and the entire town, she would humble herself and say it. In this closed universe of the Delta South, where white good ole boys had cut off every avenue and sucked out everything but their souls, Elaine needed this long overdue win.

Despite the man being a total stranger to this place, he must have sensed it. "We never had this conversation."

Marleen whipped her arms around his and squeezed him tight. "Thank you, brotha. Merry Christmas! God bless you."

He let out a low whistle. "Congratulations again. That's... wow. Damn."

That same astonishment ricocheted through Sunday. "Thank you."

"I was coming here to say I should leave and get back to my family, so I can't do the girls' hair."

A small piece of Sunday had looked forward to those zooming noises, and weird voices he made. "They'll be disappointed to hear that, but I understand. If you want breakfast, Paris will likely have hot buttermilk biscuits, bacon, and grits back at the house. You can stop through and fix a plate to take with you."

"I'd appreciate that."

He didn't take off.

Her feet were planted.

What was happening?

"Mr. Hardcastle, ya got anything else you want us to check out?" One of the soil techs arrived who'd been with him yesterday.

Seven's eyes hadn't left Sunday's. "Not if we plan on leaving here with our limbs. I don't think Ms. Sunday would allow it even if I did."

Grinning, Sunday shook her head. "Nope. Ms. Sunday would not."

He offered his hand, and when she graciously slid hers inside, he wrapped his around it. Hardcastle clearly lived a life free of hard labor. Those smooth hands may have been ashy and dry, but they weren't rough. Like her own. Out of nowhere, she wondered how her skin must feel to him.

"Good luck with everything. Sincerely." He still hadn't let go.

"Same to you. With the things you want so bad you can't bring yoself to speak on 'em." She hoped he understood what she was referencing.

He loosened his grip. Suddenly self-aware, Sunday slid out her hand. With nothing more for them to say, he pivoted for Principal Overton's truck.

Mama Piggee swerved her entire body to face Sunday. "Go on. Run after him and tell him you wanna screw. What went down between Friday night and now that me and some six hundred odd people around here missed?"

Sunday chuckled and the two walked to her truck, arm in

arm. "He got to know Elaine, Miss Marleen. As for me, I'm a multimillionaire now. It's loads of Bank Men out there I can choose from."

* * *

SEVEN

The little one's eyes tearing up nearly changed Seven's mind. Livi's "mama," Paris, had gotten her all excited to have her hair styled just like Victoria's. The scent of butter, bacon grease, coffee, and fresh bread filled their compact kitchen brimming with activity. However, now, Seven understood why. That small Christmas tree in the corner wouldn't look so forlorn for long.

As badly as he wanted to bless the girl's heads, he had children of his own. And a wife. Though they were all most likely fine, he was responsible for making sure of it. The bright side was they were going to France later this month. He and his wife could use that to springboard their marriage back to the fun they used to have.

"I'll be callin' ya office some time this week, Mr. Hardcastle." Paris held her toddler in one arm, and extended a hand to Seven with the other.

"Full disclosure, I work for the bank. You should also be calling an attorney, Ms. Conklin. I can recommend a couple I know who are licensed in Arkansas, too. But I'm glad to lay out a few financial options or answer questions over the phone."

She nodded. "Thank you."

Her mother joined her. "Mr. Hardcastle, I know things didn't start out smooth, but we did enjoy havin' ya this weekend."

That was funny. "I apologize for how I came in. I probably should have just used the front gate or called or something."

"Sho' did make things interestin'. That much I know. You have a safe trip back."

On his way out the door, the morning music of hearty laughter, chairs squeaking against linoleum, forks scraping plates and pans, and kids screaming, roared on.

He stepped into the sun and faced field after field of green leaves sprouting from the earth. Young Reggie started the truck to drive Seven and his soil techs the better part of a mile across *part* of the Conklin Fields, past planted winter cover crops, likely turnip greens, peas and cabbage. Seven had arrived here on Friday evening in pitch dark, and yesterday, when he returned to meet Paris, he'd been focused on work— checking soil quality and health, whether it was contaminated with pesticides, too clayey, whether there were signs of illegal plants somewhere. Only now did the vast, green loveliness capture him for the first time, so tranquil one could lie down and nap in those rows.

For the second time in two days, Reggie drove Seven to the front gate where the goofy iron frog in a Christmas wreath saw him off with that ridiculous smile. The gates snapped closed behind them, and Seven felt he was being shut out of the secret society of southern souls.

"That sure was a good time, wasn't it?" One of the soil techs started the car and took off.

In full daylight now, on the ride down Highway 44, Seven cringed at what he was seeing.

"Hold on before we roll out. Make a turn down this Main Street," Seven instructed the tech.

He thought rundown places like this only existed in cheesy scary movies from the eighties. On the East side of the highway were railroad tracks, and on the West side was a tiny, vintage town square that had been dropped off in the 1920s and left there.

Elaine's Main Street resembled more of a business cemetery, its single-story brick storefronts with prism glass had to be at least a hundred years old. Only four or five of the match box buildings were actually in use. All the other doors were boarded up or newspapered over, like somebody along the way had deliberately tossed the keys so no one else could find them and reopen all this.

A yellow sale sign had been left in a shop window a few decades too long. Inside another, a spider crawled over a faded "Open" sign. These dark shops, warehouses, and cafes told the story of a forgotten town that once breathed with promise. Main Street led from an old train depot, where trains no longer ran, down to a working-class cluster of humble houses that had seen brighter days. Over Seven's head stood Elaine's water tower, so rusted over that anybody might have thought the sky dropped mud on it regularly. He hoped it was just an antique and they didn't drink from that.

"This your first time in Elaine, man?" One of the techs asked.

Seven's heavy heart bolted him into the passenger seat. He'd seen healthier third world countries. This degree of neglect and blight stretched beyond racism.

Yet, the land itself—what state officials couldn't ruin, oppress, or destroy easily—was an undeniable gem. On his ride back to Helena, Elaine's quaintness began withdrawing its comfort from around his shoulders. He wanted to snuggle in the bed linens of Delta quietude just a bit longer, even while he collected his things in his hotel room.

There on the nightstand lay his own lottery ticket he'd left behind yesterday morning. A chuckle escaped him. That rough-around-the-everything woman, mowing down any object in her path, was a millionaire now. The thought of

Sunday packed tight in her jeans last night excited him all over again, so much so that his blood was a river rushing through his groin. Seven had better reach his wife quickly.

He started to throw his ticket away, but Nick would want it for family games over Christmas. He tossed it in his carryon with his personal effects.

Now that he finally had his phone charger, text after text rolled through his screen. He scrolled for Arista's. She should have found her Christmas surprise by now, and had likely been trying to contact him.

He swiped up his messages, ignoring every name, in search of hers. Where was it?

Finally.

ARISTA

How's frog land?

He swiped up for her previous messages.

That was it? Her only response to him taking her overseas?

He had spent weeks planning this France trip, down to showing the kids the spot where, seventeen years ago, he'd promised their mother her life would feel like France everyday.

Disappointed, Seven stopped scrolling any further. What were the two of them doing? What was the real reason he'd felt they needed a trip in the first place? Seven shoved his phone in his pocket. No other messages looked urgent. She and the kids were obviously fine.

He would use these final two hours to absorb a new and unexpected place that was growing on him.

Planted along US-79 were remnants of plantation society. Multiple cotton gin houses teetered to the side, dilapidated wooden boards stubbornly refusing to collapse, their ongoing existence a loud promise from deceased owners. Silver grain silos stood tall and proud, their galvanized steel glittering like they'd been Windexed, boasting prosperity Black farmers could only dream of.

Despite these holdouts of oppression, Seven was far more relaxed than when he arrived. The never-ending bridge from Arkansas into Mississippi soothed him, in a region that was deceptively tantalizing to be this simple.

On the other hand, Seven wanted to vomit in his mouth. There were so few main roads leading into Eastern Arkansas that most access to all those small, Black towns required traversing this one bridge through Helena. It may have been due to the expense of building another bridge over one of the biggest rivers in America. Still, this smacked of deprivation, where Arkansas had cut off the Blacks of the Arkansas Delta from the rest of the world.

Friends of the Delta Savings and Loan had probably helped finance this insular institution. No way in and no way out, unless it was through Friends. And Strom Adler. And all his good ole boys.

Like most other Black people who weren't interested in revisiting America's former slave society, Seven had always avoided the Delta. But the lack of support had left the Blacks here defenseless.

Sunday deserved that money. Elaine deserved the lottery, and it still wouldn't be enough.

Seven's phone rang with Nicky in the caller ID, and he declined it. He needed this little while to think. He might not have it again for a long time.

He'd go see Ian. There was no way Seven could keep doing business as usual. How would the bank remedy this? College scholarships? Farming grants? Housing aid? Financial education or free services? What Band-Aid could the bank place over this cancer?

If Friends did nothing, Seven couldn't keep working there. This was not the kind of talk for him and Ian to have in the office. Ian didn't live too far from Seven, about five miles. He was so disgusted over this Elaine situation that, after dinner with his family, he would go there and speak with him tonight.

He'd have to tell Arista. They had the money and resources to handle their household in case Seven needed to quit and look for a different bank. If he stayed after what he had seen firsthand, what was he teaching his children about trading moral character for money and status? Aside from that, he'd been with Friends nearly twenty years. Now that his children were older, maybe it was time for a change in Seven's life anyway.

A few hours later, Seven was still holding the last few minutes of countryside solitude that had just loved on him in a way he wasn't ready yet to let go of. No calls, no texts, no social media. Seven just appreciated the odd vacuum in which his body was still suspended, all the way until the rideshare car stopped in front of his house, dropping him back at his well-manicured life.

Fourteen

YOUR DIRTY WORK

SEVEN

No dinner smell greeted him. He turned on the lights. The familiarity of arguing, phone conversations, and TV didn't welcome him in.

"Ri? Ray? Ash?" He was surprised to find his house completely dark.

He scrolled through his phone for where his wife and children were.

RAY

Dad, when u gettin' hm?

DILLON

Dad, cn u send $20?

ME

For what? Where u at?

DILLON

Ant's. Need lunch $

ME

Check ur Zelle. Where's Mama?

DILLON

Aunt Erin's

ME

On a Sunday night?

Why?

DILLON

Don't no.

ME

Know.

Where u at?

RAY

Auntie Fran

ME

Cn u hang in there 1 more day? Almost finished.

RAY

I guess.

ME

Ray I'll make it up. Promise.

Leaving his luggage, he ventured upstairs with his mind spinning. Arista had clearly arranged for the kids to land at other places, but where was she? This made no sense.

He switched on the light in their bedroom, and the final light in his heart switched off. The paperwork for the France trip lay exactly where he'd left them Friday morning. She hadn't been here all weekend?

If she was out having a good time with her sister, or

accepted a news story, it would explain why her texts were so few and responses so short. But she hadn't spoken a word about any of it to him. Sometimes, she did that, though. Excited over a lead or a new development, she'd take the occasional day's ride across the state for a story that was promising. In their early days, sometimes, he'd gone with her.

Now, from where he stood, he saw just inside their closet. The shoe box for her crystal Christian Louboutins lay slightly ajar on the top shelf. Seven walked over and lifted it easily. The three-thousand-dollar, rhinestone-encrusted shoes had been missing Friday, also.

The stillness of their house, the untouched tickets, her not acknowledging his dick pics yesterday, her priciest shoes being missing all weekend... Seven pulled out his phone and dialed.

"Hey, babe!" she answered. Relaxed, she sounded in good spirits, maybe even like she'd had a drink or two. So she hadn't been abducted. "How's frog land? Are you actually out there? What's it like? Are they everywhere? What's the owner like? Are they nasty? Do they keep the frogs in their house?"

Staring at the tickets, Seven rubbed at the gnawing in his chest and took his time. "It's actually not too bad out here. There's a pretty lake, giant trees, and these long fields of crops. I see now why they call Arkansas, 'The Natural State.' Words don't do it justice. What are you into back at the house?"

"Oh, Erin and me, we took us a little trip to Houston, so I could check out a spa she's been telling me about. We didn't plan it or I would have let you know. Once you told me you were going out of town, I figured I'd use the weekend for a little TLC on myself before the holiday season fires up. We'll ride back tomorrow. I should get home about noon."

Oh. "How do you like the spa?"

"Oh, my God, they've got these twenty-four karat gold facials that are everything." An uncontrollable giggle bubbled up from her. "I love it here. They've got a new restaurant down here, too, with dancing floors. So we broke out last night, busted a couple moves. It's been cool, so I stayed one more day. You home yet?"

He was glad she was enjoying herself. Arista did work hard as an executive for the station. Only...

Melancholy rang through him. If she was with her sister, had Arista shown Erin his pic? Why didn't she ever respond? His mind began writing stories it shouldn't have.

"No. Not yet."

His heart twitched with guilt. Why did he just do that? Some feeling, some instinctive voice just told him to hold his cards. Not to be so readily accessible for her to know where he was at all times. If she was out having fun, maybe he needed to start having more himself.

And he was the one who had the security camera app on his phone, not her; so she didn't know he was in the house.

"Oh, wow. I'm sorry, babe."

"No worries. Like I said, this area is a little different than what I expected. I'll need to see the results of that facial on you. Pronto. I know your body's gonna be lookin' right, too. Listen, uh, there's something we need to talk about when we're back at home."

"Oh, yeah? What's up?"

"Um, this place I'm at.... I like it. A lot. We should bring the kids."

"You mean the frog place?"

"Elaine. The town is called Elaine. And... it'd be good for 'em."

"Oookaaay.... I thought we always said our kids won't associate poverty with being Black? They would only experience accomplished spaces."

"Like I said, let's hold off until we're face to face. You're at your spa gettin' even finer. I'm...where I'm at, feeling nice and relaxed. Let's leave it where it is for now and get into that later this week."

To entertain the possibility of losing one of their jobs, even just for a while, would be rough. They had more than enough money. For Arista, it was the status.

She had come to love their membership at the country club, which they'd acquired on *his* position and banking relationships. Country club members—oil barons, real estate tycoons, sports team owners, lawyer family dynasties, and doctor offices—didn't care about TV personalities.

How could he explain to her why they should upset their cushy status quo? Seven being unemployed meant Arista having to tell her circles and family members her husband was jobless. Not that he was a real estate executive handling lucrative deals and had access to banking credit and underwriting. How would that land for her over Sunday brunch and Saturday mani-pedis? Moreover, how would it affect him if he was black-balled and another bank didn't pick him up right away?

Did he even want to keep working at a bank?

On the drive to Ian's house, Seven's phone rang and he sent his sister's call to voicemail. Was approaching Ian about Elaine the right move? He was literally risking his job just before Christmas. If Ian said it was too bad for those folks, then what was Seven's next move?

He'd reached Ian's house, beautifully decorated for the holidays, decked out with massive bells over the entrance of his driveway, an illuminated Santa and all eight reindeer landing on top of his roof, giant candy canes and elves in the yard, complete with toy trains and bows. Seven wasn't surprised the community wasn't gated. Ian *wanted* strangers to drive by his house and gawk.

For some odd reason, he'd stopped three houses away and parked on the street, instead of just entering Ian's driveway. It was a Sunday night and Seven suspected he might try to dodge a guest from work. Seven certainly would have. But he saw movement in the house. A few lights were on. At the very least, Ian's wife and the kids were there.

Still questioning this, Seven decided he couldn't cast a blind eye on what he'd just witnessed, and felt. After this weekend, if he returned to business as usual, he was complicit and part of the problem. His conscience wouldn't let him go back home.

Walking past the glowing ornaments, and up the porch one more random thought crossed Seven's mind before he punched the doorbell.

"Seven, whoa, buddy!" his boss spoke through the Ring camera. "What the he-he-hell gives, man?" His laugh sounded like he had indeed been surprised. "You just showed up here! No appointment, no phone call, no text, nothin'. Seems you got your days and location mixed up, don't ya, pal?"

"My bad, man, but since you *did* interrupt my weekend with this unscheduled trip to a situation that's not mine, I figured one interruption deserves another. You know what I'm saying?"

"Any chance we can schedule this little hoe-down for tomorrow?" Ian asked through the Ring intercom.

"If it wasn't serious, I wouldn't be standing here. I'd be in the comfort of my own warm house with my wife and kids, ya know? I can't discuss this around employees. And it needs to be addressed. It'll only be a minute."

A few more seconds passed. Why was Seven having to beg to speak with Ian after doing *him* a favor? Ian should have been more concerned than Seven. The very least he could do was open the door.

In his pocket, his phone rang with Arista on the line again. Seven silenced it. She'd gone all the way to Houston on yet another spa weekend rather than accompanying him to do something different. Quite frankly, it bothered him.

"Ian. What gives? You sent me to do your dirty work. Open up."

For a few more seconds, Seven could have sworn he heard running and scurrying inside. The door finally cracked open. Seven was somewhat astonished. Even for this to be the weekend.

"You all right?" Seven laughed.

Ian flicked his wet hair around and wiped what appeared to be sweat off his face that matched the glowy red Christmas lights. Ian looked like he'd just ran a marathon. Breathing heavily, skin splotchy, red patches on his arms and neck as if he'd joined fight club, he and Misty had clearly been engaged in high-intensity activity. That must have been why Ian wasn't opening the door fully.

Figuring it out, Seven cracked up immediately. "Man! Why did you even answer the intercom? I see you and Misty are indisposed."

"Oh, no, man. I, uh, went huntin' this weekend, got caught up in some bushes that weren't too nice, and now you just happened to catch me in the middle of a workout. What's goin' on, brother? Whatcha got for me?"

"Yeah, whatever you say. So listen, you wanted me to look into these Conklins in Elaine, see what they might want in terms of selling, and I spent the last couple days with them. I got to know 'em some, and they're not the average farm owners, so the package deal can't be average. They have unique needs, and I think we can m—"

Seven fell down all seven levels of hell. The questions from this weekend clicked together instantly and he stepped inside the door.

Ian reached to escort him back out. "You know what, brother, I think we can go over this to—"

Adrenaline and fury gave Seven the strength to throw Ian back. Lying underneath a sprawling desk in Ian's office was a very recognizable $3200 Christian Louboutin Kate Max Eternity stiletto.

Every single crystal scraped his esophagus on the way down while he swallowed each one.

"Whose is that?" Seven didn't wait for the answer. Misty was into cowboy boots, not stilettos.

"Seven, man, I'm *tellin'* you to get outta my house! *Now!*"

Instead, he stomped to the desk, picked it up, and stared at the inner sole. No.

France for you every day.

He'd had them especially inscribed for Arista.

"Seven! What the hell are you doin'? Get! O—"

He hadn't clocked somebody in a long time. Seven's body enter the furnace, and inside it he went numb. Hurt and humiliation melted in the flames of fury. After Seven's second punch, Ian looped his arm around Seven's neck in an attempt to fling Seven to the floor. Seven stomped on his bare foot with the heel of his cowboy boot. A bone cracked somewhere down there.

"Aaaggh! Aaahhhh!" Curling over in pain, Ian managed to grip Seven in a bear hug and push him into the giant Christmas tree, both of them tumbling down with it.

He felt nothing. Only wrath. "Arista Goddamn Hardcastle!"

How in the hell had be been so dumb? Seven kicked him in his shin and punched him in the throat. Charging up the stairs with the shoe, three at a time, he left his wife's fuck buddy where he still choked.

He went for the closed door. It was her classic M.O. when she was pissed.

All it took was one kick with the heel of his boot to knock off the knob and rip it open. There she stood, the mother of his children glistening with sweat, just like her lover. In raunchy leather straps and a red wig slicked into a spiky bob, she held the phone. "It's the police, Seven! So calm down. Just be cool. All right!"

"You had my boss to send me out of town so you could screw him!" He rushed toward her.

In an instant she switched from authoritative and in control, to softly crying. "Seven, what did you think was gonna happen, huh? How long did you think I'd go without? You can't have sex with me anymore. You can't..." She waved a hand in the direction of his groin. "...*do* nothin'!"

Her husband slipped into a seventeen-year time portal so deep he heard himself cackling from some far away place on the other side of it. "Do nothin'? I can't do nothin'? Let me see that phone. You know what? We'll use mine, too. Since you like attention so much."

"Seven, what are you doing?" Ri shrieked.

He opened his Instagram app and pressed "Live."

"You wanna bring outsiders in this marriage, huh? Go on then, superstar!"

"Seven, stop it!"

He held the phone up to her mortified face. "Tell the police to sleep next to you every night for seventeen gatdamn years with them long ass toe nails scraping their legs. Tell 911 how you snore loud enough I can't leave the window open at hotels cause people think a fucking coyote is outside! Tell 'em you shop like you ain' got no..." He grabbed the woman he'd given his *whole* heart to. She slapped at his arms, face, shoulders, anything to break free of Seven's grip. Too far gone, Seven felt none of it. "...your clothes. All them damn clothes. A bunch of worthless shit. You're a fucking hoarder. You materialistic...*parasite!*"

Arista tried to beat him with a leather whip. "Stop! I tried to be with you, and stay faithful. How am I supposed to fuck a man who can't get it up? Huh?"

He lunged to smack her. Ri dodged and her cowering position brought him back to his senses.

He'd never want a man to touch one of his girls, or even tower over them. And for *their* sakes, he wouldn't want them seeing their mother hurt.

"No, Arista, I can't get it up for *you* anymore. I fell out of love with your selfish ass years ago. But here I was trying to make it work over my better judgment." He laughed. "Out here seeing a therapist, trying to force myself to want you again. Do you know how much pussy I could've had by now? How many interns felt me up while they're still in college? How many secretaries and temps flashed me at holiday parties? But I *always* brought it home to you!" At the memories of how stupidly faithful he'd been, he cracked up. "*No*, Ri! As always, you got it all fucking wrong! I can get hard for literally *any* woman, *every* woman. *Except* you."

"Seven..." When those lips quiver...right before sob stories come out of it, that used to hook him. "Baby, I'm sorrrryyy..."

"Shhhh. Shhh. Shh. Sh. No, you're not. Not as sorry as you about to be. You never loved me."

"That's not true. I do. I do. It's just been hard."

"Mm mm. You only thought it was hard. Not nearly as hard as it's finna be. Those are *my* kids. I'm going for full custody. You can keep the house. You won't wanna see my next one."

"All right, sir, time to go."

Seven had been so lost in the "how" and the "why" of his stupidity, he hadn't heard the cops arrive and come in.

His arms were strapped behind his back and his wrists confined in handcuffs.

"Sevennnn..." She cried, following down the stairs behind

him and the police. "Seven, baby, I'm coming to get you out. We'll work through it. I'll go to therapy with you."

"Leave me in there. I'd rather sleep on a musty bench than in the same bed as you now, Arista. We're past therapy now. I want a divorce."

"You don't mean that! You're upset and I understand, but we been together too long to just throw seventeen years—"

"And you assumed I was your house mutt and I wasn't going anywhere. How many others were there, Arista? How many of 'em did you let shake my hand and smile in my fa..." He broke down half-laughing, half-crying.

"Sir, watch your head." An officer guided him into him the back of a patrol car.

Two hours later, once they'd processed him and placed him in a cell, he lay there all night staring at the ceiling, reliving every time she took off on an assignment. Had she really been doing her job? Did his friends know? No, certainly not his uncle, Nicky. Nicky would have told him. But their associates? The ones who weren't real friends.

He didn't worry with the phone call. He knew his lawyer was coming.

He wasn't lying when he'd told Arista that jail was better than their bed. It was the best place to figure out his life—how they'd work out divorce, his position at Friends, the kids, holidays and summers as a divided household. At the end of that line of priorities was the question of *him*.

He'd been wearing the "devoted husband and dad" hat so long, who was he?

Fifteen

WE SOME MILLIONAIRES

Sunday

"It's the most wonderful seeeeasonnn of allllll," Sunday sang, and this morning, she really meant it. "That van pulls out in one hour!" Today was the day.

"I can get ready in ten minutes," Nookie mumbled into his mattress.

Sunday snickered. "It takes you ten minutes just to shave them two whiskers you got. I'm not waitin' fo' you!"

"Auntie, are we goin' to Li'l Wock wit you?" Vanessa's four-year-old mini, Livi, asked. Seeing her sister's eyes on her daughter now was bittersweet.

"You sure are. We're all goin' together, baby girl." She wished Nessa were alive so they could act up in this triumph together, squeeze each other, disappear in the trees, smoke a joint and act stupid until they came back home and passed out in the garage. If this blessing had come five years ago, Nessa would have had money to leave her husband and she'd still be alive. But Sunday had to believe everything happened for a reason. "Come on. Let's go get your dress on."

"Towi said we gettin' us a big Christmas twee. Are we? Fo' weal?"

Sunday escorted Livi to the girls' bedroom where she and her sisters once slept. "That's a surprise, Miss Ma'am. Tori needs to quit ear-hustlin'."

An hour later, their suitcases packed for two nights, Sunday herded her mother and the children out the door. Paris and her husband would follow with the girls in their car. Friends and family from around Elaine who were "in the know" lined up to see them off.

This was the rough part for Sunday. She wasn't good at this stuff—being reminded of who from their village was still standing here with them, and who wasn't.

"Come here, gal." Mama Piggee threw her arms around Sunday and rocked her from side to side. "Look at youuu."

"Aht aht. You know this ain' what I do, Miss Marleen." But sixteen years of bottled-up tears crept out anyway, already making Sunday Conklin out a liar. "Okay, family, let's hit this road."

In their rearview mirror, Sunday could still see the neighbors waving as they turned the corner. With Nookie behind the wheel, the first Christmas song to set off the concert was TLC's "Sleigh Ride." For the next two hours, they introduced Reggie and Victoria to the old school Christmas jams and rap songs while the kids wrinkled up their noses.

"Ooh, that's the Capitol! We came here on a field trip one time!" Victoria pointed from Interstate 630 through downtown Little Rock.

On their ride into the capitol city, her heart nearly burst for a different reason than the last time she'd come here for taxes. Sunday rarely brought the kids here. Their lives back at home were frugal but happy, and she didn't want that joy spoiled by them seeing all the things they couldn't access. That wouldn't be the case today, though.

"I love coming to Little Rock. Everything is so much bigger here." Tori took Sunday's hand on their way into the building.

"Wait until you see New York." Sunday couldn't wait to take them and Mama.

Minutes later, the lady in the Arkansas Scholarship Lottery office beamed and held up the ticket. "Yep, this is it! Congratulations, folks! I just need ya to sign the back, take out your photo IDs and I'll line up your paperwork."

Their hands shaking, Paris, Sunday, and Mama all passed the pen from one to the other. Mama signed to receive her own funds, as well as Narado's and London's. Sunday was already Reggie and Victoria's guardian, and signed to receive their share on behalf of her brother, William. Paris was Olivia's guardian, and signed for Vanessa's share. They would split the money six ways, and even after taxes and the smaller lump sum, that would still be a handsome payout.

"Now, will you stay anonymous or will ya share who ya are?" the administrator asked.

They stared at one another. "Anonymous," they all replied. This was Arkansas and they were Black.

"All righty then." After almost an hour of processing driver's licenses, their addresses on bills, and photos, the lady smiled at them. "It should take about two to three weeks to arrive in your accounts."

"Hold up." A deflated Nookie stepped forward. "What? Y'all don't have it to give us right now?"

"The Powerball is operated by all the states," the lady explained, "and it takes several days for the money to come in from every state. Plus taxes will be removed before the lump sum is disbursed."

Fortunately, Sunday's attorney had forewarned her, and since the money was guaranteed, Dorinda's firm had wired Sunday a $25,000 loan to have cash for pre-celebration ahead of Christmas. The lawyer had explained her firm sometimes loaned out money to her clients who were waiting on settlement funds from a lawsuit. It had been one of the calls Sunday had made Saturday while the others were partying at the lodge —figuring out how all this works.

"Nook, we're good. We're gonna have a good time. Let's go check into our hotel." She squeezed his shoulder.

As they spoke, her new lawyer and old accountant were working with Broadway Federal, a Black-owned bank, to set up separate accounts for Sunday, her siblings and their mother to manage their funds without Helena's interference. Plus, Sunday would meet with her attorney while she was here, a financial advisor, and at long last, a farming consultant to discuss hi-tech improvements and tourism.

Peady bumped into Sunday gently. "I won't lie, Sun. I didn't believe you were really gon' share this with us."

"What did you think I was gon' do, P? All we've ever had is us."

"I don't know. It's just always, 'whatever Sunday say is what go.' I didn't know if you would be on those same vibes, or what. But I like this Sun. I hope this is the Sun we keep gettin'."

Sun rubbed her sister's belly and leaned over to talk to the baby inside. "You's the first Conklin born into this world as a rich kid! We're about to buy you the best crib and stroller money can buy!" Sun gazed at her younger sister, the way Nessa once gazed at her. "And yo' mama's gonna have the flyest hair salon in all the Delta."

It was good to see all of Peady's teeth for a change, not holding back or serving a suspicious side-eye. They could relax. The bills would be paid in full, no need to call the utility companies and wheel and deal, or beg to make partial payments. The three-hundred and thirty-thousand-dollar plus bills hanging over their heads wouldn't be there for long.

Three blocks away, they pulled into the driveway of the Capitol Hotel and one of the attendants threw open the door.

"Hello there, ma'am! Welcome! You have a reservation with us?"

Sunday took out her phone to record the wonderment all over the children when attendants slid back the doors of the minivan and extended white-gloved hands to help them out. A few moments later, they were followed by an attendant who rolled their luggage on a gold trolley into their suite.

"Whoaaa!" Reggie's eyes nearly left his head.

The kids ran from one room to the other, and Nookie unlatched the sliding door to the terrace.

"This is big! Aw we gonna live here?" Little Livi joined him on the porch to peer at the downtown scenery.

"Liv, be careful on that patio. Nook, take Liv's hand!" Peady stroked her belly and fussed.

"Is this owa house now?" Livi asked.

"No, baby, we're goin' back home. But we'll be fixin' it up real nice, so we can have a high view, too," Sunday explained.

Tori must have expanded from the bigness she was taking in. Let's stay here forever!"

"She got a point." Nookie studied Little Rock's city skyline on one side and the tranquil Arkansas River on the other. "We ain' gotta stay in Elaine no more. Look at all the condos and houses out there. Already built. We ain' even gotta wait. We can just buy one."

"Yeh, but Elaine needs us." Mama joined them in admiring the city view, but she held back. "Folks always goin' out, but ain' nobody comin' in."

Sunday agreed with her mother, but she wasn't having any discord today, and changed the subject. "I'll give you guys fifteen minutes for a bathroom break and then, let's roll out for Christmas shoppinnnn'!"

Livi couldn't handle it. "Yes! We goin' to Walmawt!"

Peady and Sunday swapped long-awaited fulfillment, eager to upgrade their girls' standards at long last.

"No, baby," Sunday explained, "you're going somewhere even better than that."

On their way into Park Plaza Mall, the "O" in Little Livi's mouth said it all. She couldn't hold her attention in one place for long, her gaze dancing around giant wreaths, large trees, the massive rocking horse, candy canes, and reindeer.

"Train!" CiCi, Paris's baby, pointed at the life-sized miniature train around the eating area. "Mm go!"

Their first stop was the toy store.

"Do this cost too much money, Auntie Sun?" Livi asked. "If we get this, we can't have nothin' else?" Livi gazed up at Sunday.

With the children running from aisle to aisle, her sister and mother recorded proudly. Sunday had stood in the fields and wondered if she would ever get to see this.

"*Does* this cost too much?" Sunday corrected Livi. "And we can't have *any*thing else." Kissing the top of her head, Sunday tugged Livi's cap on for the cold. "Today, baby, you don't have to worry about the money. You can have this truck, *and* you're still receiving your other Christmas presents."

Flabbergasted, the children eyed Sunday as if she had two heads.

"Hold up. These aren't even for our Christmas?" A stunned Reggie asks. "This is a trick, right?"

"Nope," she told all of them. "You don't have to wait for your birthday or Christmas. You deserve nice things all the time."

Tori's eyes widened so big they could have popped from her head. "So I can have this car? In *red?*"

The moment she realized Sunday was serious, and the toy electric Mercedes Benz truck was hers, the stars in her eyes shined brighter than those fancy McMansions and gated yards they'd passed on their ride through Pulaski Heights.

Livi got her own version of the truck in pink. CiCi got a life-sized train set that Peady and her husband would need to set up around their apartment. Reggie chose the latest version of Playstation with online gaming privileges and a virtual reality headset. Nookie snagged two pricey pairs of Jordans, complete with a matching hat and two warmup suits.

"Now, Sunday," Mama murmured so the children didn't hear, "You ain't got your money, yet. And even when ya do, don't just spoil 'em. They need to learn some responsibility. Plus, you said ya had thangs to do for the farm."

"Mama, I'm with you, but this family's been to hell and back. Too many times to count. Let's take a minute to *not* brace for the worst. We will make sure they learn how to manage their money and grow it. But for now, we won." With Sunday's heart about to explode, she squeezed her mama. "We some millionaires. *Us.*"

While stocking up on basic undergarments they'd scrounged on for too long, Peady turned to Sunday.

"Let's have a boots n' tiaras ball for Elaine Day. With a parade, too."

"A what?" Sunday asked.

"A Christmas ball for the kids of Elaine. Boots for the boys. Tiaras and ball gowns for the girls. When was the last time Elaine had a gala or something fancy? Where the boys need to act like gentlemen, and the girls can spin around and be precious?"

"That would be dope. We can even have it in town on Main Street. Plus, we can reopen Elaine High. We can decorate it really pretty and trick it out. Ever since the state shut it down, it's just sittin' there idle."

Peady jumped with an idea. "We can do horses and carriage rides through town. Elaine Day this year can be Elaine

Days. A game night, a read-in with Santa at the library that Saturday morning. We can also have a toy and food drive before Christmas to help the families that need it."

A new realization lifted Sunday's eyebrows way up. "Maybe we can finally get Elaine a new water tank."

Her sister processed the thought of a lifelong issue finally being resolved. "Yeah. But we don't have to do it all ourselves. We can put up billboards, use social media and ask people to help us." Peady shot Sunday a side grin. "You know what, though?"

"What's that?"

"If we have a ball, that means *you* gotta wear a dress." She stuck out her tongue.

"Tuh." How long had it been? "It's gonna take way more than money to make *that* happen."

From President Clinton's library to pictures in front of the Christmas lights at the state capitol to pizza and games at Chuck E. Cheese, the youngest Conklin children finally met the world. And Sunday could at last break bread with the business team that would help her turn her family's farm around.

For the final and most important bit of business—the private investigators and archaeologists. An excavation on her land required far more cash than what her lawyer wired her, but Sunday intended to pay every cent in pursuit of justice. That would be the ultimate Christmas.

By Tuesday evening, it was hard to believe their two days had sleighed by. After they'd finished their brisket from Sims Barbecue, she climbed into bed with farm projections for the cover crops and organic planting techniques. The kids watched cable channels they hadn't enjoyed at home.

"You guys, ten more minutes and then, lights out," she called out. "Y'all will be going to school tomorrow, so we're getting up early to drive back."

"Aw, man." Reggie huffed. "We rich now. Why do we need school?"

"So you can learn how to keep this money you're gettin'," Sunday's mother replied.

"Flyin' Comb Man!" Tori pointed at the TV.

"Whatchu say nah, girl?" Her grandmother asked.

Fantasizing of high ceilings, two stories, a curving staircase, and a reading nook, with one of those circular windows, Sunday wasn't paying attention.

"It's Flyin' Comb Man, Meemaw! He did my hair! He's on TV!"

Sunday's jaw dropped once she switched focus to CNN.

"*Local News Reporter Discovered Cheating on Husband With Husband's Boss,*" the headline read. There was also a byline. *Husband loses it on Instagram Live.*

There was no mistaking it.

"No, Arista, I don't have a problem BLEEP. I can BLEEP for any woman, literally every woman. Except you." The channel censored whatever he was saying that he could do with anyone but his wife.

The news story sat Sunday back. She wondered if this was the trauma-bonding he didn't want to do.

The video footage was turbulent and shaky, displaying mostly his wife, leather-clad, her makeup runny. Baby girl appeared to realize she'd gone too far, and had screwed up her situation *real* good.

"Ohhh." Mama did some knitting, her gaze now locked onto the TV. "That's too bad. Why do women with good ones show their behinds like that?"

The footage captured brief b-roll of Hardcastle. Those hands Sunday had inspected behind his head out in the field, were now fists at his wife's throat. Arms thick and taut underneath his Henley, veins popping out of his neck, shoulders rounded out like he did real work every now and again, frustration rubber-banded along his lips, he jerked his wife around like she was a rag doll. Sunday's mind switched to the flashback of him pinning her in the dirt a few nights ago.

The footage cut back to the news anchors. Sunday peeled her attention from the screen, to find her mother studying her.

"What?" Sunday asked innocently.

Mama shook her head. "I ain' said a word. What *you* over there smilin' 'bout?"

"I ain't smilin'."

"Mmhm. And I ain' knittin' neither."

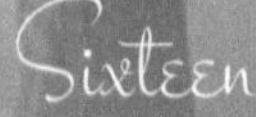

Sixteen

JUST A BIG MESS

"Hardcastle." Two mornings later, one of the officers approached with the keys. "Get on up. You're headin' out."

Seven knew it was only a matter of time before Nicky showed up. He headed to the front desk to sign papers and collect his personal effects. He was astonished at who was waiting for him.

"Bro, we've been looking high and low, scared you were in a ditch somewhere." His sister, Charian, threw her arms open. "This explains why we couldn't find you."

Seven pulled his only sibling in for a bear hug. Since she still lived in Chicago with the rest of their family, they hadn't seen each other since the last holiday season. "I didn't think you'd show up until court. Where's Nick?"

"What you mean 'you didn't think I'd show up'? We're kabillionaires now, and I got my lottery ticket. You thought I was gonna stay in Chicago? Hell nah." They headed to her SUV. "I see you already wildin' out."

With his children on his mind, he was only halfway paying attention as he threw his things in her backseat. "You talk to my kids?"

"You already know Ray called us, crying, begging me to come get you. On top of ya mama. She and Dad fly in tonight for your arraignment tomorrow. I'll ask the judge to give you permission to head back to Arkansas. You didn't cash it in already, did ya? And why didn't you call anybody?"

Were they having the same conversation? "What are you... are you talking about Ri and me? Cash in?"

From behind her steering wheel, his sister returned his blank stare. "Hold up. Don't tell me Nicky made me fly all the way to Memphis and drive down those long ass roads, go through Mississippi, and cross the Pettus Bridge, and you weren't even in Arkansas. Were you just lying or something?"

"Char, the Pettus Bridge is in Georgia."

She shrugged. "This is the South. Aren't all these racist bridges the same?"

Seven fell against the door. "You went to Arkansas?"

"When you stopped answering our calls, and you had just won the lottery, me and Nick thought somebody did something to you, so we flew out on Sunday and started riding around, asking about you. The next day, you were on CNN losing your shit. I'm sorry, by the way. But I'm glad we couldn't find you because of marital issues and not somebody unaliving you for that ticket."

Won the lottery? Ticket? "Wait, huh, Char?"

"What you mean, 'huh'?"

Confused, they stared at each other.

"Speak English!" Seven snapped. "What are you talking about, 'I won'?"

"You didn't know! We're millionaires now!" Hyped, she slapped his shoulder over and over. "We won! We need to protect you and that ticket with our lives. Apparently, you haven't cashed it yet, so that's what we gotta do now, bro!"

Her phone rang over the Bluetooth with Nicky on the line.

"You got him? He there?" Nicky yelled throughout her vehicle that reverberated out of the car and into the parking lot.

"Dude, calm down." Seven worked to push aside his marital concerns and sort through this nonsense. "I don't have a winning lottery ticket."

Char bounced up and down in the seat. "Yes, you do! We called you all weekend after Nick found out. Why didn't you pick up? I thought the Klan had run up on you in them backwoods."

"The reception is bad there," Seven explained. "It was hard keeping a connection so I gave up. But what's this about the lottery? Which lottery?"

"*The* lottery!" Nicky's energy kept booming everywhere. "You said you played, right? Lewis Sheridan's birthday?"

Seven put the pieces together. Oh, wow. Did they really think...? "Yeh, but that was back in Elaine. Which one you talking about? I haven't played anything else."

"That's the one. Those were the winning numbers!" An ecstatic Char started slapping his arm again and screaming at the top of her lungs. "Lewis Sheridan's birthday won!"

"So what I want you to do," Nicky started, "is head on over to the house and grab that ticket with the same energy you was grabbing that trifling ass wife o' yours last night! And bring yo ass on back to Arkansas!" All thirty-two of Nicky's teeth had to be on display wherever he was. He was smiling loud even on the phone. "Run me my eighteen million dollars! On the double! Ya *feel* me? I'm gettin' laid by four or five women per day between now and Christmas. Imma have the railroad put a turnstile outside my house, so every fine woman can grab a ticket and line up to board this train. He... is... a... *fast* mothafucka too! Big Nicky 'bout to get him a new name —Bullet!"

Seven started to speak.

And closed his mouth.

How? If Lewis Sheridan's birthday won the lottery, then how did Sunday believe *she'd* won?

"You sure you're not getting this mixed up with something else?"

"Hell, nah, just mix me up with my eighteen million!" Nicky boomed at the entire world. "Where'd you put it at?"

Seven's mind ran amok. Where *had* he put the ticket? The last time he'd seen it was on the nightstand at the hotel. Had he thrown it away?

"My luggage. It's in my carry-on." There was one big problem, though. "I can't see Ri right now. I'm not there, yet. " But the children were at school. "We can go by the house, but you'll have to go in our bedroom and grab it. Don't mention anything to Ri about a ticket. Just tell her I want some clothes for the next few days, and you need to use my bag."

Once their lawyers met, they would sit down with the kids, explain this to them, and come up with a schedule for him to move out.

"Oh, damn," Nicky said. "My boy ain' wastin' no time. He said it's a wrap."

Over the last two nights, Seven had made up his mind about whether he would really take his children through this. But the respect he expected his daughters to command for themselves was the same respect he would teach them to give a good man. Love required balance, and it was time for him to admit he had become a side character in Ri's story. Their son also needed to see that being walked over and taken for granted was not the definition of a "good" man.

"What if I can't find the suitcase?" Char asked, pulling into the driveway. "What if Ri unpacked it already and found it or something?"

"I doubt it. She's likely been on the phone the last two

days with everybody in town, trying to get our friends on her side. If you have a problem, FaceTime me. I'll talk you through it."

Char used his keys to go inside while he waited in the SUV. Moments later, Arista padded out in a robe and her slippers. Her sister, Erin, came to stand on the porch and observe. Seven clicked the doors locked.

"Don't be unreasonable, Seven. I get it, all right? I have never been with anybody else. That just happened. You and me, we haven't been too active. You've been dealing with… your issues. And the station's been up in the air with this new president and the governor monitoring every segment we do. All these conservative white women are pitching for my spot. It's been rough to just come home and play the happy mom and wife when you don't know if you'll be workin' next year. I needed an outlet." Cue the water works. She banged her palm on the door. "Seven!"

Silence.

She took that as her cue to keep going. "We've been together seventeen good years. Look at everything we built, and our kids. I know you won't turn your back. You need us as much as we need you. Baby, I'm *sorry!* I saw the tickets you got us for Europe. *Of course*, I'll gooo." That last line was a screech as she realized there was no way he intended to do that now.

Char came back out, dragging his very expensive luggage across the pavement and he cringed. The moment Char opened the back door to shove in the bag, Seven reached back to help her and Arista squeezed herself inside. She clutched his head.

"Baby, just give me two minutes, okay? It wasn't anything! I don't love him. I love *you*! It was dumb. I was stupid. I just needed to get the itch out of me! It was just a tiny stress-reliever. That's all!"

Char jimmied her arm between the two of them. "Ri, you tripping! Give him space and get out the truck."

"Get your hands off her!" Arista's sister, Erin, rushed to the melee.

Seven peeled his wife's hands off his face. "Arista, move back!"

Her eyes red and puffy, she grabbed for something to hold onto. "You haven't stopped loving me! Not in one night! You're being a fool. We got a family. We can go to therapy and work through it!"

"Oh, *now* you want therapy. I'm done!"

To create space, he shoved Ri's forehead with more force than he had intended, and between him and Charian pushing her, Arista stumbled several steps backward. She nearly fell. Seven had never put hands on her like that, not even last night, and it stunned all of them.

"I didn't mean to push that hard. I stopped loving you years ago, Ri. You screwing him is fucked up, but it might have been what we needed. We can finally say it out loud. There's no 'us' anymore."

"Ri, baby, come on." Erin held her up, and mad-dogged Seven. "He'll be back. He's not about to ruin all this here. His kids, his home, his good life with you. He's not about to break all that up *and* have to pay you alimony and child support. It's about to be Christmas, too? What that child custody do? I'll give him a week. Two max. Y'all live in Texas—a community property state. Everything he's got coming will be yours, too. For the *rest* of his life. He'll come to his senses." She pulled her sister away, who hugged her stomach, dry-heaving silent sobs.

Driving away, Char checked in with him. "You good, bro? You just threw everybody for a loop. You've always kind of let Arista have carte blanche. 'Happy wife, happy life' and all that."

His stomach twisted in knots, despite her betrayal. He'd

watched Arista bring his kids into the world, showered her with jewels, private getaways, and furs, to her heart's content. They'd cheered for each other and celebrated as their careers moved up. For a few years, social climbing had been enough. But now, that's all she cared about. For him, there had to be more. "Not anymore."

Char drove up the road a ways and pulled over, so Seven could unzip the bag and tear it apart. Practically on cue, Nicky called again.

"What I miss?" he asked.

Seven tossed around the clothes in desperation. Finally! A piece of paper that wasn't a receipt. He and Char cheesed as hard as kids under the Christmas tree opening their presents again. Overjoyed, they unfurled it together, and held it up to read aloud for Nicky.

"Zero...nine...three..." Their reading slowed. "Four... six..."

"That's not Lewis Sheridan's birthday." Char's enthusiasm melted.

"I thought you said you played it." Nicky's complaint echoed through the Bluetooth.

"I did! I don't know how—"

Spiraling, Seven wondered what on Earth could have...

Oh... hell.

"Seven, what?" his sister insisted.

He squeezed his head. This was even more disgusting than anything Arista could have done.

I am so sorry. My bad. I wasn't payin' attention. My head was somewhere else.

This couldn't be happening.

"Seven." Char was ready to pound him. "Talk!"

How did he tell his family? Should he tell them?

"It's the wrong ticket." He couldn't tell them.

"What do you mean, 'wrong ticket'?" Nicky sounded like

he was one more breath from full blown tears. "Bruh, how? It's yours. How do you buy a 'wrong' one?"

"Sev, this isn't passing the smell test. You didn't really buy it. Did you?" Char inspected the date and time stamp. "Nah, this here is the right date. Wrong number, though."

He had been distracted, worried about his children, wondering about Arista finding her trip, irritated to be in Eastern Arkansas in the dark. And quite frankly, he hadn't given a rat's behind about the lottery. What were the odds?

At that moment, Charian's phone beeped. His parents were on the other line.

"Seven?" Mom cried the moment Char merged the calls.

"Yeah, Mom, I'm here."

"Oh, thank you, Lord! Seven, it's everywhere. All over CNN. Good God, everybody was calling all day yesterday, asking if you'd had some kind of nervous breakdown. Family wanting to know if it was erectile dysfunction. They suggested medication and exercises you could do."

"Mom, you know what? That's not necessary. I'd really appreciate it if you'd just tell folks to..." Telling them to mind their own business was hard since he'd put his business in the street. "Fall back."

Dad piped up. "A couple folks were askin' if your condition was hereditary, but I told 'em, hell nah. Ain' no way. Must've gotten that from ya mama's—"

"I'm good, Dad. Don't worry about it, all right? I didn't mean to worry you guys. This is just a big mess."

"It sure is," Dad replied. "We're just glad you're all right, and nobody got seriously hurt. Plus, you have made it up in spades with this lottery ticket! Whewee! One hundred and ninety-six million split *thirteen* ways is just over fifteen million before taxes. I am good with *that!*"

"We're at the Chicago airport now," his mother added. "We'll fly in tonight so we can support you at your arraignment tomorrow. Once you get permission from the judge to leave the state, we'll ride to Arkansas."

Charian ate her lips, and Seven knew she was trying not to lose her cool.

"I don't know," Nicky insisted through the speakers. "Seven, did you buy a ticket off Lewis Sheridan's birthday or not?"

"What?" Dad exclaimed. "Come again?"

Seven took a breath. This was the right thing to do. "Yes. I did. But I dropped the ticket in the gas station lot while I was busy calling the kids. Apparently, when I picked it up, I wasn't paying attention and grabbed the wrong one." Technically, it was true.

He couldn't do it. Not to the people of Elaine. He remembered this past weekend, how their rejoicing had brought up the sun. Who would tell them they hadn't found jubilee?

"Where were you when you dropped it?" His lawyer-sister now dove into the case.

Now it was he who was dry-heaving. "I wasn't paying attention to the name of the place. It was dark."

"Seven, we're talking almost two hundred million." Dad sighed. "Was it a gas station, a liquor store?"

Doubled over in his seat, he hung his head nearly between his legs, recalling a drunken, hurt Sunday in front of him again. The owner of one of the few Black farms left in America was fighting for the little she still had.

"Gas station. It's a lot of gas stations down those rural roads, though. We'll probably never find it."

His tenacious lawyer-sister inspected the ticket. "Hm. What are all these numbers across here? One of them must be for the store that sold this." Charian tapped it into her phone and started researching. "I'll contact one of my lawyer colleagues in Arkansas so she can associate with me. Oh, don't worry, I'll find it."

Seventeen

YOU'VE BEEN SERVED, MA'AM

SUNDAY

"Been a long time since I had me one of these." Sunday's mother stepped inside the Black-owned Amani Bath Spa like she'd found the promised land.

They had driven to Memphis for the day to do more celebrating. Sunday wanted to shower her mama and sister with a long overdue and much-needed surprise. While Paris's husband, Kevin, took the kids to Dave and Buster's, Sunday drove her mother, sister, Mama Piggee, and Mother Fordham out for ladies' afternoon.

"You still got somethin' to say 'bout how much money we spendin'?" Sunday asked her mama.

"Well, when ya start showin' me all this, I suppose we can wait a couple days on them responsibilities."

"Baby, God bless yo' sweet heart." Mother Fordham eyed the facilities with concern. "This ole body don't need no massage. They might break somethin' and can't fix it back. But I sho would like to soak my feet."

Sunday ushered her back to the locker room with the

others. "I already thought about you, Motha, and they've got a massage that's only for feet. Ain' no way we'd leave you out."

The elderly woman slapped her hands together and waggled her head. "*Hot* diggity dog! That's what I'm talkin' 'bout."

Peady cheesed for the pregnancy massage. "Ooh, somebody's gonna rub my belly besides Kevin?"

Hot mineral baths, facials, scrubs, deep-tissue massages, and a catered brunch followed.

Peady sipped non-alcoholic apple cider. "You better watch it, Sun, I could get use to this."

"As you should. We definitely deserve it." Sunday ate her French toast and drank. "When the money clears our account, we're doing things for Elaine, too. Narado is back home pulling it together as we speak."

Mama Piggee eyed her. "Whatchu talkin' 'bout?"

Peady and Sunday grinned at each other.

"We can turn Elaine Day into Elaine Weekend, with a Boots N' Tiaras Ball for the kids." Peady clapped. "They can dress up, get cute, and be little dolls and gentlemen for Christmas. It'll be on Main Street, with a parade."

Sunday wasn't into cutesy stuff like that, but even she was gushing at this point. "And horse-drawn carriage rides."

Mama Piggee fell into the fantasy. "That's gonna be so precious." Her crocodile tears were as big as her eyes. "Look at Elaine."

"And that's not all, either. We're doing Elaine Weekend—opening up the high school again for game night, buying books for the library, and doing a toy and food distribution for our vulnerable families."

"God blessed the right people with this money." Mother Fordham held her champagne glass up for a toast. "Y'all the only ones I'll drink this nasty mess for. But I'm glad I lived to see it."

"Amen." The others drank with her.

Relaxed, thoroughly bathed and pampered, there couldn't have been a more perfect ride back to Elaine. Tomorrow was Sunday, and she'd need to do actual work. The farmed frogs in tents needed to be boxed for delivery to restaurants, hotels and schools. She'd check them to ensure their quality and health before they were killed, skinned, and packed on ice for shipping. Quality assurance was never a task she turned over to anyone else.

Mama Piggee gazed out at the fields on their way down Highway 44. "Oh, my word! Sunday and Peady Conklin! Y'all did all that out there?"

Narado and some of his friends had begun putting up the large Christmas trees Sunday had ordered earlier in the week.

"They'll be lit up come Christmas. That's what Nookie's been workin' on. After our money deposits, and we've paid off Friends, we'll light them trees up and it's gon' be a real show-stopper."

They rode up to the gates of the farm.

"Honey, I can't wait for them Adlers to get a look at this. I hope now, you got mo' money than all of 'em put togetha!" Mama Piggee jumped out to transfer to her car.

"Money or not, we got more heart than all of 'em put togetha." Sunday exited to help them with their things. "That's why they mad. They thought we'd be gone by now."

"Sunday Conklin?"

She spun around for an unfamiliar voice speaking her name, and bumped right into a stack of papers.

"You've been served, ma'am." The young white man walked away quicker than he'd appeared. "Merry Christmas."

Stunned, she took a moment to process what just happened.

"Say what, nah?" Mama Piggee craned her neck.

"What's that, Sun?" Peady asked.

"Look like court papers. A summons, and..." she mumbled, trying to figure it out, "...a complaint."

Seven Hardcastle, et al., vs. Sunday Conklin, et al.

Vertreese Conklin
William Conklin
Sunday Conklin
Paris Conklin
London Conklin
Narado Conklin
Please be noticed that the Hardcastle Family has filed a claim against you concerning the lottery ticket bearing the number 071899. The matter will be heard on Monday morning, December 18, 8:30 a.m., at the Phillips County Courthouse. An injunction has been temporarily granted, in which you are hereby ordered to cease any and all use of any monies you cannot return should the court rule against you."

Sunday's chest imploded. Like a sinking hole she didn't see until right before she fell into it. Grain by grain, her life caved in.

"Hardcastle?" *What?* How could anybody other than her...?

"Sunday, what's wrong?" Mama pressed.

She slapped her forehead.

No, no. "Nooooooooooo!" Her throat couldn't handle all the screaming her heart still needed to let out.

Mama Piggee took the paper and read. "Oh, Lord. Oh...."

Why? Why couldn't they breathe for even a little while without the sky coming down on their heads?

"Sunday." Mama's face bore the weight of the words on

the notice. "It *is* yo' ticket, idn't it? You sure you ain't mistaken?"

That Friday night, she'd had enough alcohol in her to start a forest fire. But there was no denying she'd been rushing. In her haste to buy Nookie's ticket, and still start the tour on time, she'd bolted into Hardcastle. He was distracted and talking on his phone. In that stupid Friends of the Delta polo shirt. She'd almost considered him a possibility until she eyeballed that bank logo. That much she now remembered.

How could he say which ticket was which? He couldn't. Nobody could.

He wound up with the wrong ticket, and now he was salty about it. He'd probably just lost his job after that beat-down on his boss and his wife, and now, he planned on causing problems for Sunday. She'd be damned.

"Of course, it's mine, Mama. Ain' no way he can prove nothin' else."

She should have followed her first mind about him last weekend. A lackey. Strom Adler *had* to have sent him here, just to screw with her and her family.

"Hardcastle. Sheridan. Sherman." Mother Fordham squinted, seeming confused.

But Sunday wasn't.

"Yeah. We actually brought that triflin' Negro on our land, fed him, gave him a place to lay his head. We let him play with our kids." Sunday aimed her finger straight at Paris. "And that's on *you* for invitin' him here in the first place. You trusted one of Adler's coons over your own sister!" Sunday had been feeling it burn for a week, and had tried to be the 'bigger person' about it. There was no better time to address it than right now. "And look where that got us!"

Caught in the glare of the truck's headlights, Paris went wide-eyed, with no comeback.

"Sunday!" Mama warned.

"No! You weren't thinkin' about family, Paris! As always, you were thinkin' about your*self*! You don't ever wanna do the work, but you always got somethin' to say! Don't you worry, though. As always, *I'll* fix this! While you and Nook go talk shit about me and scheme behind my back." Tripping on rocks and dirt, she charged around their Daddy's truck and jumped in. "I got lawyers, too, now! If Hardcastle wants *my* money, he'll have to come through me and take it!"

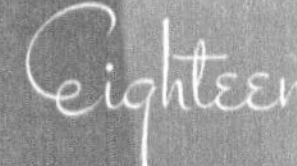

Eighteen

WHOEVER YOU MET LAST WEEKEND

SEVEN

"Seven, Ashlyn is calling." Seven's mother handed him her phone. Since Arista had resorted to using the children as cover to entice him to the phone, his mom screened his calls for now.

"Hey, baby girl, how much does it cost?" He kicked off the call with a joke, excited to hear his baby's voice. Just over a week had passed without seeing her.

"Seven, it's me," Ri started. "I understand you need time, but I found a good marriage therapist who'll help us work through our differences and—"

He cut the phone off. Frustrated, he pressed it to his forehead.

"Arista?" Dad asked.

"Baby, it'll calm down soon," his mother reassured him.

They had just arrived back in Helena, Arkansas, last night. Only, this time, he wasn't working. His family was on the hunt for the lottery ticket, and who'd claimed it.

His back and neck were wooden after one night in an

177

antique bed at the dated Edwardian bed and breakfast. Massaging the stiffness in his shoulder, he scrolled his phone to see if his divorce lawyer had finalized a visitation and calling schedule for him and the kids. His lawyer had also started drawing up divorce papers to serve Arista next week.

Char's phone rang and disrupted his marital fog. Seven noted her caller ID, just before she grabbed it. "Brenda Graves - Arkansas Attorney."

Rather than talk in front of everyone, Char left the hotel dining room where they ate and stepped outside. She rarely did that. They didn't see each other often, but when they were together and she was on the phone, Char had no qualms about rudely loud-talking and disrupting the conversations around her. Why hadn't she done that now?

When she returned to the table, his family members seemed to hold a conversation with their eyes that Seven wasn't included in.

In a bit of dinner table suspense, Char shot Nicky a slick-but-not-quick-enough wink, and resumed forking her country fried steak. Seven read their uncomfortable silence.

"Who is Arkansas Attorney Brenda Graves?" Seven thumbed his nose over his barbecue ribs. "Why couldn't you talk to her here, the way you do everybody else?"

Obvious in her shifty eyes was that Charian had done something.

"A lawyer here I'm associating with for this lottery ticket thing."

Seven waited. "And? That can't be all."

"It's not a big deal. We'll handle it," his father said. His intervention only bothered Seven more.

"Apparently, it is a big deal, or Char would have answered her call here, and you wouldn't be covering for her. So what happened? What did this Brenda Graves do that you all obviously discussed without me, and Char needed to handle out of my presence?"

His family members held another awkward exchange.

"He'll find out anyway." His mother sighed. "Just go on and tell him."

Char pulled out her phone and scrolled to a photo that had been texted to her. Seven held it up for a better view.

"Please be noticed that the Hardcastle Family has filed a claim against you concerning the lottery ticket bearing..."

Nauseous once again, he grew more furious with every name on a complaint bearing the stamp of the Phillips County Court Clerk.

"Vertreese Conklin

William Conklin

Sunday Conklin..."

Sunday.

Seven flung his sister's phone on the coffee table. "Where do you get off?"

His sister clapped her eyelids at him and sipped her rosé. "Bruh, are you serious? Our family's been playing this lottery our whole lives. We *finally* won, and you think we're letting that much money just walk out the door? The hell planet are you on? The rest of us are here on Earth."

Seven returned his attention to the complaint in the phone. Harsh and callous, the words on that paper were as caring as butcher knives. He scoffed at what else he discovered on that pleading.

"Char, you forged my signature on this thing? You're an attorney. You know better. Why wasn't I included in all this? I'm the one who bought the ticket."

"Boy, don't play with me." Char popped back. "You know the rules. Everybody who buys a ticket *owns* the one that wins. We all play this *together*. That ticket is all of ours, not just yours." She poured herself more wine. "Besides, you seem real soft on those folks, like something went down between you and somebody over there. Is that why you ghosted us last weekend?"

In his mind's eye, Sunday was still standing in the lake, sunrise bouncing off her dimple, radiant while she held up a large American bullfrog with her bare hands. "No."

Nicky side-eyed Seven. "You sure, nephew? You sho' seem to be healin' pretty fast after your wife was hunchin' on ya boss."

"Careful," Seven warned.

"He's right, though, Sev," Char added. "What Ri did was jacked up. You can't act like it was nothing. You have to deal with your wife at some point. You and her have kids together. We'll take care of this lottery thing. While you handle your home situation, we'll address these Arkansas people."

How had Sunday handled being sued? Just seven days ago, she was wiggling her toes and relaxing at her lodge. Secretly preparing for a whole new way of life. In her element, comfortable in her skin, tending and growing her part of Earth, she was a chalk portrait. Truth be told, her full and generous figure, molded on the pottery wheel of life, would have translated artfully in any medium.

But Sunday Conklin was *too* raw. Too unhinged. Brazen, out of control, uncivilized, uncouth, un-every damn thing. So why did he even care? His family would flip if he told them she'd held him at gunpoint.

"Seven, you still with us?" His mother asked.

"I'm right here at the table."

"Not judging by how you were just stargazing. You sure your mind isn't somewhere else?" Dad pressed. "Is Char right? You meet somebody over there?"

"Y...no." Seven's inner turmoil spilled out of him. "Look, I don't think we should 'give our money away.' Completely. But you didn't have to be dirty about this, and run up on her in some sneak attack."

"So it *is* a woman?" Nicky leaned in. "Because none of us said anything about a woman."

"I'm thinking of the person responsible for that place, who let me stay there when it stormed, even though I was there to buy her out. And yes, that person happens to be a woman." He thought another moment. "Maybe we can split it."

"Split my behind," Seven's dad piped up. "We won it, fair and square. Claiming what's ours won't feel good, but we're not doing anything wrong."

Seven stared out at Helena from the window of the Edwardian. "You haven't been there or spent time with them. It's different once you breathe in the Delta. After you wake up to sunrise over a serene land. You're on the edge of a lake, fish are playing, ducks are taking a bath, and these crickets and frogs are making music. Or you're just a speck in row after green row of soybeans. You're not on some rich white farm. None of that food was put in the ground with machines owned by rich white men. You're standing on ground tended by Black people. Everything around you looks exactly the way it did when our ancestors grew it a hundred and fifty years ago. And a part of you might even feel like they're roaming out there with you in the moment."

His family deadpanned on him. Seven questioned where those thoughts had come from.

"Damn, nephew, that's beautiful. I didn't know you had all that in you." Nicky raised his Cognac glass to Seven. "One thang Imma do once I get this money is hire me a poet. He gon' stand there and say some shit just like that while I'm screwin'. So her mind'll be totally in another pretty ass place. You know what I'm sayin'? Not that what I'm givin' her ain' a beautiful experience, but you gotta set the scene and shit, ya feel me?"

"Seven, your cell is vibrating." Char picked it up and held it toward him.

He had forgotten to turn it off again, but didn't bother looking. "If it's not one of my kids or my lawyer, don't worry about it."

"Who is Strom...." His nosy mother peered at the caller ID. "Adler." Her face sank.

Seven peered at the phone in disbelief. The screen displayed "Strom Adler."

"Seven, don't." Mom warned him too late.

He'd already clicked and put it on speaker. "Seven Hardcastle."

From the angst on her face, Seven would have thought she'd seen the Grinch.

"Mr. Hardcastle. Strom Adler here," a gravelly older voice paved their ears. "Was wonderin' if ya had time to come join us for supper this evenin'. Got some duck braised with brandy and mushrooms, mashed potatoes, fresh vegetables. Blueberry pie. Nice an' hot. Finish ya off with some of the finest bourbon money can buy."

"Wheeew-ee, that sho' do sound good." Nicky rubbed his hands together. "These the kinda friends I like. Ask him what time we need to be there."

"I see somebody there likes to have a good time," Mr. Adler continued. "There's a whole lot more good time where that comes from if you're willin'."

Seven glared at his uncle.

"I'm here with my family right now, and it's Saturday. May I ask what the nature of our meeting would be?"

"I'm sure you know, Mr. Hardcastle. It's what brought you to Arkansas to begin with. I believe you had a job to do, didn't ya?"

Sunday. Mother Fordham. Paris and her babies. Narado and young Reggie.

"Mr. Adler, I'm not currently in town on Friends of the Delta business. If you need information about work, Ian is your best point of contact."

"I beg to differ. You spent the entire weekend there. Tested her soil. Talked to her people. Broke bread at her table. It's my understandin' you and her may have even become... friends. I'd say you are the perfect contact. I'd like you to come and share how she intends to pull herself out of financial ruin."

How had he known all that? The soil techs from Friends's real estate department must have reported it. What had *they* told?

Shame snaked through Seven's chest. The techs had only been analyzing Sunday's property because of him.

Now her fiery words rang in his head like warning bells. *They ruin everything! And you're a fool for lettin' them use you to take down anotha Black person! That damn bank has destroyed Elaine! Ain nothin' in this world worth me givin' up this land. You'll need a missile to take me out.*

"Mr. Hardcastle, you still thah?"

Seven's answer could affect not only his career and future, but his children's situations—their cliques, summer camps, where they were invited and where they weren't—all he'd worked hard to set up for them.

"I can't tonight. I'm not free until morning."

"Due to the urgency, I'm afraid I must insist on tonight."

Seven's mother shook her head.

"Mr. Adler, I appreciate the invite, but as I already said, I must decline." Errand boy, no longer.

"Mighty unfortunate. I am also familiar with *your* family's past here in Phillips County. Particularly the role of one Lucas Sherman, son of Cane Sherman. Before ole Lucas disappeared in thin air when his neighbors needed him most. Was never seen or heard from 'round these parts again. Until his people were drivin' his body back here from Chicago, some seventy-five years later."

What on God's green...? Seven mouthed to his mother, *Who is Lucas Sherman?*

"Pray tell, Mr. Hardcastle," Adler continued, "how is your motha? It's been a long time, but I believe I met her once. She was with her daddy at the courthouse. Right when Lucas Sherman was buried. They were lookin' up their property records."

Across the table from Seven, Ascencia Hardcastle clapped a hand over her mouth in an unwilling confirmation.

From the hazy fields of his memory banks, wasps and butterflies resurged in Seven's mind. Barbecue smeared on his shirt again, and running around someone's yard holding a popsicle...Seven also remembered. Last weekend, the land seemed to welcome him back. He *had* visited Elaine before. As a boy, his mother had brought him with her.

You is kin to somebody 'roun' here. I just ain' put my finga on who yet. What's yo' motha's name?

Mother Fordham had called it out. Several times.

Yo' spirit ain' no stranger. You ain' come here for no business. You came here 'cuz you got debt to pay.

The town's wisewoman had spoken of a bloodline apparently lost to Seven. Now he wondered what was the debt.

Char rushed to their mother and glared at Seven for talking to whoever was upsetting her.

"You sure you can't find a little time for me, Mr. Hardcastle?" Mr. Adler jarred Seven back to the present. "It certainly will be a shame if Ms. Conklin finds out who you really are."

Stumped, Seven and his family all searched one another for answers.

Sunday...how would she be affected? She'd already been through enough.

"Fine then." Seven braced himself. "I'm on my way."

"You will *not* go to that man." His mother banged the table, her upset flowing through the blue veins knotted in her fists. "Hang it up!"

She reached over and clicked off Seven's phone, shocking him. She hadn't gone that far to make his decisions for him even as a teenager.

"Who in the hell is that?" Seven's dad also stared at her. "That man sounded like he was the damn Grand Wizard!"

"Mom." Seven faced his mother, who had obviously lied to him over the phone when he'd asked if their family knew anyone around here. "Adler's telling the truth, isn't he? Who is 'Lucas Sherman'? What happened here? The people in Elaine keep telling me my face looks familiar. How does Strom Adler know who we are?"

A sea of red bathed her eyes. "Let's just find that lottery ticket and get out of Phillips County. There's a reason people leave these parts and don't come back."

"You said that like you know somebody who left and didn't come back." Seven remained firm. "Who? What are you hiding?"

She and her brother, Nicholas, shared a moment too loaded to be ignored.

Nicky tried to blow it off with a sip of his Cognac. "Nephew, don't worry about all that, man. Or none of these Arkansas folks for that matter."

You ain' come here for no business. You came here 'cuz you got debt to pay.

Mother Fordham's voice, spritely and curt, reverberated through him now, as clearly as if she stood there.

Seven stared at them all. "Was our family involved in something around here that hurt Elaine? What was Adler talking about when he said Lucas Sherman abandoned his neighbors when they needed him?"

His mom massaged her forehead. "It's Christmas time. You need to be with your children, Seven Mitchell Hardcastle. Stop worrying about Elaine and *whoever* you met last weekend." She pointed outside at her son's truck with finality. "Drive yourself back to Dallas, figure out this problem between you and *your wife*, and start finding you another job."

The dilemma tore Seven in two. She was right. He did have children to raise, and Christmas was coming. But, hanging over him like a large, black cloud was also Arista, and the drama she would rain down on him. The kids didn't deserve that emotional upheaval either.

The truth called you back here, son. Now he itched to know what truth Mother Fordham had referred to.

Adler had said his mother and grandfather had been at the courthouse researching property records, so her family had owned land here.

"I don't appreciate you guys forging my signature on a lawsuit I didn't consent to. I won't go to the courthouse and challenge it. I'll let your lawsuit ride. But only if you tell me everything. And then, Mom, you'll have to do something for me."

Nineteen

BECAUSE I WANT YA

SUNDAY

"Sunday, get over here! Come grab one of these beers and take a load off!" another farmer called to her.

In silence, Sunday kept pushing. She, Reggie, and Narado unloaded large steel tubs of live frogs in the town square on Main Street. Sunday threw her entire back, legs, and behind into picking up one tub by herself.

"Sunday!" Principal Overton yelled from some distant place where people still thought rationally.

She managed to move the oversized tub to the edge of the tailgate.

"Somebody, help her! Nook!" Mama Piggee cried. "She's gonna hurt herself. Sunday, sit down!"

That was impossible. Too many unfulfilled dreams and almost-coulda-wouldas simmered in her belly, bubbled up her core, and now threatened to erupt from her. She needed an outlet to grieve this latest death.

They had come so close. *So* close.

"Sun." Her younger brother approached so he and Principal Overton could take over the big tub. "Move so I can—"

"Don't touch me."

Sunday's little brother apparently knew her well enough to understand that was more than a threat. He tried to assist without touching her, and spotted Sunday instead, while she toted the tub of frogs from their truck.

"Sunday, it'll be all right." Mama Piggee followed her. "This town ain' never needed money to make do. We don't need none now."

"Bull jive," Sunday muttered, marching back to her truck. "That's what po' folk say so bein' broke don't kill us as qui..." That last word got caught on the tripwire of her electrically charged heart.

The rest of the town continued unloading their wares for the next three weeks of Christmas festivities. The mood had nosedived since last Saturday when they'd all gathered at the Conklin farm. Tonight, it felt as if Christmas had already come and gone.

Just as word of Sunday's winning ticket had flown from field to field like a wildfire, so too had word of the lawsuit. From the interloper.

"Don't act like we lost already," Nookie insisted in the middle of lifting a tub. "They can't prove that ticket is theirs, no more than you can. We've got just as much chance of it belonging to us."

"That man works for Friends, and Strom Adler is behind them. I'm sure he'll have something to do with this," someone else added.

One brave soul finally grabbed Sunday's hand and shoved a mason jar inside it. "There." Up to the quarter line of the jar was blessed whiskey. "Go on and take that to the head. You's justified tonight."

The others returned to setting up for Elaine Weekend,

from Christmas decorations, to knits and quilts, cookies and pies, dolls, and winter baskets of fresh, organic produce.

Sunday's half-decorated Christmas trees stood at different corners of town, lifeless and dark. Staring at the celebration that almost was, she turned up the jar and took a swig of whiskey.

In a move that surprised even herself, she spat it into the dirt. Liquor wouldn't change anything, and on top of that, she'd still feel like hell in the morning. If she didn't find a solution or workaround, her family would be in trouble by Christmas. She set the jar down and went to find more heavy objects to lift.

Somewhere beyond her own worry, in the distant minefield of people she cared about, mutters floated to her.

"Who is that?"

"Don't that look like...?"

"Them license plates say...?"

"Sunday."

She was helping to unpack the goods of a disabled resident. Whatever it was, the others would figure it out and come to her if it was serious. She just needed to numb herself with work.

"Sunday," Nook insisted.

Sick of everybody trying to pacify her and force her toward fake happiness, she swung around. *"What!"*

Sixteen years of heartache found its target.

What words did she hurl? How loud should she scream? Did she punch, or slap? And how hard? Unable to decide, Sunday couldn't move from over-analysis paralysis.

"Leave," she finally managed.

Though he stood half a block away where he'd parked up the street, the entire block of people had fallen so quiet they all heard him.

"I came here to see you, so we could talk face-to-face."

"You got a lotta nerve comin' anywhere near us, fool."
Nookie fisted his hands over and over.

"I figured that's how you'd feel." Bank Man moved to the
front of his sleek, white truck, so brand new Sunday had never
even seen that model. "And I came here anyway."

Sunday's eyes nailed this traitor to the cross in her head.
"Reggie."

"Ma'am," her nephew answered.

"Bring me Earl."

* * *

SEVEN

Who was Earl?

What must have been a quarter of Elaine stood gathered
on Main Street and Highway 44 tonight. Seven's eyes tracked
Reggie to the Conklins' truck and watched the kid reach
inside the bed. Long and slim in Seven's LED headlights, the
silhouette of a rifle couldn't be missed even in the night.

Reggie walked it to his aunt and placed the gun in her
outstretched hand.

"That's not necessary." Seven stretched his arms wide.
"I'm not carrying any weapons, Sunday."

"Careful, Sun," Mama Piggee called out.

Sunday ignored her, and without hesitation, cocked it.
Seven looked around at what must have been a hundred and
fifty people, to see if any rational person would take the gun,
reason with her, or help him in some way. Not a soul broke
ranks.

"I told you to go."

He was a damn man. Not some boy she could boss
around. "And I told you we need to talk."

Shocking him, her finger squeezed, and she fired. Seven

jumped. She'd blown out one of the headlights on his brand new Ford.

"Sunday!"

"Now get back in it and ride." Brandishing more than hurt on her face, she cocked the gun again. "*Right* now."

Brazenly, Seven stepped forward. "I'm not the one who…"

She squeezed, and Seven dodge. His other headlight exploded.

"Will you *stop* that!"

Sunday cocked and aimed. Despite her madness, though, something else ricocheted between the two of them that wasn't bullets. Seven took another chance. He pushed his new boots ahead.

"Dumbass," one observer muttered.

She fired straight at his feet. He leaped back and the bullet hit the pavement right where he'd stood.

"Gatdammit, Sunday!" Seven thundered. "I did not file that lawsuit! I know you're pissed. But I'm *here!*"

She fired again, and fortunately, he'd already jumped.

"Liar! Get away from me!" she screamed. "You takin' me to court? A judge? You need them white people to protect you! You came here to take from me and give the little I got to them white people! One way or the otha! You no betta than Strom Adler!"

"That's *not* true!" Another shot shut him up, and Seven ducked.

"He sent you here! And we fed you! Let you sleep under our roof! You played with our children!"

"You're right, I did. And you and them don't de—"

"Say *one more* word to me about how sellin' my farm is in our best interest, and I *swear to God* I'll— "

"It'll be paid off. You won't have to sell, Sunday."

Already mid-cock when she heard the words, she hoisted the gun again and stopped short of squeezing the trigger.

"What kinda lie is this?" Nookie asked.

His hands still out, arms wide open, Seven stayed focused and tried not to think of his mother having to pick out his casket. "It's not a lie. The loans on your property will be paid in full, and once they are, Friends can't get hold of it."

Shaking her head, shaking the gun, she stood firm. "I don't believe you. Why would you do that? You up to somethin'."

Seven crept forward a few more steps. Sunday aimed, and he halted.

"I'm not. I don't know how much longer I'll be at Friends after what happened with my boss. What I do know is I respect what all of you are doing here. Black town. Black farmers. Black businesses and families. This place brought me a lot of peace last weekend. Before I came here, I didn't know Elaine existed."

Sunday clutched her gun tighter, as if it was one of the few things left in the world she could depend on. Seven's truck headlights spotlighted the battle being fought behind her forehead. "Then you *sued* me. Now you come out here talkin' about don't worry?"

"My sister filed that lawsuit. Not me. I felt like that wasn't the way to handle this, so I came to work it out for you to enjoy your land, free and clear of any debt."

Though it was chilly outside, Sunday was sweating. Her eyes projected fear her mouth would never admit to. "What would I have to do for you? I'm not givin' up *my* lottery ticket. Once I get my money, I can pay off my own house. If you and them white boys did somethin' with my money, you got anotha thing comin'!"

Though, she squeezed that rifle, she was clinging to protection.

Seven stepped forward and took the risk, walking until all

that remained between them was their hearts. Her gun was now imprinted in his chest.

"No strings. No conditions. You won't owe me a thing, Sunday. Once your land is paid for, it'll be yours to do with as you please."

"Why would you do that?"

Her exterior may have been tough, but not every part of her was made of steel.

"Because I want ya."

"Oop." One lady neighbor couldn't help herself.

"Last weekend, you asked me what I lay next to my wife and want. You told me I must lay there at night wanting something."

The windows of Sunday's eyes flickered as if they had been tapped by her own words coming back to visit her. She may have even been stunned he'd remembered.

"I didn't answer at the time. I was still trying to respect my vows. But I've been hard for ya ever since I laid eyes on you."

All eyes in the town square switched back to the other end of the rifle.

"If you lose in court?"

"I'll still want ya. I wanted you before I knew anything about that, and I want you now. Ticket or no ticket."

"You a married man." But she relaxed her arms, and the gun slipped from where it was mounted to her breast.

"I am. It's a good thing I'm not asking ya to marry me tonight."

"You tryin' to get even with your wife? We saw you on the news. I'm not the one to be your rebound woman. You won't be usin' me." She was running out of objections.

"It's been a mighty long time since I've wanted *any* woman the way I want you. Including Arista."

"Oh, my Jesus." Despite the night chill, Mama Piggee had found a fan.

"My stories ain't even this good." One of the aunties drank from her mason jar and kept viewing.

"I just want some time with ya. I want to feel a woman who's real. With herself and with me. No pretending, no games between us. Just us." He wondered if he should say the rest, but hell, why not? He'd come this far. Might as well. "So your toes can wiggle. To see you suck your top lip after ya drink something you like. See the dimples in your back when you bend over and your shirt goes up. To stand back and look at ya all proud of your land when the sun is comin' up."

"Apparently, he intends on doin' somethin' with ya right *befo'* the sun come up." Mama Piggee rocked back on her heels and quipped to the others.

"If she's willing," Seven added. "And not just that. Maybe I can be the one to take ya to Paris...draw how the whole city looks on Sunday."

Naked. He kept that part to himself for now. Until then, he would be satisfied with more of this simplicity here in Elaine, particularly in her.

At this point, Sunday's only sign of life was that she was still standing.

A townswoman nearby stomped the dirt. "Lemme go find me two hundred million dollars to lose."

He eased her barrel off his chest, and leaned into their electricity that could power every Christmas tree in town. They weren't standing near mistletoe, but Sunday's parted lips looked ready and that was good enough.

She whipped her index finger up to push back Seven's forehead. "Where you think you goin'?"

A soft chuckle fell out of him, because of course, she did. "Nowhere until you kiss me."

Sunday Conklin turned up her nose. "Then, I guess you won't be goin' nowhere for a while, huh? That lottery ticket is still mine. Even if that judge say it's not, I'm holdin' you to yo' word. You *will* help the folks in this town on our loans with Friends. And even then, I *still* ain't yo' rebound tail."

Clapping her barrel back in her palm, she strutted off and left him where he was.

Seven grinned. He was still breathing.

A win was a win.

Twenty

A WOMAN WHO'S REAL

SUNDAY

I've been hard for you ever since I laid eyes on you.

Paying attention to the details of her, it felt as if he'd peeked under her dress and seen her with no panties on. Hot coffee slid down Sunday's chest.

Maybe he hadn't lied when he'd said he wanted the real her. Who was that even? Sunday had been in survival mode so long, she could no longer tell the survivor from the woman. A lot of time had passed since that girl left here eighteen years ago thinking she'd come back as an engineer, expecting that all the faith and hope she poured into life would churn out her deepest desires. That girl was now an auntie, with responsibilities and children who she'd ensure would have a better go at life than she had. There was no space now for silliness or fanciful thinking.

Even if Hardcastle had the best intentions, Strom Adler would never abandon the generations-old problem that lay squarely on her family's land. Over a hundred years bore down on Elaine, and some days, Sunday felt the weight of every one of them.

As if the heavens confirmed it, decisions waited for her at the kitchen table.

"Mmhm." Mama's house slippers scooted into the kitchen. "I suppose the answer is all over you."

"What you mean?"

"Don't play with me, girl." Vertreese Conklin poured herself a cup of coffee and started up some oatmeal. "I heard what happened out there. He's still married with a whole family you don't know nothin' about." From the stove, she peered out of the corner of her eye at her child. "Where's his kids at? What about that wife? You think she ain' gon' have somethin' to say? She just gonna move out the way?"

I want to feel a woman who's real. With herself and with me. No pretending, no games between us. Just us.

He had said that out loud.

"Mama, who said I was thinkin' about him?"

Because what would happen if people found out gun-toting Sunday Conklin was walking around here daydreaming about love and France?

"I know my children. Whatever comes off that silver tongue of his, you make sure he means it."

"Ain' nobody studdin' that man." Sunday said that even as she closed her eyes and relived *his* eyes scanning her when she stood on the porch last weekend.

"And one mo' thang. Be nice to ya sister. Y'all were gettin' on so well a couple days ago, when ya didn't think ya had to worry 'bout money anymore."

Sunday's mood hardened at the mention of her sister. "I wasn't wrong, though, Mama. She had no business trustin' a stranger from the bank to tell her about our land. Somebody could tell her anything she wants to hear, just so she'll sell."

Her mother stood in front of her. "Sunday, you gotta remember. Paris never left for college the way you did. She don't know as much as you do about business and land and banks. Sometimes, you can be intimidatin' and she don't always have the heart to ask ya. Same with Nook. They don't know. Be patient."

Outside in the yard, a flashlight searched in the dark. Sunday rushed for one of the guns, checking that it was loaded on her way back to the window. A heavy knock on the backdoor startled them both.

"Yes?" Sunday's mother asked. "Who's there?"

"Seven."

The two women groped at their head scarves and house coats since they weren't proper, yet. Unable to believe he was really at her door, Sunday cracked it.

"Good morning." His voice, still thick with sleep, drifted through the opening. He hadn't fully awakened, yet.

"What you doin' here?" She hadn't been ready. "How'd you get past the gate?"

"Overton. I came in with him." He shifted his weight on his feet and rubbed his hands together. Those hands looked different now that Sunday had seen him snatch up his wife. "Is that coffee I smell?"

Only two people besides Sunday and her family could access their gates and their home—Principal Overton and Mama Piggee, both unemployed since the Arkansas Board of Education had closed the Marvell-Elaine School District. While younger school staff packed up and headed for Little Rock, Memphis, Pine Bluff and bigger towns, Overton and Marleen were older, so they retired. They now pitched in to help Sunday when her workers needed off days or during harvest and planting season.

Hyper aware of herself now, she stood back and let him in. Along came Principal Overton behind him.

"Mornin'. I was telling Mr. Hardcastle here about your

frog sales before Christmas, and how you get 'em ready ahead of spring," Overton explained, apparently nervous as to how Sunday would react. "Sunday here pulls frogs from the swamp, keeps 'em healthy and safe for the next few months, and breeds 'em in April. He's here to help with your tents."

Hardcastle stared at her directly. "Ms. Sunday. Seven Hardcastle is the one who showed up today. Not Friends of the Delta."

Now it was Sunday shifting from one foot to the other. "How we supposed to know that?"

He opened his coat and showed her. "No shirt. No techs. No equipment. Just Seven."

"You bring ya wife with ya, Mr. Hardcastle?" Her mother returned fully dressed and poured herself another cup of strong black coffee, sans sweetness or light.

"Mama." Why had she opened her mouth to defend him?

Hardcastle planted his gaze firmly in Sunday's. "I understand, Mrs. Conklin. Sunday is somebody's daughter. I would have the same concern for one of mine. I'm not promising the world or pretending to know what I'm doing. I just came to help you with your frogs."

Somebody's daughter. Human. Precious. To be loved, and treasured, not just worked to death or screwed.

Sunday gave a slow nod, and that pushed forward the lever that started up the morning.

"'Scuse me?" The intercom unit at the front gate cracked to life. "Anybody home? Ya got a bunch of folks ready to gig us some good frog legs one last time this year."

"Y'all, looky what I got." The screen door slammed behind Mama Piggee, who marched in carrying an object wrapped in gold foil. "Somebody gave me a ham last night, but me and Tootsie can't knock this out by ourselves. Who else want some?" She referred to her poodle.

Daylight streamed through the blinds, and one of

Sunday's workers slid in and fired up the stove with grits, eggs, ham, and Texas toast. The kitchen came alive as Elaine was waking up. Not fueled by Christmas, nor by money, but by their devotion to each other.

"Say Mr. Hardcastle," Mama Piggee started in her voice that indicated she would give him hell all day. "Ride us over to the Kwik Stop for a lottery ticket. Oh, yeah! That's right. Ya got transportation problems, now, huh?"

Bank Man took it in stride. "My real problem is not transportation."

His focus drifted over his coffee cup. Up Mama's house slippers Sunday had borrowed, over her old nappy pajama pants, up her faded Elaine High School Class of 2003 t-shirt that got lost in her fat rolls since she was several sizes bigger now than when she graduated, along her bare, unwashed face, where his eyes told hers that he had seen everything and he still hadn't run back to his pristine lawn in Texas.

This was...these weren't...no. Something besides her coochie was responding to him.

Sunday backed up to go wake the kids.

How *did* she look? She stopped by the bathroom to see what he'd seen.

Oh, Lord!

Her bonnet had a stain on it. This t-shirt was way too tiny, and there was a little bitty hole just over her belly. Damn. Her chin hairs were growing back too fast. Slamming on the water faucet, she rinsed the boogers out of her eyes and scraped the dry skin from the crevices of her nose.

What was he doing? Playing a game? Distracting her, fooling her into believing he liked her, so she wouldn't fight so hard for the money?

Coming out of the bathroom, she bumped into a figure taller than her.

"I plan on fightin' for every penny that's mine. You bein' here actin' all sweet don't change that," she blurted fast.

Seven stared down at her. "Fine. We talked about this last night." He aimed a thumb behind him. "A little later, I need to use your landline phone to call my kids when they get out of school, check in on them. Plus, I need to make a couple of other calls and the reception around here isn't always the best. You good with that?"

Sunday nodded. "Yeah."

"Thanks." Before he pivoted, his eyes took a final sip of Sunday. A tiny smile frolicked at the corner of his lips.

Since he was going there, she needed to see something herself. Sunday let her gaze slip. What was she *doing?* This was crazy. But her eyes kept traveling.

"Satisfied?" he asked once her attention landed at its destination.

Brother man was *not* lacking. She couldn't just validate him, though. "Not that you'll be usin' it over this way anytime soon."

He swung it away from her, and headed back toward the kitchen. "Last time I read your reports, you needed heavy machinery to clear all them bushes you got."

* * *

SEVEN

"One, two, three, up!" One of Sunday's workers counted so all of them would hoist up the large box of frogs at the same time. It was part of several deliveries to local restaurants across the South.

"People really do order truckloads of frogs." Seven wiped the sweat from his forehead before returning to the tent.

"Most folks are not going out in the woods with a stick,"

Principal Overton explained. "They'd rather us do all that. But they loves to order some garlic butter frog legs at them food stands and nice restaurants."

Seven no longer needed a gigging stick. To fill the next box, he reached into the nets, scooped up several live frogs, with a few escaping his hands, and took them to the ice chests so they'd chill and become desensitized over several hours. At a table, two workers processed chilled frogs for boxing.

Principal Overton toted some frogs to a chest. Seven held open the lid, Overton threw them inside, and they quickly snapped it shut before any could leap out.

On their way back to the nets, the older man stumbled, and Seven quickly grabbed him to help him stay on his feet.

"Thank ya."

"Don't mention it."

"Ladies and ladies, time for lunch." Sunday smiled behind them. In dirty jeans, boots, and a cranberry henley, she advertised quintessential country living. "We brought turkey sandwiches if you interested. And if you ain't interested, don't be lookin' at me to pick you up when you drop. Mr. Overton, why don't you sit out this afternoon? Lookin' like you're on your last leg. I'll take your spot after we eat."

"You won't hear me arguin'." Overton took a long swig of cold water.

Sunday offered a glance at Seven. "One of your kids called. A girl. Is it Raegan? Asked for you to call when you get back."

"Appreciate you letting me borrow your phone."

She passed him a bottle of water, their fingers hugging, stoking his itch for more of her. He almost took her wrist but thought better of it.

"You're welcome." Had her voice softened, or was it only in his head? "How many kids you got?"

Why was she asking?

"Three. Sixteen going on thirty. Fourteen, and nine."

They started a lazy stroll to where she'd parked her truck.

"This is none o' my business. I know you unhappy with ya wife. And I know you not interested in trauma-bondin'." She rolled a gigging stick back and forth under her boot. "But your baby girl didn't sound good. How come you not there with ya daughter?"

The others had cleared out to eat at one of the outdoor picnic benches, leaving the two of them alone under a slate sky.

Seven inhaled the scent he'd been inhaling the past two days, of woods, dead leaves, reptiles, and propane.

Sunday finished her thought before he answered.

"I'd give anything to have my daddy back here with us. Things wouldn't be so hard." Sharply, she spun away from him so that Seven only faced the back of her head. On the other side of it, she was wiping.

"With respect, Sunday, you can't say how things would've gone if he was still alive."

"I know our lives would have been better."

"Your life *is* better." Seven stared across her acres of land. "Appreciate it. How many kids out there had parents with anything to leave them?"

"You might have a point."

He grinned at his walking companion. "What is the world coming to when Sunday Conklin gives me a point? As far as my children, if I did my job right, a few days of me taking time for myself won't knock them off course too much. They shouldn't be hitting up liquor stores or breaking into houses anytime soon. Ri and I have a solid village. Besides, they're at the point where hanging around Mom and Dad isn't hot anyway. I'm mostly their chauffeur nowadays."

They let down the tailgate of the truck and scooted on with their sandwiches, their legs dangling over the dirt.

"Why are you here? Elaine ain't Dallas. We ain't got nothin' on the city."

"Your town does something for me." He bit into his sandwich, essentially Thanksgiving turkey and dressing with all the flavors melting onto two pieces of bread. "This hits. You couldn't have made it."

"Why not?"

"'Cause it actually tastes good."

For a blessed moment, all the fields brightened in the whites of her teeth she let him see. Even the dimple came out and smiled. "I can cook!"

"Mmhm." He took another bite. "I haven't seen you light up nah stove."

"When do *you* cook? I bet your old lady do all the cookin', don't she?"

He served her the side-eye he gave his kids when they talked smack. "So, you're saying you want to go head-to-head? *Do* you want to go head-to-head? Don't talk loud if your skills are only a whisper."

"Taahhh! What they makin' over in Dallas? Weenies?" Sunday stood her ground, despite clearly being taken aback at his confidence in cooking.

"You've seen for yaself, ain't no weenies over here. Let's keep this easy for you. Pancakes." Aiming his sandwich at her, he remained unfazed. "Tonight at the house. Breakfast for dinner. We won't tell the kids who made which ones, and they can decide whose are best."

"Oooh! I want some! I'll be a judge!" One of the workers piped up.

They had started talking loud enough for the others to hear.

Sunday sized him up. "What's this with you talkin' country now?"

The spontaneous observation caught him off guard. "What did I say?"

"Nah stove," she repeated, teasing him with a side grin, "and ain't."

The laughter and bonding in these open fields had indeed relaxed him. "I guess my hosts make me comfortable."

"Imma have to give you more work to do then." She swallowed a bite and savored it, nibbling her top lip a moment longer. She was doing it again.

"My back is ready when you are."

"I said I wasn't gonna be your..." Sunday choked, and started coughing.

He reached over and gave her a hard slap on the back. "Can't handle too much meat in your mouth at one time, huh? You need proper guidance on how to swallow?"

Laughing choked her up more and tears crammed her eyes. "I don't need squ—"

"Yeah." He passed her the water. "Sip."

She fought accepting it until she had no choice. Crying and coughing, her voice was still weak when Sunday finally managed, "Forget you."

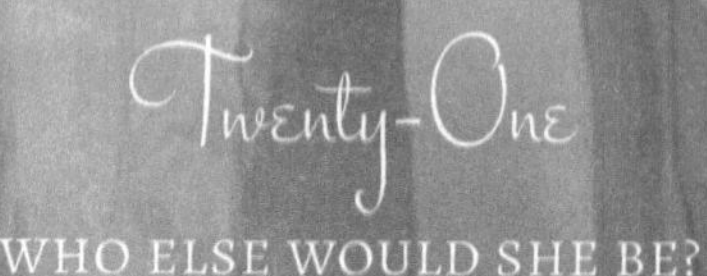

Twenty-One

WHO ELSE WOULD SHE BE?

SUNDAY

"Don't be lookin' over here," Sunday muttered to Seven while she whipped her batter.

"What I'm lookin' at is *wrong*. That's too much milk. Throw in one more egg, a little more flour."

Sunday shoved him at the counter. "Get outta my business. You just do yours."

"All right, I tried to tell ya."

"You can't tell me nothin'!"

"Come here. You got some on your face." He licked his thumb and came at her.

Sunday cringed. "Oh, no, you will not!"

Throwing an arm around her, he pulled her into a playful headlock before she could escape. "It's just spit. You go through worse than that out there with those nasty frogs."

Feeling his wet thumb slide over her cheek, Sunday's laughter erupted even as she squirmed. Maybe she should have questioned if he was fully healthy and didn't have any STD's. After all, his wife *had* cheated on him.

But as she opened her mouth, the moment dropped Sunday off in another era of her life. Back when her older brother William came home from school, he and Vanessa would gang up on her. One of them would tickle Sunday and the other pinned her down so she couldn't run. This way and that, she would wiggle from side to side, tickled so hard she couldn't breathe, unable to escape. Vanessa was the best tickle-fighter. For the glorious few seconds that she could relive it, Sunday returned to a time when life was more fun, and safe, and the weight of her loneliness lifted.

"We hungry!" somebody called from the dining area in the lodge.

"Yeah! Y'all in there playin'! When we eatin'?"

A few minutes later, Sunday threw her hand on her hip and leaned against the stove, staring down Seven who tossed a kitchen towel over his shoulder and parked against the refriger-ator. The two faced each other.

"You can come and get 'em now," Sunday yelled.

Nobody had been allowed in the kitchen, so nobody knew which of them had prepared which pancakes. The plates were numbered "one" and "two." Only Seven and Sunday knew that Sunday was "plate one" and Seven was "plate two." The people would decide which stack tasted better.

Mama Piggee entered to pick up the plates and take them outside. Sunday started to follow her, and Seven shot an arm across her chest to block her from leaving.

"Aht aht. Don't go out there so you can signal to your people. Stay that tail here and wait." His lips spread over perfect teeth. Walnut complexion, roasted nuts, Christmas katydids. Eyes genuinely amused. Soft laughter tickling her ear. His grin was grinning. "You're gonna get your little heart broken right here where I can see it."

Were Sunday's bones relaxing? "Bro, don't get cocky. You about to find out."

His arm stretched over her head, he still leaned on the wall, blocking her direct path. What began as an effort to stop her from cheating now sealed their proximity.

"I was born cocky. When you know, you just know."

"And what do you think you know?"

Endless brown closed in. Brown eyes, brown lips, brown skin, a five o'clock shadow, with plenty of ash after the fire, a whole new excursion for one Sunday. His mouth stopped. Close enough for his warm breath to heat her skin. Intimate enough that her body was reacting to a caress he'd only started with his eyes.

"This really mean, violent, country ass woman held a gun to my head, blew out the headlights on my truck, fought me out in a field." His mouth spoke against hers. "And all I wanna do is..." His tongue brought Christmas to her bottom lip, trailing wet heat along its edge.

The drip into her panties was her body's answer, but Sunday's mama wasn't wrong. Sunday deserved a man who wasn't compromised. Possibly even, dare she think it, a husband one day.

"Why don't you go home and do it to yo' wife?" Why was Sunday tripping? She'd had plenty of married men. What in the world held up her show now?

"I tried that already. Plenty times. She ain't what I lay awake and want at night. Somebody around here asked me what I *do* want."

Sunday's heart flipped. *Urghhh!* Why did he have to have a family? Why did everything that fell into her life come with four or five sets of terms and conditions? Damn. *Don't do it, Sunday. Don't do it. Be smarter than this.* "You've got a lot on ya mind. It's obvious you goin' through a lot. Maybe you shouldn't be standin' here with me after all that stuff on CNN."

The pupils in his eyes focused until she saw her reflection

in their centers. "Maybe you're right. I think you want me standing here with you, though. Or Sunday Conklin wouldn't let these legs stand."

Seven took her bottom lip between his teeth, and sucked Sunday in the rest of the way. Those broad hands she'd seen that first night engulfed her face, and held it inside them, as if his words from a few days ago weren't idle talk, but actions carrying intention. The cornstalk shooting from between his thighs, the subject of much discussion between Arkansas and Texas the past few days, introduced itself against her belly. Sunday's curiosity wouldn't allow her hand to stay where it was. The same hand that expertly palmed her rifle slid over the wood on another shotgun now. Long and ready, it didn't disappoint. Over his jeans, Sunday squeezed.

The pressure evoked a small moan from Seven's throat that told her he was in his drought season. One that might not have been so different from her own.

Their attraction opened the gates of her, and in her mind, she tiptoed toward the possibilities. What *would* Paris look like on Sunday? Who else would she be without so much work, stress, and worry?

Like he ached to show her, his hands disappeared from her face and slid over her hips to her behind, clenching her butt. His manhood pressed into her harder and his zipper cut into her flesh, but his tongue tasting hers muted the pain. Each time he pulled her in, Hardcastle yanked her booty up and down, as would a man who'd indeed lied awake in want for a long time.

She kissed men, romped in the sheets, enjoyed nice hard-ons all the time. Only now, she allowed herself to be fool enough to kiss with thoughts of a future.

"Auntie?"

Dammit!

Seven, the father of three, was first to heed a child's voice.

He thumbed the spit from his mouth, shot her a promising glance and headed down the hall.

"Is that what we do with boys?" Victoria asked on their way down the corridor.

"No!" So hot she'd begun sweating, Sunday dabbed at her forehead and cheeks with her sleeve. "That is not what *girls* who are still in school do with *boys* who are still in school. That is what very old people do a long, long time after they've graduated high school, college, and graduate school, they've got good jobs, and their parents can't tell them what to do anymore."

"I see the high school girls doing it on the back of the school bus," Victoria retorted.

"But you're not in high school, and you're not thirty-six years old, so you don't have to think about any of that for a long time. Right?"

A few seconds of silence passed while Victoria must have been assessing it in her head. "Okay."

What kind of example was Sunday setting?

"Plate two is the winner!" Principal Overton called out from the dining hall. "Plate two! These pancakes didn't miss a beat! Fluffy and soft, with the buttermilk flavor just right, we need to be selling these at Elaine Day! We know this isn't you, Sunday. Sorry, baby!"

Seven immediately reached out and brought Sunday to his chest, laying a kiss on her forehead. "Good job, sweetheart."

Did he say that to his daughters? Was this how they always felt? Comforted even when they were disappointed or a situation didn't go their way? His arms enveloped her shoulders so easily, and it was obvious he'd done it so many times it came naturally for him. Affection humanized Seven in a way Sunday still processed.

Though Seven's arm covered most of her face, she

managed to peer over it, at Mama Piggee and Peady, both wearing uncertain expressions.

He released her and went to join Principal Overton. A handful of people sat with him to pick his brain about their home loans and other debts with Friends. Other townsfolk still hadn't decided on him, and kept their distance.

"This is weird," Peady whispered.

"What?" Sunday asked.

"Why's he here huggin' on you when he's suin' us for our millions?" Peady eyed Seven, now at one of the tables explaining something, using his hands to emphasize. "I'm surprised you ain't already made him leave, Sun."

Sunday took a breath. It was time to level with her siblings, starting with this one. "That ticket just might have been his."

"How you figure? *You* signed the ticket and cashed it in already."

"I was drunk. And all of you know it. I remember some of what went down, but not all of it," Sunday confessed here and now, just her and her sister.

"Shhh. Don't say that out loud. He don't know that."

"The surveillance camera at the Kwik Stop will show the time he bought his ticket and the time I bought mine." Sunday had to be honest out loud now. "The judge will compare the purchase times on the video against the times on the tickets to see whose is whose." Raw and real, she dispensed with the tough talk that defined so much of how she often approached peril. "I was rushing to buy Nookie's ticket and get back here. I was pissed and worried after the bank told me I was out of chances. And I bumped into Hardcastle. Knocked his ticket clean out of his hand. I dropped mine, too, picked 'em both up, and didn't look at 'em first. I could have accidentally given him my ticket while I took his, Peady."

The truth didn't feel any better once it was out of her.

That monkey now jumped on her back rather than in her stomach, but it *did* feel as though she'd been freed from it some, now that it had been set loose.

She was sorry to watch it jump on Peady now.

"Why didn't you say somethin'? Instead of lettin' us believe it was ours?"

"At first, I didn't know. I don't think he knew either. One of his folks obviously said somethin'. I'm guessin' they wouldn't have filed a whole lawsuit unless they checked it out and they're sure." Tired of holding her head high all the time, she now let it fall. "Then, when I did realize it, I ain't have the heart to tell y'all." Sunday didn't bother holding back the tears she cried alone any other time. "I feel like I always let y'all down. You said it yaself. I'm not 'Nessa."

One hundred and ninety-six million dollars sleighed off of Peady's face the longer Sunday talked. "No. You not 'Nessa."

Sunday accepted that. "Before you go to court and see it on video, you needed to hear it from me."

For the next few moments, the sisters wrestled a heavy truth sinking in for both of them. Though they faced each other, they stared into an uncertain future.

"Thank you for tellin' me."

Her sister's disappointment dragged the weight back onto Sunday.

"I'm sorry you have to hear it at all. I was happy to finally give you all somethin' good."

"You *been* givin' us somethin' good, Sun. You might not be Ness, but you kept us here. Daddy been gone a long time and we ain' lost none of this, yet."

Their tears slid into their mouths.

"We deserve better," Sunday creaked.

Peady nodded and stroked her belly. "We do. Bein' millionaires was fun for a little while anyway. More fun than we've had in a long time. Not worryin' about them fields and frogs twenty-four-seven sho' did feel nice." The younger Conklin both laughed and cried. "That woulda been a dope life."

Sunday shared Peady's melancholy. "It can still happen. But if we don't win the money, I'll find a way for us to get outta here more. Go see otha things. So the kids know it's a whole big world out there."

"So *we* remember what's out there."

"And so *we* don't let the world forget Elaine is here." Sunday wrapped an arm around Peady's shoulders, pulling her sister in for a hug and kiss on the cheek.

On the other side of the dining hall, their mother was watching, her fist covering part of her face so she didn't give away her own emotions.

"So, this man coulda called you out for takin' *his* money, but he didn't?" Peady asked between sniffles.

"We don't know for sure it's really his," Sunday thought aloud. "But, pretty much. Yeah."

Her younger sister exhaled her upset. "We can tie him up in one o' the cabins until after court."

Sunday chuckled. "The Adlers would just love for me to go to prison and have me outta their hair."

Since it was a school night, the pancake wars had to end early and they said goodbye to the children filtering out.

Hardcastle approached Sun, no humor or comedy on him now. "Hey, if it's all right, I'll use your landline at the house to check on my kids. I'd rather do it early, before I drive back to Helena."

"There's a phone here at the lodge. Look underneath the emergency supply counter in the auxiliary room for the old phone. It's got a jack to plug into the kitchen."

"Thanks."

Principal Overton also took Sunday aside. "I'm glad you're not mad at me for bringin' him back here. I know he's married, kids, and all that, but he's a solid man. He started off wrong, but he owned it. Ya daddy woulda befriended him."

Sunday nodded and squeezed his hand. "I know."

"What ya say, after we get the rest o' them frogs on the trucks, we go out and finish up decorations for Elaine Day?" Eager, restless, he beamed as bright as Christmas lights. They needed to show the town Elaine didn't need two hundred million dollars to celebrate.

Sunday's heart felt as if she were holding it under water, but he was right. "Let's have us an Elaine Day."

She waited a few minutes to give Hardcastle privacy with his call before she headed to the back to pass him the key for locking up.

"It doesn't matter what anybody else says. What do you say?" His voice emanated down the corridor. It had shifted, from sensual and cocky to firm and supportive. "Your grandmother and aunt shouldn't be talking to you about that. That's a conversation you have in private with a therapist of your own, who looks out for you and nobody else. Your mama shouldn't be using your grandma and aunt to put pressure on you. I'll discuss that with my attorney so she can warn your mom's attorney that she should stop it."

Sunday backtracked. He clearly wouldn't be finished for a while.

"No, baby, I can't do that."

But Sunday didn't exactly hightail it out of earshot.

"Your mom and I needed a cooling off period. I needed time to think and clear my head, same as when you and me don't see eye to eye, and you go to your room to tune me out. I'll be home in a couple days."

A few moments passed.

"It's a little bitty town called Elaine, Arkansas." Another few moments. "There's not much here as far as buildings and shops or entertainment, but not every town is supposed to be full of stuff. Some towns are meant for us to find peace. Towns have identities, just like people. This town has an incredible identity—Black farmers who've been around a long time, since before slavery ended. They have good stories to tell, and we still need places like this to teach us history and how they've been living off the land. It's pretty and the people are nice. I can draw it once I have my chalk and pencils. If that's what you want, of course, you can." Another few moments. "No, baby girl, we'll talk about that when I get back. Your mom and I have some things we need to go over with you all. Our family will..."

The big sigh that came out sounded like resolve. And maybe release.

"...will be moving different pretty soon. It doesn't mean we don't love you or won't be there for you. Just that you guys aren't babies anymore. Your mom and I can support you differently now."

Knowing she was outright disrespectful at this point, Sunday turned and crept the rest of the way out of the corridor.

Twenty-Two

NOTHING ON HER

SEVEN

Seven hung up the phone, a slightly victorious smile on his lips. As he'd anticipated, his children were giving their mother and aunt pure hell. Arista was getting exactly what she deserved. They were mad at her and acting out that she'd driven Dad away. The main reason he had no qualms about staying gone a few days longer was so she could sit in it. Despite his sentiments falling a bit on the childish side, this still felt good.

Wrapping Sunday's phone back up and putting it away, he headed through the corridor, and was surprised to find it shrouded in darkness. The lodge had completely emptied out. Where was everybody?

"Sunday?" He was drawn to the crackle of flames.

In front of the fireplace now sat a large rocking chair, a red and brown flannel blanket inside. But there was no one around. On the floor lay a flattened cardboard box, and crayons on top of it.

A door opened along the wall. Out strolled Sunday from the restroom, into the dark. Nothing on her.

Except for the cowboy boots Seven had been wearing when he'd first snuck onto her farm. He remembered tossing those boots in the trash. Topping them off now, Sunday donned a black Stetson. Other than that, she strutted across the floor in her birthday suit.

Her full breasts swung ahead of her, their stretch marks speaking of her age, her defined calves filling out the boot, the slopes of her thighs sculpted day after day in her fields, layers on layers of hips and butt that boasted suppleness for a man to lay more than his head. Light from the flames two-stepped on one half of her and the shadows jigged off the other half, a countryside angel all aglow in natural Rembrandt lighting.

Seven's manhood stood up, ready to worship on Sunday. Two weeks before Christmas, Heaven and nature weren't the only ones singing.

In those brief seconds she came toward him, the dust of his marriage and vows blew across his mind. Whatever he did next, was he really ready to stand ten toes down and activate a whole new life for himself that his children would have to adjust to? And say goodbye to an old version of Seven and the old pretense of manicured lies.

Sunday took a seat in the rocking chair, slid one side of the blanket over her shoulder, and the other side around her curvaceous waist. The sight of her leaving him breathless, he knew where he'd put his face first.

"Do I come sit over there with you, or am I about to get a show, or what?" he asked.

"You said you wanted to draw me. I found you some tools." She waved her hand over the crayons and cardboard beneath her.

He snort-laughed. "You think those are tools?"

She flung one cowboy boot over an arm of the chair, exposing the hairy valley between her thighs, and draped just a smidge of flannel to cover it. "A real artiste can work with whatever he's got." She drew another part of the flannel so it barely concealed her nipples. "You better make me look good, too."

Amused, he pulled off his jacket. "This is kind of impromptu. I might be a little rusty."

"No excuses."

He dragged over a chair and found a small card table.

"How much am I getting paid for this?"

They eyed one another.

Firelight revealed her dimple next to her devious half-grin. "Oh."

He licked his lips and sat down. On his first time drawing in a few years, he started with a chocolate crayon to sketch out her outline.

"Why didn't you become an artist if that's what you wanted?" she asked.

"I like money too much. Not that it isn't possible. You just never know how that will turn out. Even if you do gain some notoriety, the jobs and pay are unstable, and I'm not about that feast-or-famine life. I'm not sure it would have always brought fulfillment."

"What brings you fulfillment?"

With black, brown, and white crayons, he outlined the figure that had been tempting him from the first night. Slopes of her shoulders, smooth and at ease, dipped into her clavicle and curved down her breasts. Folds of flannel prevented Seven from seeing the rest of her.

"Traveling to different places around the world and receiving room service. Late mornings. Moving on my own time and nobody else's other than my kids. Watching my money work for me, and showing other people how to maximize their own money and land values. Learning interesting topics, like frogs absorbing the environment into their skin." He grinned while blending red crayon with orange to create the firelight playing off the flannel. "Learning that was dope by the way. Connections with people that are more than surface-level. When you walk away from them, their words or something they've taught you stays with you. What brings you fulfillment?"

"We're still talkin' about you." Her chest rose, like she was sucking in a big breath, and out fell her next question. "What did Elaine teach you that stuck so hard it brought you back here?"

Seven stopped drawing, and shifted his focus from her body to *her*.

Their only disruption was the sashay of fire and an owl hooting in the distance.

Sunday continued, "Why didn't you call me out for knocking that ticket outta your hand that night?"

He answered the question in his head, but hadn't reached enough strength to utter it aloud. Illuminated by the fire, Sunday's eyes deepened as if she'd heard his answer anyway. Like she'd felt it. Seven put the crayons down and moved toward her. Failing marriage and past pretense be damned. Sunday dropped the flannel. What remained were two souls tired of existing for everybody else.

The only question now was who would go first.

Before he could dip to his knees, she beat him to the punch.

"Imma do you this solid 'cause your need is screamin'."

With strength, she gripped the top of his jeans and jerked his bulge to her. She was a pro. Not demure, highly unlady-like, she expertly maneuvered the zipper up, outward, and down. She shoved his briefs aside, and Seven's full length sprang onto her face, over her forehead and disappeared under her hat.

The tip of her tongue wet his balls, and she wasn't shy or prickly about it, either.

Long-awaited ecstasy closed his eyes at the feel of Sunday.

Sunday licked and sucked gently and firmly. She opened his pants wider, and pulled them down with his briefs for more access to him. Then, she started over again, laying her whole tongue over his nut sac like she was reading his *every* fantasy. She massaged his dick so thoroughly Seven was ready to become a country man full time.

He refused to scream. He would *not*. No matter how her fingertips rubbed spit over his balls that she held. No matter that she worked from the base of his shaft and dragged every one of her moist taste buds up each vein and nerve connecting him to the stars above.

The cowboy hat was barely clinging to her head now. Her naked, smooth back poked from underneath the hat, and extended to her bare bottom on the edge of her rocking chair.

Needing to see the pivotal moment he'd played over and over in his mind, he slipped the hat off her head. Right in time to watch his tip disappear between her lips that were thick as sugar sacks.

Pulling and tugging him, wetting, licking, savoring, she teased him just at his edge. At the same time, she massaged spit around his base, squeezing and releasing to coordinate with her tongue action at the top. She escalated her motions, from tastes and taunts to unhinged head action.

Seven almost gave up the ghost when her head shoved fully forward, consuming the rest of him. Sounds of gurgling in her throat, her head tugging him in one direction and then the other, were a kind of restoration, a Christmas gift no other present would compare to for a long time. Sunday's fat lips, long tongue, and full cheeks suctioned Seven's manhood like she was sucking out his spirit.

"Eee!"

Still standing in boots, his toes had nowhere to curl. The tip of his wood scraped the back of Sunday's throat, her gnawing and licking and tonguing as if she was coming for his life, and she just might take it. And anything else she wanted.

Sunday must've known she was driving him to the edge. One of her thumbs stroking the nerves under his shaft, the other playing with his balls, Seven rolled his eyes toward the sky for her to take him all the way up. Feeling like a reindeer kicking through the clouds, he believed Santa just might be real.

In the warmth of her mouth, Sunday suctioned out every drop of cum he didn't know he still had. He would not squeal again. Clamping his mouth shut, he jerked through the torture.

When he opened his eyes, hers were waiting underneath him. Sunday slid her mouth off, got up and walked to the bathroom to spit out his cum. He joined her to wipe himself off.

It had been a long time, and Seven was ready for *her*. Rubbing and stroking himself, he inspected locations around the lodge where he could get the best leverage. But Sunday started putting her clothes back on, suddenly focused hard on her jeans. What was she doing?

Her mouth moved, as if she was talking to herself in some internal dialogue.

He stood behind her. On the rise again, he pressed himself against her back. "You just left me hanging."

Sunday stared at him in the mirror. "I did it 'cause I feel bad for you and wanted to help you out. You've still got a wife and kids you're going back home to, though."

"So you gave me some pity head?"

"Yeah."

He nodded sharply, irritated at how she was being cold and transactional. As if he was just another man and she did this all the time. As if this was just business, and they could go back to their regularly scheduled programming.

"All right, let me give you some pity dick then. I've seen your man options you're working with out here in the boonies. They ain't stellar."

The two cracked up.

"Bank Man, whether you stay with your wife or not, I'm not interested in a casual bang to help you get over her. I ain't interested in bein' your rebound if y'all breakup, or your side dish if y'all stay together neither."

In an attempt to understand what was going on here, he stretched an arm over her head to anchor himself against the mirror. Faces side by side, their reflections held one another.

"What are ya interested in then, Miss Sunday? Because right now, you're acting like nothing just went on here."

His reflection examined hers long enough to see her unful-filled Christmas dreams. Her gaze darted everywhere but at him. Not answering, she began fumbling with her underwear.

So that was the problem. Her sudden nonchalance was protection.

"I'm coming back, Sunday." He stopped her arms from moving, her mind from evading. "You have my admiration and my respect. You're the bravest person I know. Out here making bricks out of straw, standing for something even when you've got nothing. *That's* what Elaine taught me that stuck with me even after I left. *That's* why I didn't call you out on the ticket. I've got money and resources. So does my family. If the judge rules against us and says it's yours, we'll be just fine. I know you'll use it to do right by the Delta."

For the first time in the short week-and-a-half he'd known her, she let him see her fear. "And if the judge doesn't rule in my favor? What about then?"

"Then, *I'm* gonna do right by *you*. And that's on my chil-dren *and* my mama. The liens on your house will be paid."

He turned her so she faced him directly. Seven removed his wallet from the back of his jeans, slipped out his credit card, and held it between them. "Elaine Day is coming. And a little bird told me you wanted to have a Boots N' Tiaras Ball for Christmas, so the kids could dress up." His goatee brushed her chin when he sucked her lips. "Plus, you left all those damn Christmas trees out there with no lights or ornaments in 'em."

A stubborn smile unfolded from her mouth, stretched across her forehead, and on down through her hips that shifted between his legs. Giggling, she asked, "You payin' me for what I just did?"

Seven burst out laughing. "I hadn't thought of it like that. Did you wanna be paid for what you just did?"

"No, but I do think it's worth somethin'."

"I think it's worth something, too. But money ain' what I had in mind." He cupped her neck and kissed her again, his adrenaline sleighing everywhere when Sunday slid her tongue in his mouth and kissed him back.

She accepted the card and shoved it in her bra, in the same spot where she'd placed the ticket.

"Go easy on that thing, will ya? Make sure you don't drop it or mix it up with any other ones this time," he cautioned.

Tonight, the way Sunday Conklin beamed, maybe even hoped, she couldn't have hid her dimple from him if she'd tried. "I'll think about it."

"If you need anything, call me. I'm here for you and for Elaine." He trailed an index finger down her neck. "If you'll let me without shooting me."

Twenty-Three

WELCOME HOME, BABY

SEVEN

"Daddy!"

Seven hadn't been in the door five seconds. With barely enough time to set down his bag, his favorite girl ran to him from where she did homework in the dining room. Seven spun her in the air. His back screamed in pain, and he had to set her back down. His sun ray was becoming a little woman, with weight on her, not the five-year-old shrub running around on the soccer field.

This back thing couldn't happen on his next visit to see Sunday. He'd need to be more consistent in the gym so he was ready when he headed back to her.

"Damn, how many cheeseburgers did you eat while I was gone? How much junk has your aunt been shoving in that belly?"

"Nunya!" Raegan crowed happily for "none ya business." "You weren't here, so it didn't have anything to do with you!" She repeated one of his refrains.

Seven snickered. "It's awfully strange, though, how you're

not at work making money with me either, but my money's got plenty to do with you."

"That's right!"

Feet pounded down the stairs. "Dad!" Dillon squeezed him in a bear hug, and the pressure sent another sharp pain up Seven's back.

He would definitely need an Epsom salt bath or some Icy Hot. Maybe both.

"Who is this grown man hugging me? Where did you get all that strength?" He kissed his son's forehead. There was only one hug missing now.

From where she sat in the living room, his oldest served him her side-eye and returned to her homework.

"Hey, Ash Bear," he called to her.

She remained on the sofa. "Hey, Dad." Her eyes didn't venture toward his again.

He was in hot water.

"Daddy, I baked you a chicken and rice casserole," Ray gushed.

"You mean you heated up a Cosco dinner?"

"Same difference."

Seven massaged his own back, wondering how he was able to do several days of field work in the Delta countryside but caught a cramp the moment he stepped foot back in Dallas.

Their mother descended the stairs. "Welcome home, baby."

He stared up at Ri in silk pajamas, no bra underneath, once his weakness. "How you doin', Arista?"

"Can you guys give me and your daddy some time?" she asked them.

"He just got here," Raegan objected.

"Ray is right." Seven went to wash his hands. "Let me catch up with them." For the children's sake, he left out the rest—that while he was gone, their lawyers had negotiated a schedule and sleeping arrangements, and he expected Arista to comply with it fully.

Over dinner, Seven's younger children chattered his ear off, catching him up on all the school drama, particularly when he'd gone live on social media.

"Dad, the girls at school had a lot of jokes," Ray reported. "I didn't like some of it. It was really disrespectful."

"I'm sorry you had to go through that. It was wrong of me to put mine and your mother's business out in the street. I would never tell any of you to handle a situation so childishly."

"No, Dad," Raegan piped up. "Some of my friends' moms sent their phone numbers home. They said if you really do mean 'you'll get hard for any woman but mom,' they could use help."

"Raegan Monique!" her mother snapped.

Ignoring her, Ray took out several slips of paper, and with a fat, cheesy smile that displayed every piece of metal in her mouth, Raegan dropped six phone numbers on the dinner table.

Seven did a backflip inside. He could always count on his Sun Ray. "Don't disrespect your mother, Raegan."

Behind his glass, he and his second-born swapped devious grins. Ash was still icing him out, and stared into her plate.

"So, how was Arkansas?" Arista asked. "The kids mentioned how nice you said it is there. Maybe we can go for a family vacay this spring or summer."

"You wouldn't like it. Not your scene."

"Why not?" Arista frosted on her 'interview' face. "I'm down for a different experience. What did you say was there? A farm? Some snakes or something like that? Pigs? Isn't that all they've got over there? I think your mother mentioned history, like some sort of killing went on? I'm not too sure what's so special about that, but you know me. I'll try anything."

The children fell silent since the energy at the table was plummeting.

"Kids," Seven started, "let's clear the air on some things."

His heart was already cracking.

"Seven, not tonight. You just got back," Arista argued. "You and me, we need our own sit-down first. We haven't been alone in nearly two weeks."

"We talked about this already, Ri."

"We haven't talked about nothing! Your lawyer shoved a piece of paper down my throat."

"Either way, it's been planned and agreed on. We would do this tonight."

"No, *you* agreed, Seven Mitchell!" With that, she shoved the table. "You forced me! Signing it was the only way I could get you to come home."

Ash finally lifted her gaze to level her father with it. "Daddy, you didn't want to come home?"

"Girl, hell yeah, I wanted to come home to *you*, not some bullshit." He hit Arista with his most violent stank face. She had strategically blurted that, just to get a rise out of Ash.

While he took some time in Elaine, his lawyer had drawn up the divorce papers and served Arista. Since he'd blocked her number, the only way she could communicate was through his mother, his sister, or his lawyer. And later, through Sunday's landline.

"Arista, I'm not playing these games. Now we can talk to them together, or I can pick them up from school tomorrow and tell them myself."

"Mom, will you cut with the drama?" Ashlyn intervened and turned to her father. "Daddy, are you leaving us?"

Seven couldn't let that one ride. "Ash, I understand your frustration with your mom. Believe me, I do. But she's still your mother. Keep it cute. And I'm never leaving you guys. I will be here regularly, but yes, I am moving out."

"See, Mom!" Ashlyn shoved her plate away.

Their sunken faces, particularly Dillon laying his head on the table to cry, nearly compelled Seven to take it back. The words skied to the tip of his tongue.

"Look at what you're doing to them!" Arista teared up. "I know I was wrong, but at least they never knew about my private moves. I never interrupted their lives, until *you* aired it. So who's more selfish? Me or *you*?"

"Mom, it's you," Ash muttered. "You're the problem."

Seven took a breath. "So that's what you were counting on, Ri, huh? That you could do whatever you wanted as long as you kept up pretense for the kids, but what about me? What about your marriage? And *my boss*, Ri?" He hadn't intended to do this, but the mere memory of her—leather-clad, her stiletto *he'd* bought her lying on the floor, in another man's house—had Seven hot enough to commit a more serious crime.

"Like I said, we need to talk."

"No, we don't. I really don't care at this point."

"Seven, I'm sorry. Please, let me fix it. We can fix this. I found some good counselors. One is a man and he's Black."

His kids were snot-crying now.

"Ri, stop it!" Seven slapped the table and sent every butt jumping in their seats.

Ash shot up. "Mom, you can't even satisfy your own husband. You don't have authority to tell me anything ever again! I *hate* you!"

"Ashlyn Hardcastle!" Seven called after her.

She marched upstairs to her room and slammed the door.

"Happy?" Arista asked. She took her plate and threw it in the sink, hard enough for the plate to shatter. Moments later, another bedroom door banged shut. Ash was definitely *her* child, straight up and down.

"Dillon, Ray, come here." He opened his arms for his two younger children to come to him and sit on each leg.

"Daddy loves both of you. You guys know that? I even love Ashlyn sometimes."

Raegan chuckled through her tears.

"Then, why are you leaving?" Dillon sniffed into his father's shoulder. "You've been gone almost two weeks already. Did Mom make you hate us, too?"

"I could never. No matter how we get on each other's nerves. I love you guys more than anything, but your mother and I are not doing a good job holding this down anymore. I've thought long and hard about this, and *I'm* not okay. What have your mom and I always taught you to do when you're not okay?"

Dillon sucked back his upset. "To ss...to stop hanging around people if you don't f-feel good, or if you're not number one, also."

"That's right. As long as your mother and I are in this house together and one of us is not okay, we'll be fighting constantly. And our arguments will make you just as sad as you are now. Nobody deserves that. It's time for us to find a new way where *all* of us can be good."

For a long time, to keep the peace and his kids stable, he'd sacrificed himself. But he wouldn't hold his tongue any longer. He would hold Arista accountable, and no longer be the doormat for her to walk over in the name of her superficial friends and social status. That was how he'd felt *before* he found her at Ian's. But now? There was no way he and Arista could stay under one roof, go visit friends, and pose for pictures while people questioned where were his gonads.

"Are you moving far?" Dillon asked.

"No. I'm looking into some condos a few miles up the

road. Close enough that if you wanted to take a Lyft or ride your bike over there, you could, any time you want. As long as I'm in town. When I was in Arkansas, you wouldn't believe I met a thirteen-year-old who's driving already."

"Really?" Dillon sniffed. "So I can start practicing?"

"Let's see how your grades turn out. But over Christmas, I'll take you on some dirt roads and see how you handle yourself." He turned to Raegan. "Sun Ray, talk to me."

"I get it, Dad. Mom's not your vibe anymore." She laid her head on his. "But I'm still sad."

"Me, too," Seven said.

"I want to go with you, Dad." Raegan eyed him.

"Go with me where?"

"I wanna live with you."

He squeezed her shoulders and took that in. His and Arista's lawyers had already started working out some custody scenarios and pickup-drop-off options. Meanwhile, Seven wanted to adjust his children one step at a time, starting with his being here at the house for the next few days when they got home from school.

"What about your friends, and basketball?"

She shrugged. "I want to go somewhere and start over as the new me."

"Ah, I see." He chuckled. She was indeed his. "Can we talk about it with a therapist while you're on winter break?"

She nodded, and a wicked gleam appeared in her eyes. "Are you going back to Arkansas?"

Seven suppressed a smile. "What you wanna know for, nosy?"

She lowered her voice. "When I was looking up you and mom on the internet, I saw an article about you and Aunt Char fighting some lady in court for a lottery ticket. Did you really win the lottery? Was it a real story or was that an AI article?"

Pressing his index finger against his lips, Seven shushed her. "Let's keep that one to ourselves for now. We've got enough popping off as it is."

Raegan opened her mouth wide in astonishment, and then, she shut it.

Hurting his kids hammered nails into him. But the Band-Aid had been ripped off, and a bloody wound that had refused to heal was finally getting air.

A few times that evening, while he, Ray, and Dillon stuffed their chimney socks and hung them over the fireplace, hunted down their matching onesies and ugly Christmas sweaters, and pulled out their childhood board games, he almost caved under the memories. Everything he once excitedly imagined he and Arista would become, now rushed at him in waves of failure.

He nearly fell into his old routine of going to her and patching it up. *Damn that.* His children deserved a whole mother *and* a whole father. Even if they weren't necessarily whole together. Seven finally walked them upstairs to their rooms for their regular round of 'goodnights.' After he closed their doors, awkward silence filled the hallway between him and those last two bedroom doors. He'd give that more time. However, no longer would he give away his own fulfillment.

Trudging downstairs, he went to where he'd now be sleeping when he came here—the guest room.

Desire stirring in him, he waited for another hour to pass so the kids were good and knocked out, with no "last minute" requests. He finally took his cell phone, and scrolled to the name of the woman who'd brought him back from the sexual dead.

ME

Wyd?

Suddenly, the door knob shook and he shoved the phone

under the covers. Remembering he'd locked the door, in case Arista tried sneaking in, he exhaled his relief.

"Seven," Arista whispered on the other side. "Seven, I know you're up. I saw a light." She jiggled the knob again. "Please, baby, I wanna try." Silence. "Seven." She wrapped on the door softly so as not to disturb the children. "Don't be like this. We don't have to do anything. Let me just explain."

He lay back against the covers and waited for it to be over. No matter how she'd hurt him over the years, he still had love and compassion for her. It had not died completely. Hearing the mother of his children beg wasn't a "win" for him.

Yet, on the other side of that, Sunday had nearly sucked him raw, a promise of what his future could be. There was no going back to obligatory intimacy.

He closed his eyes, and instantly returned to Old Town Lake, the forest surrounding him and morning glory ahead. He was serenaded by the chorus of chirping field crickets, barking American bullfrogs, owls hooting, and mallards fighting in the water. At his side, poised with Earl, stood Sunday.

* * *

Outside the bank president's office, Seven sat in the waiting area and placed three items in the digital cart. Ensuring he'd entered the correct locations, he clicked "submit order." Then he called up Stillwell's and made a reservation for two.

"Seven!" Tom McIlroy, or "Mac," president of Friends of the Delta Savings & Loan, came out and threw open his arms, as if today were payday. "Welcome back! Come on in. It's mighty good to see ya. How was Arkansas?"

"Eye-opening." Seven took a seat.

"I would imagine so. You have had quite an eventful past

two weeks there, sir. Over in Elaine and Helena. Made yourself some new friends, I hear."

Seven chose his words with the strategy the situation required. "I certainly gained some new experiences and knowledge. That's for sure."

"Well, let me start by thankin' you, because the stats you brought us in our soil analyzers and data chips on them Conklin Fields was pure gold! We now know what all her fields can grow, what she's been doin' on 'em, and what *we* can do on 'em!" Mac laughed.

Seven's chest caved in from the weight of regret. They now knew so much about Sunday's land use and value because of his actions.

"It's also my understanding you're in good with maybe two of the Conklin siblings, and they're interested in selling their shares. Genius!" In a victory gesture, Mac swung his clasped hands from one shoulder to the other. "You are a genius, my man! Hell, I heard you even got your pretty self in them woods and gigged for frogs with 'em. Now *that* is what I call bringin' our money on home."

Every word was another boulder falling onto Seven. "And now what's the plan?"

Mac wagged an index finger at him. "For all your good work, the bank knows that prosecutor on your criminal case, and we might be able to work something out so your charges are dropped. I already spoke with Ian and he'll agree. Mighty unfortunate bit of business there. But if you bring the *entire* Conklin property under the bank, I will give you Ian's job. It's mostly Black over in those parts. There should be a Black executive overseeing those loans and accounts. And since you connect with them, that would suit everybody perfectly."

Ian would be punished by Seven taking his place? That thought was immensely gratifying. "So, you would fire Ian and give me his spot?"

Mac's raised eyebrows answered before his mouth did. "No. I didn't say fire him. You'd take his job as head of real estate financing for both the southeast and southwest divisions, and he'd move a little closer to me. He'd be out of your hair, and you wouldn't have to worry about him. Now—"

His blood starting to boil, Seven sat up taller in his seat. "To clarify this, Ian won't suffer any consequences for sleeping with the wife of his colleague? He used his authority as my senior to send me out of town, so he could bang my *wife*. And he'll suffer no consequences?"

And why would he? The entire incident had played out to the bank's benefit. They were closer to acquiring Sunday's property. Their Black bank executive had gained inroads into the Elaine community. And whatever secrets the Adlers wanted to keep hidden from the public, Ian would help them destroy.

"Well, now, Seven, that's between you and him. If he'd had an affair with *you*, let's say, a fellow employee, we'd be having a different conversation. That's a clear conflict of interest. But there's nothing in the rule book about spouses who don't work here." He turned his mouth upside down. "Best I can do is separate the two of ya, and everybody move on. Back to these Conklins—"

"I'm leaving Friends. Effective immediately."

Mac's oversized eyeballs could have been meme-worthy. "What'd you just say?"

"I said 'I quit.' I've already packed my things." For the past two days, Seven had snuck them out in a large gym bag he'd brought under the guise of increasing his workouts, which he had. He wouldn't hang around for the next two weeks for them to act "weird," as his kids often said.

"Well, just hold on a minute." Mac's easy-going façade evaporated. "I've been hearin' about some kinda lottery ticket. That what this is about? You've hit it big, and you think you don't need ta work anymore? Because, tuh, I assure you, that's far from the case. We gave you your career, son. We've done quite a lot for you. You're only over at that country club because of us. They don't just let any ole nig…"

Seven leaned forward, his heart suspended, ears canceling out every other noise in wait for the rest.

Mac's brain must have labored so hard for his next words that the inner turbulence shook his lips. "They don't just allow any ole person to come in off the street."

At this point, the "n word" was as good as spoken. It still reverberated behind Mac's eyes and came out in his arrogance that expected Seven to be the humble Negro.

"'*Gave* me'? You've 'done for me'? *Son?*" Thinking of his degrees from Northwestern, Seven had to come back to himself. "I'm curious to know, Mac, why *wasn't* a Black person in charge of the southeastern division?"

"For the same reason you've never cared. Who wants to be assigned to the Delta? Ian has always been the most willing man. Talented Black finance folks like yourself are more interested in the wealthier Black accounts, in the larger cities—Houston, Austin, Tulsa, Jackson—whereas the Delta is smaller and more…economically challenged."

Seven couldn't fight him on that one. He was guilty as charged. Returning to the rural South brought up in accomplished Blacks the "Post Traumatic Slave Syndrome" Joy DeGruy wrote about, and they'd rather move on from.

Seven assessed how much truth he should speak. "Where guys like Ian can prey on them," Seven added, "and bleed them bone dry. Where good ole boys like Strom Adler can run a nepotism mill, so white kids get the best jobs and Black kids are shuttled away from the opportunities."

And that was putting it lightly. However, Seven kept a lid on most of it, out of fear he'd say something to trigger Adler retaliating against the people of the Delta.

"Now, now, Hardcastle, we don't need to resort to that kinda talk," Mac added. "It would be wise to leave Mr. Adler's name out of such mean-spirited conversation. I don't know what bit you, or what they told you over there. But you've never talked like this before. You've always been very reliable, an excellent performer. I must say, Mr. Adler will be disappointed if you refuse this role. He personally requested you for the job." Mac leaned against his desk with a "danger ahead" sign in his squinting eyes. "Don't be no fool. You could do a lot of good for them Black folks over there. Or either you could find yourself in a lot of trouble."

Seven recalled what his mother had told him back in Helena, about Friends's involvement in an event that was so abhorrent Seven had gone to the bathroom and vomited.

"This bank could have done good for them whether I was here or not. I've made up my mind. Of course, I expect my stock options, vested stocks, retirement, vacation pay, and bonuses to all be transferred to me without reduction."

"Seven, you stay here, and we will certainly make it worth your while. If you did indeed win the lottery, and you park your winnings here, you will be rewarded very handsomely."

Like a butterfly that floated into his mind from nowhere, Sunday was suddenly standing in front of him again, by the fire, in nothing but a cowboy hat and his ruined boots. A living, breathing paradox, her toughness and softness conjured a grin in him now. If Seven was decided as the winner, he knew exactly where he planned to park his money.

"I've already been rewarded. *Beautifully.* I'll see myself out. Merry Christmas, Mac."

Twenty-Four

WE ARE STILL BLESSED

SUNDAY

"Let's put this gold here, and put the blue over there." Director Peady spoke into her megaphone and instructed her crew for the all-important Christmas trees. "Every window on Main Street should have fake candles and Black angels! And where are my big brown angels at? They should have been here already! Horses! Who's bringin' my horses?"

Sunday and her workers rolled their eyes while hauling the ski ball machine out of the trucks and setting them up on the street. "Somebody take that thing away from her."

"Let me see you take it." Mama Piggee dared her from the food booths. "I swear that chile was born to be a show director or some kind of Academy Awards producer."

"Next thing ya know, we gon be puttin' on Elaine's Got Talent," Sunday's mother added.

"Elaine *do* got talent." Mama Piggee laughed. "How long's it been since we had a talent show? We can do it next spring. And invite the kids from Snow Lake, Helena, Memphis, and Stuttgart. We can have us a Delta's Got Talent. Now that we

237

got us a rich gal around here, we can actually get them some-thin' nice for a prize." Mama Piggee winked at the others and returned her attention to Sunday. "Why you so quiet?"

"I'm not."

"I'm not," Nookie mocked his sister. "She's quiet because she mixed up our lottery tickets! You'll never live that down."

"If I hadn't bumped him, the ticket would be one hundred percent his. Right now, we've got a shot because of me."

"Where else did you bump him besides the Kwik Stop?" Mama Piggee licked her lips jokingly and eyed the others.

"I don't wanna know," Sunday's mother complained.

"Well, I do," Mama Piggee shot back. "How's his bumpin'? Is it any good?"

Sunday almost blurted that they hadn't, but if she confessed that, the others would make it their business to keep checking until she reported otherwise.

"Nookie," Peady blared his name through her megaphone, "one angel goes at the front of Main Street and the other goes right in the middle. I wanna see that first one from 44."

Their little brother cracked his knuckles, apparently tempted to crack her. "Why don't you go put it over there then?"

"Whewee, whose town is this here?" Mother Fordham stepped out of Principal Overton's truck, and slapped her hands together. Peering up and down the street, gob-smacked, she seemed to be meeting a different Elaine. "This the prettiest I ever seen us! Where y'all get all this stuff?"

"We got some help from a secret Santa," Sunday answered.

"He ain' no secret," Mama said.

Sunday sucked her teeth. "It was a nice gesture, anyhow. He didn't have to help us."

Mother Fordham admired the "Mustang Wonderland" they were creating, so named for the old Elaine High School mascot, its colors royal blue and gold. The Christmas parade would travel from the old high school gymnasium where Vanessa, William, Sunday, Peady, and their parents had graduated. Their younger sister, London, was in the final graduating class.

"You talkin' 'bout that Hardcastle man?" Mother Fordham asked. "He comin' back? I think I done learnt somethin'."

"She don't know if he comin' back." Sunday's mother chewed her snuff. "Or if he went back to that wife o' his and that bank."

"Mama, you the one who told me to be nice to him."

"I told you to lose the attitude, not lose ya mind. When I said that, he was just the man from the bank, befo' your eyes started crossin'."

"It's all right, Sunday." Mama Piggee steered back to the positive. "He do seem like he ain' too bad. His pancakes fa sho' licked yorn. And your face is a wonder, baby girl. Imma really pray he do right by you, or me and Obie, we goin' to get him," Marleen said, referring to Principal Overton.

Sunday chuckled. "I appreciate you, Miss Marleen, but that won't be necessary. I'm good eitha way. Man or no man. I ain' never needed a man to bring me joy, and I won't start lookin' for none in a man now."

"I know that's right. But I'm still sendin' a prayer to ya daddy anyway, 'cause good lovin' from the right man pours honey in the right places, and you deserve all the honey, baby."

Sunday was feeling the sweetness already but she kept it hidden in her belly. "From your lips to the ancestors' ears."

"Amen." Marleen smacked a kiss on Sunday's jaw. "I'll see ya tomorra mornin'. We havin' us an Elaine Day this weekend."

"And it'll be the best we've ever had! Money o' no money," somebody else chimed.

Before they rode off from Main Street and back to the farm, Sunday peered out the window of their truck a final time while Nook drove.

Downtown Elaine was a postcard, sprinkled with trees from the forest, wrapped with twinkling lights, and guarded by golden mustang horses lining the streets, positioned so they appeared to roam among the Christmas trees. Lovely, quiet, quaint, Elaine was a Christmas carol in Arkansas, its hymn quiet as a whisper, sung by a choir for a world that didn't hear them.

If only her daddy and Nessa could have seen this.

Sunday lifted her phone and snapped a picture worthy of being forwarded.

ME

Look at what you did.

Since the phone reception often took its sweet time, the photo would probably take forever to be 'delivered'. She didn't want to wish too hard, but anticipation brewed in her chest, steamed by hope that he'd make it back for them to continue what they'd started.

Inside the house, Sunday nearly levitated from the floor.

"Oh, good grief." Mama snickered, but even she couldn't resist stopping at the table and sniffing.

A giant Christmas bouquet had overtaken their little kitchen table, full of cranberries, cinnamon sticks, pine cones, and red and white roses. The scent of Christmas spread throughout the house.

"Auntie, is those from the Flyin' Comb man who was gettin' yo booty?" Tori dipped her head bashfully, but she wasn't so bashful that she couldn't ask.

Sunday's mother glared at Sunday. "What is yo' problem? When did she see that?"

"Go to bed, nosey!" Sunday opened up the note.

No reason. Just because.

As long as Earl's not on you next time, I can't wait to see you again.

With the note pressed to her chest, Sunday spun away from Mama and hurried to the first empty room she could find. Closing the bathroom door and locking it behind her, she reread the words. Several more times. And imagined his voice saying it in her ear. They hadn't spoken over the phone since he left a few days ago, and Lord only knew what those days must've been like for him and his children. Despite it all, he'd made time to send this.

ME

> They're stunning. Maybe I'll leave Earl home next time.

* * *

SEVEN

The limousine driver called to tell him they were arriving, and Seven walked outside Stillwell's. As soon as the car stopped, he opened her door himself and extended his hand to help her step out. His sixteen-year-old mad-dogged him, and seemed to evaluate if she would join him.

"Come on, Ash, Christmas is coming so you can't do the silent treatment forever."

"Oh, I can. I'll text you my list." She glared at him from behind her bouquet of roses he'd had delivered to her at school. "Since you wanna be an absentee dad now anyway, we can do it all via text and email."

"What about your permission slips, last-minute funding

emergencies, or you sprain your ankle in dance again and need to be run to the doctor, or if you break up with one of your friends and you don't want your mom to know she was right so you need me to talk to?"

Wrinkling her nose, she gave him the evil eye.

He mocked her and gave it back. "Yeah. Tradeoffs."

Inside, he took her coat, and held out her chair. Yes, his child was absolutely high-maintenance, and he performed these acts so she would stay that way.

"How's school going?"

"Oh, *now* you care?"

"Wait. You mean you needed adult supervision while I was gone? 'Cause let you tell it, you're grown."

Nobody could roll their neck like Ashlyn. "Well, if I do need some, I know where *not* to look. I won't start on CNN. You and your wife just out here having a good ole time."

So she had probably inherited some of his humor. Once they'd ordered their four courses, she proceeded to serve him the third degree for the first few minutes, no matter what he asked.

"Did you really have to go *live?*"

"No, I didn't have to, but it felt good. I wasn't thinking about you guys, though, and how embarrassed you'd be."

"Dad, my classmates kept talking about...you and your junk for days. In the cafeteria, they were making jokes about my parents' bedroom. How Mom was dressed in leather like a hooker, and how you were all mad..." She stopped and stared at the ceiling so her tears could defy gravity. Gravity won.

For both of them.

"Baby girl, I'm so sorry."

"And you weren't even here. You weren't *here!*" That fury balled into her fist against the table. "So, I couldn't look at you, and be mad at you to your face. How could you do that to us? I'm not saying Mom didn't have it coming. She definitely did. But that was, like, between the two of *you*. Why did you have to be out here ruining *our* lives?"

He nodded. "Everything you say is valid. I should have moved different. It caught me off guard. I wasn't ready, and everything I did after that was not at all from my rational dad mind. Not even close. I came unhinged. It was unacceptable, and I'm sorry for what you had to go through as a result of mine and your mother's actions."

She sipped her sparkling water. "I'm glad you whooped the skin off him, though. He didn't look too good when somebody took a video of him in his yard and posted it on social. He was limpin', so good job there."

For the sake of his criminal case, and because Seven didn't know who was around, he didn't acknowledge the violence. "Have things gotten better at school? Hopefully, the car picking you up helped."

"It was a nice start, but I'm still experiencing emotional trauma." She folded her hands, making it clear she came to negotiate. "It'll take some more apology behavior for us to get past this."

Even though she was Arista's child, those occasional flashes of himself in her made him cringe. "What? You need a new tablet for class or to get your hair done or a new skirt or something?"

"Yeah, ha, that's funny, Dad. No, I was thinking we might go look at some cars. Mustangs, Challengers, Teslas."

"Tesla drivers have Tesla grades and Tesla SAT scores. What kind of car you plan on qualifying for?"

"The one for aggrieved children of parents who give us bad news over the holidays."

"It's only been two weeks out of an entire semester."

"Those two weeks are over exam time, which is the most crucial part of the semester." With high drama, she grabbed her napkin and dabbed at fake tears. That part of her was all

Arista. "And whew, chile, is that rough. So upsetting and devastating how you came back and told us you and Mom are getting a divorce. These next few months will be so hard for me to manage at pickup and drop-off. A few of my dance teammates are still cackling."

"This is where you develop character. Life often takes a wrong turn, and you won't get a car or a gift every time it does."

"But those will be situations I get myself into. Not situations forced on me by my parents who don't know how to act."

Ash sipped her soda and studied her dad, with a gleam in her eye. Seven dropped his head and laughed. Deep down, her skills filled him with pride.

"Baby, that was good, but your *worst* problems will sometimes come from somebody else's screwups. Just know that." He sighed. "All that said, once I see grades and tests, we can go look. *Look* only. I'm not making—"

She almost knocked over her chair when she jumped up. "Thank you, Daddy!"

With her kissing him on the cheek repeatedly, how could he not do it now?

"Ash Bear...Ash...I need something from you, too."

She returned to her seat and resumed her adult role. "I'm listening."

"Since your mom and I are separating, I will be coordinating with you guys' schedules so I can have more time for things I enjoy, too. I might even start my own real estate gig, or I was thinking about a savings and loan of my own. I've been wanting a business for some years with other Black professionals."

"That's cool, Dad." Her eyes lit up and she was fully engaged, leaning over her soda.

"You think so?"

"Yeah, we only have like one Black-owned bank around here, so that's a good thing. We need to see more of that."

"I'm glad you approve." He took a quick moment for the next priority. "Our family time will look different, though, Ash. Your mom and I won't be going to parties, or having get-togethers, or the same friends. I won't be at all the family functions on her side. I may show up sometimes to support you guys, but not all the time. I'm looking for my own place that's close, so you can come whenever you feel like it. But there will be two separate households in a few weeks. I'm at the house with you all now, because it's still my home and you're my family."

The light dimmed on her face, reality being a shade drawn over her window. "I get it, Dad. It is what it is, I guess." She stopped swirling her straw in her glass, set her elbows on the table and buried her face in her sweater sleeves instead of her napkin, wiping away real tears now. "This is just a lot."

"I know. It's a lot for me, too. But you mean the world to me. That will not change."

"Does this mean you'll start messing with somebody else, too?" She stared at him head on. "You're bringing another woman to our house? Is that why you were in Arkansas?"

"I was originally sent to Arkansas for work." He swallowed his lighter fluid for Ian, all over again. "But while I was there, I did meet a lady."

"So while Mom was cheating, you were cheating, too?" In frustration, she smacked the table.

"No!" He shut down her speculation with his index finger. "It's the opposite, Ash. I stayed loyal to your mother, in spite of my issues with her. I will not discuss the details of our marriage with you, but I went to Arkansas and handled my business." He also wouldn't crap on her mom for conspiring with Ian, regardless of how that burned. While I was there, I met *many* people in a very special Black town. I learned we actually had ancestors there, and it just so happens to have a fierce, bold woman who's a farmer with her own family business. She lives close to a lake you just need to see. She's got wooden cabins on her property, and—"

"You're gonna be dating her?"

Why did he feel like he was the child now, having to explain himself? She certainly was coming at him like the parent.

"I don't know what'll happen. I still need to unpack what went down between me and your mom, so I won't put too many expectations on the future. But I did want to clear the air for all of us first. Make sure we were good. I'm being transparent with you, Ash. Like the adult you are becoming. Things will be different in the new year. New for everybody. It doesn't mean our relationship changes, just how we do it."

He reached over and thumbed the last few tears from her cheek, the way he did for her early gymnastics meets when she didn't place.

"You've been a good daddy. I want you to be happy, too. So I guess I can't be selfish and say I don't want anybody else to have you because you're mine. Just, don't be pushing anybody new on us right now."

Seven nodded and opened his hand over the table. "Understood."

"And the next time I call you, you need to answer."

"Yes, ma'am."

She slid her hand in his and he kissed it.

"We are all still blessed, Ash. Even with divorce and some of the pain we'll feel at times, we still have fantastic lives. Going to some of these rural areas in the Delta reminded me. You've got a strong foundation so many kids don't. How many teenagers can pull up here in a limousine, eat a four-course meal, and negotiate with their parent for a car? Remember that, okay? When your brother and sister have their sad moments, remind them. I'm gonna need your help, because they'll take some of their cues from you."

It was her turn to focus her teary eyes on him and nod. "Okay."

"I love you, Ash Bear."

"I love you, too, Daddy. But whoever you love next, just remember I loved you first."

"Yes, ma'am."

She started in on the first course the wait staff had set down. "So we had ancestors in Arkansas? I thought you said our family is from Chicago."

"Yeah, that's what I wanted to talk with you guys about." Seven thought of everything he'd coerced his mother to disclose at the dinner table last weekend in Helena.

"You said the town is special. What's special about a place where slavery happened?"

"A lot of strong people stood up for themselves a hundred years ago and did a brave thing. The sad part is history has hidden it. Now, they need help because Arkansas pretends they don't exist. I plan on helping them with my real estate and tech savings and loan."

Ash made some foreign gesture at him that he hadn't learned yet. He figured it must've been good since she smiled between bites. "My daddy's gonna own a bank? That is ssssick!"

While he told her about his idea, his phone buzzed. He waited until later, once Ash started scrolling her phone, before he stole a peek at his. Sunday's name did things to him that almost had him rolling his eyes into his head here and now.

He opened her message, and was slightly disappointed. He'd hoped for a different kind of photo. The kind with her legs open in the rocking chair by the fire. But he'd settle for one of the prettiest towns he'd ever seen.

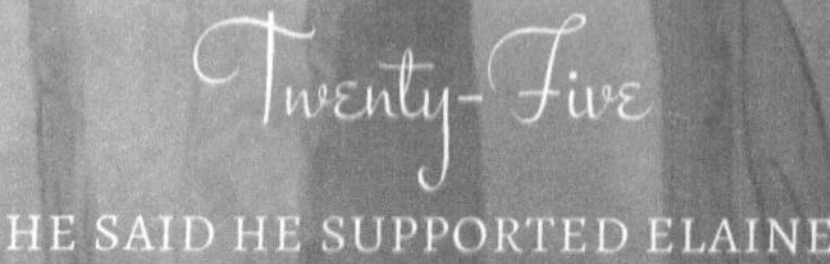

Twenty-Five

HE SAID HE SUPPORTED ELAINE

SUNDAY

This morning, the long list of to-do's didn't jolt Sunday from sleep. Nor worries of how she'd meet bills, how creative she could get with her sob story, or what hustle she'd have to drive over to Mississippi and work so the children could afford one of their field trips and not be embarrassed at school. Rather, today, she woke up to the smell of Christmas. Fragrant and sweet, her bouquet summoned her from her bed in the converted garage.

A few minutes longer, she snuggled under the bed covers. *No reason. Just because.*

On a cloud, she drifted into the house and the moment she entered the kitchen, cinnamon and winter fir took her to the heavenliest of places. The halls breathed joy, instead of hardship. She went for her fragrant bouquet first, not coffee. Just a bit of water in the vase would prolong her giddy moment, and then, she'd come back to reality.

Switching on the spigot, no water came out. She tried it again, and this time, it stubbornly sputtered what could have been mud water. Once she'd filled a glass, particles floated around in filthy liquid that appeared to have arrived straight from the swamps, rather than an aquifer.

"I just got a text from Frank over at the Dollar General." Mama scooted into the kitchen, her face melting. It was clear she had more to say, but hesitated.

"What?" Sunday insisted.

"He was ridin' through town on the way to open the store, and he say Main Street is messed up. The pictures ain't come through my phone, yet. But he say ya might wanna get over there."

Tripping on a floorboard, Sunday was already out the door.

"Sunday, come back in here and put some clothes on!"

Her mother nearly fell down chasing her, and hobbled to the passenger side. She threw the door open and barely managed to jump in before Sunday's house slipper hit the gas.

"Now, Sun, whatever it is, we'll be all right. It ain't the end of the world, okay?"

"Mama, just…" She sped down the dirt road, over the field as fast as Daddy's old engine would take her, cutting corners so hard she skidded into some of her growing peas.

"Slow down, Sun!" Though she'd managed to strap on her seatbelt, Mama held onto the dash so she wasn't tossed around the passenger seat.

"C'mon, c'mon…" Sunday talked to their creaky gate. The tires spun the moment it opened wide enough, and she flew the two-and-a-half miles from her fields down Highway 44 to the town square.

"Oh, my Lord." Mama spoke for them both.

The wreckage was so widespread she couldn't turn onto Main Street, and instead, needed to park on the side of the highway.

"My God, how did this happen?" one of the neighbors walked from down the residential area.

Peady's Black wooden, life-sized angels were splashed with red paint. At the base of one angel were sprayed the words, "Niggers ain't angels."

The wire mustang horses were spray-painted red, and the lights cut up and pulled apart. Booths and games smelled of feces.

"Ugh!" One neighbor backed away from a game booth.

Sunday went to see it, and instantly cringed, backing away. It wreaked of urine and animal manure.

"How come nobody heard this happenin'?" Sunday's mother asked the others.

"How could they?" somebody else asked. "This the kinda stuff that don't make no noise. Ain't nothin' smashed or beat down, so they didn't use no bats or sticks or no loud weapons. All this here is paint mostly. Crap. Trash. Stuff they could just throw on there without makin' noise. They coulda snuck over here for ten, fifteen good minutes with no lights, and been gone befo' somebody noticed."

"That's 'cause they knew if one of us had heard 'em, their behinds woulda been beaten raw," Mama replied.

Elaine's Black residential community started just two blocks away from Main Street, so she was correct. These vandals had to know that too much noise would start a war.

"Who do you think it was?" Sunday rummaged through the desecration, assessing what could be salvaged. Some of it could be repainted, but many of the manure-filled gaming booths would be ruined once hosed down with water. Even then, Sunday wasn't sure the stench would disappear. And would she touch them or let the children and parents do so?

Her mother's firm hand scrubbed Sunday's back.

"Let's just cancel it," Sunday muttered. "This is too much to clean up in two days."

Mama swung her head hard. "We can still have somethin' small. Even if it's just a cookout. It don't have to be nothin' big and fancy. Elaine Day is for Elaine. Nothin' else."

"Any idea who coulda done this or why? Was there some kind of argument recently, or a fallout somewhere?" one of the Elaine police deputies asked a while later.

Sunday had her suspicions. "They had to come from Helena."

"How can you be certain?" the officer asked.

"It's always Helena. Right as they see us doin' somethin' big, here they come, tryin' to keep Elaine under their boot."

The officer raised an eyebrow. "I'm afraid we'll need harder information than that."

Sunday muttered to her mother, out of the officer's earshot. "You can't convince me it wasn't one of them Adlers."

Sunday's phone rang since the reception was much better here in town than out in her fields. One of her workers appeared in the caller ID.

"Hey, Sunday, you might wanna hurry on here to the lake." He struggled to breathe, his words stumbling over each other. "We came to get the new breedin' frogs for the tents, and they skin ain' lookin' right. Plus, they ain' jumpin' like bullfrogs s'pose to."

She no longer had the energy to run for the truck again. The world spun around her. It weighed too much now for her head and shoulders to keep carrying the load. Somebody else had to drive her this time. On the way back to the farm, she scrolled for one number. He had offered to help. She didn't know how he would, but he'd said he supported Elaine.

* * *

SEVEN

Raegan passed Seven a stocking after she stuffed it with her prank gift, and he hung it over the fireplace. The mood had certainly fallen from last year. The laughs, jokes, and burn-clapbacks from every other year had fizzled into awkward conversation.

"Seven, babe, you want me to spike up your eggnog?" Arista asked, touching him on his back when she brought the tray of mugs in the room.

Everyone else grabbed theirs, and he did so as well, without looking at her. "No, thanks."

"You know you always like a little rum in your drink."

"Not tonight." He would keep a clear head.

In his pocket, his phone vibrated again. But he'd been with the kids nonstop all day. He'd allowed them to stay home from school so they could have personal time after the big announcement.

The situation between him and Arista had never been so intense. Now, he guarded every one of his moves, especially when he received a text. If he took his phone out, she would jump up and play innocent to see who was texting. Then, he'd have to snap at her to mind her business, and the kids weren't used to that kind of conflict between them. He was working to maintain as chill a vibe as possible, for Dillon in particular. Seven's girls were over their mother's games, but not the youngest.

He snuck off to the bathroom while they flipped through a streaming service for the next corny Christmas movie. One peek at Sunday's name, and his sweats were already on the rise.

SC

Hey, Bank Man. We got a prob. Elaine Day trashed.

What? The beautiful setting she'd texted him yesterday evening was the stuff storybooks were written on. In the photos popping across his phone screen now, he hardly recognized the place. Was that paint? And was that brown stuff...? He hated to think it. But the photo that triggered him most had started with the "N" word.

ME

Baby girl, who did this? Will come back asap.

With him supporting his children and being present for them, he calculated how soon "asap" could be.

SC

U got connects w Adler & at Friends. Help find who did it.

Seven nearly dropped the phone as more photos came through. In the swamp lay dead frogs. Either they were dead or close to it, from their sickly pale skin. Who would do something so foul?

SC

Pesticides. Want my own investigation.
Help?

The door-knock almost knocked him from his bones. "Dad?" Dillon called out from the other side. "Movie's ready. The cookies cooled off. Ray said if you don't hurry up, she's changing it because she doesn't want to see *Friday After Next* anyway."

"She's not changing a thing! I'm coming."

Sunday's question still lingered, unanswered. A woman whose electricity powered up all of Elaine must have charged Texas, too, because Seven's thoughts had summoned her call.

Quickly, he flushed the toilet and murmured, "Hey—"

"Oh, you picked up! I didn't know if you'd gotten my—"

"I can't talk right now. Gotta call you in the morning. Those photos are sick. We'll find whoever did that mess and lock them *under* the jail."

"Do you have friends who deal with vandalism? An insurance person who can tell us what to do?" Distraught, heavy sighs came out with every other word, and Sunday sounded like a Monday.

"Seven!" Arista stood at the door now. "Babe, we're waiting for you. Are you all right in there? The chili didn't agree with your stomach?"

He pressed the receiver to his chest. "Just give me a minute. I'm almost done." He flushed the toilet again, feeling like a damn fool for having to sneak. "I'll see what I can think of. I'll get there soon."

"Will that be tomorrow? You're gonna be here for Elaine Day?"

The toilet was almost done flushing. What was he doing? This weekend had to be for his children. As far as they were concerned, he still belonged solely to them. He would be an idiot to leave them for somebody he'd known less than three weeks.

"In a few days," he whispered. "See you soon." He timed his conversation to the final swish of the toilet. With Christmas tree pine needles clawing his chest, he had to cut off the call.

He opened the door, and every set of eyes waited expectantly for his next move.

What *was* Seven's next move? How often had he done this over the years—capitulated to Arista's version of what their family should be every single time?

Troubled and disturbed, he couldn't return to the sofa, or to the way things used to be, and stared at his family from the archway.

His Sun Ray took notice and sat up. "Daddy, what's happening for you?"

How often had *he* asked *them* that?

Rather than respond, he took out his phone and showed Raegan the photos Sunday had texted him.

"The people I met in the town I visited for work have been hurt. Vandals are trying to stop them from celebrating Elaine Day."

"We'll say a prayer for them this weekend at church." Arista sipped her wine, and tucked her feet under her.

"That's horrible." Raegan scrolled the pictures. Her mouth dropped the moment she glimpsed the Black life-sized angels and the quote with the "N" word.

Seven's finger stopped the scroll before she swiped too far back. He hadn't yet deleted his pics he'd sent to Arista a couple of weeks ago.

"This is where you were? What you were talking about on the phone?" Raegan asked.

"Yeah. They have a Christmas parade every year to celebrate their history. The town dates back to the early 1900s, and in 1919, something really terrible popped off there. They've never risen above that because their state doesn't do anything to help them."

Seven caught Ash's attention from across the living room in hopes she would jump on. Whatever happened next needed to be *the kids'* idea.

Ash got up and came over to scroll. "What's the bad thing that happened?"

Good job, Ash.

"That's what I want to talk to you guys about. There's something important you all need to know about our family's history, and our ancestors. Mom told me while we were in Arkansas."

"Seven," Arista interrupted, "it's Christmas and you

should wait for all that. This is probably a good Black History month lesson."

"What are ancestors?" Dillon asked.

"Okay, let's start the movie, you guys." Their mother tried redirecting them.

"They're our dead relatives who gave birth to our grandparents and great-grandparents a long time ago." Raegan pulled out her phone and checked. "Elaine still hasn't found the people who did this. Dad, this is super not okay. Why don't we go help them?"

"That's not a good idea, Ray." Their mother tightened her mouth and silently threatened Seven with payback for starting this. "This has been a rough week for us, too, and your dad is finally back with us. We're having our own time together. Besides, that town doesn't sound very safe for you guys to visit until you're older."

"Wait, Mom." Raegan piped up. "Are you saying we're not mature enough to handle that? And are you saying we're not exposed to racism here in *Texas?* Besides, we're not doing anything but sitting here watching Christmas movies while this Black town can't enjoy *their* Christmas."

Arista would certainly get her revenge on him now. "You're very smart and mature, baby, but your daddy and I worked hard to protect you guys from poverty and racism. Now he wants to take you to the heart of it? No. If he thinks he's driving you across the state line and putting you in danger, my lawyer will file a motion for sole custody first thing in the morning. And I will call the police and report that he's absconded with you all."

It's how she had grown to be since she'd learned she was pregnant with Dillon—using the children to get things done her way. After she agreed to have him, she'd begun acting as if she was the sacrificial lamb who was owed for keeping a third child she hadn't wanted. Everything in the house had needed to be on her terms, because in her eyes, her career had suffered for another kid. Never mind the global travel, fun and sense of adventure Seven had sacrificed for her to elevate professionally. Over time, he'd lost interest.

"So this is how it'll be, Ri? You dictating our lives to us? You always being the final decider? Any little disagreement and you call your lawyer?"

Arista sat back and eyed him over her wine. "This is how *you* wanted it, Seven. Divorce and lawyers and visitation schedules...doesn't feel too good, does it?"

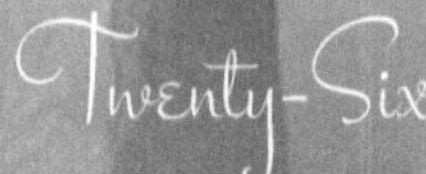

Twenty-Six

THE STUFF STORYBOOKS WERE WRITTEN ON

SUNDAY

"Everybody, bow your heads," Pastor Thompson instructed them. "Dear Heavenly Father, thank you for bringin' us all together, despite every enemy who tries to attack. None of them is mightier than you."

"Amen," Vertreese Conklin murmured next to her daughter.

Her daughter's eyes were not closed. Sunday was in no mood for yet another sorrowful prayer, or to let another 'amen' roll off her lips and into deaf skies. She sought justice. If the One up above was truly so mighty, why was Elaine never protected?

A mile up the road, she'd had to burn her dead frogs, set up holding tents to observe and nurse the sick ones, and kill those that were too frail to live. She hadn't found them all. Her workers had started putting down pesticide-consuming mulch to absorb the chemicals poured in the swamps. Even then, contaminated parts of the land might not be healthy for her frogs for the next two to three years.

She couldn't bring herself to bow her head out of some misplaced loyalty to a higher power that was never loyal to them.

"You hear back from your man?" Marleen asked.

"Yeah, where's he at?" Nook rolled his eyes. "He was out here talkin' about he wants to help Elaine. He's just another punk who shows up on his own time. When it's somethin' in it for him."

"He said our house would be paid for, free and clear. And he came to the fields and helped us, Nook."

"And you believed him? That's what they all do. They make all these promises about what they'll do. Push their 'help' on us so they can take pictures for their social media. News reporters, newspapers, politicians, celebrities, historians, everybody wanna come to Elaine and fake-help and talk good until we actually need help. We don't know what kinda information that man was takin' back to that bank. How do we even know he wasn't involved in this vandalism. How come it didn't happen while he was here?"

"That don't make sense." Sunday stopped herself from reminding him that he and Peady had allowed outsiders onto their land before she ever had. A back-and-forth exchange would only infuriate them both. Besides, for a moment anyway, Seven seemed to mean what he said. He'd showed up with intention, and the energy behind it had been hopeful... dare she think it, joy-filled.

The Elaine Day parade consisted of the Marvell-Elaine Mustangs old marching band, the Black dance team from Helena, youth choirs from Clarksdale, Pine Bluff, and Memphis. The floats had been locked in the high school, so they were safe. But there were no games or decorations. The celebration went on, even if Elaine's intruders had escaped without accountability once again. Like her mother had said, Elaine Day was for Elaine, and nobody or nothing else.

They hadn't been able to parade down Main Street, since much of the mess remained. The last couple of days, they'd focused on salvaging what was left of the parade. They hadn't had time yet to gather the destroyed items and transport them to a junkyard or incinerator. Rather than having it on Main Street among the old shops, they paraded down College Avenue in front of the high school.

Miss Marleen rubbed Sunday. "It's all right, baby. We doin' good. It coulda been worse."

That refrain was as reassuring as mud Sunday couldn't stop spinning her tires in. Black folks always had to nickel and dime for a little bit of joy out of the Benjamin Franklins they paid in upheaval.

"I'll see y'all." Sunday headed for her truck. "I've got work to do."

"Hold up, Sun." Peady tapped her arm and pointed down the tiny street.

"What?" Sunday snapped.

Coming down the highway, a large caravan of headlights illuminated the dark roads. A line of trucks turned onto College Avenue leading to the high school. In front of them all, a sleek, shiny black F-150 led the way. Trailing behind it were several wide flatbed trucks transporting scores of bare Christmas trees and decorations.

Peady's hand flew to her chest.

The moment he stepped out, Tori left her friends and her legs couldn't race toward him fast enough. "Flying Comb man!" Flinging her arms around him, she jumped up and down so fast her feet didn't seem to touch the ground. "Can you do my cousins' hair, too, this time? And my friend, Adrienne, wants hers done, too."

Sunday's insides were having the same reaction. But running and jumping on him would have been too...not the kind of thing she did.

Her grandmother called out, "Tori, get back over here. He's not your—"

Bank Man held up a hand. "It's all right, Ms. Conklin. I brought helpers with me this time." He reached and opened the back door. Out stepped younger versions of him.

"Hello," the older one said tentatively. "What's her name again, Daddy? Paris? Is she around here?"

Peady walked forward carrying her daughter, Sienna. "Hello. I'm Paris, but you can call me Peady."

"I'm Ashlyn, but people call me Ash. My dad showed me the pictures of what happened to your decorations. But don't worry. We're going to make it all like Christmas again. We hired a decorator person, too, to help you get ready for your Boots N' Tiaras ball."

The other mini-Seven extended her hand to Peady. "I'm Raegan. People call me Ray, and I looked up some Ring cameras and security systems you can hide in secret areas so the town can see what's happening and who's doing bad stuff."

"There's an independent investigator coming. He'll look into who bought all that paint and would have had access to that much manure," Seven added. "That way, the police can submit any evidence we find to the Phillips County prosecutor."

"Yeah, and if the prosecutor doesn't do his job, we'll blast them on socials, too," Ash said.

Seven side-bumped her. "We'll talk with the mayor first, though, and the locals about whether that's safe for Elaine. There's a lot of racial tension here in Arkansas. These residents have jobs to hold down and customers to keep. We don't want to make things hard for them or cause bad blood."

Ash nodded like they'd talked about it on the ride in and she was remembering. "Right."

The third mini shoved his hands in his coat pockets, clearly more reserved than his sisters. "I'm Dillon, and I'll be helping the lady with frogs? I've never heard of a frog farm. How do you frog farms?" He shook his head. "I mean, how do you farm frogs?"

His dad squeezed his shoulder, and the people around them chuckled.

Sunday's mother tapped Reggie and murmured something to him. He then went over and offered a fist pound.

"The name's Reg, my guy. I'll take you out there and show you in the mornin'. It'll be real early, though."

"How early?" Dillon's eyebrows reached for his hairline and the adults couldn't stop cackling.

"Early, bro."

"Can I hold your baby?" Ash asked Peady. "She's so precious. What's her name?"

"Sienna." Peady looked at her two-year-old. "You wanna meet Ash, baby girl?"

Ash opened her arms, and little CiCi hesitated a few moments, checking with her mama that this new person was safe. Then, she leaned forward and fell into Ash's arms.

Vanessa's four-year-old daughter, Olivia, went into Raegan's arms.

"Get on over there."

Sunday peered next to her and found Miss Marleen wide-eyed, staring at the truckloads of Christmas trees and decorations.

"He's earned it," she finished.

Sunday didn't know how. How did a girl so used to striving and fighting for every little thing simply step forward and accept the blessing, no strings attached? Without suspicion. Without her gun.

Seven's eyes found hers. Rather than the lust from two weeks ago, tonight, they poured hope and promise into her that may have generated stars in her belly. He refrained from joining her, only offering her a respectful nod from where he stood. Sunday returned it. He shifted his attention back to Peady and the mayor to discuss arrangements for the Christmas trees. Sunday understood. His children were present.

"Them's sho gon' be some good pancakes y'all whip up next time y'all get back in that there kitchen, babaaay," Marleen sang under her breath.

"Mmhm," Sunday's mama chimed. "That griddle gon' be hot."

"Greasy," Marleen added.

"Bacon and fat meat gon' be everywhere. Y'all ain' greasin' down the lodge neither. Go bump somewhere else."

Sunday stood openly embarrassed. Her people had never discussed her sex life nor what she did when she had to drive over to Mississippi. But this was different. Nothing else had ever held meaning.

"Y'all nasty," Nook complained, sucking on a toothpick.

"I know you ain't, when you only wanted to win the lottery so you could pay to have kids," his mother shot back.

"Nook, will you help Peady with those trees?" Sunday instructed him to change the subject. "Reggie, go over to the house and get some cabins ready. Make sure they're in order. Fresh sheets, fragrance, clean towels, clean showers and facilities, you know the drill."

"Yes, ma'am." Reggie fished the keys from his pocket, jumped behind the steering wheel of his grandfather's truck and slid down the window. "Big D, you wanna come? We'll see if we've got enough room for you to have your own cabin."

Dillon's eyes practically fell from his head at the sight of a thirteen-year-old doing such adult things. "My own? I won't have to share like at camp?"

Sunday sensed anxiety rising in Seven, his jaw clamped, nerves in his neck twitching.

"Be careful out there, Reg," Sunday called out. "No showboatin'. Straight to the farm, please. No detours. Easy on the gas."

"Yes, ma'am."

Across tiny residential College Avenue, Sunday read her own question on her neighbors' faces. Could this finally be the Christmas that redeemed so many others?

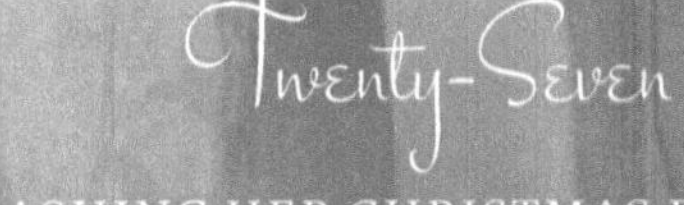

SMASHING HER CHRISTMAS PRESENTS

Sunday

Sunday and the cleanup crew picked up the leftover mess on Main Street. In a separate group, Seven helped with lifting the heavier gaming consoles and booths onto the flatbeds he'd brought. His daughters filmed footage and took photos of the damage, especially the "N" word, and posted to multiple social media sites, something Sunday had little time for. But she was realizing how social media had essentially replaced newspapers and the nightly news in terms of spreading the word.

"Hello."

She spun around from tossing trash. Seven's younger daughter stood behind her, hands clasped as if she were doing something she wasn't supposed to be.

"Good evenin'. You're...Raegan, right?"

"Yes, ma'am. I just wanted to meet you." She shot out a hand. "The other folks were saying you're, like, a badass. That you grow all these crops, and you actually raise frogs yourself, and you have this big gun named Earl, and you're a really good shot. That is super sick.

Like, you're not doing girl stuff at all. You're just out here doing your thing and not worried about gender roles, or other people telling you how to act, or what you need to be."

Sunday laughed at that. "Other folks try and tell me how to act all the time."

"They do?"

"Of course. As long as we're Black women, people will treat our lives like theirs to govern—family or otherwise. I just ignore 'em is all. Sometimes, I feel bad. But everybody gets in their feelins every now and then. It's who I am. I don't know how to be anybody else. And I don't quite care to, frankly. One of these days, you'll see that can't anotha soul step into your skin and carry your heart but you. You're the one who'll have to bear the weight of your heart and answer to it before you die."

Raegan shocked Sunday when she very quickly swiped at forming tears. Baby girl was going through something. "Later on, if I see you again, will you take me out and teach me how to shoot? That sounds fun."

"If it's all right with your parents, sure. We can do that."

A throat somewhere cleared, and Raegan and Sunday looked up at a stern-faced Seven eyeballing his child. With his head, he motioned for her to get on.

Her smile turned shy, like she'd been caught. "Bye, Miss Sunday."

"Bye, Miss Raegan."

Seven gave her a chastising side-eye. "What did we talk about on the way here?"

Apparent in their vibe was their playful relationship.

"I was just saying 'hi'."

"You were just being nosy."

The moment his daughter was out of earshot, his eyes flipped the page back to the Sunday hymn.

"What about me?" Sunday grinned. "Am I in trouble, too?"

Without a word, he slid his tongue over his bottom lip, and returned to his own work. Sunday's mind immediately dived to the gutter of where he would put it.

Around eleven, Seven placed his daughters in Miss Marleen's car to be taken to their cabins. While he said goodnight, Marleen came over to Sunday for a last word.

"Y'all ain' even gon' make it to the lodge."

Most of the town had cleared out, and only a few men remained, still taking away the heaviest gaming machines.

"Goodnight, Miss Marleen." Sunday grinned and swept the street while venturing down memory lane, recalling the games she and her own dad played when she was a child.

Before she'd fully made it back from her childhood, she was shoved by a hard object. He pushed her toward the final game booth. Sputtering her laughs out loud, Sunday stretched her arms across the doorway and stopped him from pushing her all the way inside.

"Check it first and see if it's one of the messy ones."

"Already did. Scoped it hours ago. I told the boys to leave this one." With his pelvis, Seven bumped her the rest of the way inside. He swung the bottom door shut, and then snapped the two top doors, closing them into the tight space, outfitted with shelves of stuffed toys.

"How we gon' do it in here?"

He fumbled for her zipper in the dark. "Where there's a will, there's a way."

In the dark, Seven didn't have to fumble for her face, though. His fingers slid underneath her chin as easily as if he'd committed their height difference to memory.

Somebody's loud truck rode down the street, blaring Robert Nighthawk's *Merry Christmas Baby* just as Seven started the slow tease of his tongue across her lip. With

Nighthawk's spicy base guitar in the background, and the harmonica and banjo serving an unmistakable Delta twang, Seven's lick ignited every nerve from the most vulnerable tip of her womanhood right up to her belly button. His mouth was a magnet dangling from her mouth, letting the kiss hang open, like he needed to be reminded of how it felt to do this again.

"Hurry up," she fussed. "Don't do that shit."

"You like this shit."

She did.

He lifted her sweater, shoved down her bra and grabbed a nipple. Sunday wrangled the zipper over his years of longing and dissatisfaction, the full weight of his erection thumping into her palms. Seven covered her hand with his over his manhood that couldn't wait any longer, evidenced by his precum leaking in her fingers. He squeezed out some of it and rubbed it on her nipple, pinching, thumbing it back and forth. Like he'd thought of nothing but this, he tasted her tongue, and kissed Sunday the way chocolate frosting kissed cake. For this sweetness, Sunday pushed her chest out so he could keep massaging. Tasting him back, she let herself fall into the foolishness of not caring what happened after this.

Only, she liked to suck. And bite.

Now it was he who begged softly from his gut for her not to do that. His fingers picked at the button on her jeans that shielded him from her. Sucking while unbuttoning, he shoved them open.

"Take these off." He only removed his mouth from hers to squat as best as he could.

In the cramped space, she lifted a leg and he heaved off her first boot.

"How am I gettin' these back on?" she asked.

"We're not worried about that right now."

She lifted her other leg.

Outside, a loud knock on the booth doors threw them both for a loop.

"Sundie? Hardcastle?" Principal Overton said on the other side of the doors.

Both of them froze, Sunday's leg in mid-air. From the other side, her retired principal tried the doors and Seven suppressed his outburst, holding them closed from inside.

"I know y'all are in there. I seen ya go in. Ain't no other way out. Unless y'all some David Copperfields all of a sudden. Hardcastle, ya truck is still out here."

Several more seconds, and he gave up.

"Fine. Y'all, just be mindful. I suppose I'll see y'all in the mornin'."

They heard the footsteps walking away. Relaxing, Seven moved to her other boot and tugged it off. One leg at a time, twisting and jumping inside a sardine can of space, she maneuvered for him to shove her jeans all the way down.

"Spread your legs," he whispered.

"Spread 'em where?"

"Out."

"That's funny."

In the dark, he lifted one of her legs and he tried squatting, but struggled in the narrow space.

"Yeah," Sunday said. "Looks like you gon' have to get on down there."

He was already on his way down when she clamped his shoulder and shoved him the rest of the way to his knees.

"Don't do that too hard. I won't be good for much else." He threw her leg over his shoulder.

She suddenly felt self-conscious that she'd been working all day. The auntie and farmer twitched to know she was finally doing it with somebody she liked, for the first time in years, and she wasn't ready. She tried to take her leg down, but he held on.

"What?"

"I've been workin' and busy all day. I don't know how I smell," she confessed, incredibly embarrassed now.

"Hold on. Let me see." He shoved his head between her legs, and into all her nakedness.

She burst out giggling when he sniffed, long and hard. He nuzzled his nose deeper into Sunday's row crops and smelled the yield.

"Musty."

The snort-laugh she snorted almost hurt her nostrils.

"Froggy. Like the swamp," he added.

Sunday grabbed onto a shelf to keep her balance, and the entire booth rocked. "This thing's not stable."

"You're strong. Hold it tighter."

With his first taste of her, his soaked tongue on her flesh sent Sunday's back against the wooden boards. She tilted her pelvis up to give him more access. Seven went in with all the motivation of a man who'd lied in bed fantasizing about it. He pressed her pleasure pearl between his two fingers so it bulged out further, and started with soft strokes. But that didn't last long.

As if he wasn't between her thighs deep enough, he threw her other leg over his other shoulder, clawed her butt cheeks and held them up like a bowl of cake batter. Sunday grabbed hold of whatever she could for Seven to shove his face in her bowl and lick until they both rocked.

The sound of his throat swallowing rolled Sunday's eyes upward.

Whatever he hadn't been serving in his bedroom at home, Sunday opened wide and received now. He plugged his tongue into her, and she thrust harder on his face. If the man was hungry, she would make sure he ate. She needed as much of his tongue in her as she could get. Sucking and slurping like this was his first meal in years, Seven met her every buck.

"Mmmpph..." The sexual goddess who'd had plenty couldn't believe that had come out of her.

Holding the wooden shelves together, Sunday rode his face hard until she was good and satisfied that his neck was screwed on tight enough. His tongue too.

Neither of them coming up for air, Seven plunged his tongue down to her asshole, and that final lick shot a flame through the rest of her that squirted liquid fire back on his face.

"Haaaaaah!" Sunday was a cowgirl, riding his face right on to glory, determined to stay on this orgasm and not lose a millisecond of this. Back and forth, she threw her back and he held on, licking his bowl, tongue-screwing her to ecstasy with Sunday squealing all the way into Sunday morning.

"You're a squirter? Why didn't you say somethin'?" He couldn't wipe himself since he was holding her and she was holding the booth together.

"I ain' nevah did that. My bad, yo."

Lips and legs trembling on her way back down, she felt her arms giving out from clinging to the shelf and door latch. Her nerves were still tingly and tender, and Sunday hesitated to move, longing to curl up and go to sleep.

Something in the wooden booth cracked, and one side of the wall caved in. Nearly colliding on her, but he caught it and held it back from falling.

"Look at you, breaking shit. Let me hold it."

"How do I get back in my pants? We don't have enough room."

He laughed. "You're just gonna have to leave like this."

"I beg your pardon."

"Stand against this and push it up. I'll grab the truck and pull around. Just wait."

Sunday took over his spot, but he didn't know how to act, teasing and tickling her when he knew she couldn't fight back.

"Seven, stop. You gon' make me fall!"

"Whoa." He stopped and stared at her in the dark. "What did you call me?"

Self-conscious that she'd slipped up and let out a tiny hint that this could mean more than she wanted to admit, she answered, "Bank Man."

Even in the dark, her eyes had adjusted enough to see his mouth.

"Liar." He took his time backing out while she still held up the booth.

"Hurry up!"

"If I don't leave you here."

A few moments later, his headlights brushed across the door and he drove up as close to the booth as he could. Opening his passenger door wide, he ran in to take over. Sunday collected her things and bolted her naked butt straight into his passenger seat. Moments later, she heard the booth collapse and Seven's boots run around the truck bed before he jumped behind the steering wheel.

"I don't have any more cabins left," she told him on the short ride down 44. "Your children took the rest. They're cute, by the way."

"They're some knuckleheads, but they're my knuckle-heads. So where am I gonna sleep tonight then? It's too late to go all the way to Helena and get a room."

Sunday assessed his backseats. "That looks like good sleepin' right there."

He turned onto her little dirt road and threw his arm over her seat. His face had clearly bathed in her juices, some of them still on his goatee. "You gonna make me sleep back there by myself?"

"You scared of the dark or somethin'?"

He shrugged. "Depends on what I'm doing in it. Or who I'm doing. I did all right in it a few minutes ago."

Inside her gates, they drove down the dirt road that meandered through the fields. She didn't have to give him directions tonight, and noticed how he was growing more intimate with this land as he grew more intimate with her.

"Over there." Sunday pointed in the direction of the area where she'd hemmed him up that first night.

They drove to the perimeter of her fields that met the boundary of the forest. He got out and went to the trailer bed for something. While he was out there, Sunday squeezed herself into his backseat. When he returned, Seven saw she'd left the front seat, and he did a double take. Sunday waited for him in his backseat naked, save for being tucked inside his suede jacket. He couldn't wrestle his boots off fast enough. After wrangling out of his own jeans, bare as the day he was born, he got out again and switched to the back seat.

Large, deep breaths escaping as clouds out in the cold, he may have been exhaling everything he didn't want anymore and inhaling all he was about to partake.

Once he settled between her legs, pressed against her belly was his longing on those nights she'd asked about, lying next to his wife. It was now pressing from the edge of her feminine hairline, over her stomach, and curving slightly, hooking into her left breast. Sunday wrapped her legs around him.

"Is this Negro good?" she asked, motioning to his wood.

"Yeah, he's good. You good?" He replied, clueless.

She remembered he probably didn't think about this if he'd only had one partner for a long time.

"I mean, are you clean? You don't have nothin' after... all that business with ya wife and yo' boss."

"Oh." The outlines of his face in the dark now reflected that he understood. "Right. Yeah, I went and got checked after I found out."

"Good. That's smart."

"You? How 'bout all those men who were on you that day ya found out you won?"

"I just had my annual and everything came back clear. Nobody since then."

"Good."

"Yeah, good."

They kept repeating that word. Though they were talking about their bodies, they may have been symbolically affirming other things. Perhaps that their hearts were safe. And there would be no regrets in the morning.

Was he having a change of heart?

Seven touched a hand to Sunday's face, and what she saw silenced her doubts.

"Your ring is gone," she whispered.

He'd been wearing it as recently as a few days ago when he'd helped her workers with the frogs. Its imprint in his skin now marked how much had unfolded in such a short time. He pulled his attention from her to the empty space on his finger.

"I didn't want to be double-minded." Their noses kissed. "I didn't want *you* to think I was being double-minded." He laid a hand on her chest, a heartbeat away from where his dick was thumping and restless. "Not about this."

Out of the mouth of a true girl dad.

For the warmth and preciousness and protection she didn't want to trust, she snatched her gaze away, and focused it outside, among the trees. A couple of tears escaped anyway.

"I said something? What did I say?"

"No. Nothin'." She shook it off, or tried to, a sliver of her that had opened up and received the possibility from Heaven that men did this kind of thing.

"What is it?" He thumbed her tears, and nudged her face back to his, her eyes back to his. "I don't know what this'll be. I just know I'm feelin' you, Sunday."

Giving in just a smidge, she touched his lips with hers and

kissed his frankness, stroked the waves on his head with the back of her fingers. "Good thing you're not askin' me to marry you tonight."

He smiled at hearing his own words. "I might surprise ya, though, tomorrow."

"Or I might surprise *you* tomorrow."

"You are good with your surprises."

Their next kiss didn't rush. It tarried. Lips hesitant, scared to enter, two very grown adults approached new territory, exploring one another and feeling out themselves. How much did they want to give and how much would they hold back? Not even the darkness could hide Seven may have been nervous and self-aware. He'd been with one person a long time, and Sunday wasn't her.

He edged himself higher over her, and took over Sunday's mouth as if he were making a final decision. Cramped even in his spacious backseat, he wrapped a hand around her throat, tilted it up and tasted the skin along her jawline. Down her neck to the hollow, sensitive skin in the valley above her clavicle, where he sucked. He must have liked what he tasted, since his manhood bobbed on her stomach.

Sunday hadn't necked in some years, and this reminded her of when she was younger.

"Teh heh heh." She had forgotten how ticklish she was.

"Put ya neck back."

"Nah, I'm good." Giggling, she playfully raised a shoulder to block him from sucking.

"All right then." He pushed two fingers into her folds, and found her pleasure point he'd loved on moments ago.

Caught off guard, Sunday sucked in a sharp breath that put an arch in her back and pushed her chest up. He gazed straight in her eyes, studied her nose, her mouth, all while he kneaded her womanly folds that squished from being so wet.

"What you doin'?" She wondered why they weren't getting to it yet.

"Watchin' your face to see what you like."

"Huh? We 'bout to screw. I like screwin'."

He slid his fingers inside her, easing them in her as far as he could, his eyes still focused on hers. Exploring the sweetest parts of Sunday, Seven took his time. As if her pussy was a playground, he circled his fingers inside her, seeming to enjoy the *squish-swish* sounds and feel of her soaked softness. The first few strokes of his fingers in her canal, Sunday was confused and somewhat put off. Normally, she and her partner cut to the chase, eliminating fluff or pointless lies or promises, and got right down to business.

What was this? Why was he dragging this out? Seven kept staring at her, massaging the inside of her.

"Why you movin' slow?"

"You have somewhere to be?"

She couldn't bring herself to look away from a man locking his attention into her. He curled and unfurled his two forefingers repeatedly, in a "come hither" gesture. What was he searching for?

His fingers climbing through her felt good. His eyes digging into her...

...felt good.

He murmured against her temple. "Put your neck back."

So that's what this was about. He'd taken the long way around her objections and belligerence, and his willingness to take the scenic route over her body to come back here...

... felt good.

Sunday's fight oozed out of her with her juices. Relaxing, she let her head fall aside and gave him her neck to lick the hollow, ticklish skin above her clavicle. Her body responded, creaming with lust.

"Hmmm." Her involuntary hum surprised her.

Tasting, savoring, touching, listening, he dragged his fingers at a snail's pace and let them linger in every spot that drew a twitch or sigh from her. As if he'd found a new button that opened a different doorway to her. Impatient at first, Sunday was acclimating to being opened.

She was learning. This wasn't about sex. This was about pleasure. Seven seemed to relish the discovery in that. He was teaching her to relish and not rush.

Sunday grabbed his dick and squeezed, sliding her hand up to thumb his tip. In the dark, she could see his jaw slacken, and his Adam's apple move up and down, swallowing his excitement. He fingered her faster, and she stroked him more intensely.

Her pussy liked it.

Her heart liked it.

He found Sunday's sweet spot, and she gyrated on his hand to make sure his fingers connected with the right buttons on her erogenous playground. She could get with the relishing.

"You're getting hotter." Underneath her, his truck seat was wet with her bodily essentials. "You're coming."

Bringing her to the edge again, he stopped and eased out his fingers.

Stunned, Sunday asked, "What you…?"

He slid her down, and without further hesitation, entered Sunday. Years of his longing filled up every millimeter of her womanhood, stretching every fold.

Softening, gushing, opening, Sunday widened her legs as far as she could, placing a foot on his headrest. In their push, the *swishing* sounds of bodily fluids sprung into action. No air between them, Seven's strokes weren't a transaction. He tipped up her face so her lips could reach his.

"You scared to kiss me?" he breathed.

Yeah, she thought. Because that brought her one step

closer to hoping for the impossible, and setting herself up for inevitable hurt.

Not used to this, she tilted her head and craned her neck to reach, so her mouth could touch his, and actually kiss during the act. He threw a leftward curve to one corner of her, and she felt all he'd wanted when he laid awake at night. He was making love to her like all *she'd* wanted every time she'd linked up.

Seven dove in with his full weight, so that Sunday had to take some breaths and adjust. She was pleasantly taken aback at how his thighs and butt muscles rippled under her fingers while he circled his hips. The heavy breathing, tongues dancing, Sunday pulled him in deeper.

"Mmmph." He stroked faster. They rocked harder. He craned his neck and tilted his head so he could keep kissing.

Every tiny moan and whine from Seven's throat invited her to release her own inhibitions.

He slowed down. "I'm tryin' to pace myself, but I don't think I can. You feel like presents on Christmas morning."

Though he'd paused his stroking, his manhood still twitched inside her.

"Open up yo' presents and play with 'em then." Sunday kissed him now. She trailed her tongue through his goatee and down his throat. He stretched his neck to give her more access, as if she was taking him to Heaven.

Jessie Mae Hemphill streamed through the radio and serenaded them with *Loving In the Moonlight*.

They rolled their hips back to an easy tempo. In the Delta that gave birth to the blues, there was no need to rush. Slowly, musically, they harmonized their strokes, so deep Seven was no longer pulling himself out. Sunday held on for him to keep unscrewing every doubt and fear she had.

Her legs open wide, Sunday gave herself permission to feel it all, and to give it all. Her orgasm rained from the top of her head through her titties, along her heart valves, across her lungs, underneath her navel, and on down her vaginal canal until, yes, she squirted her release onto his suede jacket. Kissing, tonguing, making love, she soared over the tips of the trees outside and rode the stars. It was Christmas.

A climaxing Seven was crossing his own personal threshold, running his own sexual race. In the buck of their butts, they breathed it out and rediscovered electricity. He laid his mouth on hers again, and Sunday trusted it. Shockingly, another orgasm was charging up in her.

"Don't stooooo...aaagheee!" She didn't know she could scream that high. But here she was.

Seven kept pumping, his mouth kissing her forehead, his goatee scraping the bridge of her nose. Their proximity, the intensity of their stride, had her clinging to the seat with one hand and gripping his ass with the other. Ecstasy bolted through her again, just as powerful, kicking and screaming up and down her body.

He held on, not letting her go. Not ready to let her go?

Exhaling the storm, full and satisfied, they settled down together.

"You good?" he whispered.

Still too weak and enthralled to talk, she nodded. He finally pulled out, and their separation broke the spell.

"You weren't wrapped up. Why didn't you ask me about birth control befo' we started?" she asked.

He nestled behind her and wrapped an arm around her waist. "What are we, Sunday? Kids? Same reason you didn't. You wanted me like I wanted you, and you know I've got the money if any issues come up."

He was already snoring before she could react.

She set the alarm on her watch to ensure they moved out of here early enough in a few hours that they didn't get caught.

WHAT'S GOIN ON AROUND HERE

SUNDAY

"Sunday!"

"Mmm…" This massage felt so good in her canopy bed. Breakfast was on the way, and the pigs-in-a-blanket with pancakes smelled like Heaven. Seven's hands on her back hit every spot just right. She snuggled deeper into the covers and puckered her butt out.

"Sunday!"

"What!" She resentfully opened her eyes and saw that she was not under a canopy.

Seven's hand kept shoving her in the back to wake her up, not massage her. "We overslept!"

Leaping up from his backseat, she flung the covers off and realized they weren't covers, but rather, his suede jacket.

"Oh!" Sitting mere footsteps away was a big, yellow bus filled with tourists.

"Get back down!" Seven shoved her. "You're in my truck! My kids can't see you in here."

"What are tourists doin' here? Ain' no tours scheduled for today!" Nevertheless, she did what he said and lay back down.

He tossed his jacket over the top of her and his sweater over the bottom of her, right on time to hear a knock on his window.

Ugh!

"Hey, Mr. H." Reggie!

"Hey, Reg, my man!"

"Dad?" Dillon! "What are you doing parked way out here?"

"You guys took all the cabins last night, and I didn't have any place to sleep. It was too late when I finished working to drive over to Helena. I came here, so nobody would mess with my truck out on the highway. Anyhow, I'm gonna head to your cabin now and wash up. I'll see you guys back out here in a bit."

"Okay. We're takin' some tourists out to the lake," Reggie said. "You want a walkie talkie so you can radio if you get lost tryin' to find us?"

"Yeah, sure. Thanks, good man."

"Are those Sunday's boots?"

Good grief! Go on, Reg!

"Oh! She asked me to bring some of her things back with me last night, because she had to..."

Come on, Bank Man, I had to do what?

"...go to Helena and handle some business. She said she'll be back this morning."

"Oh." Reggie didn't believe it. Sunday could hear the smart-ass in his tone. Besides, she'd taught him better than that. "Well, if you see Sunday, will you tell her she got an important call this morning?"

"You'll likely see her before I do, but I sure will. You boys, take it easy out there." A few more seconds passed. "They're gone."

Sunday rose again and shoved him back. "You don't want people seein' me with you?"

"Sunday, my kids just learned days ago I'm divorcing their mother. I'm risking my custody by even bringing 'em to Elaine. Will you cut me some slack?"

That was the reality. Both of them had entire lives to safeguard. "Don't think hidin' me is somethin' you'll do all the time."

His frustration melted into a cocky grin. "So you're thinking about doing this all the time?"

She cut her eyes. "I didn't say that."

"You literally just said it."

He passed her underwear to her. She reached for her panties, and he held on, tugging back on them.

"Hush up."

"Sunday, I wouldn't dream of hidin' you. Just let me figure out *how* I'll do this if we wind up doing it all the time. Fair?" He looked sincere.

Sunday nodded. "I have to get back and find out what's goin' on around here. Gimme my panties."

He released them and they smacked her in the lip. Since he laughed a little too hard, she pushed him.

"Let's get your mean butt back to the house." On his drive over the fields, he purposely bounced her around in the backseat while she struggled to put on her clothes.

"It was good, wasn't it?" He stared at her in his rearview mirror.

Her lady parts were indeed feeling like Sunday morning, but she wouldn't tell him that. "You were all right."

Seven jerked his steering wheel, and flung her into his headrest. "Liar. Or you wouldn't be talking about 'doing it all the time.'"

"You got one more time to—"

He snatched his steering wheel in the other direction and Sunday flew, face first, into his seat.

Unable to keep a straight face, she held onto the headrest the next time she got up.

"You can stop here. I'll walk the rest of the way." Before she opened the door, she couldn't help eying him through his rearview mirror. "Court is tomorrow."

"I know."

The two eyed one another a final time. Sunday wished they could just keep being careless and making love, and that there had never been a lottery ticket in the first place.

"Baby girl, you're gonna be good, no matter what. I'll see to it, like I told ya."

It wasn't two hundred million dollars, but she supposed that would have to do.

In the house, the others were up and going when she walked through the back door.

"Why do we have giggers on the property when gigging season is—"

A big surprise awaited her at the kitchen table. "London!"

Her youngest sister shot up from eating breakfast. "Sunshine!"

Sunday's heart was on overload, after the Christmas trees arriving last night, Seven coming with his children, and now her sibling crew was almost complete.

"When did you come in?"

London's effervescence already livened up the entire house, and they would certainly need her energy for tomorrow. "Last night." This twenty-year-old kid stared her big sister up and down. "And where were *you* at? Why are you comin' in here at eight-thirty in the mornin'?" London mimicked the way Sunday once chastised her when she'd come home late.

Their nieces giggled as they went back and forth.

Standing there in front of everybody, Sunday was at a loss. "It don't matter. I am grown."

London held a glass up to her eye as if it were a magnifying glass. "Are ya now?"

"Yes. But if you must know...I had a very important meetin' with a potential buyer in Helena."

A wicked gleam in her eye, London kept turning the glass on Sunday. "Is that why your sweater is turned around backward?"

Sunday looked down and the tag sat right at her throat. The entire kitchen burst into laughter.

"I hope you wudn't at your meetin' lookin' like that," Nookie added.

"No, but really, what was that bus full of tourists doin' out there?" Sunday asked, accepting a plate.

"Folks been hearin' about y'alls lottery ticket," their mother explained. "We been gettin' calls from people everywhere, wantin' to know what frog giggin' is. We got some last minute bookins'. That Hardcastle's daughters been tellin' all their friends what happened here. Folks is offerin' to help." The lines on Mama's face deepened. "Sunday, it's somethin' else. You might wanna sit down." Her mother began rubbing her own chest, and swaying from side to side. As if she were about to break into a holy dance.

Sunday already felt it in her belly. The woods last night had been too quiet, too solemn, mimicking the pause before a resounding grand chorus. "No, ma'am, I'll stand."

Tears crept down her mother's face, and her lips crumbled as if she was too afraid to smile. "We found 'em, baby girl. We found 'em."

"Found what?" London's confusion didn't last long.

"The bodies?" Apparent disbelief slackened Nookie's jaw. "Them investigators Sunday hired..."

The divine replied where their mother could not. On the

kitchen radio, Helena-born songbird Roberta Martin came on, and the Arkansas Delta silt flowed through her vocals and into their souls, telling them all to *Ride on King Jesus*.

"...found the victims." Those words tasted sweeter than honeysuckle nectar on Sunday's lips.

The Conklin siblings exchanged disbelief.

Her knees already weak from Seven, Sunday's legs gave out. Nookie grabbed her so she didn't hit the floor.

Twenty-Nine

ANTICIPATING FIREWORKS

SEVEN

"Oh, sweet Mother of Christ! This here is a plum mess!" Seven's mother twisted her hands on her way into The Edwardian once his parents touched down back in Arkansas. "Why did you bring the kids here and it's about to be Christmas? They ought to be in school. Not here in this racist town. You actually took them to Elaine? There's nothing around here but horror. I'm with Arista on this one. She called me, ya know."

Seven's father squeezed his own neck and issued a silent warning not to argue with his mother. "Son, the news folks are crawling all over the place. They're already standing outside the courthouse."

Charian entered with her luggage, but she and Seven didn't acknowledge each other, not on speaking terms since they both felt betrayed by the other.

"It's only a matter of time before they find out who we are."

"Mom," Seven said to his mother, "maybe you shouldn't

go to court tomorrow. If this is taking that big a toll on you, stay here at the hotel."

"This is my family's name, and I'm going. I just wish you would have listened is all. I did what you asked. I deeded the property over to escrow so we can help your friend out, this Sunday Conklin woman or whoever she is."

"I appreciate that." He held his mother's hand. "And as far as the kids, I will not have them learning about their heritage in the news or the internet, or even worse, from their schoolmates. They need to hear in an environment where I can provide context and understanding. And they sure as hell don't need to hear it from Arista's family spitting lies about us."

"It's Christmas, Seven." His mother's eyes were red, as if she hadn't slept since the last time she'd been here. "They should be thinking about Christmas things. Their gifts. Seeing their friends. Fun. Not any of this."

They headed upstairs to their rooms.

"In the time I've gotten to know the folks around here, Ma, I keep asking myself, 'damn, how much could I have done for these people if I had known some of this thirty years ago?' How much could you have done for them?"

"You will not shame me for protecting you," she snapped back. "You will *not* make this my fault! We didn't make these people poor!"

Seven breathed slow. "No, we may not be responsible for the Titanic, but we sure as hell never came back with rowboats, either."

She swung around at the top of the stairs. "You've done *enough*. Let. It. Go! That Conklin woman is blessed to have met you. We're selling our land so she can keep hers! She ought to be *damn* glad for that. Our family agreed to it so you could *move on* from this business. Take your kids home to

Dallas." She tried to jam some sense into him with her finger in his chest. "Before you *lose* them to Arista!"

He picked up her hand and kissed it. "I'll never lose my children, even if she gets custody. Ri can't handle them by herself. And they'll always call me before her."

"Mr. Hardcastle!" a strange, yet familiar, gravelly voice called behind him.

He and his mother pivoted. Instantly, Seven recognized the face he'd only seen in the pictures on the bank's walls.

"Strom Adler."

"Pleasure to meet in person after all this time." The old man offered a veiny, leathery hand filled with brown age spots.

Seven wasn't interested in touching it. After working at Friends for seventeen years, this was his first time crossing its most prized patron. Seven's hand remained in his pocket. "What do you want, Mr. Adler?"

"Looks like you and your family are in quite the pickle. I'm sure ya heard the news. There's been a discovery over on the Conklins' property. You might've won the lottery, but you's about to be found out, Mr. Hardcastle. The descendants of Lucas Sherman, a traitor to his town and to his race." The old man edged closer, smelling as if he'd brought his attic with him. "I wonder what kind of Christmas this'll be for your children?" The man waggled his head. "Especially when it spreads all over TikTok."

"You leave my children's names out of your mouth, or I'll keep them out."

"Seven," his mother shakily muttered.

"Don't you threaten me, boy. You clearly don't know how things work 'round here."

"Seven, let's *go,*" his mother warned.

Despite his heart running faster than a bullet train, there was no way he would let that stand. "I'm none of your boy. And I wonder what'll happen to Strom Adler's empire when the world learns you paid to cover up genocide and oppression."

"You ain' got the proof." The old man's blue eyes sharpened. "*Boy*. The old man's blue eyes sharpened. "And here I thought you's a pretty smart fella. But I see yo' intelligence don't go outside them books. You be careful out there, ya hear me? No amount of money you got, or people you know, will change this here respectful... *Christian*... community. That's how it's always been. That's how it's always gon' be. You have yaself a fine Christmas." His eyes tight, the old man backed up. "And good luck out there findin' ya next job. Let's hope it ain' spoonin' soup over at the soup kitchen. You *and* Miss Conklin."

Seven's mother clamped a hand to her mouth the moment Adler was gone. Seven tried to bring her into his arms to calm her down, and like lickety split, her hand caught his cheek.

"How dare you put us through this! Over some woman!"

His cheek stinging, Seven stared at her. She'd never raised a hand to him. "Mom, you had no problem with me working at the bank he patronizes just a month ago."

"As long as you work there, get your check, and go home, like you've been doing, no!"

"If it wasn't for me coming here, we wouldn't have two hundred million dollars to claim in the first place!" He said it to her backside while she marched off.

Was he truly off his rocker this time? Had Seven been outright dumb to think there could actually be healing for Christmas? That he could use his financial negotiation skills to bring closure for Elaine *and* his family?

SUNDAY

"Welp," Nookie started, "either we eatin' frog legs for Christmas again, or we eatin' caviar."

Their mother marched onward. "I ain' never eatin' no fish eggs. I'm havin' me some chitlins eitha way." She sized up her oldest daughter. "Sun, no matter what that judge say, you've done good. We real proud of ya. Just know that. And hold ya class. Regardless of how it goes in there, don't let 'em see you come apart."

The Conklin family walked arm in arm up the concrete steps of the historic Phillips County Courthouse, where over a hundred years before, the Elaine Twelve had been sentenced to die.

"These kids should have gone to school," Mama Piggee muttered. "They shouldn't see this place where so many Black folks been wronged."

"They should see, and learn now to hold their heads high, no matter what the world tries to take from them." Sunday declared this even while her own spirit shook in her Sunday heels, the only pair she owned.

"Ms. Conklin!" a news reporter shouted. "Is it true the graves have been discovered from over a hundred years ago?"

"Ms. Sunday! Over here!" another reporter yelled. "How many bodies have been found?"

"Ms. Conklin! Will you be filing a lawsuit against the State of Arkansas?"

A lone voice called above all the others. "Conklin Family, is it true you have a survivor from 1919 hiding in your house?"

That question stopped Sunday and her mother in their tracks, but Mama Piggee tugged them onward.

"Keep goin'," Miss Marleen muttered.

The same reporter remained undeterred, following them up the steps. "Sunday Conklin, do you have a relationship with Seven Hardcastle? Has he told you his ancestor is Cane Sherman, the man who betrayed the sharecroppers of Elaine that night? Are you dating a man whose family escaped to Chicago and never came back to own their part in the ruin of your town?"

No. Sunday couldn't believe it. Not him. He was there for Elaine. It's what he'd said.

"Sunday, girl, keep movin'," Mama Piggee coached her.

At the top of the stairs, Seven and his family were entering from another side of the portico.

"There's Seven Hardcastle!" one reporter noted.

A handful of cameramen rushed between Sunday and Seven, shoving their cameras and microphones in their faces.

Everyone on the portico quieted, in anticipation of fireworks popping off between the two families, minutes from finally learning who owned the ticket, and whose lives would change this Christmas, one way or the other.

How could he not tell her about his history?

"Hold ya class," Mama reminded her.

Sunday hadn't seen him since he dropped her off in her fields yesterday morning.

He'd picked up his children and taken them to Helena, apparently once his family had flown in, led by his sister, a hard-charging Chicago attorney whom Peady had looked up on the internet.

Today, his easy goofiness from yesterday, when he'd tossed her around in his truck, was nowhere in sight. The situation was wearing him down. Bags under his eyes, his five o'clock shadow begging for attention, Seven held the courthouse door open for her. "Good morning."

Eerily, Sunday stepped through it, and carried on, if only to be an example for her family. Though, her heart weighed even heavier now.

"Excuse me?" A well-dressed lady came toward her, the

picture of grace, her style elegant, everything Sunday once thought she herself would become. "Sunday, can you and I speak a moment? From one Black woman to another?" Unmistakably, she was Seven's mother.

"Mom." His voice was thick with exhaustion.

She ignored him. "I don't know if Seven told you, but we are paying off your house. My family is doing this on behalf of the Shermans. The proceeds from selling land we own here will be used to pay off...your situation." Her smile matched the white ladies' smiles at Friends Savings, where smiling was more an act of tolerance than of kindness.

"My situation might also be paid if the judge rules in my favor today." Sunday held her class.

"But he won't," Seven's sister intervened. "That number, 071899? That belonged to our great-great-great grandfather, Cane Sherman. So there's no way that lottery ticket could be yours. It's nothing personal, sis. We're just reclaiming what is rightfully ours."

Sunday's hope and faith and wonderment, and all the loveliness she'd started to believe in for the past few days, she now tossed back at Seven, standing a few steps away.

In silence, she straightened her shoulders. On her way into the courtroom, she held her class.

Thirty

FOR ALL OF THE DELTA

SEVEN

Seven entered a courtroom more packed than a church on Easter. Standing room only from wall to wall, fans fanning, arms crossed, all six hundred and thirty-six of Elaine's residents might have arrived before him to snag their seat.

He chanced a glimpse of Sunday across the aisle. Her defiant face couldn't mask that she was holding herself together. She had mastered her poker face, but Seven saw her nostrils flare when that reporter blurted the truth. He'd almost gone over to embrace her, but had doubted if she would have let him. And he refused to give the media a show. Now she avoided eye contact.

"All rise. Court is now in session. The Honorable Laureen J. Childress presiding."

When the woman emerged, Seven nearly plunked into his seat. From the heavy thud in Charian's chair, she was equally as shocked. The chorus of murmurs and gasps from the gallery revealed an equally astonished town.

"Good morning, good folks of Phillips County. My name

is Judge Laureen Childress, and I will be temporarily hearing cases this week." A *Black* woman judge?

Seven had researched the judge online, and he looked like he could have been Strom Adler's cousin.

Judge Childress continued, "Unfortunately, last night, I received word that Judge Huckabee had a stroke and is in the hospital. We send him and his family our warmest thoughts for a speedy recovery. Let's go ahead and get this ball rolling. I'm sure that, like me, many of you have last-minute Christmas shopping to do, and don't want to be put out of your house for not getting it done."

Sunday's face lit up brighter than a new set of Christmas lights.

"Our first case of the day is Hardcastle Family versus Conklin Family for injunctive relief and a suit to settle owner-ship over...a lottery ticket. In the amount of one hundred and ninety-six million dollars. I read over the moving papers and the arguments already." She held up a brown envelope that was sealed. "I have also received this subpoenaed package that was mailed to this court, and it has only been in the possession of the clerk, preserved in the file. I will now open it on the record."

"Yes, Your Honor," Charian started, "that is likely the video footage we subpoenaed from the Kwik Stop."

Judge Childress opened the envelope and passed the hard drive to the bailiff who turned on the television.

"Your Honor," Charian said, "I'm asking to mark that video as Plaintiff's Exhibit One, and my first witness that I'd like to call is the Defendant, Sunday Conklin."

Her chin up, as brave as she ever was, Sunday pushed up.

"Charian," Seven whispered. "This isn't necessary."

"Before you get started, Counsel," Judge Childress replied, flipping through the documents, "One question I have is who in the Hardcastle family actually purchased the ticket? There are twelve names listed here. They couldn't have all purchased the ticket at the same time."

Sunday's attorney placed a gentle hand on her arm to sit back down until this part was finished. Seven peeked over his shoulder, at his children seated behind him. They all listened intently for what their aunt had to say. Raegan leaned forward.

"Daddy, why is Aunt Charian calling Miss Sunday to the witness stand in front of all these people? Why didn't Auntie just call her and ask her the questions on the phone?"

"This is what people do when they don't know or trust each other."

"Your Honor, my brother, Seven Hardcastle, purchased the ticket. However, our family has a longtime oral agreement that—"

The judge reviewed the court papers. "And here is his signature."

"Although the ticket was purchased by Seven Hardcastle, it belongs to all of us," Charian explained. "That's an oral contract our family has always abided by."

Over the rims of her glasses, Judge Childress addressed the bailiff. "Let's have a look at the video first, and I'll see what questions I have from there."

On the other side of the aisle, Sunday's shoulders shrank, as if she were bracing to meet another part of herself. That hadn't been the free-wheeling woman out in the fields whose kinky hair blew around in the wind while she rode in the back of a pickup truck.

Seven stood up.

"Seven, sit down," his mother muttered.

He walked over to the other side of the aisle. "Excuse me." He stepped over legs, purses, canes, and fans among the townsfolk of Elaine, managing to squeeze right behind Sunday.

Judge Childress cast a long, suspecting glance at him. "All right then, let's begin."

"No." Seven cleared his throat and stood again. "Your Honor, we don't have to do that. We should be able to work this out among ourselves."

"Bank Man, let her play the tape." Sunday stared up at him. "Whatever is on the video, I accept responsibility for my actions. So far, though," Sunday said, a toughness in her that refused to quit, "I think it's a reason that ticket was won in Elaine, and not Dallas." She studied Seven. "Or Chicago. And why you and me bumped into each other the way we did. So, why don't we see how much further God will take me? And let this play out."

Sunday's mother grabbed one of her hands, and Peady laced her fingers through the other.

The video began, and Seven relived the night along with her.

He made his purchase first. He was waving his phone around in the air trying to catch a signal, irritated to be there, frustrated his marriage was on the rocks, reevaluating his life and what he wanted out of it, still trying to convince himself he wanted Arista and her Barbie dream house, too afraid of what awaited him outside of her bubble, scared that he didn't really love her as much as he thought now that he knew her better. Seven observed the man in the video walking around in circles, looking for a signal, a sign.

Wham. A bullet couldn't have shot into him faster. He almost dropped his phone, but he was more concerned about Raegan, and he let the ticket fall. Stumbling some, dazed, Sunday picked them up, and without either of them checking, she passed him one and pushed hers in her bra.

The bailiff stopped the video, and the judge studied the timestamps on the video for both their purchases.

"On the video, it appears that Seven Hardcastle purchased

his ticket at 6:33 p.m., and Sunday Conklin purchased her ticket at 6:36 p.m. I'm now comparing the two tickets. 771899 was purchased at 6:33 p.m., and 059847 was purchased at 6:36 p.m. If we accept all factual inferences—that the timer on the ticket machine was working properly, as was the video security system—that means Seven Hardcastle purchased the winning ticket."

Seven's family erupted on the other side. Agony plagued the Elaine side, as if Christmas had upped and left the Delta.

"Please, let me finish." Judge Childress held up a hand. "The trouble here is that Mr. Hardcastle is not the one who turned in the ticket. Nor is he the one who signed it. In fact, once the winning number was announced, Mr. Hardcastle never even filed a police report for his missing ticket. Charian Hardcastle did. And that was five days later. Here in Arkansas, a lottery ticket is considered a 'bearer instrument'. Much like a check. Meaning until somebody signs it, it's open for anyone to go and cash. To claim a possessory interest over it, one must act like an owner—search for it, turn it in, file a report if it goes missing. That's what people do when something of ours leaves our possession."

"But, Your Honor," Charian interrupted, "that ticket belongs to all our family. Not just Mr. Hardcastle. That's the way our agreement works. Our family should not be punished and deprived of our winnings because of Mr. Hardcastle's error. I would call the court's attention to the Arkansas case of *Sharon Duncan vs. Sharon Jones*. That court ordered the money to be turned over to the original purchaser, because she had not abandoned her right to that ticket by throwing it away."

"I'm familiar with that case, Ms. Hardcastle," the judge replied, "and she threw away her ticket because she checked it in a machine that incorrectly informed her she had lost. She was given mistaken information. That's not the case here. Mr.

Hardcastle never bothered to follow up on his ticket for days. That is not consistent with exercising a possessory interest over a thing you own. Nor did he exercise due diligence by double-checking to ensure he had his ticket when he dropped it. He was more concerned with his phone call."

"But when his family—the other owners—learned of this, we took every measure available to us," Charian argued.

"Well, now, about this 'joint ownership' argument, I'm not sure I buy that either."

Sunday and her clan grasped each other's arms, stiffening with shock. Low murmurs turned Seven in his seat. Around the courtroom, townsfolk bowed their heads, their lips moving, eyes closed, praying quietly.

"Ms. Hardcastle." Judge Childress removed her glasses and peered at the attorney once again. "Did Seven Hardcastle file this lawsuit?"

Charian froze where she stood, like a deer caught in headlights. "N-no, Your Honor, our family did."

"And everybody else signed it but him, huh?" the judge asked frankly. "For him, you must have used a digital signature. I can tell from this uneven penmanship that looks computerized on here when you zoom in on it, whereas everybody else's signature is smooth like they did it in ink."

Charian blinked more times than a child caught red-handed. "Yes, Your Honor."

Seven hadn't snitched on his sister. He understood how the family game was played, so he wouldn't defy them outright. But Charian had plagiarized his signature without his permission, and when he'd learned about it at dinner a couple of weeks ago, he'd been hot.

"So the actual person who bought the ticket did not bring this action. And you don't have legal standing to bring this lawsuit."

"We are co-owners with him—"

"Yes, yes, I know." The judge waved her hand around. "But technically, *he's* the purchaser, and I'm sure you know where this is going, Ms. Hardcastle. If you want your co-ownership with him legally recognized, you will need to first sue him to be named as a legal co-owner, and *then* file your claim against Ms. Conklin. Until then, the only person with standing to sue Ms. Conklin is Mr. Hardcastle."

The judge peered over the bench. "Who, I will note for the record, happens to be sitting right behind her. If he wants that money from Ms. Conklin's bank account, he needs to get it himself. But from where I sit, looks to me like they don't need help. The lien placed on the Conklin family's bank accounts as a result of this action is hereby lifted. Since no one with standing has filed this action, I have no jurisdiction and I must dismiss this case. I will not make any rulings on the substantive issues. This is not a ruling that the money belongs to Ms. Conklin, only that the proper party has not challenged her for it. This lawsuit is dismissed. Next case."

The pronouncement snapped Sunday's body.

Today, Christmas showed up and showed out. For more than just Sunday. More than the Conklins. But for all of the Delta.

The ruling may have technically been a "non-win," but this meat tasted like justice. Fair and square. No good ole boy network or white wall of resistance. Justice.

Seven's chest overflowed. Their tears, yelps, hugs, and squeals, filled him up, too. This had been purposed. Nobody could tell him different.

"Dad, what happened? Did you really give Miss Sunday almost two hundred million dollars?" Ray asked.

"No, sweetheart. She and I will work out how to distribute the money. I'm trying to right a wrong from a long time ago. Long overdue. Come on. Let's go hear how awful I am, and how I'd better not ever show my face again at another family event." Despite his family's anger, no part of him felt the slightest guilt. His conscience light as a feather, he started off.

Before he left Sunday's side of the courtroom, something tugged at him.

Seven turned and there she stood, more festive than Beale Street, her teeth a strand of pearls too invaluable to put a price on them. Sunday extended her hand, and Seven knew she was offering more than a handshake. They had reached an upper level of respect.

"You got a minute?" he asked her over all the celebratory noise.

Sunday followed him to a small meeting room, and as soon as they closed the door, she closed in on him. "Seven, why weren't you real with me? You just saw me yesterday. Why'd you let me find out like that?"

"I only learned myself. That night you shot up my truck, my mom had just told me. I drove to you right then, and started trying to figure this out. I wanted you and me to have our own rapport before you started judging me on what happened in the past. Be honest, Sunday. If I had told you, would you have dealt with me?"

Conflicted, she mulled that over. "But at least, I would have had the truth, and you know how important that is, with all we go through around here, not knowin' who to trust. Right now, I feel like you played me."

"You would have suspected I was up to something, or plotting to take your land from you, or that I had motives. All I mostly wanted was to learn about Elaine, and teach my children about it." He moved in and closed the distance between them. "And have fun with you."

Sunday's reaction to him was instant, her forehead smoothing out and her jaw relaxing, whether she wanted them to or not. "Don't ever keep anything from me again."

Seven picked up where they'd left off in the courtroom, offering his hand for a shake. "Deal."

Sunday accepted it. Still holding on, he stroked it with his thumb, drawing her to him.

"But there will be an 'again', though?"

She rolled her expressive, intense eyes that could chisel somebody better than an ice pick. "Imma have to check my schedule with the frogs. See what they say."

"You know how they feel about me, girl."

"So?" she asked. "Are you? Suing me in your own right?"

"Will I need to? Or will we be having an 'again,' so we can work something out?" Seven made a show of thinking. "It just so happens I'm out of a job." Licking his lips, his gaze sleighed down her figure in a dress that was far too little and too tight. "Maybe you've got some things around here that need fixing, or soil that needs plowing...holes that need filling...odds and ends jobs I can do."

Sunday's dimple was back. And put a dimple right in the middle of him. Chuckling, she played along, "Oh, you mean you wanna be paid for what you do?"

He shrugged playfully. "I think it's worth something." He pulled her hand to feel the bulge in his pants. "I think what I do *for you* is worth something."

Tough-talking, gun-slinging Sunday Conklin surprised him when she stood on her toes and reached for his face, bringing it down to hers. Her mouth on his was definitely whipping up Christmas vibes.

As if Sunday's joy couldn't joy any harder... "Come over to the lodge for some Christmas celebratin' and plannin?"

"I should take the kids home. They've still got the rest of this week left for school."

"Seven!" a voice cried on the other side of the door. "Are you in there, baby? It's me! What's this I hear? You're giving away *my half* of our lottery earnings?"

Seven and Sunday stared at each other.

At first, Sunday was stunned. "Is that...?"

Seven's head fell and he closed his eyes.

"Seven!" she banged on the door. "Are you in there with her now? You're not even divorced, yet! I'm *still* Mrs. Hardcastle!"

Softly laughing, Sunday covered her mouth, utterly tickled.

"I'm glad you think she's entertaining," he murmured.

Sunday patted his chest sympathetically. "I'm so sorry."

"Me, too. I'll come back after Christmas? Maybe we'll do something for New Years?"

"Oh, we'll definitely be doin' it for New Year's. And I'll have somethin' with the family, too." She grinned.

They snatched one more kiss before he took a last deep breath, and flung open the door.

"Arista, really?"

"No, Seven, not really. Why'd I hear about this ticket from my sorors and not you?" She eyeballed their children. "Or our kids?"

One of the townsfolk observed. "This Negro got mo' drama than Young & The Restless. Somebody pass the pig skins."

Arista clocked Sunday standing behind Seven. "You brought *my kids* to see another woman, who you're splitting lottery money with!"

"Shut it, woman. If you'd been here in Elaine supporting *me* for a change, that day I asked you to come, *you* would have picked up the ticket when I dropped it. But our ticket together has been punched out, Ri."

His wife aimed a well-manicured hand at him. "Half of that money is mine if you're the one who bought it. I want *every* red cent." She side-eyed Sunday. "And you must be one crazy broad if you think I'm not suing that cheap dress off you to get my money."

Sunday nudged Seven from between her and Arista, and stepped toward her opp.

Dillon pushed in front of his mother now. "Please, don't hurt my mom, Ms. Sunday. She can be a lot, we know, but she doesn't deserve to die."

Her thumb strummed her fingertips while Sunday sized up Mrs. Hardcastle, apparently for whether she could fight. The entire courthouse—media, news cameras, and relatives—all waited for Sunday's next move.

"Don't worry, Dillon, I won't hurt your mother. Not right now anyway." Before she walked off, Sunday stopped at Arista's side. Covering her mouth, she whispered something. As Sunday patted her shoulder sweetly, Ri's face seemed to dive through the floor. With that, Sunday joined her family and walked out.

Arista glared at Seven. "You will never bring my children here again! You'll be hearing from *my* lawyer. Ash, Ray, Dillon, let's go."

"No, Mom," Ash replied.

"Excuse me?" Arista cocked her neck. "Young lady."

"Mom, Dad didn't bring us to see Ms. Sunday," Raegan explained. "He brought us to see a Black town. We're meeting good people here."

"And even if Ms. Sunday does become Dad's girlfriend, do you blame him?" Ash tilted her head inquisitively. "You schemed with his boss to get him out of the way so the two of you could screw. If it hadn't been for you, Dad might not have even met Miss Sunday. It's not like she tried to take your man. You literally gave him to her. You only have yourself to blame, Mom. No, I'm not coming. You don't want to take me from here to protect me. You're taking us to be spiteful, and so you don't have to admit what you did was wrong."

"That's what you always make us do." Raegan picked up where her sister left off. "You make us own what we did. But you never want to. You think you can get away with anything. While you fuss at everybody else. If you sue any of these people in Elaine, or try to be unfair with Dad, I don't want to stay with you for Christmas. You can't use us to hurt him."

It stung Seven to see the humiliation in Arista's eyes. Disconnection from one's children had to be a cold Christmas present.

"I'm your mother," she snapped through tears. "Not one of your little friends. I am *not* asking you."

Normally, when their daughters copped an attitude or clapped back, out of habit, Seven would back up their mom.

"Not tonight, Arista. They're going to their first country Christmas celebration. I'll be sure and have them back for school tomorrow." That was a six-hour drive from East Arkansas to East Texas. "We'll talk then about how to do this civilly."

In disbelief, Ri stood still as a statue, her husband and children facing her. She seemed to shiver from nakedness after being disrobed of what she'd always taken for granted, the kind of love and devotion no social status or money could replace.

Poor, vexed Dillon seemed divided between his mom and his sisters. Like a man, he made a man decision, and walked over to take his mama's hand. Batting his eyes many times, Seven's son was holding back the flood. Dillon's mouth tightened into a determined knot, and he offered a silent explanation to his father: *some*body had to stay at his mama's side, regardless of what she'd done. Seven's chest swelled at witnessing that maturity. He offered his son a grip and pulled him in for a hug.

"I'm proud of you, son. Love you."

"Love you, too, Dad."

"See you back at the house."

"K."

Practically out of thin air, Principal Overton appeared, ever the gentleman, and held out his arm to Arista with a kindly smile, giving her a way to pick up her face and leave the courthouse gracefully. She looped a hand through the principal's and allowed herself to be led out.

"So, Dad, how did I do?" Ash asked on the way out.

"I was proud of you, sweetheart. You spoke well and you had a good justification for your decision. But don't make a habit of disrespecting your mother. We're still a family. Just moving different now. There's something else, too." He wanted to check in with her. He'd brought the children to Elaine for their history and heritage, not to witness him moving on from their mother. "I promised you wouldn't have to meet a new woman so soon, and that's not why I brought you here."

"Say less, Daddy. You're keeping it PG for us. Sunday seems like a solid lady, but I'm not ready to be besties with her, and I'm glad you're not going there. I understand you have needs, though."

"Exact--" Seven stopped himself and eyed her. "So long as we're all keeping our needs in check, though."

"Noted. So what my Tesla do? Because I think my speech deserved a Tesla."

Seven rolled his eyes, mimicking her. "You don't get a gift every time you do something you think I'll approve, Ash."

He would not encourage her defiance toward her mother, or start a parent war where Arista used Dillon to defy him. Suddenly, footsteps rushed back toward them.

Dillon popped up at his Dad's side again. "Dad! Reggie just said they're having a big party with cakes, and pies, and homemade Christmas candy! Can I come with you and we just run over there for a few minutes?"

So much for loyalty and devotion to his mama.

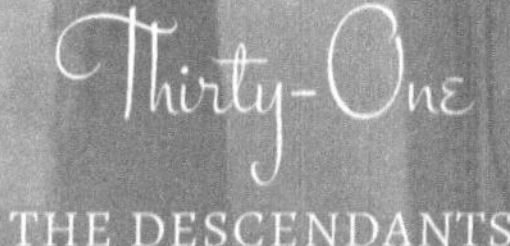

THE DESCENDANTS

SEVEN

"You can do it, Dad!" Raegan pumped her fists, jumping up and down. "Go on!"

At the celebration back at the Conklins' lodge, Seven was sick to his stomach. Nauseous from the smell alone, Seven paced in one spot to work up his courage. He was starting to feel like he'd rather accept defeat now.

"Come on, Dad!" Ashlyn prodded. "Swallow and don't think about it."

In front of him sat a small bucket filled with slimy, greasy, jiggly pig chitlins. Seven stared at the intestines and the intestines stared back. The stench nearly flipped his stomach inside out. On the other side of the table stood a freaked out Narado, who might have been girding his own loins.

Sunday held up the timer. "All right, gentlemen, you have the next five minutes to eat as many chitlins as you can. Everybody has seen the scales. These buckets weigh the exact same right now. Your bucket must be lighter when this timer goes off, and you must hold down the chitlins for *ten* minutes!

Whoever does that is our winner. The winner gets a trip to the Hot Springs bath houses and Magic Springs. The loser's gotta ride the electric bull in front of everybody, *and* shell the New Year purple hull peas, wash the greens, clean the chitlins, and wash the frog tents."

"Okay, Daddy, we got this!" Raegan clapped, imitating how Seven clapped for her at her basketball games.

"We?" Seven asked her.

"Y'all ready?" Sunday glowed, her dimples showing out. Her gaze bounced from one side of the table to the other.

Narado scratched his chin. "I don't know about all that. Let's just get it over with."

Seven swallowed. "What did these kids drag me into?"

"On your mark. Get set." Sunday flashed them a final glance. "Go!"

Seven dug his hands into the bucket, scooped out as big a pile of cooked chitlins as he could and shoved them in his mouth. He pressed his eyes shut.

Chew, chew, chew...swallow.

He kept shoving and repeated the cycle.

"Eat! Eat! Eat! Eat! Hordes of townspeople cheered so loud Seven had to be going deaf.

"Faster, Dad!"

Seven chewed fast and swallowed, moving continuously to keep his mind from drifting off course. More chitlins. Don't think. Jaws chomping. As many in his mouth as he could.

"One more minute, Dad! Keep going! You're doing it!" Ash coached him.

His gut was filling up, but he kept his jaws chomping, if for no other reason than his children were animated and super hyped.

"Stop!" Sunday cried. "Don't forget. The winner will not be declared for another ten minutes. You must keep it down the entire time."

"Ugh." Seven's stomach rumbled already.

They took the buckets to the scales. Narado's weighed one point three nine eight. Seven's weighed one point four one. He hadn't shoved fast enough, and it was over.

"No, Dad, that's okay. Just hang in there." Ray urged him.

"His bucket is lighter." Seven wiped grease from his mouth. "He was raised on this stuff and he'll keep it down. That was too nasty. I can't." Now that he paid attention, the chitlins stench overpowered everything else. He would be wearing this smell for the next two weeks.

"Don't give up, Dad." Dillon patted his arm.

His children were growing more than he had realized. They were now repeating back to him things he often said. Eight minutes into the waiting, Seven was hanging it up.

"I'm going to eat some real food." The macaroni and cheese, pigs in a blanket, greens and pot liquor, and cornbread were all calling his name.

Behind him, out of nowhere, he heard coughing and heaving, and then a giant splat hit the floor.

"Oh, my God!" Raegan cried, laughing.

Narado hated chitlins so much he couldn't keep it down and gave it all back.

"That makes Daddy the winner!"

His kids wrapped their arms around him for pictures and tight hugs.

"Look at Mr. Hardcastle, turnin' into a genuine Southern man," Principal Overton teased.

"This was fun, Dad." Ash's long nails cupped her mug of eggnog. Looking over his shoulder, she froze. "Oh, wow, guess who came!"

Seven pivoted to find his family walking in the door, terse and uneasy, but they had come. Across the room, one of the neighbors also pointed them out to Sunday, and with her expression, she asked Seven a silent question.

He strolled toward his folks.

"Grandma, what are you doing here?" Dillon beat Seven to the inquiry.

On edge, she wore her nervousness, her eyes scanning the lodge and all the faces who were scanning her.

"Mom..."

Nicky and Charian were serving some feelings that they weren't speaking on, and Seven appreciated it because he had a few sentiments of his own.

"I couldn't just leave here." His mother unwrapped a cloth bag she was carrying, and unveiled boots so distressed and curled up no person could have put them on. A musty stink on them, they were so worn out that the wooden soles contained large, gaping holes, and had thinned past their nubs. The holes and square frames stared back at Seven. Its front leather uppers had severely separated from the soles of the shoes, so whoever had worn them would have touched the ground with their open toes while walking. She stared up at the toys hanging from the ceiling in the lodge.

Somebody passed them a chair. Seven helped his mom stand on it, and when she could no longer reach, he took over the task of hooking the shoes to the ceiling by the old shoe laces.

"Granny, what's that?" Dillon asked when they came back down.

She wrung her hands, the way she did with an uncomfortable situation. The entire lodge awaited.

"Those shoes belonged to your ancestor, my great-grandfather, Lucas Sherman, son of Cane Sherman. When Lucas finally arrived in Chicago, October 13, 1919, after two weeks of hiding in the woods, people hauling him on wagons, and folks putting him up in their attics, he changed his name to Lewis Sheridan." She faced the people of Elaine, the descendants. "Took us a long time to get here. But we're here. This is our heritage, part of our story. We're not running from it anymore."

"You been here befo'." Mother Fordham remembered. "When you brought him back home and buried him. Thirty years ago."

Seven's mother swiped at tears while she nodded. "Yes, ma'am, we did. Back then, my daddy was alive, and he didn't think we should bring it up. Sunday said something today that stayed with me. She said that lottery ticket didn't sell in Chicago where I live, or in Dallas, where Seven lives. It sold right here in Elaine, while my son only happened to be here by chance. We all saw it on that video. When Sunday picked up the ticket, and Seven didn't really care." She studied her grandchildren. "Maybe this is how it was purposed. For the next generations to start the healing. They're not scarred like the older people."

Seven's children encircled their grandmother.

"We love you, Granny."

"Proud of you, Granny."

"Do you eat chitlins, Granny?" Dillon asked her. "I didn't even know what they were, but Dad just ate a lot."

His mother's face fell and she shook, disgusted. "He didn't learn that from me, baby. Let's skip that part."

"Welcome home, baby." Sunday's mother approached Seven's with her arms outstretched. "What you wanna eat? Somebody, fix her a plate."

Sunday's sisters came to greet Seven's mother and siblings.

As always, Sunday knew how to corner Seven. On the stereo somewhere, one of the elders turned up Leon Bridges' *A Merry Black Christmas*, a playful tune perfect for how she lightheartedly walked a circle around her target. "So…"

Tickled as a kid the night before Christmas, he anticipated what this particular gift might become.

"What will we do with *our* money?" Dimples showing up

on both sides of her cheeks, she continued strolling around him. "Which is in *my* bank."

Her hips were thick in those jeans under an accentuating sweater that was doing what it needed to do. It wasn't wise for him to make important decisions under this kind of pressure.

"How about half to Seven and his family, and half to Sunday and her family?" Peady suggested.

"Or everybody gets the same cut," Nicky countered. "It can be split eighteen ways to everybody involved."

"After taxes, the lump sum is one hundred and thirty million dollars." Charian stood in the middle and lawyered, as she had since she was a kid. "Seven point two million for each of us. And if somebody wants to contribute a portion to the town of Elaine, they are encouraged to do that. But that's each person's choice." She glanced at her brother. "I will contribute a portion of mine—five hundred thousand dollars."

Seven nearly dropped at the words coming out of her mouth. Regaining his composure, he nodded. "I'll give five hundred thousand to the town of Elaine, also."

Their mother rubbed her hands together. "Me, too."

"Well," Nicky started. "I'll give fifty thousand."

"Nick," Seven admonished him.

"I don't want to hear a damn word outta you. I'm not no rich real estate cat, and I'm not some school administrator with a fat pension," he said in reference to Seven's parents. "The rest of it is mine for me to soar into outer space. Several times a day." He surveyed the ladies in the room. "For those fine women who are interested—especially if you wear a size ten and up— lift-off times are at eleven in the mornin', six in the evenin', and ten at night. Imma invest in me a good launch pad, too." He took off toward the buffet tables. "Now, what kinda greens y'all got? I don't eat collard."

Charian checked in with her family and glanced at Sunday's. "So it's settled? Even split?"

Narado, Peady, Sunday, and some other young lady Seven hadn't seen until the courthouse today, all held their own exchange. She must have been the sibling before Narado—London.

Sunday moved to accept, and halted, as if hit with a sudden realization. She turned to Narado, and apparently passing on the torch, she motioned for him to do it instead.

Flabbergasted, the Conklins' youngest stepped forward, and extended a hand to accept for his family. "I guess seven point two million dollars is way more than what I had yesterday. So, yeah, even split. Agreed."

"Mighty fine thang ya did here, young man." Mother Fordham shocked Seven right at his side. "That coulda went a whole notha way, but you let ya soul do the thinkin'. I told ya you had business to settle here."

He kissed the elderly woman's soft cheek. "I guess you knew the whole time, huh?"

Her eyes took a tour of all the generations of toys hanging from the ceiling. "I guess you guess right. One thang 'bout bein' alive this long is it ain' too much 'roun' here somebody my age ain' gon' know."

Seven eyed the toys as well, and quietly paid respect to all the passed away souls who still watched over Elaine. "Maybe one day, you can share more with my children and me. We've got a lot to learn."

When no response came, he turned to one side and the other. Mother Fordham was gone. He smiled. It was for him and the younger generations to define what Elaine would be going forward.

"Bank Man." Warmth returned, and wrapped around Seven's arm. He was steered from the excited energy. Back down the corridor they went, where they'd cooked pancakes and he'd first kissed her. She turned him around, and kept a hold on his arm. "Thank ya."

"You're welcome." He'd had a pressing question on his drive over here. "What did you say to Ri over at the courthouse? Why'd she get so quiet?"

A cute side grin turned up on Sunday. "It was woman business. Not for you to worry about. So..." She peered around for whether anybody was close. Seeing they were safe, she examined him, her eyes hooded. "You gon' be here this weekend?"

"I'm invited here this weekend?"

Her dimple issued Seven's invite. "Your children comin'?"

"You want my children? Or you want me?"

She laid a hand on Seven's chest, never unplugging her eyes from his, and slid her palm down his belly. Seven's soul slid with it, dancing through his blood cells, all along the way. She stopped beneath his belt, and answered his question. "Who you think I want?"

Seven's head fell. "You ain't right."

Massaging him over his jeans, Sunday applied the perfect amount of pressure. He dared to look over his shoulder and see if anyone was coming.

"Don't worry. I got you." Over his jeans, she palmed his shaft, and played with the tip, lowering her voice. "I asked are you comin' this weekend."

Sunday was so adept at this that she could play with his life.

"I think I'm comin' now."

Her smile flirted with his goatee. "You comin' this weekend?"

"I'm comin' then, too."

Her thumb circling around the head, his girth between her fingertips, Sunday owned him.

"When you back in Dallas, who's climbin' on this here?"

"Mm..." Seven had slipped into a delirious state. "Nobody."

"Nobody? Where's Bank Man sleepin'?"

"Downstairs. Guest bedroom."

"With who else?" Her hot breath warming his neck, her thumb still circling, Sunday stood on her toes and set her open mouth on his neck. And sucked. Hard.

A teeny giggle flew out of him, young and haughty and hopeful all over again, their heads softly collided on one another.

"By his damn self."

She stroked him to the edge.

"Good."

Sunday drove Santa's sleigh up Seven's chimney, and unclogged him.

"Mmph...*fuck*," he squeaked, climaxing right where he stood. "You're no good, Sunday. You're real dirty."

She licked him and rubbed the hickey she'd left on him. "Sunday's also sweet. Especially when she's gettin' what she wants."

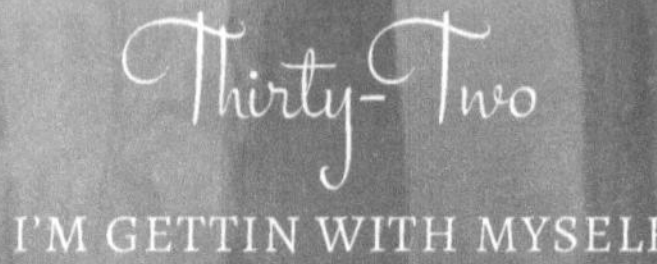

Thirty-Two

I'M GETTIN WITH MYSELF

SUNDAY

A cold snap had finally reached the Arkansas Delta. At forty-one degrees, winter was making its grand entrance.

"The ground is harder," Sunday noted.

"I'll start turnin' up the heat on the water in the tents. Check the frogs, make sure they're good," Nookie offered.

"Fine." Gazing across the fields, Sunday took a breath. "And then, that'll be your last time."

That stunned him.

"What you mean?"

"Nook, now that we've got resources, I'm gonna hire folks to do this stuff. This ain't your responsibility anymore."

Nookie studied her sideways. "Say what nah? Ain't nobody else gon' take care of all this around here like me." Indignant, he stared out at the same fields he'd wished away so often throughout his life. Just as Sunday had eighteen years ago. "You firin' me or somethin', Sun? You gon' try to buy me out? I might not always like bein' here, but that don't mean I'm sellin'."

She faced him. "I want you to go to a better school than Helena. You're gonna test for the Arkansas School for Math, Sciences, and Arts. Finish your last two years strong so you have a shot at the best universities."

He shoved his sentiments into his coat pockets. Condensation curled from his mouth, out into the morning chill, like it was already clearing the way for him.

"What if Iown want to? I was thinkin' 'bout buyin' me a couple strip malls in Little Rock, and rentin' out space to some shops."

"Nook, you don't want to go? Or you're scared of leavin' what's familiar?"

He turned his head in another direction.

She continued, "Don't take the easy road 'cause you too scared of doin' what you really want. Think bigger than that. Vanessa, and me, and Peady, we're here because we had to be. After Daddy died, all we had was each otha. You've got options now. Don't think small. Be big. Learn dope things we ain't never heard of before." She closed her eyes, and relived that feeling of leaving Elaine. "Go see what's possible." Tears rolled out of her. "Get you a degree so you'll always have somethin' to fall back on. Start ya business while you in college. If it's profitable and growin', and you wanna drop out, I swear, I'll shut my mouth. If it don't do too good, I'll clap for ya anyhow, Nook. It'll be a lesson for you to do better next time."

He leaned on the hood of their father's truck. "What if I'm not..."

"You got it honest, Daddy's curiosity and love of nature. You're one of the smartest people I know. He would be so proud of you. So am I."

A range of emotions fluttered across him. She watched him realize for the first time that their necessity no longer needed to frame his identity. Freedom of money meant the freedom to discover who he truly was.

"What if it ain't for me?"

"You won't know unless you go find out. And don't run at the first sign of trouble either. Fight for what you want. Learn how to fight with your head. Not your hands. You deserve it as much as anybody. Maybe more."

"What about you?" He peered at her. "What you gon' do? You gettin' with that Bank Man?"

She cast her eyes at their dirt road, its many twists and curves winding toward the gates of their property, at the highway. 44 lay too far ahead for her to see it. But she'd traveled all these turns, bumps, and holes enough to know how to find the exit. A twenty-year-old kid when Vanessa had picked her up from the bus station to grieve their father, Sunday now remembered riding through those old gates. Back then, she'd had no clue that she wouldn't be going back out of them to return to Clark Atlanta.

"I'm gettin' with myself." She and herself had some lost time to make up for. Maybe not lost. Rather, accumulated.

Narado tipped his faded Arkansas Razorbacks baseball cap to her. "Respect."

While the sizzle between her and Seven couldn't be denied, it wasn't all bad that he was still tied up in Texas, or that he was asking for their communication to be sensible. She'd appreciated his honesty. Their different commitments allowed them to get high on each other without overdosing, and then come up for fresh air. Their own air. She could enjoy this new connection *and* enjoy herself. A grown-up attachment without lies, cheap thrills, or unreasonable expectations could be a perfect fit in her new wardrobe of freedom.

She reached up and pulled Narado's head down to her level. Laying a kiss on his cheek, she quietly wept.

Daddy, I did my job.

She'd just said all to Narado that their father had once said to her.

* * *

SEVEN

"A hickey." Arista clocked it two minutes after Seven had brought his things in the house. "So you take our children with you to see somebody else, and you kept them out of school all day yesterday? Then, you bring them home after midnight on a school night and *I'm* the bad parent?"

It was two in the morning, and the children had slept for much of the seven-hour drive. They were having so much fun, Seven felt bad finally pulling them away at seven in the evening. Now the kids trudged up the stairs, more than ready for bed.

"Nobody said you were bad, Ri."

As an afterthought, Ray came back down. Sleepily, she grabbed Seven and kissed him. "This weekend was one of the best ever, Daddy, meeting our new relatives and winning the lottery. Thank you. Love you, Dad." She started to take off.

"Ray," Seven called. He knew what she was doing, but he couldn't let it happen. If Arista caught even a whiff of gamesmanship, she would ramp up the pettiness. Right then, he motioned for Ray to acknowledge her mother.

Ray cut her eyes. "Goodnight, Mama."

Seven cleared his throat.

Ray backed it up. "Love you, too, Mama."

He nodded, and she dragged her exhaustion up the stairs. Instead of cutting off conversation and escaping to the guest bedroom, he took a seat at the dining room table and pulled one out for his wife.

After serving him a particularly stank eye, Arista brought over her wine. "You're wearing another woman's hickey on your neck around our kids. If you think I'm okay with that, you—"

Her gaze crashed on his ringless hand. "When did that happen? How long have you been walking around with no ring on?"

"Ri..."

"Don't 'Ri' me, Seven. How long?"

"Damn, Arista, the kids. Turn it down some. I took it off before I left here this last time."

"Oh, after you bring them in here at two in the morning, now you want to think about the kids?" That must have chipped off another piece of her. "You're sincere about not working on our marriage." Arista's declaration brought him back. "It's really over for us. Just that quick?"

He wasn't trying to hurt her, but deeper pain was guaranteed if he delayed the truth. "Ri, it's been over for us. Only now, I'm accepting it, instead of booking another vacation to convince myself I'm still in this."

Her face crumbled. "All right then. So, that money you just won?"

"You can half my portion with me. Half of seven point two million. Full fifty-fifty split of custody. And we equally split all our other assets."

"Or, what if I feel like that ticket only belongs to you and me?" She sat back and stared at him. "Nobody else's. That's one hundred and thirty million dollars you and I could split. Maybe I should sue your new lady friend myself. Since you apparently feel something for this chick, maybe you're being too friendly to these people. Someone who's thinking more clearly should undertake the lawsuit."

"Somebody thinking more clearly, or more vindictively?" Seven braced himself for the mental chess they'd play.

Across the table, his longtime chess partner did the same. "Either way, it's my right. As your *wife*." She moved the king piece—her legal entitlements. "But you've turned our children onto those people now. That was clever, taking them there, getting them attached to that town, the way you are. So if I sue any of them for what's rightfully mine, I'm the villain."

Seven found comfort in how these mind games, the constant jockeying to outthink each other, would one day come to an end.

She circled her wine in her glass as if it turned the wheels of her mind. "Half of your 401k, half of your pension, half your stocks."

He'd expected to lose those pawns. "Yes. Half. As of the date of the divorce filing. But that will be it, Arista. No alimony. No child support. One lump sum payment of everything, and we're done financially. Whatever you do with your share, that's it. No coming back later for anything I build in the future without you."

That knight moved in an L-shape across her chest. A tear slid and splashed into her wine. She drank. "And you've told me about every penny. You're not hiding anything?"

"Not one red cent. And you don't touch anything I inherit from my parents."

"I know." Arista's face was now so tear-stained she could no longer *not* wipe her cheek. "You're sure you don't want to go to therapy and at least try. I want you, Seven. I do. It just got rough when you couldn't..."

"For you." He was quick to correct her. "When I could no longer perform *for you.*"

She sniffed back the question he suspected she desperately wanted to ask, and what he knew she didn't want the answer to.

He pulled a glass from the table setting and poured himself some of her wine. After guzzling the entire glass, he set it down. "Yes."

"Hrph!" It was a shriek that didn't quite match the ones

she'd screamed during childbirth, but it was just as guttural. "You fucked her?"

And that night with Sunday had rocked him more than all his exploits with Arista put together. Though Seven now held his silence, he must've still worn Sunday on his face.

"All this time, you were waiting for me to screw up so you'd have an excuse to do the same?"

"Hell, no. I was still trying, Ri, *until* you screwed up. It turned out to be the confirmation I needed. That part of us is over. Couples therapy won't fix what's not there. But we can go to family therapy and address how to do this divorce with respect. For the kids' sake *and* our own." He reached out to her over the table, an olive branch. "We can still give our kids a nice Christmas. This doesn't have to make us enemies, sweetheart."

He watched the pendulum of her thoughts swing between serving a petty swipe or capitulating.

"Seven, I was wrong for taking you for granted, and I'm owning it." She waited for his forgiveness, and some indication he understood. "We can still go to Paris. I promise, you won't be sorry."

Silent, Seven waited for her to take his hand and shake on a civil, mature divorce.

Stunned all over again, his wife stood up in her new reality. Gathering her glass and the bottle of wine, she left his hand where it was at.

"I'm not there, yet, Seven. Just give me some space with this."

He grabbed her wrist before she walked off. "What did Sunday say to you at the courthouse yesterday?"

Whatever it had been, it must have fallen short of 'congrat-ulations,' judging from his wife's scoff right then.

"She said, 'Don't you worry, sis. I'm gonna fuck your

husband so hard I'll put a dent in him and you won't recognize him.'"

Seven's chin fell to his chest where he hid amusement.

"I can't say I blame her," Ri continued on her way out. "If circumstances were different, me and her might have been friends."

SUNDAY

The morning of the Boots N' Tiaras Ball, Sunday stepped into a place she didn't recognize.

"Oh, Peady and Lon, you outdid yaselves." Their mother's wonder danced all over the Elaine High School gymnasium.

"You like it?" Peady was more giddy than Sunday had ever seen her.

"Girl, what kind of question is that?" Sunday couldn't study one scene too long before she jumped to another.

Flabbergasted, Sunday and her mama linked arms, winding their way through the candy cane forests, life-sized snowmen, Black nutcrackers, and Sunday stopped in her tracks.

Black farmers. Black women and Black men in straw hats and overalls, holding shovels, hoes, and proudly extending their arms toward baskets filled with food. They didn't resemble ignorant Sambos, either, or give way to the common stereotype of rural Black folk. These figures held poise, stature, and formidability for the value they provided the nation.

Among them stood replicas of the Delta's great blues musicians who'd called Arkansas home—Odessa Harris, Frank Otis Frost, Sonny Boy Williamson II, Robert Lockwood, Jr., Robert Nighthawk, and so many others. Seated on bales of hay laughing, or their eyes closed mid-hum in a honky tonk, pressing everything they had into a guitar, banjo, harmonica, or horn, they were belting out the glory, trials, richness, and promise that was the Arkansas Delta.

"Oh!" Sunday's hand flew to her mouth.

In the next section, soldiers on horses as heroes, looked out over the farmland. Sunday realized what Peady's arrangement depicted—the heroes from the night of September 30, 1919, the farmers, many whom were returned soldiers from World War One, who'd bravely fought back that night. Tonight, they were protecting Christmas for the children of Elaine, still protecting the Delta.

Right there among them, on horseback, between the trees, was First Lieutenant Earl Conklin, Sunday's great-great grandfather. He carried a replica of his historic gun. He'd shot and killed many of Elaine's invaders for six days straight from where he'd hidden in the swamps. The real gun now belonged to her.

Sunday couldn't have loved Peady or Elaine more than she did right now. "How'd you pull all this together so fast?"

"Donations. I called up Black museums and high schools in Mississippi and Tennessee. They was happy to help and loan some of it. I got a few replicas, like the Earl Conklin from a man in Mississippi who makes stuff like that. He already had some soldiers on hand to sell us. When Elaine finally gets a museum, we can store these there for the future."

While Sunday had been laboring on the farm with Deanne and Principal Overton to save as many frogs as she could, Peady had been here creating an entire world.

"And we will get that museum," Mayor Hicks reassured them all.

Sunday nodded her agreement, and turned to Peady. "When we do, Miss Paris here will be the Event Coordinator or Museum Director or somethin'. I'm so proud of you, sis. You've had Elaine lookin' good these last few weeks. You about to raise us to some whole new levels."

Peady returned Sunday's hug, but her vibe seemed off, as if she were here but not fully present. Their embrace missed all the energy for this kind of an accomplishment.

"You okay?" Sunday nestled her chin in Peady's shoulder.

"Y-yeah. Sunday?" Peady took her hand and led her away from the others, through the winter decor.

"What's wrong, baby? You all right? The baby's okay?"

Peady seemed to shrink. She struggled to find Sunday's eyes.

"You not feelin' good?" Sunday asked. "If pregnancy sickness is botherin' you, London can—"

"I'm leavin', Sun." Paris wriggled in her sweatshirt, like she was trying on those words to see how they fit. "I've been offered a job somewhere. On a reality TV show, decoratin' sets. And I'm gonna take it."

Sunday clapped her hand over her mouth, so her heart wouldn't tumble out. Not that that made any sense, but it was all she could think to do.

Panic gripped Paris, and Sunday's little sister appeared to instantly start second-guessing herself. "I'm sorry."

"No! Don't you dare be. I'm so so proud of you, P." She couldn't be the strong big sister on this one, and the breakdown was coming. "You're gonna be the best set-decorator they ever had." Stretching out her arms, she went for Paris, and Paris clung to her. The two hugged like they were holding onto their longest-held dreams.

"Thank you for everything, Sun," Peady sobbed. "I'm not

tryin' to leave all this on you, but if I don't try, then I might re—"

"Baby, you don't have ta explain nothin' ta me. And if anybody mess wit you, you jus' call, and me an' Earl gon' be there like Johnny on the spot, you hear me?"

Peady nodded like the little sister she'd always been—cherished, held, spoiled, and protected, no matter what they had in the bank.

On her way back to the house by herself, Sunday rubbed her chest for the joy, and also the melancholy.

As inspired as she was by Paris's bravery, Sunday tried not to think of how, with all her siblings gone now, she would indeed be left to hold this together alone. That was terribly selfish, but she couldn't shake the sudden loneliness. With the departure of another Conklin, the world had just gotten a little quieter.

"A package came for you, Auntie."

Sunday threw the keys on the counter. "From who?"

On his way out to chores with a snack, Reg was already bolting through the door.

"Boy, don't let that screen door—"

The door banged against the frame several times.

Sunday didn't have to search for her package. It found her first. A lovely gold jacquard box, embellished with silver trim. She slipped out the card tucked underneath the soft silver ribbon.

I'm only coming if you've got this on.

Even in her melancholy, laughter rolled out of Sunday as naturally as the waves tossed off the ocean floor.

No signature on the box, only one person possessed the audacity to tell her what to put on. Easing the box open, she unwrapped the paper and almost couldn't bring herself to touch what lay inside.

Countless sequins and sparkling crystals awaited her on a strapless, body-hugging showstopper, champagne-colored and complete with a full skirt of organza.

"My Lord..." Who was supposed to wear all this?

A few hours later, Vertreese and Ira Conklin's third oldest child stood in her parents' cramped bedroom, staring at herself inside the dusty old mirror nobody had had time to clean.

"It's sho' 'nough pretty," she said to herself.

Bank Man had good taste.

"The woman in it is prettier. That's likely why he bought it."

Sunday hadn't known her mother was standing in the door. She came over to wrap her arms around her daughter, like she must have suspected Sunday was wondering what to do with herself in this thing.

"You wear that dress like you the First Lady or the Queen, 'cause ya is. You hear me?"

Sunday wiped away an onslaught of unexpected tears. "Yes, ma'am."

Nevertheless, Sunday squirmed in all these crystals and would have been far more comfortable in her overalls, flannel, and mud. But she supposed if she was pushing other folks to grow, it was time for her to do some growing of her own.

"Sunday!" Nook called from the front of the house. "Ya ride's here."

"What you mean my ride?" she replied.

"Yo' *ride,*" Nook repeated, agitated as if that should have cleared it up.

Sunday stared at Mama, who shrugged.

"I thought we's all goin' togetha."

Her mother gave a short, quick head-shake. "I gotta get these kids ready. You go on."

Sunday checked herself a final time. Unknown territory glimpsed back.

As if this Christmas couldn't have lifted them any higher, outside awaited a black carriage with gold trim, and twelve shiny, black horses in elegant coats.

"Go on," Mama urged her, and didn't seem all that surprised, her tone insistent enough that Sunday wondered if she'd had a hand in it. "Get in there. Gon' 'head nah."

Sunday stared back at Mama, Nook, Reggie, and the girls, all peering at her from inside the kitchen. Sounds of a triangle instrument tinkled the beginnings of *White Christmas* from their tiny radio, joined by the soft, cotton plant voice of Sister Rosetta Tharpe.

Now, whose turn was it to fear leaving?

The driver jumped from his bench and opened the door. "Ms. Conklin, good evening." He held out his gloved hand.

Sunday stepped forward and took it for him to help her up the step. At her other side, her mother gathered her dress. In the cabin, she paused.

A pair of long legs were draped in velvet-lined tuxedo pants, patent leather oxfords, and the same long fingers from their first night. No wedding band. Its imprint in his flesh had faded some, so he hadn't just slid it off right before he came. Freshly shaved, smelling of rich, spicy oils, his hair lined up with new waves, he affirmed himself to be the gift that kept on giving.

His gaze in a chokehold, he sucked his bottom lip and his eyes praised Sunday. He slid one hand toward her across the seat, while he readjusted his machinery with his other hand. "Good evening."

Her mother finished sweeping her skirts into the cabin, and Sunday settled in next to him. "Good evenin'." A thought dawned on her, and she turned to her mother. "I'll see y'all over—"

The door shut. Her mother didn't wait around to wave them off, in a clear message.

Excited, nervous, scared, she turned to the other side of her.

Seven's eyes zoomed in and drank her up, forcing Sunday to be overly self-aware.

"Stop starin' so hard."

"No," he said from underneath his trimmed mustache. "It looks good on you."

Rather than going to a ball, she would have preferred just sitting on his mouth. He had used it so expertly the other night.

"It's way too fancy. You probably spent a lot of money."

"The proper response was 'thank you.'"

She would have to learn that. "Thank you. You don't clean up too bad yaself."

"It fits all right?"

"Perfect. It's perfect. Mama gave you my size?"

"Peady." Of course, her little sister was making plans for Sunday to find some happiness, while she'd been secretly making her own.

Seven set his hand atop Sunday's thigh and opened it. It wasn't really asking or insisting or offering anything. Just there, minding its own business. Holding hands with a man, these small gestures could lead her to taller heights she might eventually fall from. Why would she climb way up there?

"If it makes you feel any better," he started, "I'm nervous, too. I haven't done this with anybody but Ri in a long time." He gazed at her with genuine understanding in his eyes.

With giddiness floating around in her belly, Sunday placed her hand in his. They scooted closer, until their hips were locked in.

Their nerves must have been intertwining, talking to each

other, figuring out what to do with themselves at ages thirty-six and....

"How old are you?" she asked.

He smiled. "Forty-one. Where did that come from?"

"I was just wonderin'."

"Why?"

She shrugged. "We did the nasty. We should probably know somethin' about each otha."

Their chuckles were soft, and he leaned in closer.

"I know what side of your pussy heats up fast when I hit it."

Sunday snort-laughed.

"It's snowing," he whispered on her forehead.

"What?" She was still wrestling the mental and emotional American bullfrogs hopping their big behinds all over her.

He stared past her out the window. "Look."

Snow flurries were cascading from the sky. "It's been a long time since we had a white Christmas."

"Too bad you won't be here for it." He stared straight ahead.

"Huh?" Sunday hadn't noticed that, once the carriage left her gates and turned onto Highway 44, they rode in the opposite direction of Elaine High School. The further the horses galloped, the more distance they put between her and her farm. A tiny sliver of panic shot through her. He was taking her away from her cocoon. "Where we goin'?"

Studying her, he wielded the same audacity she'd seen on him the first night they met. The same sense of adventure, curiosity, and purposefulness, with which he'd snuck onto her property, snatched her gun, wrestled her, dove into the mud after her frogs, walked toward her while she shot at him, and then defied his career and his wife, all of his fiery energy now bubbled next to Sunday.

His lips twitched with humor. He sucked her jaw, and

worked his way down her throat, beginning to worship on Sunday.

"Some place where you can fuck me so hard you'll put a dent in me."

The two of them cracked up like kids. This time, when Seven Hardcastle rose again to kiss her, Sunday gave him her lips to do with as he pleased. Her heart opening, world expanding, she kissed him back with no restraint.

THIRTY-FOUR

The Gift of Us

IF YOU WISH TO CONTINUE YOUR CHRISTMAS
PLEASURE READING, CONSIDER PROTECTING
YOUR PEACE AND SKIP THIS CHAPTER.
YOU WILL NOT MISS A MAJOR EVENT.

SEVEN

"Sorry, not sorry, I forged your signature for a hundred and ninety-six million dollars," Charian said once they'd gotten out of their cars.

"Sorry, not sorry, you're only getting eight million instead." Seven couldn't hold his poker face and was already laughing at her.

"Now, the two of you hug each other," his mother instructed, the way she did when they were kids.

Seven threw an arm around his sister and hit her with a forehead kiss.

Their father waved everybody on. "Let's hurry up, folks. The choir is starting."

That Christmas Eve, the Hardcastles joined other descendants of Cane Sherman, as well as the descendants of Earl Conklin, the Johnston doctor-brothers, the Hicks men, Frances Hall, and other sharecroppers and families whose lives and sacrifices would be acknowledged at long last. And not just in another magazine or newspaper column, either.

In the ultimate Christmas present, today, the State of Arkansas would finally issue an official apology for 1919. Talks had already begun over what forms of reparations would be most helpful for Elaine.

People had flown in from all over the country to see an event that only happened once every generation. Extended relatives, well-wishers, historians, professors, news reporters, and even celebrities had traveled after receiving a phone call and being informed they had ancestors involved in the Elaine Massacre.

When the Hardcastles arrived to sit in the descendants' section, Sunday's mother welcomed them with open arms, introducing them to the other families.

Seven searched for his favorite gun-toting avenger somewhere in the crowd, and when he found her, his heart fired.

"Dad." Raegan tugged on him. "Look at Sunday! Is that a World War One uniform she's wearing?"

He wouldn't tell her he was already looking. Hard. "It sure is, baby girl."

"She's such a badass," Raegan gushed. "Who does all the stuff she does? Nobody," she asked and answered herself.

Seven started to correct her language, but her admiration put a smile on his face. He let it ride. She was right. Except for one thing. "You will, too."

Mama Piggee, a descendant herself, took the podium and addressed around six thousand people gathered in the open field of what once was a town called Hoop Spur.

"On behalf of Elaine, I'd like to thank all of you for coming here on your Christmas Eve. On the night of September 30, 1919, brave Black sharecroppers secretly gathered to form a union and protect their rights. Their secret meeting was intruded upon by two white men. They stood up for their right to meet without interference. Within three days, hundreds of Black souls were slaughtered and their bodies dumped. For over a century, this state looked the other way! This stain on humanity has gone ignored and overlooked. Our ancestors were terrified into silence. But no longer!"

Mama Piggee gazed at Sunday and the other Conklins.

"Thanks to the devotion and perseverance of the Conklin Family, this will be one Christmas that Phillips County *never* forgets!"

"Amen!" several people shouted.

Mama Piggee wielded her finger around like it was a sword. "The mass graves of our beloved ancestors have finally been discovered! And the truth is, at long last, set free!"

"Finally!" Raegan yelled with the others, her fist in the air. Elaine was all she'd been talking about for days. She'd already decided to write her history paper on Elaine, she planned to start a podcast, and interview some of the historians and archaeologists who would be working at the mass grave sites next year.

Seven and Char swapped a prideful moment.

"We never lost hope! We still got vandals! They still bring us their crap! Their great-grandsons still try to kick us down. And Elaine never gave up! We're still here!"

"Yes!" They jumped to their feet.

"I said, we're still here!" Mama Piggee laughed mockingly in the direction of the governor who sat in the audience, rather uncomfortably. "*We* are the hope of our ancestors! *We* are the future they dreamt of! We are the lives they prayed over! And as I stand here and look at all we've endured, what an astonishin' Christmas gift we are to the world! Us! Come hell or high water, rain or snow, we's the superheroes and sheroes of the Delta, baby! The amazin' gift that keeps on givin'! The gift of *us!* Tell the world Elaine said, Merry Christmas!"

SOMETHING REALLY VALUABLE
— TWO YEARS LATER

SUNDAY

"All right, everybody, class is dismissed. Don't forget to clean up your area," Sunday reminded her students a few days before Christmas. "For tomorrow, don't forget to bring your seedlings and frogs. We're heading out to the forest to compare the frogs you've been raising in your house to the ones that have been in the swamp. I want to hear some really good analysis on the soil quality and texture, based on the skin of the frogs."

Sunday glanced at her watch. She was late for a meeting with her new farming partners in Africa.

"Miss Sunday?"

She wondered if one of her workers were around to give her a lift.

"Miss Sunday?"

Sunday spun around to see her students still seated and confused. "I forgot somethin' again, didn't I?"

"Tomorrow is Tuesday. We're goin' to Mr. Hardcastle's

336

bank for farm financing to learn about how all this gets paid for."

Their teacher sighed. "Right. Of course, you are. See ya in a coupla days."

While shoving herself into her coat, she radioed for a worker to come and give her a lift since Reggie had dropped her off at their state-of-the-art Ira Conklin Plant Science Center.

Nobody answered. She tried her mother, hating to disturb her. Now that they were set financially, Vertreese Conklin rarely came out to the fields anymore.

"Mama?" A few seconds passed. "Mama?"

Now, she was late and irritated. "Where was every...?"

Sunday exited the building and entered her fields. What must have been the whole town of Elaine, and her students, and her family were gathered on the roads and standing in the crops.

Sunday's mouth almost fell off of her.

"William!"

"Hey, baby sis." Her legs couldn't carry her fast enough into his arms.

"When did you get out?"

"A few days ago."

"A few days? And you just now comin' to see us?"

"He wanted to keep it a secret so they all could give you a bunch of Christmas gifts at the same time. But it's good to be home, baby girl," her big brother murmured in her ear, squeezing her extra tight, like he'd longed for this more than she had. "I can't thank you and ya mans enough for fightin' for me."

He finally put her down, and Sunday couldn't tell left from right.

"What are y'all doin' out here?"

"They're waitin' to see what you're gonna say." An all-too familiar voice approached her from behind.

Sunday turned to see her man's all-too familiar swagger, expensive boots, felt cowboy hat, and impatient intensity, all wrapped in love that kept her wide open.

"Well." Sunday sized him up. "Usually, my answer is 'no,' so they won't have to wait too long."

He removed a box from his jacket. Every belly in the fields shook with laughter. Even his lady busted up. He held a Cracker Jack box. Out of it, Seven pulled a cheap gum-ball machine ring, and he lowered to one knee.

"I am holding something really valuable now, Miss Sunday. I am holding a promise to make you laugh, roll your eyes, swat at me—and you will miss, just like you always do—shoot at me, cuss me out..." His face softened. "Keep teaching me how to love you, keep inspiring me to be a better man, keep exciting me to wake up and find new ways of exciting you, and to keep loving me back. Forever. Until our last breaths." He held out the Cracker Jack ring.

"Oh, my God, you guys, that's my daddy," Raegan gushed.

Seven finished, "So, I'm hoping now will be one of the days you say—"

"Yes." Sunday set her bag down and went toward him so nothing was in their way.

Seven took her in his arms, but she didn't throw in all her weight to avoid throwing out his back again.

"Absolutely, yes, Bank Man. Yes."

Merry Christmas!

When you are ready, please continue reading for how you can learn about and support the real-life historic town of Elaine, Arkansas.

To The Negroes of Phillips County

BIBLIOGRAPHY & RESOURCES
WHEN YOU'RE READY

What happened in Elaine

Many historians, professors, and amateur students of history have written on the Elaine Massacre, but due to the scare campaign carried out by Arkansas farmers and former plantation families, Black residents of Phillips County were terrified into silence.

As a result, the mass public still has no idea of the Elaine killings, and that they may have been more brutal and larger than Tulsa and Rosewood.

BIBLIOGRAPHY

The Arkansas Race Riot, Ida B. Wells-Barnett, Chicago, 1920.

In the days after the massacre, Ida B. Wells went to the scene and investigated. She wrote a pamphlet where she covered the killings and the trial. It is available online for free.

Blood In Their Eyes: The Elaine Race Massacres of 1919, Grif Stockley, 2004.

Grif Stockley is considered by nearly every person I interviewed on the subject to be the preeminent historian on Elaine. He passed away unfortunately before I got to meet him. His book is available on major retailers and in Arkansas bookstores and libraries.

THE ELAINE MASSACRE AND ARKANSAS: A CENTURY OF ATROCITY AND RESISTANCE, 1819-1919, GUY LANCASTER, 2018.

This is a collection of historians and professors who write on the subject matter from different perspectives. I reached out to Professors Brian K. Mitchell and Dr. Cherisse Jones-Branch, who included a piece about the sacrifices made by women—mothers, wives, sisters, and farmers themselves. I appreciated their willingness to speak with me.

The Elaine Massacre of 1919, https://encyclopediaofarkansas. net/entries/elaine-massacre-of-1919-1102/ (Last accessed: Jan. 5, 2026.)

Encyclopedia of Arkansas was one of the primary web sites I visited repeatedly during my forays into Elaine history. At the bottom of this article, there are a ton of even more resources and periodicals listed. They are rich in information, and I got lost for hours.

What a Preacher Saw Through a Key-Hole in Arkansas, Dunaway, Louis Sharpe, https://encyclopediaofarkansas.net/ entries/what-a-preacher-saw-13911/, 1925. (Last accessed: Jan. 5, 2026)

My understanding of this book is that it is really apologetic on behalf of the perpetrators in Phillips County, but Grif Stockley found his detailed accounts of the killings to be reliable. They number in the hundreds. According to Stockley, Dunaway was sympathetic to the Phillips County power-holders, so he would not have a reason to paint them in a bad light. Thus, the high death toll and retellings Dunaway gave have more credence.

Brutal Facts About Arkansas' Elaine Massacre, "Trista," History Collection. https://historycollection.com/brutal-facts-about-arkansas-elaine-massacre/. (Last Accessed: Jan. 5, 2025)

Elaine Massacre Memorial Set for Unveiling, Moritz, Gwen, Arkansas Business. https://www.arkansasbusiness.com/article/elaine-massacre-memorial-set-for-unveiling/, July 29, 2019. (Last Accessed: Jan. 5, 2026)

Arkansas Residents Make a Case for Reparations 100 Years After the Elaine Massacre: A Small Southern town tries to come to terms with its blood-soaked legacy, Mulder, Brandon, The American Prospect. https://prospect.org/2019/09/30/arkansas-reparations-elaine-race-massacre/ Sept. 30, 2019 (Last Accessed: Jan. 5, 2026)

Troops, Elaine, Ark., during race riot. American National Red Cross photograph collection, Library of Congress, 1919. https://www.loc.gov/pictures/item/2020638852/ (Last accessed: Jan. 5, 2026)

Phillips County

Map of Phillips County, Arkansas

Map of Phillips County, Arkansas, reproduced from The Crisis Vol. 19, No. 2 (December 1919), page 59. The Crisis, which began publication in 1910, is the magazine of the National Association for the Advancement of Colored People (NAACP), and was one of the national publications that offered substantial coverage of the Elaine Massacre.

Thank you to these people

PEOPLE YOU CAN CONTACT

Lisa Hicks-Gilbert, Descendant of The Elaine Massacre and current Mayor of Elaine, AR
Descendants of The Elaine Massacre of 1919

James White, Descendant of The Elaine Massacre
Elaine Museum

Nancy Hall Neal of Snow Lake, The real-life inspiration for "Sunday Conklin"
Knowlton Farms

Harvey Williams and The Williams Family, Whiskey-Distiller and Descendant of a farm family
Delta Dirt Distillery

Kevin Dedner, Author and Activist
The Joy of the Disinherited: Essays on Trauma, Oppression, and Black Mental Health

Brian K. Mitchell, Professor, Historian & Author

Use CAUTION

IF YOU DONATE FOR ELAINE…

NOT ALL THE ACTS ON BEHALF OF ELAINE ARE FOR THE BLACK VICTIMS.

When you research the Elaine Massacre, one of the first links to appear in search is Elaine Massacre Memorial in Helena, Arkansas. Yes, a memorial was dedicated in 2019, but it was built by the descendants of the **perpetrators**.

It was not placed in Elaine, where the deaths, rape, and maiming of Black people actually happened. They built it across the street from the Phillips County Courthouse.

The memorial does not list a single victim of the Elaine atrocities.

These descendants of the perpetrators have not put up a single marker for Hoop Spur, site of the sharecropper meeting, or at any of the sites where the bodies of victims are believed to have been transported by train, dumped and buried in mass graves.

They have not paid for a criminal investigation and a full factual report laying out the events in detail, and have not called for names of every person involved to be published in newspapers nationwide.

No one has paid for an archaeological excavation to locate where their ancestors dumped and hid the victims' bodies. To this day, scores of people remain unmarked.

Rather, on the memorial, the donors put their names, as well as names of the contractors and construction company. Yet, nowhere are the names of Black victims.

The State of Arkansas has never issued a formal apology or officially recognized, or offered redress, for the horrors visited on Elaine by Army troops, called in by Arkansas Governor Charles Brough.

As I finish this novel and write this afterword on November 29, 2025, I have learned today that the Elaine Library will be closed down. Elaine High School, Elaine Middle School, and Elaine Elementary are already closed.

If you would like to know who and what to support concerning Elaine, reach out to Mayor Lisa Hicks-Gilbert at mayorofelaine@gmail.com.

Leave a review and let's stay connected!

If these characters found a home in your heart, or you made your home among these families of Arkansas, or you were all about the depth of research and history, let's be friends! Use the QR code below and choose your social platform of choice. You have no shortage of options for where to go read now. Thank you for trusting me with your time and emotions.

If you bought this directly from me, I press a lot of heart, thought, and study into the craft. If you would kindly take a moment to leave an honest review on my web site, that helps assure other readers that they too will receive more than a fantastic story, but an experience. The link to review this book is HERE.

Web site: www.lulawhitebooks.com

Email: lula@lulawhitebooks.com

Instagram: https://www.instagram.com/lulawhitebooks/

Tiktok: https://www.tiktok.com/@lulawhitebooks

LULA'S BOOKS

Books in the *Metamorphosis* series

Who's Lovin' You?

Circa 1979 (Spring 2026)

Of Warriors & Women (2027)

Of Tyrants & Terror (2027)

Books In The *Sag Harbor Black Romances*

Brown Sugar This Christmas - Maddy & Jerrell

Hot Chocolate This Winter - Chrissy & Sheldon Part 1

Flinging All Spring - Adella & Desmond

Overheated for Summer - Chrissy & Sheldon Part 2

Rouse Family Christmas - All Couples

Books in the Sag Harbor spin-off series *Explore Men of the Hamptons*

Christmas Down Under (FREE PREQUEL NOVELLA) - Keenan & Eugenia

Explore You - Kevin & Cher

One Tasty Night (FREE PREQUEL NOVELLA) - Solomon & Chaitra

Taste You - Solomon & Chaitra

Drink You - Lion & Kamila

See Through You - Keenan & Eugenia

Find You - Roland & Neeraja

Books in the *Young & Luxurious* series

Love and Fire - Korienne & Easton

Stand-Alones

The Gift of Us

A New Life for Christmas